The Epiphany of Clementine Gingersparkles

by

Sarah Shanahan-Mallows

First paperback edition December 2023

Cover design

ISBN 979-8-8684-3022-0 (paperback)

www.sarahbooks.co.uk

#clementinegingersparkles

DEDICATION

To all those who celebrate Christmas.
Make it yours.

FOREWORD

'What are you doing for Christmas?'

This phrase is one of the most common things that those who live in a western culture might ask one another. Of course, one cannot make assumptions and must recognize that, in many western towns and offices across the globe, there are those who do not celebrate Christmas Day and cannot be expected to offer an opinion on the matter. To them, it may as well just be any other Tuesday.

However, that notwithstanding, for those who do, it is an acceptable level of inquiry. No one views it as rude or personal, yet it carries an implicit, subliminal undercurrent of meaning. We ask it with an expectation of what we understand a good Christmas to be and without even meaning to, we judge the answer according to how well it meets that standard.

If it should deviate from the expected result, we are surprised. If it nestles comfortably into the shape to which we have allocated it, we are pleasantly gratified. 'Oh, just us, quiet, staying at home…,' or 'Oh, we're going up to Derek's sister in Hull,' or, 'Finn's home, but Kelly's in Spain now. It won't be the same without her,' or 'Gran's coming for a week, so that means rubbish telly and me sleeping on the floor.'

We need limited further information as to what else the day or period will include, because we already know those details. We know there will be lights and decorations and turkey and chocolate and movies and drinks and resolutions of gym membership and future weight loss, and thus those replies fit around that knowledge; and we factor in travelling and gift buying, staying with family, tensions, arguments, compromise, absent family and the void that they leave. It is all there, but unsaid.

If the replies were, 'Jim wants to repaper the living room,' or 'I was thinking of beans on toast and getting a head start on my tax return,' or 'I was going to see if the dentist could squeeze me in since I've got time off work,' we would think them unacceptable and that their locutors must be some sort of humbug Scrooge Grinch to even contemplate such a thing. To our festive and culturally-conditioned sensibilities, it just doesn't feel right. We want the world imbued with Christmas Spirit and for there to be decked halls and comfort and joy around every corner.

There are of course those random few; Mavericks, who buck the trend, go their own way – though not to the dentist. Take holidays in the sun, even. But for most, Christmas is part of who we are. Our practices and traditions shape us, and we in turn are shaped by them.

Until we are not.

Prologue

Darcy was fatigued. Not the yawning, I'll be okay after an early night kind of tired, but that full body exhaustion that leadens the tread of your feet and causes your posture to stoop like a picture of early man.

She stepped on the escalator in a strange state between numbness and hyperstimulation. How could you be both? The moving steps weren't helping, levitating her high above the store below, without any physical effort, she didn't even need to remember to put one foot in front of the other, which it often took her great levels of concentration to do. She was just rising, mesmerised, like Disney's Aurora following Maleficent's green light to a spinning wheel in a tower. Perhaps that's what she craved, to prick her finger and fall to sleep for a hundred years.

The metal teeth of the steps closed on each other like gentle jaws and a nasal voice reminded her that she was near the top. Dragging her empty wheeled basket behind her, she stepped to the upper floor, into hell.

There had been assaults on her, during the ascent, lights and sounds and animations, sending triggers and thoughts and memories like blow darts from a pipe, rapid and silent and deadly. But this level, was next level.

To her left a ghost hung from the ceiling on clear wires, its white robe wafting in the exhaust from the air conditioning unit. It hovered over a black figure emerging from a coffin which opened by itself at ten second intervals emitting a haunting cackle. Screams and sounds of creaking doors and sinister footsteps grated her nerves rather than curdled her blood and the copious amount of fake gossamer that had been draped overhead caught in her hair. To her right, a small man stood and sang to her. His voice was deep and low and sounded much like her husband's when he calls from the car in a particularly patchy part of countryside known for its poor signal strength, the words stretched, the vowels elongated, and the intonation rising and falling like a boat on a choppy sea. On closer regard, Darcy recognized the man to be Santa and his song to be *Joy to the world*. Allowing herself to engage with him for a moment, she considered this rather odd. She would have imagined his pre-recorded melody to have been a secular song like *Santa Claus is coming to town*, rather than a carol which was determining that Jesus was the Joy that the world was waiting for and that the earth had now received their king. Although, she reckoned, his manufacturers probably thought that without Jesus, there wouldn't be a Christmas, and therefore not a Santa and so it was permissible for one mystical deity to big up the other one.

Thwack! One of the blow darts hit her on the back of the neck. Carols. What did she make of those now? Could she sing them with the same fervour that she had always done? Could she even utter the words at all now that their meaning had lost meaning?

As she moved through the displays of baubles and trees and three-feet high nutcrackers, and snow-covered reindeer and tinny singing things that played jingle bells; and then actual jingle bells that rang in the tiny hands of a small girl in a pink coat who ran before her and then stopped dead, sending Darcy forward like a dummy in crash-test simulator She felt her heart palpate. The little girl was Kitty apparently. Darcy knew that because her mother kept calling her from the other side of the aisles. Although Darcy wasn't sure whether the purpose of that was actually to locate her daughter for safety or to prove to other shoppers that she wasn't a neglectful parent. The woman was studying the boxes of lights so closely that it seemed as though she was revising for a GCSE in festive illumination. The man who stood with her looked like he would rather stick candy canes in his eyes than calculate how many boxes they would need to go all around the front of the house and down the front drive. They needed to be the connecting ones, she said, and they only had three boxes of warm white, the other was a bright snow white. She kept huffing and searching the shelves of multi-coloured lights and projectors as if that would suddenly yield the missing two boxes of warm white. The woman was getting increasingly frustrated that Christmas would be ruined if she was not able to source the items she needed. The man suggested Amazon. She gave him a withering look as if he had intimated that the world was flat, and explained that buying online was too risky because how could you tell whether they would be the right warmth of warm white? Her sentence concluded with a silent word, 'imbecile'. Venturing to speak again, which Darcy thought was bold and stupid, in equal measure, the man said that if there weren't enough on the shelves, there was no choice really but for her to accept the three boxes – that was still three-thousand lights after all – or accept that they were getting more online, or trying somewhere else, perhaps the garden centre. She said that the garden centre was way more expensive, and that there was no way that three thousand were enough (silent word – idiot); they wouldn't even reach to the garage, let alone go down the driveway and across the front fence. The man mentioned something about outdoor cables, weatherproof housing and power supply. The woman huffed again at this as though he was deliberately spoiling what was supposed to be a nice Christmassy experience by pointing out practical obstacles. Kitty continued to wander up and down the aisles, setting off all the singing toys that someone had wisely sought to stack at toddler height, and was only a step away from getting lost or abducted by the jingle bells that she shook at the singing Santa. His jaunty animation consisted of jutting his hips from side to side whilst keeping his feet rooted to the spot. Kitty did the same, accompanying his off-key tenor, with her own minor harmony of *Toy to the girl*. Makes sense, Darcy thought to herself. It seemed far more comprehensible to a three-year-old that Santa would sing a song about bringing toys to girls, rather than joys to worlds. Darcy had only popped in for a couple of cleaning supplies, but the houseware section was in the back corner. Traversing the winter wonderland without getting lost in the snow seemed as impossible as the Pevensys finding their way back to the wardrobe in the spare room.

A smell of food reached her, provoking a mix of hunger and nausea. She wasn't aware that she was hungry, she didn't really find much enjoyment in food anymore and was getting by mostly on breakfast, a sandwich, and a glass of wine at night. But she suddenly felt that a sit down and cup of tea would be nice. She glanced at the café area, it was quiet. No one there, only a couple of attendants in black outfits with catering trilbies on their heads. One was wiping the counter while the other put up posters about their upcoming festive menu. Having paid for a cup of tea, she wondered whether she should add a bun or a teacake. Perhaps she did need something, a sugar boost to lift her energy levels. But then, she thought back to how her efforts at exercise had failed her in the last few weeks, and how the toning that her diligent daily yoga practice had yielded had now slipped back into flabby slackness and cellulite and determined that she didn't need the sugar after all. A range of Halloween cookies decorated as pumpkins and bats, witch's hats and ghouls sat pre-wrapped in cellophane looking pallid. Without even trying one, Darcy knew how they tasted, the mass-produced child biscuit that was either soft and stale, or rock hard and brittle. Neither appealed but she could imagine Kitty loving one. Please, she prayed, please let me have a cup of tea in peaceful silence before Kitty Jingle Bells comes and gets pumped up on Halloween cookies.

The café space was open-plan and looked over the Christmas shop and the balcony to the lower ground. She watched people walking thought the door, getting their baskets in eager anticipation of what to fill them with and heading up the escalator. Friends, meeting for coffee perhaps, chatting pointing and laughing as they passed the singing

Santa; parents and children, excited and gleeful at all the lights, pretending to jump scare each other with the remaining Halloween display. What was common among them? Darcy thought as she sat alone and sipped her tea. Joy. Perhaps Santa had a point?

Yet she had felt nothing. Anxiety perhaps? Another Christmas, not knowing what it meant to her anymore. Tiredness, certainly. Everything just felt so overwhelming now. Where was her energy? Where was that sense of fun and expectation and anticipation, looking at all the new decorations with delight? All she could see was excess, and cost, and the pointlessness of it all. She had always loved Christmas and had never understood those who didn't. She could get annoyed if they said, "What the fuss, it's only one day." But now she felt the same. So much fuss, just for one day.

She wished that she could just sleep and like Aurora, be awakened by her true love's kiss when it was all over.

Paying for her disinfectants, she braced herself for the sensory onslaught. From this direction, she had to walk through the special Christmas bed linen, bathroom accessories and sofa cushions, the festive spiced candles and room sprays.

Thwack! Another blow dart, carrying with it a cinnamon orange clove mix that reminded her of a pot pourri her mother had bought when she was little. It always went in a gold bowl on the coffee table, next to a box of Turkish delight and a stemmed crystal dish of satsumas. The thought had jumped unbidden, raked to the forefront of her mind simply by the smell. And with it, nostalgia and satisfaction. Not all of Christmas was draining, Darcy allowed. There were some good bits.

Large rolls of wrapping paper stood in tall boxes, lining the walls like a festive picket fence. Extra-long and Extra-wide, they were for those presents that were extra. The big, special, grand gestures, the ones that had the wow factor, the Santa presents like bicycles and tricycles, dream houses and remote-control jeeps.

Her basket knocked into a chair leg, knocking the table and shaking the three tall dinner candles that were placed along the centre. Darcy readied herself to catch them, but they remained upright, looking fresh and ready to begin their duty, like soldiers awaiting posting to active service.

Thwack! Another blow dart – another memory. Next to the table was an A-frame, displaying a perfect Christmas dinner, the turkey bronze and shining. She felt a glimmer of pride. She had always produced dinners like this, as had her mother, photos from Christmases throughout her childhood, evidence of domestic achievement. Always the perfect bronzed bird. Always huge; the main event. The stuffing and cranberry sauce and soft white sliced bread, suppertime; cold slices with piping hot bubble and squeak and gravy; the delicious soup, the carcass in a huge pot with carrots and onions. She made a mental note to check when the ordering opened at the supermarket, feeling a sigh of burden at the prospect.

The shelf stackers were surrounded by boxes on pallets, new arrivals from Lapland, or more probably, China or Taiwan. Darcy smiled to herself. She wondered how many Buddhists and Taoists had worked on the manufacture and shipping of these baubles and dancing reindeer to meet the ever-present need for more, to countries far away and cultures more than oceans apart. She acknowledged that she had been guilty. Every new year, buying a new decoration for the tree, the children eagerly choosing one, which she had to allow either in accordance with the colour scheme or for their own trees. She didn't do that as a child. It didn't seem necessary to change things so frequently. The same old decorations came out each year and if there were breakages, her mother might buy some more, but there was never a theme to follow. Indeed, it took a good few years to move away from tinsel and foil concertina pieces.

She noticed how ordered these were, they were even pre-themed, the classic red and gold being called "Victoriana", the midnight blue and silver, being called "Starlit night". The whites, "Frost wonderland", and the gold, "Three kings". Her mind span. Should she stop and peruse? It did seem as though there were some lovely baubles. She knew she didn't need any, but since when was Christmas about what you needed? It was about what was new and shiny. Perhaps she should try a new theme, rebuild her whole look. One year, she had painted the lounge walls a duck-egg blue to coordinate with the design in her gold Chinese lamps with black shades, the tree of course had to be black and duck egg blue too. Since moving to the new house, the lamps didn't suit. The walls were "Chatsworth beige" and the black and blue baubles have stayed in the loft ever since. No, it was just more expense that they didn't need. Thwack! When she passed the Victoriana display, she considered the large red and gold theme they had had for years. Then, in the years that followed, they had chosen burgundy and jewel colours; after that it was white and silver, then all white, then just silver, then just gold, then glass. She could probably create a display at home that would rival this one, the themes of her past, her age and taste measured in baubles. She could give them names too, "Byzantine", "Ice", "Mercury", and "Prism". New names for old things. A way to make the same – different, the traditional – innovative.

Darcy edged past the table, steering her wheeled basket carefully. She smiled as she looked at it, set up with so much decoration there would be no room for food. It was a small table, a modern one, made of some sort of veneered chipboard. A broad runner ran down the centre, oblong mats in each of the six places, then placed on top, a plastic charger plate, silver, but they came in red and purple and gold too. A dinner plate then supported the rest of the items like the base position of a cheer squad, everything else piled on top of it in a pyramid, the side plate, then a bowl, filled with baubles. A table centre ran down the middle with the three soldier candles standing to attention, an arrangement of holly and ivy at their feet, as if their drill-sergeant had thought it sensible to hold parade on the forest floor. It was plastic and frosted with artificial snow. Crackers lay at the head of each place, vying for what narrow piece of territory they shared with the dessert fork and spoon. A printed, cloth napkin in a gaudy ring was laid to the left and above it stood a place holder in the shape of a Christmas tree. Large wine glasses with small holly leaves marked the boundaries of each place, like traffic lights at a county line. Beyond here, the open road, or at least, four square inches of unencumbered tabletop.

Darcy imagined a fraught host on Christmas Day, ceremoniously bearing the turkey platter aloft, to the appreciation of the assembled and then having to perch it on the corner whilst asking all the guests to chuck all the baubles out in order to make use of the bowls, and then chuck out the bowls to make room for the plates to put the food on.

Thwack! Another blow dart. Her mother's table service. Wedgewood. The large dining table being the big thing to do a few days before Christmas. They had always had a separate dining room for special occasions. Just looking at this little table now, Darcy considered that if this was your everyday table where homework was done, and fishfingers and peas were eaten, and where football boots were cleaned, you wouldn't be able to lay it up three days in advance. But, when she was younger, they had. Removing the silver cutlery from their individual little bags and taking them out of the mahogany coffee table, the secret cutlery store was her favourite bit. She loved how the little coffee spoons had tiny sleeves. The fish knives and forks they never used. She loved that table and making up everything nice with the Waterford glasses, the Irish linen tablecloth, with a weave so fine you could see your hand through it. The cut glass, shimmering in the dancing light. This is what she had grown up with. This was Christmas and it was what she took with her into her own family life. Christmas was special, extraordinary, and having the table arrayed with elegance was a significant part of that.

So many memories, flooding unbidden, triggered by the sight of the festive displays. Yet, for some reason, instead of providing comfort in recollecting happy times and reassurance in the familiar, it did nothing but the opposite. It just felt overwhelming and exhausting. It felt trite and routine. A reminder that another year had passed, and she was another year older. That, instead of feeling a sense of shared belonging with those who shared her culture, she felt as though she were in a dream, on the outside, looking in at them. She envisioned herself in the dark, like on the outskirts of a fairground. The people are all laughing and squealing with fun, as the big wheel goes up and the hurdy gurdy music of the carousel carries smiling children and parents on its shiny horses. There are lollipops and candy floss, and the smell of popcorn and bells that ring when the strongest wields the hammer. And the lovers go giggling into the ghost train. Yet, her feet are held in some sort of glue. She can't get there to be part of the fun. She sees herself in a cartoon dream, the strands of adhesive stretch as she lifts her shoe, yet she cannot move. Those around her are moving and smiling and happy, but she is just stuck. Then the glue changes to mud, as cartoon dreams do, and she is sinking lower into it, the ground giving way to nothingness beneath her. Why can't she get to the carnival? Why can't she enjoy the fun? A sadness overwhelmed her. She watched everyone else smiling and laughing and singing along to the carolling Santa. What was wrong with her? Why could they see fun and joy and she could only see confusion? How were they so in control and she so out of it? How could they see Christmas as a fun winter festival filled with good cheer and she could only see, thinking, planning, uncertainty, money, debt, expectation, disappointment and inadequacy? It wasn't like she could just decide to cancel it and go on a cruise, like the *Kranks*. There were traditions. Things to do. The tree to get; the new bauble to buy; the movies that had to be watched. The ice skating that had to be done; the hot chocolates that had to be drunk; the Christmas jumpers that had to be worn; the goodies to eat; the gifts to exchange; the stockings; the carol concerts; the decorations to have; the baking to do; the games to play; the crockery and cutlery to clean; the table to dress; the table centre to make; the turkey to order; the menus to plan; the guest room to be prepared; the visiting to do…

For some reason, tears welled in her eyes. This had been happening more frequently recently. She supposed it was menopause. Having weathered most of that storm, she felt she was through the worst of it, and it had left some emotional debris that she was still trying to clear up. But this felt different, this deep, gluey, muddy, ground destabilising carnival that everyone was enjoying except her.

It would be fine, she told herself. She was completely fine. Just tired. She would have an early night and be alright in the morning.

Thwack!

She had seen a film once, about the exploration of the Amazonian jungle, the explorer paddling their raft down the river. One of the party had earlier fallen overboard and had succumbed to the snack requirements of the piranha, as a reminder to the viewer that the water offered no sanctuary from those who would persecute you from the land. Then there were the rapids to consider too. As they had emerged from a bend in the river, a silent and deadly blow dart shot through the air to meet with the neck of another of the doomed party. These were interlopers who had no business being amongst the natives. The leader of the exploration peered into the dense jungle, it was just possible to pick out the bodies of the dart blowers, their loins covered but nothing else, save for some strings of beads and leather pouches full of darts. But they were mostly concealed. You dare not go closer, to seek to challenge the hostility or seek friendship. You must just go on, slowly, meandering, letting the river full of flesh eaters carry you along its course, a floating target practice like ducks at a funfair.

Darcy allowed the river to carry her through the Christmas shop, as exposed to the memorial darts of her native Christmas pasts as if she were on a raft, drifting with no agency of her own, no water to escape into, and no fight left to resist being hog tied and taken to the chief of the Christmas tribe. She would have no language with which to negotiate her safe passage, she no longer knew the cultural etiquette. She may as well just hand them the Tabasco sauce and climb into the cooking pot. The darts in her neck had pretty much tenderised her anyway. Christmas had her beaten and it was not yet even Halloween.

'*Joy to the world*' Santa sang as she descended the escalator.

'Oh, fuck off, Darcy said, as she stepped off the escalator. Christmas was coming and she just didn't have the resources to deal with it. A festive well that had run dry. She wondered, not for the first time in recent months, where the hell, in these stores filled to the rafters with every conceivable Christmas thing, did they sell any sodding Joy?

THE EPIPHANY

PART I

The advent of Advent

BEHIND EVERY DOOR

THE EPIPHANY

Black Friday

25 NOVEMBER

Jason pulled into the supermarket car park and turned off the car engine, relieved to be free of that wretched song about Santa coming to town. He didn't have anything against it per se, merely that he had been listening to it for weeks already. As soon as Halloween was over, all the Christmas stock, that had been accumulating on the back shelves since September, had made its way to prime position. The tins of Quality Street had first appeared in August. Even before August bank holiday. He couldn't believe it and had never noticed it in the past. But now he worked there, he had become more aware.

As each seasonal item arrived, it was placed at the back of the store and then edged up little by little week by week, in tiny incremental steps like the coins on the nudging machines at the amusement arcade, dropping to the back, and then, in infinitesimal movements, shifting and jostling and nestling, sliding over the other coins until it is teetering on the edge, until it falls forwards, bringing with it an avalanche of silver.

That's what it was like at the store. The suitcases came in first, just before the Easter holiday; the Easter things following hot on the coattails of Mothers' Day, whose merchandise appeared just after Chinese New Year. Valentine's day appeared somewhere between; and then from Easter to October, there were 'back to school' items, uniforms, stationery, alongside leftover bikinis on sale. Halloween followed closely, arriving in early September, two months before Samhain itself. And then Christmas, the Quality Street tins finally finding themselves the forerunners, the dropping off point of the coin-shelf; vying for place with inflatable kayaks and cheap useless wetsuits, and picnic rugs.

Nudge, nudge, shuffle shuffle, until they are pride of place, in all their shimmering shining glory. Enticing you with their sparkle and glitter, promising a Christmas of excess, the coins tumbling in a waterfall of plenty.

The toys had begun to fill the shelves; the tinsel and wrapping paper; the decorations and fairy lights. Banners floated overhead with photos of tables groaning under the weight of food, and happy families seated at coordinated place settings, wearing crowns, pulling crackers and laughing. Family, young and old. The perfect family Christmas.

Marketing gold.

It was what everyone wanted. The perfect family Christmas. A convivial atmosphere of laughter and plenty.

No one wanted grumpy grandpa; or fights over the television; or finding batteries for the toy; or wishing that they hadn't found batteries for the toy. Sprouts that no one wants anyway, or chocolates that everybody wants; kids tearing open boxes in a present frenzy; kids finding more delight in the box in which the toy arrived than the toy itself, despite its ninety-three quid debit on the credit card statement.

No one wanted a real Christmas like that. Everyone wanted the dream as shown on the boards that swayed gently in the soft exhaust from the heating control unit overhead.

No one, except for Jason.

Walking through the staff door at the side of the supermarket, he nodded to a colleague leaving and made for his locker. He passed a notice on the break room wall about a briefing regarding Black Friday. The briefing was held yesterday evening. A call to arms. A grouping in readiness for the assault. His manager had stood solemnly before them, conveying as much gravity as she could at the prospect of impending doom, as if she were a military officer preparing troops for battle, which of course, she was. There would be chaos, she had warned. Crowds. Queues. Pushing and shoving. She had looked at Jason knowingly and he had nodded. A slow nod of recognition, a shared understanding of his role in the mission, and her expectations of, and trust in, him.

She had instructed the floor staff to manage the crowds. To herd them, separate them, thin them out, keep them moving; dispersion being the preferred approach. They must be disallowed the opportunity to swell numbers and form a rising tide of bodies surging through the tills, like a rip current through rocks. The till operators would have to be vigilant too, focused, checking that the sale price made sense. She had admonished them. They were not going to have the same debacle as last year, where the barcode was wrong, and people snapped up the latest air-fryers for £10.80 instead of ten times that much. The team nodded their assent. They would heed her and be ready. They would each play their part, like loyal infantry soldiers on the front line.

Jason had suddenly felt the inequity of the odds. He saw himself, standing sentry alone, filling the automatic door space like a keeper in a goal mouth, small before the stares of a stadium of supporters quick to praise or judge his efforts. The store manager, pinning all her expectation on his quick eye and lightning reactions to spot and apprehend thieves or to intervene when things looked set to become physical. He knew that he was good, but were they better? Would he move to the bottom right as the penalty-taker shopper took a shot to top left? Would he bear the disappointment of the rest of his team for failing them all at the last minute as the shoplifter walked away with their trophy bargain?

And before she finished her pep talk with a rallying cry of solidarity and purpose; with the invocation to Ares, the god of war and Soteria, the goddess of protection, she reminded all present of 'the incident'. It needed no further clarification, nor name. Everyone in retail knew of it and dared not speak of it. Such as actors who will not utter the name *Macbeth* in theatre, referring to it only as the Scottish play, or the Bard's play. And that is enough. Whether there be real or imagined sorcery amongst its words, no thespian would take the risk of inviting disaster to either stage or company by tempting the Fates. And no one wanted to invite knife attacks over a cut price television.

So let it rest, unsaid.

Part of him wondered though, whether his role was, in fact, the last line of defense as the store manager led him to believe. Surely, if someone was of a mind to steal something, they could do it anytime. Why wait until Black Friday to sneak out with a massive telly? It wouldn't matter that it had been reduced in price. It was free to them anyway. It was probably more to do with the chaos than the theft, he assumed. Social order was lost in such entropy, and it was easy for any inexperienced security guard to be distracted from the main focus of attention. He likened it to the observation exercise, where the gorilla walks behind the basketball match, or the trampoline gym, and you don't even notice because you are counting the hoops, or the bounces. Who would notice someone casually walking through the barriers with eight coffee machines in their trolley when there were people physically assaulting each other over a discounted suitcase? If it went the way of 'the incident', it could bring new meaning to a 'bag for life'.

Whenever there was the potential to obtain; whether it be from a scarcity of resources or a surplus, the human need to have what others had - or indeed to have so that others couldn't have - was too powerful a force to quell; and too blinding a motivation to observe such societal norms or social niceties of waiting, turn-taking or putting others before oneself. Jason had seen that for himself with the Covid toilet roll episode. But, could it really be as bad as the store manager had warned? He wondered. She would know, of course. It wasn't her first rodeo. As she had outlined the behaviour that they were anticipating, Jason's other colleagues, also veterans of the retail phenomenon, had joined in with their own recollections and anecdotes. Each eager to share their past experiences. Their witness to the tramplings and the crushing; and even as per 'the incident'…, the fatal stabbings.

Whatever its origins (and Jason had looked them up after the meeting last night), Black Friday had become code for retail warfare and Jason was feeling neither adequately trained, nor armed, for the prospective combat.

Taking his station by the doors, like William Wallce facing the English army, he watched anxiously as the crowds assembled on the other side, jostling and unsettled, raring to get loose. Only a sheet of glass separated them, its transparency unwelcome as he tried to avoid eye-contact with the enemy, or for them to sense his fear. He glanced at his watch, wondering if there was time to go to the craft aisle and pick up a set of blue face paints. He might feel better prepared to engage with the marauding hoard, if his face was a mask of warring righteousness.

The minute hand ticked to its o'clock home, and the doors opened.

Eight hours earlier, the digital doors had opened, and keypads and laptops had launched a similar attack. Raw animal behaviour (the likes of which is seemingly most adopted by humans whenever purchasing or consuming is on the line), triggered in them the basest foundations of hunting, and as the minute hand had ticked away from its o'clock home, the feeding frenzy had begun.

Eight hours later, it was over. To the winner, the spoils. To the latecomers, bare shelves. There had been no stabbings, but Jason had felt sick as he witnessed the wanton desire to consume.

After the Black Friday rush, the rest of the evening had passed by in a blur. It was quiet, which he was glad of, being a double shift. The late-night shoppers, mostly staff from the hospital, starting or ending their own shifts, probably doubles, like his. A couple of couriers popped in to use the toilet and get a coffee to wake them up, the harsh florescent lighting awakening the synapses. There were those who had forgotten advent calendars, running in to get whatever was left. They had been reduced in price, the stock managers realizing that another significant moment had passed. An advent calendar had twenty-four days. It was possible to buy one a few days into the period and catch up, but that wasn't the done thing. You had to be there for day one, or else it didn't count.

'Shit!' he whispered under his breath, suddenly snapping out of his reverie. He had been so taken away, watching other people shopping, that he hadn't considered his own. He needed advent calendars too; for when the kids came to visit. Ellie had always used to get them in the past, and it wasn't on his radar. Once he had become aware of it, he was consumed, eyeing each new customer warily as they crossed the threshold. It seemed that every person walking through the door was getting a calendar. There weren't going to be any left, or if there were, they would be the rubbish ones. He watched nervously as the hunters contributed to the gradual depletion of the stock. He was desperate to finish his shift so that he could secure a couple for Skye and Tim; though by the time he had, he was right. The only ones left were the rubbish ones. Well, not rubbish – more inappropriate. He didn't want to imagine what Skye, nearly sixteen, and ten-year-old Tim would think of *Paw Patrol,* or *Hello Kitty.* They couldn't even switch them. Hopefully they would just appreciate the chocolate, Jason told himself. That's all anyone wanted anyway, wasn't it? It wasn't like they were counting down to the birth of Christ, with anticipation of the birth of the Saviour, as he himself had been raised. Not unless, Jesus meant more chocolate, like he did at Easter.

*

In his research on Black Friday, Jason had learned that one of the reasons for its name and purpose was that in the US, the first week-end after Thanksgiving was the official beginning of the Christmas shopping season, and that shops that had theretofore been in the red, in financial terms, began to reap in the cash, shifting their bottom lines into the black. He could empathise with them. His own bank account trod that line as precariously as a tight rope walker.

He had no idea how he was going to afford to compete with Ellie and bloody Darren when it came to Christmas. Skye had told him that they had planned to move into the new house before the holidays, but also that Ellie wasn't too worried if it didn't happen. Getting all the finishings perfect was more important in your perfect home, her mother had explained. Although Jason thought that it was more to do with the fact that if you were sleeping with the developer, there was no cause to worry that the sale was going to fall through. Not that he said that though. As much as it took all his self-control, he didn't want to malign Ellie to the kids. She was still their mother.

So, it was likely that they would still be at home for the foreseeable future. Their family home, the one he had created with Ellie and the one that their children were raised in. He knew that he wouldn't be able to afford to keep it, once they had moved. It was too big for him alone, and it would feel too sad to see and hear them in everything. Their splashing in the bath, their cries from falls on the patio, Happy birthdays sung in the kitchen and bedtime stories read at night. That would crush him, he knew. The emptiness.

No, he would have to move. But it had been a council home. There was no capital asset to be sold and apportioned. There was nothing. He hadn't for a moment, ever thought that he would be here considering such things, a week before December. This time last year, he was planning on fixing a new light display on the roof because Ellie had watched a

Christmas film and wanted to re-create their version of it in Osborne Gardens. Their happy Christmas home.

Whilst he was mindful that Christmas was around the corner, he had not been able to save anything. With the rent on his new place, the van to maintain, and child support, he had hardly anything left out of his salary. His main job, as a roofer, was fine in the summer months, but the winter weather; the cost-of-living crisis, and the rise in mortgage rates and energy costs had battened down the majority of hatches and people were holding onto their money. It was an honest profession but, as with most of that kind, it couldn't always be relied upon to be financially reliable. There had been a time when he had thought it might be nice for Tim to have joined him and the business could be his legacy to his son. Yet, not only did it seem that the ten-year-old rather fancied himself a professional footballer at the moment and was unlikely to follow in his father's ladder steps; the miserable thought had crossed Jason's mind that he might even follow Darren into property development, seeing the lucrative lifestyle it offered. Not that money was the most important thing in the world. Except for the fact that it was.

The combination of factors had led him to the security guard job. He had originally thought of being a driver for the supermarket but then thought that he might have to carry shopping up flights of stairs to flats. He spent all his roofing days going up and down steps, so the idea of doing the same in his additional job was less than appealing. When the security guard option came up, he grabbed it. Extra money for standing by the door? Yes, he could do that. No climbing or lifting or crouching on his aging knees. Being out in all weathers or driving down dark country lanes or busy high streets.

Yes, he thought. Standing by the door and having a stroll around the foyer would be great. It wasn't like they were in a bad neighbourhood; it should be fine.

Well, it had been until today. Black Friday. Then Jason had seen humanity at its worst. The fighting and greed and roughness portrayed by people just to get a few pounds off. He understood it to a certain extent. Money was tight and people needed things, but when he reflected, he had to admit, they didn't need these things. Needing would be like the food lines in Ukraine, or during Covid when then shelves and freezers were bare. He was glad he hadn't been on security then, having to wrestle toilet rolls out of people's hands as trolleys were filled. It was true, humans showed their true colours when resources were limited.

There were those who had both cared and shared. In those early days, when the elderly were in isolation and friendly neighbours left whatever groceries were available on doorsteps, two metres apart, and where bags were wiped with sanitizer before they could be touched by the vulnerable. These people had echoed the Blitz spirit that his grandfather had told him of. Rationing and sharing and making do with nothing. When coffee was ersatz, and stockings were gravy browning. He guessed that people were just used to wanting more now. To having what they needed, yet it not being enough. As his mother used to say, "much wants more".

To be fair, he was guilty of that himself to a certain extent. He had a roof over his head and food on the plate. Granted, they were mostly ready meals and packet noodles but that was because he couldn't see the point of cooking nice meals for one. He would rather just refuel his body in the cheapest and quickest way possible. He had a car, could support his children and was able to spend time with them. He had his health and could work. He was lucky compared to many.

But not compared to Darren.

Shit. It just wasn't fair. He had schmoozed into their life one day, like a wave creeping up the shoreline and had schmoozed out and taken everything with him. How had it all gone so bloody wrong? And how could he not have seen it coming? All his life was now, was struggling to make ends meet and barely getting by. Was that living? he asked himself. Is that all that anyone was doing? And if so, what was the point?

Pushing the door open wearily, he got out of the van and pointed the key fob over his head to lock it behind him. It was mild for the last days of November. But it often was, feeling autumnal rather than Christmassy, with short days that were dull and dark, the last of the fallen leaves swirling around. There wasn't even snow to look forward to. Not like in New England, or New York.

He liked that romantic idea. The images that he had seen in Christmas films. Ice skating in Central Park; the huge tree outside the Rockefeller centre; Santa on every street corner, ringing bells, collecting for charity; warm department stores on Fifth Avenue, with big windows displaying festive tableaux, or artfully arranged wares, enticing the eager shopper inside. It was no different to London really, he thought, giving some cinematic credit to his domestic capital. A huge tree in Trafalgar Square; the glamorous windows of Regent Street and Piccadilly; Fortnum & Mason; illuminations spanning the boulevards; and ice-skating at Somerset House. London did Christmas pretty well, and offered as much to the tourist as New York, if not more, because it had the Houses of Parliament too, and the Tower of London, Hampton Court and Westminster Abbey. Places whose stories were held in the walls of stone that had, for hundreds of years, observed those who had dwelt and served within.

As all homes did.

As his home had.

As he walked up the scruffy pathway in the foreground of his flat, on that last day of November, he let himself get whisked away to New York-New York, so good they named it twice. The city that never slept. The place where his Christmas would outshine anything that Darren could cook up. He could keep his villa in Marbella, Jason thought. What was so good about that? There was nothing to do there but work on your tan and lounge in the pool. But New York? That was a full life-changing experience. The kids would never forget it.

Flicking on the kitchen light, he placed the advent calendars on the worktop, hoping that his failings in that department would be mitigated by the prospective trip/present of a lifetime.

Something other than hunger pulled at his stomach. What was the nagging doubt? Money? Of course, but he would come to that later. Passports? He acknowledged the thought. They might prove to be a problem. He couldn't remember whether they were still in date. He was pretty sure they were but how would he get them? Not without Ellie knowing what he was planning. Then she would probably say no. It was highly likely that she would just love to veto him taking them out of the country. Or worse, she could tell Darren and they would take them. His very own idea would be snatched away from him, and the credit given to someone else. How was that fair?

The stomach nagging reminded him that as fanciful and romantic as this motion was, there was the small matter of funding it. Who did he think he was fooling, even considering the notion of an expensive trip? Himself. He was the biggest fool.

While the kettle was boiling, he picked up his phone. It wouldn't hurt to just look at the prices, he told himself. Just to see what he was in for, ballpark. What could it be? No more than a grand? £1500 maybe? No, he reasoned, probably £2500 with accommodation and spending money. It needn't be long.

This represented memories that the children would have, not just objects that they would eventually grow out of. Whatever happened in the future they would always be able to look back and know that their dad loved them and had never wanted this divorce, and Ellie would know that he wasn't the loser she thought he was. That he wasn't just a waster roofer who wouldn't amount to anything or couldn't offer her the life she wanted. And Darren..., bloody Darren, this would wipe the smug smile off his face, his self-satisfied, 'I'm the king of the jungle' attitude, peacocking around showing his feathers at every opportunity.

It didn't matter how much it cost, Jason determined. He would get a loan out if he had to. He just had to do this. Santa be dammed. It was more important that his kids knew what lengths he would go for them.

The toaster popped, launching its incumbent gluten- heavy occupants up and out onto the counter. It had always had a brazen ejection. This was one treat he allowed himself. Ellie had always insisted that they have wholemeal or granary bread, which he didn't mind, and he valued her concern for their collective health. But every now and again, he would give in to the seductive call of the gluten and indulge in thick white toast on which the butter melted like icebergs slipping into the surface of the sea.

He yawned and debated whether to see if there was anything that caught his eye on Netflix. But the flat was always cold by this time of night as he didn't leave the heating on when he was out. The lure of his bed with a hot water bottle was preferable, and he had a new crime book that he had got from the charity shop.

After re-reading a paragraph a few times, he realised that he was too tired to read, plus he was distracted by his disappointment about the cost and the demise of his New York dream. He would have to go back to thinking about what else he could get with his meagre savings and how they were to stretch to not only presents from him, but from Santa too; and presents that would if not rival, be equal to, presents from Ellie and Darren, and *their* presents from Santa.

'Bloody presents! Bloody Christmas! And Bloody Santa!'

Jason's heart shouted inside him, twisting like an animal in pain.

Who made it so hard to just have a family and love them? Why did love have to be measured in pounds sterling, or American dollars or any other currency that wasn't just hugs and kisses and time?

Tears welled in his eyes as he sent Skye a good night message. He didn't expect her to answer it, it was late. He just wanted her to know that they were the last thing he thought of at night. Tim didn't have a phone, so Jason had to rely on his digital love being passed on in real terms by his daughter. Tim had been asking for one for a while now. He said all his friends had phones. Jason had challenged him on it asking why he needed a phone when he spent all day in school, all evening at home and never went anywhere without Skye or an adult. Apparently, the phone wasn't for phoning at all. It was for games and apps. It was for Snapchat and accessing the internet and Minion Rush and some other such things.

Jason felt fairly certain that Ellie would get Tim a phone, either from them, or from Santa. It stuck in Jason's craw that they were in a position to get him what he most wanted, but the upside would be that he could message him too, then. At the moment, he could only hope that Skye passed on his nighttime messages in a timely fashion and were relayed at some point between breakfast and the following bedtime.

He would be seeing them on Sunday. They could open their advent calendars together and at least relive some part of their Christmas traditions. Although, he knew that, here too, he had failed, again. All he had managed to get were some crappy left-overs, when Ellie had probably bought hers in October and had got the perfect ones for whatever would most impress the kids.

His phone pinged. A notification, from his mate, Mike, inviting him out for a drink on Saturday at the White Lion.

While he was on, he thought he would check Facebook for a quick scroll through of the updates. There were a couple of adverts for loans. Typical, he thought, the all-seeing AI 'eye' in the phone, monitoring his interests and engagements.

His eyes were nodding, and he was tired, but something caught his attention.

He sat up and strained his eyes open. What was that? Last minute Christmas deals? Lapland.

It was cheaper than New York. Closer. And there was nothing like it on Regent Street, or Fifth Avenue. He could not believe it. That would be amazing. He could just see Tim and Skye's faces. Of course, Skye was a bit too old and didn't believe in Santa anymore but, it would be a wonderful experience and something that she could always say she had done. He could imagine her as an adult, at university, saying, "Oh, yes, I went to Lapland when I was younger. My dad took us?"

He simply had to go. Excited, he clicked on the link and looked at all the details. This would be incredible. The money was still a worry, but then as he clicked back out of the page, there was another advert asking the reader if they had ever been refused a loan. "Low income? Low repayment amounts. Is there something that you desperately need money for now? Repay at affordable monthly payments over a term that suits you? Don't delay, complete our quick and easy application form now and we will get back to you with our answer. No questions, just cash in your bank right away when you need it most."

Jason wasn't silly, he knew not to fall for such advertising gimmicks, particularly when money was involved, but these guys sounded legit. They said that they were underwritten by a team of solicitors so that all sounded above board. And as long as the term was long enough, the monthly payments would be affordable. Well, not affordable at all, actually, but necessary. He had to have this trip and this loan, and how he paid for it was a problem for future Jason.

And how else could he prove to his children that he was a good dad who loved them and didn't want them to miss out on things? He would get the loan. Calculating the cost of the trip, he totted up the amount to request. Then it struck him. He had got so carried away with the Lapland idea and poking Bloody Darren in the eye with a Christmas gift to rival his, he had forgotten about Santa again. As with the New York idea, Tim would be expecting a present from Santa as well as the trip. More so, if he had actually been to see the man himself, in his hometown. There would be no doubt about it. He would have to factor more money in for that, and he made a mental note to ask Tim what he had put on his list. He let himself hope that they might be able to write it together. Then they could post it, like when they were little, and he would lift them up to the post box and take photos of them dropping their letters into the box and hearing them drop down onto the pile of other wishful papers.

He loved them so much and wanted them to have the best. And not just from Darren but from him, their own actual flesh and blood dad.

The Lapland thing was stupid, he told himself. Too late, too impractical and too fraught with problems. But the loan idea still had legs. Two stripy legs with pointy toed shoes with bells on. He would get the loan and then just get them whatever they wanted.

The phone beeped in his hands. It was from Skye.

"Gnight dad. Love you. Looking forward to seeing you on Sunday. BTW Keely got a nose piercing, do you think I should get one? LOL. Tim got a prize at school today for neat handwriting. 😊 Hope you had a good day... You should see this cool advent calendar that Darren got me. I wasn't supposed to see it yet, but mum showed me hers and I saw it. It has beauty products in each door. It's so awesome. He got Mum one that has little bottles of different gins. She got him one that has different coloured socks. Tim has two, one with stationery in each box the other has a picture of him on the front so it is personalized. It has packets of popcorn in it. We have the chocolate ones too, but everyone has those. XOXO

Jason did three things. First, he breathed in to raise his sunken heart back up to its rightful position, and replied to Skye, asking why she was up so late and still on her phone after midnight, even though it was Saturday the next day (knowing that she got cranky without enough sleep).

Secondly, he re-read the text and contemplated why Darren would have got Tim a stationery advent calendar. That was a bit weird. Perhaps Skye made a mistake, or it was predictive texting. She probably meant to type science kit or something. Or maybe not. Perhaps Tim was developing other interests that he wasn't even aware of and only Darren knew about because he lived with them and saw him each day. Could it be that Darren knew Tim better than his own father? Jason's throat closed at the thought of it.

And finally, he completed the loan application, and hovering over the submit button for a moment, asked himself whether he was really doing this, arranging a loan off the internet. Yes. He told himself. Yes, he was, because it was Christmas and because he loved his children more than anything in the world. It was only money after all, and although they say it can't buy happiness, or buy love, or affection or show them that you're not such a loser as their mum makes you out to be…, it bloody well helps.

By the time he awoke tomorrow, he would be £5000 richer and £5000 closer to a bumper Christmas for his kids.

He closed his eyes and stretched to the cold corners of the bed. Instead of this contributing, as it usually did, to his feeling of lack and disadvantage that he had a cold, damp flat, and that his bed was empty without Ellie in it, it actually felt revitalizing and refreshing. He had something to look forward to. He sighed a contented sigh that might have said, "Well Santa, we may hit your big month next week. Your time to shine. But you're not the only guy around here now who can make Christmas dreams come true."

And for the first time in a long time, Jason felt that not every day was black.

Do donkeys eat oats?

29 NOVEMBER

Lucy returned home, tired and drenched. The train had been cancelled and the bus replacement service had got caught in an endless tailback caused by the contraflow set up by the cinema. She had thought it would be quicker to walk than to crawl along the high road on a steaming bus stopping and starting every two minutes. She was right. It was quicker, but it was wetter too. Her telescoping brolly was struggling to stay upright in the wind and the drips soaked her shoulders. As she turned off the highroad and down her street, the traffic flowed more freely, and she had been splashed twice by vans who seemed to favour the kerb rather than the centre of the lane, sending walls of water up against her legs. The tops of her boots and the hem of her coat sat equidistant from her knees, and her tights were getting waterlogged, dragging her gusset further down with each step, until they hung from her like the H bar of a rugby goal.

Raindrops had settled on her glasses, and she was struggling to see, which was made harder by the fog that was descending. Though she couldn't make it out clearly, it seemed, from her position, three houses away and across the road from her Victorian terrace, that there was something on her doorstep. She wasn't expecting a delivery today. And what was there looked nothing like her usual Amazon parcels.

Stepping over it, she put her key in the lock and opened the door. She shook off her umbrella and placed it on the hall floor, open, leaving it to dry out. The radiator was on, filling the hallway with that inimitable swaddling warmth that only central heating on a rainy day can offer. Instinctively, she reached to hang her dripping coat on the rack, as was her daily habit, but seeing it shedding rain into puddles on the floor, she carried it into the kitchen, placing it over the back of a chair instead.

Returning to the doorstep, she studied the package warily and leant out into the street, looking left and right, for clues as to who may have deposited it there. It was not a usual boxed parcel, taped with the branding of the vendor, or labelled with delivery instructions for the courier. It was a Bag for life and looked already into its middle age, according to the creases and wrinkles that had formed on its body. Its long webbing straps had been tied in a hurried bow in an attempt to close the tops together, but with no more secure form of fastening, the top edges remained open as if in a wonky smile.

Peering inside, Lucy could see what looked like a wooden carving of some kind. There was a hoof. Was it a horse? Her mind asked her in incredulity, sending a frown to her forehead as if to strengthen the question. Who on earth would put a horse on her doorstep? Her brain raced, showing her images of the horse head in *The Godfather*, and she racked her mind to see whether at any point in her life, she might have unconsciously made any connections with the Mafia. Finding none, but still cautious, she gingerly separated the lips of the bag, easing them apart to peer inside. Filed within a clear plastic document wallet, was a piece of paper, and nestled in the crumpled corner sat a Ziplock freezer bag with what looked like a bundle of virgin tealights, their wicks untouched by flame. Lucy was certain this wasn't for her. It must have been left her door by mistake. She told herself that she shouldn't open it, or take it inside, because if someone returned later to correct their mistake, they would see it missing. But that notwithstanding, it was lashing down, her shoulders were getting wet, and above all, she was curious.

Flicking on the kettle, she took a mug from the cupboard and spooned a measure of coffee mix from her homemade mix of coffee, milk powder and brown sugar, then poured the boiling water over, stirring until it frothed into a creamy, non-Barista latte (but about £3.50 cheaper). She slipped off her wet shoes and slid her feet into the slippers that were under the radiator then took the bag into the living room. Curling her foot under her, she settled into the sofa and sipped the warming drink.

She would have to open it, Lucy decided. Perhaps there was a note that would explain. If there wasn't and she was no wiser, she could just leave it back outside and see if anyone came to get it. The thought crossed her mind that it could be important. Someone could be waiting for it. But who could be urgently waiting for a wooden horse…? No one, except the Trojans, and this wasn't big enough to fit an army inside. In fact, it didn't even appear to have an inside, it was flat. Two dimensional, as if it had been cut around a stencil with a jigsaw. It was mystifying.

Chilled from her wet walk, Lucy walked into the bathroom and turned on the shower. She would just open it quickly to check and then return the bag to the doorstep. After all, the handles were only loosely tied, it is not as though someone had gone to extreme lengths to maintain the horse's privacy. Once she had satisfied her curiosity, she could put it back out to pasture on her doormat. Then at least if someone did come to claim it, leading it away by its bag-for-life bridle into the night, she wouldn't forever be wondering what it was.

Drying herself with a fluffy towel, she had considered that, if it was a case of mistaken identity, and the horse had been intended for another house or flat in her street instead, it would be neighbourly of her to do a quick check by knocking on doors. But hers was a downstairs flat in a row of Victorian terraces, each with long pathways and brick walls separating their front gardens. She would have to go up and down each path, making what seemed like only a few feet, more like miles. While she thought about it, the rain beat heavily against the window, as if someone was pointing the garden hose directly at it. Lucy was dry for the first time in an hour and a half, and the thought of going out again, even just to the neighbouring houses, was enough to make her shiver. She would go when it eased off a little, she told herself. Pulling on some loose sweatpants, a soft jumper and some slouchy socks, she sauntered into the kitchen and opened a bottle of red wine. Deciding on a simple chicken pesto for dinner, she planned to curl up with a good book and wait out the storm by the fire. The perfect plan for a rainy November evening.

The horse bag stood quietly in the corner, as horses do when they are turned out in sodden field. Anthropomorphising the creature, Lucy imagined it grateful to be in the warm kitchen and giggled to herself at the thought of it sitting at the breakfast bar and sharing a glass of Merlot with her. Surely, whatever it was, could wait until the morning and leave the poor animal to enjoy a nice bowl of pasta. Lucy decided. She was not going out again tonight. She would allow a little extra time before going to work tomorrow and pop around a few of the neighbours in the morning. Usually, she left earlier than most of them, who were either elderly or families; whose working day began later than hers. If the travel situation in the morning was anything like it had been tonight, she was in for another wet walk and the thought of it made her relish her current state of dryness even more.

She invoked Alexa to resume her playlist and set about blitzing pine nuts and garlic in the food processor. After her meal, Lucy lay some kindling in the log burner and curled up on the sofa. As she picked up her book, and turned to her marked page, her phone beeped. A new post. She would ignore it. No, she couldn't, it might be important.

No, when was it ever important? It would just be the same old inane online stuff.

She tried to find her place in the book and took a sip of wine. Having read the same line a couple of times she realised that her mind was wandering. She would just see what the post was. It was a Whatsapp message, from Karen at work. Karen was one of those organisers. The one who sorted collections when colleagues left or got married. The one who bought more teabags and ensured the milk was fresh. The one who organised the Secret Santa.

"Hi all, it's that time of year again," the text began. "Time to get your Secret Santa sorted. We will be doing the draw at our Christmas lunch on 16th. Limit is £20. Can be fun, saucy or tacky – doesn't matter, just any old tut that will be a laugh. Ok guys? But remember, anything that is gender normative, culturally appropriating or politically insensitive will be reported to HR and you will be barred from taking part next year. Ho Ho Ho you bunch of HOs." ☺️😋🎄🎁

Lucy groaned. God, she hated this stuff. She had asked to opt out last year, but Karen had refused, saying that it wouldn't be fair because someone wouldn't get a present. Lucy had queried whether that would be such a bad thing as it was all rubbish anyway that would end up in landfill. And couldn't they all just forget it. Karen had been horrified that Lucy could be so cavalier with such an embedded Christmas tradition and told her that she was a miserable old humbug. Chocolates then? Lucy had suggested. No can do, Karen had replied, Alison is lactose intolerant, Craig had nut allergies and Maya was Jewish and so the chocolate had to be Kosher. Lucy had simply raised her eyebrows at that particular oxymoron. How could you have a Kosher Christmas present?

And twenty pounds? How had it got to that? She remembered her first Secret Santa value had been a fiver, back when she worked in an insurance company as a clerk. Their 'Karen' had asked them to make a list of five things that they would like from Santa, so that what you got would still be a surprise but would at least be something you wanted. Lucy had listed a pair of black, opaque tights, a cherry orchard lipstick from Boots, a slab of Cadbury's fruit and nut, and a box of Just Brazils. She couldn't think of anything else for £5 so just repeated the chocolates. When she had opened her gift, to the guffaws of the invoice team, she had got a knitted willy warmer.

Opening her Amazon app, she was immediately assaulted by the Black Friday deals. It was funny how you didn't think you needed something until you saw it appear on your feed. That hedge trimmer really was an excellent price but was arguably a little too much horsepower for the marjoram in her patio pots. She wondered whether there was anyone she knew that she could buy it for. Having decided not, she continued scrolling and convincing herself that she really had to find a place to accommodate every item on this conveyor of delights. Focus! She told herself. Secret Santa! She typed into the search and began to flick through suggestions, then stopped herself. No. You do not need to do this now, she told herself. It is still November. And she placed her phone back down on the coffee table and picked up her book again.

The phone sat there, a portal to all the shops in the world. It might be good to just pick something and get it out of the way. It would be delivered tomorrow, and she could have it wrapped and done before it was even December. That would show little Miss Organiser Karen, that she wasn't the only one who could be organised. Scrolling through the wacky gifts, she balked at the nonsense. Was she really going to spend twenty of her hard-earned pounds on some piece of rubbish? Particularly for someone she didn't really like. Her colleagues were mean and annoying. Nut-free Craig was a mansplaining misogynist, lactose Alison was work-shy, who had more days off 'sick' a year, than Santa himself (although Lucy had learned that these were for visiting museums and art galleries when it was less busy than at the weekend), and Maya was new to the office, and it was her first Christmas with them. She seemed nice enough but very devout and Lucy wasn't sure it was appropriate to get her a Secret Santa present anyway. A gift for Hanukkah, perhaps. She had suggested as much to Karen, when she began talking about Christmas in early September, but it was no use. She was the type who found it inconceivable that people could believe in anything other than Christmas and couldn't see the harm in everyone partaking in all it had to offer, regardless of personal opinions or religious beliefs.

A dot appeared on Lucy's email app; she opened it instinctively to find that it was a thank you message from UNICEF for the advent calendar she had bought. Each day was purported to reveal a donation of much-needed gifts for the children of those nations whose worlds revolved less around Secret Santa and more about staying alive each day. She was particularly excited to note that her contribution would be supporting the purchase of mosquito nets and polio vaccines and couldn't wait for December to arrive so that she could start opening the doors. She wondered whether to reply to Karen's text suggesting that they each put their twenty quid towards more mosquito nets, or any other type of needy charity than buying more jokey landfill crap. She might go for the idea, Lucy mused hopefully. But then realisation hit her. If they did that instead of opening funny gifts, they would have nothing to provide forced jollification at their Christmas lunch on the sixteenth. It was painful enough to find a place that met everyone's dietary requirements, let alone fill two hours finding conversation amongst people with whom you had nothing in common (whilst avoiding lapsing into work-speak and discussing who was going to manage the McArthur account), and find something to do once the cracker riddles had been read, the crowns had been laughed at, and the plastic frog had been jumped over the tableware. For a PR company, who were supposed to be ambassadors for communication, Lucy found it increasingly difficult to connect with any of her colleagues on matters that were important to her. The very nature of the company was to compete with rivals; to win contracts; to promote their clients in the loudest, showiest way possible. To maximise marketing, social media presence. To be the most eye-catching; to stage the memorable events, even if what they were promoting wasn't something worthy. It was what they did. But sometimes she felt that it might be nice to be around people whose ego came second for a change, who recognized that just because something is a household name, doesn't mean it has integrity. Perhaps it was time for her to have a think about whether she was cut out for the dog-eat-dog world and make next year about eating a vegan falafel instead.

Lucy was already nearly at the bottom of her first glass of wine and was about to pour another when the doorbell rang.

It was the lady from across the road, Margaret. She had a clear rain hat over permed grey hair and was standing stooped on her front step wearing a purple padded jacket and a pair of green wellies. The rain streamed from the blocked gutter over the window frames, sending sheets down at once.

'Oh, hello dear,' the woman began. 'I'm sorry to disturb you but I was wondering if you had found a package on your doorstep. It was meant for me, but they got the wrong house. I've been across the road and to number 27 and 31, but no luck. I was going to try to earlier, but I could see you weren't home.'

Lucy looked at the elderly lady and felt a flush run up her throat. It could have been the wine, but she was pretty sure that it was guilt and shame. Here she was warm and toasty in her fluffy socks and her elderly neighbour was traipsing up and down the road on a wet and foggy night doing what she, Lucy, had put off until tomorrow.

Suddenly she remembered herself. 'Gosh, yes, please, come in out of the rain. Yes, I have it. Well, I think I do. Is it a horse of some kind?'

'A donkey. Yes,' the woman replied stepping into warm hallway. 'Well, I won't come any further I don't want to drip all over your nice floor,' she said trying to confine herself to the coir doormat.

'Honestly, please it's fine,' Lucy assured her. 'Come in and have a cup of tea or something.'

'Oh, I don't want to disturb you,' replied the woman. 'I'll

just take it and get out of your hair. It's a terrible night, isn't it?' she said rhetorically. 'I wouldn't have bothered, coming out in this deluge, only it was important that I find it. There's been a right commotion about it. Everyone is in such a panic about it being missing. If you didn't have it, I don't know what we would have done.'

Lucy struggled to think why a donkey carving could be important and what kind of commotion could ensue from its disappearance. She tried to imagine the significance of donkeys in the daily life of most people but couldn't think of one. No rides on the beach perhaps (did they still do that? She thought that had been outlawed). Or perhaps there were panniers of Spanish carrots that wouldn't get delivered.

She took a step into the living room and picked up the bag. 'I must admit. I was a bit curious about it. I was going to do the rounds to the neighbours myself actually,' she said brightly hoping to convey her most able and proactive demeanour. She neglected to add that she had determined it to not be important enough to do so this evening, based on nothing other than her reluctance to get soaked again and had deferred her task until tomorrow. 'I thought it might be important' she added for emphasis. She realised that her cosy outfit, smell of fresh basil and the logs crackling in the fireplace, didn't really support the urgency of her mission and hoped that Margaret's polite smile didn't suggest that she didn't think so either.

'Well, like I said, I'll be off now,' the woman said. 'I must ring Jean and tell her that I've found it and that all is well. Thank you, lovey.' She turned to go, pulling the chub knob to release the lock.

'You're welcome,' Lucy replied realising that she hadn't actually done anything to be thanked for, nor to be magnanimous about. 'I'm sorry,' she added, 'I don't mean to pry, but I can't help but wonder. What actually is it? The donkey I mean – why is it so important?'

'Oh, it's just something for church. I suppose you'd think it silly,' Margaret explained. Although a devout Christian herself, she was mindful that not everyone shared her conviction, including her daughter, and particularly these – what do you call them – Millennials.

'No, I won't. Really,' Lucy said 'I'd like to know. I couldn't imagine what it was. If it was a sculpture, I would have expected it to have been in a nice box or something, or at least wrapped in paper or bubble wrap.'

Margaret peeked between the handles and noted that it had really been stuffed in quite unceremoniously.

'Well, it's this thing we do at Christmas – well, Advent really. In our church. We have this little donkey here, and he is passed from house to house, each evening. You have a cup of tea and light the candle and say the little prayer that is enclosed in the bag.'

'Oh, I see,' Lucy said, although she didn't. What was the point of that? 'Why a donkey?' she asked instead.

'It's the donkey that Mary went to Bethlehem on, you know, in the Christmas story, with Joseph, to get to the stable because there was no room at the inn.'

'Of course,' said Lucy nodding her head in recognition. 'Silly me, I didn't think about that.'

'I'll show you if you like,' Margaret said placing the bag on the floor and untying the handles. She withdrew a flat wooden carving, about the size of a tea tray and balanced the base on her palm, steadying the back as if she were presenting a BAFTA. It was the silhouette, nothing more, of a donkey shape, led by a featureless man in a simple robe and a veiled woman sat upon its back. Lucy couldn't tell what type of wood it was, but it had a kind of marbled pattern and slightly greenish tinge.

'It's olive wood,' Margaret said, as if reading her mind. 'It's beautiful, isn't it? Very simple, yet I find that is where most beauty lies – in the simple things.' She smiled wistfully and placed the object back into the bag, tying it up again. So that's it. That's our travelling crib – that has seemingly already begun its travelling, all around the neighbourhood,' she chuckled.

Lucy smiled, pausing with her hand on the doorknob, not quite wanting to let Margaret go. 'But if you want a crib, why not just use an actual crib – you know the whole stable and three wise men and things?'

'I don't know really,' Margaret replied. 'I suppose there is something about the donkey being a form of transportation. It symbolises the journey itself. So much of our lives see us rushing to our destination, we don't recognize the way we get there, or sometimes how difficult it is. It was a long and arduous trek for Mary, and it was a long way to Bethlehem. They didn't have trains in those days,' Margaret chuckled again, peering over her spectacles.

Lucy felt like saying that the cancellation of the 17:42 from Farringdon hadn't made her journey any less arduous this evening but didn't know whether Margaret would take offense at Lucy likening herself to the mother of God. She did allow herself a moment to wonder whether riding a donkey to work might be a suitable alternative to her daily commute though - fewer delays; a regular timetable; no need for a bus replacement service that edged along no faster than a snail, and the benefit of avoiding eight stops with her face in someone's armpit. It all added up to an upgrade to her mind. Not to mention the savings on fares. She assumed that the Oyster card had been so named to try to create the impression of the world being your oyster, but the proportion of her salary that it took each month was more akin to an oyster's reputation for being a luxury expensive item, it's precious pearl within, being as rare as a trouble-free commute.

Yes, she had to agree, a donkey was looking like a better proposition by the minute. How much did it cost to keep a donkey? She wondered. Would it be happy in her courtyard, nibbling on the herbs in her window troughs, or did they eat oats or something? She could just see herself ambling along to the rhythm of hoof treads under a starlit sky – well, not on a night like tonight, but in the image that she had of Mary crossing the desert. It all at once seemed quite appealing.

Although, she had to concede, it may not be if you were nearly full-term.

'My Dave carved the donkey a few years ago and it is usually kept in the cupboard in the vestry,' Margaret explained as she straightened her rain hood, 'but it was taken out yesterday, in preparation for Sunday's service and then it went missing. Ooh there was such a to-do. Everyone searched high and low.'

Lucy raised her eyes in support of the dilemma.

'Apparently, Jean, who is on the flower arranging committee had seen it looking a little battered and took it home, thinking that she would drop it into me, for Dave to give it a little TLC, but then Kevin, that's Jean's husband, well Kevin's mum took ill. She had a fall, bless her, she's ninety-two and lives in Stockport, and they had to rush off to see how she is. Well, Jean remembered that she had the crib bag and had no time to get it back to me, but she had popped to her daughter with the cat things so she could mind her and had asked her daughter to drop it round to me. But she must have got the house wrong. Jean called me this evening to see if I'd got it and when I said I didn't, Jean went into a terrible panic. We thought the blessed thing was missing and we'd have nothing for the service. We have a whole schedule of people booked onto the list. They'd all be lined up waiting, and there'd be no sign of it.' Margaret sighed, shaking her head at such an unthinkable thing.

For a second time, Lucy saw the comparison between the beast of burden and the 17.42 from Farringdon – there was a whole crowd of people lined up last night too and there was no sign of it.

'Still, all's well that ends well,' Margaret concluded. 'I'd better be going. Thanks again, Love. Look after yourself in this nasty weather.'

Lucy watched her neighbour leave, hunched over the bag, and clutching it close, protecting it from the downpour. How funny it was, she thought, the practices that people have. 'Advent donkeys!' she whispered to herself as she closed the door on the darkness. She had heard everything now.

Home Goal

30 NOVEMBER

Kayleigh drained the last of her mug of tea and leant over the balcony. It was getting dark, and it was time that Liam came in. She watched him kicking the football against the garages. The repeated thud as it hit the tarmac, then the contact with the ball then the clang as the metal door reverberated was grating on her nerves. One, two, three – one, two three– like two robots performing a waltz. She was sure that the other people in the flats were finding it annoying too, but they found everything annoying and either told in plain words or let their sidelong glances of judgment speak for them. The spoken words she could cope with, the unspoken words were worse. She knew they hated her, but what made them so special? It's not like they were much better. All the occupants were the dregs of society; the flats, like the back of the cupboard where you put stuff you didn't really want anymore. Most of them were unemployed and the majority were addicts of one kind or the other, it wasn't a case of whether you were or weren't, more a case of the extent to which you were. There were those, recently unemployed, down on their luck, turning to substance for comfort and oblivion, but managing to keep it together, or so you think. There were the others who had succumbed. Lost a total grip on reality and whose purpose was only to get up to steal something, to borrow something or to score something before climbing back to the pit to sleep off the effects. Then there were the recovering addicts, the ones who having plunged to the depths were now on the other side, trying to climb out of the pit. That was the hardest, that's what she was like (not that she was in recovery herself, but by association, as it were), but it felt as though the pit walls were sheet plastic and someone was pouring washing-up liquid down it, the glassy sides, making it impossible to find purchase even when clinging on by both finger and toenails.

She didn't like having to raise her son amongst these people, the ones who peed on the communal stairs and graffitied the walls and did deals of all kinds in the lift.

But this was the world she was in, the one which, although not choosing specifically, had been the one that her choices had led her to. A shelter would be okay if she was on her own, but she had Liam; and the refuge wasn't really an option because she wasn't fleeing for her life. And for that she was grateful. The flats weren't nice, but when she was home and she and Liam were tucked up in bed, reading stories, they were safe; and he had a room that he could call his own and have his own things in. He didn't have much, and most of that was from the charity shop, but he didn't ask for much either. He was happy with a football and a garage door. In the summer months, she would take him to the park, but it was already dark now at four o'clock.

He sometimes mentioned that his friends went to skills training, or football matches after school at the weekend and that that was why they got picked for the sides when they played at school. He was usually picked last, which he was sad about because he was naturally quite good. Kayleigh had suffered through enough football with Liam's dad, in the days before the heroin of course, to know what to look for in a player. It bored her, in truth, but her early education hadn't lasted long, he had mixed one too many pills and had so she hadn't had to watch another game again.

She called for him to come up and he begged for three more. His last kick sent the ball to the flowerpot of the bottom flat and the door flew open. Screaming at him, the man grabbed the ball and clutched it to his chest. 'You're not getting this back until you pay for the damage to that pot,' he shouted angrily.

'But that's mine, you can't just take my ball,' Liam cried.

'I can and I will. That's criminal damage that is,' the man shouted.

Kayleigh slid into her slippers and ran back through the flat to the stairwell. She took them two at a time and appeared by Liam's side as soon as she could.

'It's not criminal damage,' she said snatching the ball back out of his hands. 'It was an accident, it wasn't willful.'

'I don't care, you still need to pay for a new pot, and the plants.'

Kayleigh looked at the brown twigs and hairlike strands that she remembered had once been a petunia.

'The pot, I'll replace, but the plants are dead.'

The man didn't retort, seemingly accepting that the desiccated remains of the summer blooms made a convincing case for her argument.

'Shouldn't be bloody playing here anyway. It's a garage, not bloody Old Trafford.' He said angrily and slammed the door. The number one slipping to one side on its loose screw.

Kayleigh handed the ball back to Liam and put an arm around his shoulder. He looked hurt and worried.

'I'm really sorry Mum,' I didn't mean to kick it that hard. I was aiming at the door, but it hit the handle and ricocheted,'

'I know you didn't mean to, but you have to be careful, hun. They might stop you playing here.' Anway as if you'd play for Man Utd,' she said trying to lift his mood. 'Chelsea are the best, aren't they?' she said, picking the first name she could think of that would tease her son and take his mind off the broken flower-pot.

'No Mum, Man City are the best in the world at the moment, but I'd play for Real Madrid,' he said balancing the ball on is toes and tossing it from foot to foot as he walked. She noticed that the top of his shoes were coming away from the sole. That was more likely to be the cause for his missed shot, not the handle. She couldn't tell whether Liam knew that himself and didn't want to mention it, or whether he had really just hit the handle.

'Oh, my bad,' she said, scruffling his hair. Forget about him, I'll sort the pot out tomorrow. Come on up. I've got a surprise for you.'

'Aw, brilliant!' Liam yelled when he saw the advent calendar, the crown emblem of his favourite Spanish team at the top and a snapshot of a game on the front. The doors were hidden in the image and Liam immediately scanned it searching for the numbers.

'No cheating!' Kayleigh warned. 'You'll ruin the fun on Friday. That's the first and I'm putting it away until then. Liam planted a kiss on her cheek and ran into the living room with a packet of biscuits, flicking on the TV.

She opened the door to the cupboard over the microwave, and placed the calendar behind the tins and took out a jar of dried pasta spirals. Shaking some out into a bowl, she found three notes, a twenty, ten and fiver. The twenty – she would have to keep for emergencies. Rent, food and electricity she could use her bank card for, her benefits covered that, but this was for extras, for those things you couldn't use your card for. Things like plant pots. How much was a pot? she wondered. She didn't have a clue, and where did you even get one? A garden centre she supposed. There was one on the dual carriageway. The 265 bus passed it. She could go there tomorrow and let her supervisor know that she might be half an hour late. On second thoughts, perhaps she should take Liam there on Saturday. She wasn't punishing him for the accident, but she did want him to learn that there were consequences to your actions. As much as it pained her, it might be better for him to pay some out of his birthday money and know what it was like to have to make your money stretch to the unexpected as well as to the expected.

Which in her case was Liam's shoes.

Hail Grace

30 NOVEMBER

Liz dropped her keys into the bowl and the shopping on the counter. Grace followed behind dragging her swimming bag along the floor.

'Can you empty the bag love?' she said. 'Just pop them into the washing machine and I'll give them another spin, they'll dry faster that way.' Her daughter nodded and yawned. She was always exhausted after swimming. Liz hated it and couldn't wait until next year when she had completed her grade. The summer months were nice, and she would sit on the side feeling envious of the kids in the cool water, but now in November when it was dark and cold, she dreaded it.

She couldn't complain really. She had a car, it wasn't like she had to take the bus, and the pool wasn't really very far. It was just everything that went with it, like having the stuff ready before pick-up, including a snack which was light enough to not induce vomiting in the pool, but enough to sate the voracious hunger of the 'end of school-day' child. Then it was the lesson, where the walls and ceilings were dripping with condensation and the wet floors of the changing rooms had to be navigated keeping uniform off the floor and spending enough time to dry the hair, so it was not dripping but not so much that it was too dry to wet again in the shower at home. (Grace didn't like the showers at the pool) you had to press the button down with your back in order to wash your hair) then it was late by the time she had eaten dinner, dried the hair, squeezed in whatever homework or reading there was and had seen to the needs of Josh and Elliot, who, whilst older still always needed something; couldn't find something, blamed each other for taking it, which she then had to mediate and needed driving somewhere or picking up. Lewis was at Uni – which was one fewer child, competing for her constant attention, but this was more than made up for by her residents in the care home. They too, always needed something; had lost something or blamed someone else for taking it, just like her children. She might not need to taxi them around in the same way, but the demands on her were relentless. At least, once she had done something for her kids, they were content and sorted. With her residents she had to repeat it all five minutes later, their memory retention unable to hold on to facts and information any longer than that.

'Aah, is this for me?' Grace said as she found an advent calendar on the counter.

'Yes,' Liz replied filling the kettle, to put on some spaghetti, 'I didn't know what you wanted so I just got the chocolate one with a Santa on. That's pretty much all Christmas is about, isn't it? Chocolate and Santa.'

'And Jesus,' Grace said.

'Oh. Yes, of course… and Jesus,' Liz said, surprised at her daughter's sudden redirection in festive emphasis.

'I forgot to tell you,' Grace said, 'coz we were late for swimming. I'm Mary. In the nativity.'

'Oh wow!' Liz said, 'That's great. I didn't know you were auditioning, or anything… did you audition?'

'Er, yes, and no,' Grace admitted. 'Mrs Midden asked if anyone wanted to be Mary and only me and Kitty and Chloe…'

'Kitty, Chloe and I,' Liz corrected, squirming at the error.

'Yeah, that's what I said,' Grace acknowledged. 'Well, us and Patrick.'

'Wait,' Liz said turning to face her daughter. 'Patrick wanted to be Mary.'

'Yeah, and Mrs Midden said he couldn't because he was a

boy and he said that wasn't fair and it was gender discrimination – because it is… right? It is sooo unfair.'

Liz placed the spaghetti in the pan and added a sprinkling of salt and a drizzle of olive oil.

'Well, yes, I can see that,' Liz agreed.

'What's this?' Elliot said as he sauntered into the kitchen and opened the fridge, which is what he did at regular intervals. 'Oh, is this mine?' he asked, picking up the calendar.

'You know it's not,' Liz chided, tapping it out of his hand. 'There are two missing, so I presume you and Sam have already taken yours. And on that. I think it would be nicer if we kept them all here together in the kitchen, like we did when you were little. It's not the same if you just open them on your own in your rooms. Can you bring yours back down please?'

Elliot nodded, biting into an apple. 'Yeah, okay. Anyway, what were you talking about? What's happened? What's unfair discrimination?' he asked loving the opportunity to get stuck into rights' issues, human, civil, alien or any others.

Grace explained, pulling strands of dry spaghetti and snapping them into little pieces. They kept bouncing on the floor which added to the cause of Liz's tension headache. 'Mrs Midden said that Patrick can't be Mary in the play, the nativity, because he is a boy.'

'God, on so many levels is that wrong,' her brother exclaimed dramatically. 'Firstly…' he said sitting up on the kitchen table and placing his legs on the chair seat, it providing an upgrade to a soap box for his pronouncement.

'Oh God,' Liz thought. He was settling in for a debate. She just wanted to feed them and have a soak in the bath.

'I mean,' he continued in his most authoritative voice. 'Firstly…,' he repeated, 'they are just parts in a play. It's not like he actually has to physically be a woman. They're not really doing a live action birth scene, are they?' he challenged.

Grace wrinkled her face in a grimace of disgust at the thought.

'Secondly,' he counted on his index finger for emphasis.

'They all wore robes and head coverings in those days anyway. Men and women looked the same. From the back, you can only ever tell who Mary and Joseph are because she is in blue, and he is in brown – which is still gender normative when you think about it. And thirdly, even if they did wear different clothes, with Joseph in trousers and Mary in a dress, that is so not right either, because people don't want to be confined by how they are supposed to dress. And…,' he added, leaning forward and pointing to Grace, 'when you see Mary from the front, you can see she is pregnant; but as most year six girls aren't pregnant - year nine, maybe,' he allowed as an aside, and Liz gave him a meaningful stare for discussing such things in front of his little sister.

'Elliot,' she warned, waggling the wooden spoon at him. 'Not in front of your little sister.'

Elliot smiled wryly and continued 'They have to use a cushion to create their bump anyway, so there is no reason that Patrick can't do it either.'

Liz wanted to say that Joseph usually sported a beard but thought that might be antagonistic; and since she had begun the menopause, the wayward hairs on her chin were starting to rival his so, she thought she would keep quiet. Just keep stirring, she told herself, feeling ill-equipped to keep pace with what was and wasn't the right thing to say these days.

Grace was listening to her older brother and adopting his outrage by osmosis. 'Yeah,' she said thinking that this was rhetorical gold and how she wished she had known all this earlier. She would have sounded so woke.

'Finally,' Elliot continued, 'If Patrick wants to express himself in that way, he should be allowed to. Who said the mother of God needed to be a woman? Dads are parents too, you know? Cal, in my year has two dads. He doesn't have a mother.'

Liz nodded and wanted to say that he would have had a mother at some point, someone needed to carry and give birth to him, regardless of whether they were able to raise him. And that's what Mary was, as Jesus didn't come to Earth as a fully formed man. Unless you subscribed to the idea that he was an Alien, come to save the human race from the destruction of itself and the planet. Or that the whole of the Christmas story is a deep fake and there was no annunciation, visitation and holy birth. Again, she kept her thoughts on women with gestational capabilities to herself. Whilst it was valid, it weakened Elliot's current point; and she didn't ever want to quash his vigour for righteousness. She liked his open-minded tolerance; how unprejudiced and willing to be the voice for justice and acceptance he was. If she said something practical now, about mothers being anatomically essential for the physical birth of the child (she should know – she had done it four excruciating times), it would come across as old fashioned and feminist. She knew that there were wonderful mothers who had never given birth, and women who had given birth that were terrible mothers; and women who had neither wanted to, nor been able to be mothers; and that there were fathers who were excellent mothers… and that determining what being a mother even means was a debate to get into with Elliot on another day. But not this evening. Instead, she remained quiet, let him have his moment and sprinkled the sauce with chopped basil.

'I guess Jesus was like Cal,' Elliot mused. 'He had two dads, too, Joseph and God. And God was the father of all fathers – he was God the father – it was even in his name. That's cool,' he nodded satisfied with his discovery. 'I'm going to tell Cal that tomorrow. He's like a new Jesus.'

Liz smiled and served the food into bowls and cut up the garlic bread.

'And do you know what else…?' he continued. 'What if Patick is really secretly Trans, and identifies as a woman and wants to have the opportunity of being the most famous woman of all. Why can't he do that? It's just not right,' he said shaking his head as if the future was beyond all help.

Grace didn't really know where he was going with that

because he thought that Beyonce was probably the most famous woman of all. She must be more famous than Mary, surely. Because there were loads of people in the world who didn't believe in Jesus and probably hadn't even heard of Mary, but Everyone knew Beyonce – well her and the Queen. But she had just died, so it was still probably Beyonce holding that top spot – or maybe Jennifer Aniston.

'Oh, and guess what homework I've just being doing?' Elliot asked rhetorically,'

Liz wondered whether the homework was how to be an opiniated year ten teenager who was doing a greater job of stirring than she was with the spaghetti – in which case he should get an A star, but she tapped his legs out of the way and gave him the cutlery with which to lay the table.

'English,' he answered. See, it was rhetorical.

'I've just being doing Shakespeare, where all the men played girls parts, because – outrageously – women were not allowed on stage. And then in his comedies, when they all swapped roles, there were boys playing girls who were dressing up as boys. So, if it was good enough for him, it should be good enough for Mrs Midden. That's what I think,' he pronounced, placing the last water glass down with a flourish.

'Yeah,' said Grace emphatically, taking up a glass to toast his oration.

'So, I'm assuming Patrick wasn't allowed to do it, which left the three of you girls to audition. Is that right?' Liz asked, trying to sum up so that she could serve the Bolognese and hasten to her bath, without any further human rights violations.

'God! "girls". That's so reductive mum. You can't say things like that anymore.'

Liz raised her eyebrows, mouthed a sorry and looked to Grace to answer her question.

'Yeah, well Kitty is friends with Patrick, so after he wasn't allowed, she said she didn't want to do it anymore…'

'Respect,' Elliot nodded approvingly, 'Solidarity with her oppressed brother. I'm here for that.'

'… and then it was just me and Kitty left,' Grace explained.

'Kitty and I,' Liz said reflexively.

'Kitty and I…, and we both had to sing the song. And Kitty sang off key, so I got the part. So, yeah, Yay Me,' Grace said, allowing herself a small jazz hands in her own congratulation.

'I can't believe that Kitty was ditched just because she can't sing,' Elliot said defensively of this new patriot he had learned of. 'More oppression. Right there.'

'Well, the play has got songs in it,' Grace said simply.

'Yes, but they can autotune, or have a voice over for the songs,' Elliot pointed out matter of factly, as if it were so obvious an oversight, Mrs Midden had no business casting for the school play. 'That's what they do in the movies. They even did it in *Singin' in the Rain,* and that was centuries ago.'

Liz took the plates to the table, wanting to point out that it was hardly centuries ago, but then remembered that it was set in the twenties and that was about a hundred years ago. It was no wonder that she was feeling left behind. Would children in a hundred years to come, be sitting on a kitchen table referencing her son's words, seemingly so forward thinking now, but considered archaic to the new, young minds of the future generations.

'What if Kitty was a brilliant actor, and she is being judged on a disability?' he asked.

'I don't think being tone deaf registers you as disabled,' Liz ventured, but she wasn't exactly sure of the rules anymore – perhaps it was. She turned to her daughter and raised a glass to her. 'Well. Well done darling, I'm very proud of you,' she said, although the accolade sounded weak, as though her daughter's achievements comprised no more than the wearing of a blue robe stuffed with a cushion foetus; not having facial hair; not being a birth male; and being able to hold a tune— whether that is considered a talent or a privilege.

'Yeah, here's to you, Mary,' Elliot said joining the salute.

Setting aside a portion of the meal for Sam and Karl to have when they got in, Liz relished the first moment of silence as they ate. She twisted the pasta around the fork and felt revived by the warm food. Elliot was bent toward his plate and sucking his spaghetti through his lips. Suddenly, he splurted it out in an explosion of laughter. 'Hah!' he guffawed.

'Oh, what on earth…!' Grace cried. 'Elliot! That's disgusting! What's the matter with you.'

'I've just realised. I know why Mrs Midden picked you,' he said through the giggles. He clearly thought he was very funny.

'Yeah?' Grace asked.

'So that they could say, "Hail Mary, full of Grace," he laughed again.

'Oh yeah,' Grace said and joined in with the giggles.

Despite Liz's exhaustion, she laughed too, using the last of her remaining strength to hit him with a piece of garlic bread.

The bunyip

30 NOVEMBER

Laura bent to kiss her son's soft forehead and placed the storybook on the top of the chest of drawers. Her feet padded across the carpet, carefully avoiding the Lego, and checking him one last time, pulled open the bedroom door. It closed gently behind her, and she released the knob, carefully peeling her fingertips from the brass, as if she were completing the most crucial part of a bomb disposal. As she looked up, Jack was doing the same. They locked eyes and giggled. Complicit in the rules of the bedtime routine game. Jack settled Max, while Laura read to Briony, then they switched. Often, Briony chatted for longer, suddenly remembering things that had happened at school and sitting up to give a full account. It always mystified Laura how such facts and features could be absent throughout the walk or drive home; through homework and reading time; through the whole course of supper – both making and eating it; and bath time, and only be seemingly of enough significance to muster being raised at this point in the night, when Laura was counting the minutes to pouring a chilled glass of Pinot Grigio and sitting down for the first time since 2:30pm. It would seem that it takes six hours of decompression time for the memories to begin to surface and by then, the bedtime could take two turns. Either the high points would be so excitedly recounted that her daughter would now be wide awake and chatting garrulously and laughing. Or the gross injustices of the day, only recently recalled in the quietness, would have worsened in direct proportionality to her level of tiredness and be now an outpouring of sadness. What might begin as a small voice asking for the light to be left on, or a little hand refusing to let go, would then become silent tears, falling down the peachlike mounds of her cheeks to wet the pillow. It was in these moments where Laura found that wrapping her in her arms and nestling behind her like two spoons in the drawer, stroking her temple and softly singing the tears away was better than getting into the whys and wherefores of the event. Love and comfort were what was needed. Exploration and rationalisation could wait until tomorrow. So, regretfully, could the Pinot Grigio.

But tonight was good. It had seemingly been an uneventful day, nothing notable enough to disturb the embarkation on the boat to dreamland, and Laura and Jack were able to creep softly down the stairs and, in the confines of the kitchen, felt it safe enough to resume a low-level normal voice, rather than the mouthed whispers on the landing. The only sound, the glug of the wine from the bottle and the slight chink as the edges of the glasses kissed gently.

'So, what do we do with this then?' Jack asked, pulling the new advent calendar towards him. It was made of wood and shaped like a gingerbread house, its windows and doors, edged in thickly fallen 'snow' and numbered in the customary way.

'Well,' Laura began, 'We open the drawers and put chocolates in, just like a normal calendar,' she said removing one of the little wooden drawers. 'Although, they are a bit shallower than I expected. They're going to have to be little chocolates, which won't go down too well, I imagine.' She laughed. 'My idea was that I go to the supermarket, get some bits for the food bank and put them in the collection box by the door and write them on a little slip of paper. I got these and typed up a list. It's your job to cut them out.' She handed him the scissors from the kitchen drawer and thrust her phone under his nose for him to see the photo of the shopping trolley with all the items in.

Jack peered at the screen and made a comment about

whether anyone actually liked tinned sardines. Laura screwed up her nose at the thought of them and agreed but explained that they were one of the recommended items on the foodbank's list. 'I got nice things too,' she added defensively, 'like a couple of Christmas puddings; chocolate selection boxes; packets of stuffing and jars of cranberry sauce. I know people at the food bank might be needy, but it doesn't mean they need to be grateful for a packet of mashed potato mix, when they would really rather have a mince pie.

'So, this is what I was thinking,' she said as she opened a box of Celebrations and selected a Bounty and a Milky Way, squeezing them into the narrow box. 'We can put a chocolate in for each of the guys and then a little slip of paper that says, "Today, you have given someone in need a tin of beans", or a packet of rice, or a box of cereal. Things like that.'

'That's nice,' Jack said nodding. 'I like it. It's good to remember how lucky we are compared to others.'

'Yeah, well, that's what I thought,' Laura replied. 'I know we want to give the kids everything that we didn't have when we were growing up, but I also don't want them to be spoilt. Look,' she said, turning the laptop towards him. An Excel spreadsheet shone its face at him and spoke to him in columns and rows of neat figures and text and different-coloured highlighted titles.

'To that end, I created this. Thought it might help us keep track of which presents we've got for our guys,' Laura said with a light tone in her voice which tasted of part pragmatism and part pride. 'We can limit the expenditure and make sure that everything is fair.'

'Really?' he whined dramatically. 'I've looked at spreadsheets all day.'

Laura smiled at her husband's mock complaint and proceeded to walk him through it.

'So, we have two columns for the children,' she said checking that he was following, which seemed elementary and unnecessary, given the complex tables, graphs and statistics he was used to. But both knew that she sought not to patronize, it was merely a starting point, like finding the *You are here* dot on a map. 'Then beneath, we have this line, which is the main present from Santa,' she explained pointing to a red row detailing the item's name and cost; and two further columns whose ticks demonstrated whether it had been purchased and wrapped. 'Then the other rows are the other smaller things from Santa which they have mentioned over the last few months.'

Her husband nodded to show his comprehension.

'According to the last conversation, the guys are still set on their original choices, which is just as well, seeing as how we have already bought them. We can get them to write their Santa letters this week and then we are sorted. Then, no matter what they see on TV adverts, or in the shops, we can say that it is too late, you've already sent your letter and that's what the elves are busy making.'

'Has Briony said any more about the mermaid thing?' Jack asked as he opened a packet of olives.

'No, I've tried not to mention it and hope it goes away,' Laura said reaching for the shiny green fruit. 'It's not just the mermaids, it's the other things in that flipping Myths book that she has. She wants a figure of each thing, so she can act out legends and recreate scenarios and she can't do that if she hasn't got the figures. I have looked all over the internet and there is nothing like it anywhere. I don't know what we are going to do if we can't find them.'

'What is it again?' Jack asked, reaching for his phone.

Laura forced down a swell of frustration. She knew that he was only trying to help and was grateful that he was such an engaged father but, she knew that he would either find what she had already fruitlessly spent ages looking for; to which, she would have to put up with his proud swagger and mansplaining about how to use the search correctly. Or, alternatively, he wouldn't find anything and agree with her that they don't exist, which will then make him realise that he could actually accept what she said, in the first place, without having to check it himself.

'What about that Schleich stuff? They have all sorts of creatures,' he said scrolling through to find the page, before waiting for her response. "Yes, like that wasn't the first place I looked," she wanted to say, but didn't.' He didn't even know what he was searching for yet.

'Look here's a mermaid, and a manticore – what's a manticore again?' he asked, looking up at her and taking another olive.

'A man-lion with a dragon or scorpion tail,' she replied, resignedly. Knowing this, because she was required to keep up to date with every such mythical beast, it being Briony's current obsession and one that she conversed with Laura upon daily and expected her to be au fait with each one's characteristics, origins and abilities, particularly if they were supernatural and had extraordinary powers.

Jack had gone quiet, and Laura could tell that he had gone down the rabbit hole of Wiki searching, following the warren of hyperlinks and was now somewhere wandering around Wonderland like Alice, stumbling across no end of remarkable and interesting discoveries. No wonder that rabbit was late for every important date, Laura thought.

'A bunyip,' she said, taking a sip of wine and waiting for him to refocus. 'She wants a bunyip figure.'

'Oh, right,' he said nodding. 'And what exactly is a bunyip?'

'Well, as far as I can tell, no one knows,' she said giving a small shrug, 'which is part of the problem. I'd imagine that neither Sleich, nor anyone else can make a figure of something when there doesn't seem any consensus of what it is. Some say it is like a seal, others, a crocodile; some say it has the head of a bird and a long neck, others say it has a barbed tail like a stingray.'

'And she still wants this?' Jack checked. 'Can't we put her off and find her something else instead? He scans the page, 'like a leviathan, or a gryphon?'

'She already has a leviathan,' Laura stated patiently, and a gryphon is already on her list for Santa, and I have got one of those. It's the flipping bunyip, I can't get. How is Santa supposed to bring her a bunyip figure when they don't even exist?'

'Well, they are mythical,' Jack said wryly.

'You joke,' Laura replied, suddenly minded of a conversation she had with one of the mums in the playground that afternoon. 'That's exactly what I said to Hildy. You know Hildy? With Magnus?'

Jack nods.

'We were discussing Santa and I explained that I was having trouble finding a bunyip. She said she'd never heard of it and asked whether I checked Amazon, or elsewhere on the internet. I stopped myself from being facetious, and politely explained that, yes, I had searched the internet and had been unsuccessful. When she asked what it was. I said that it was a mythical beast, from olden days, but that it didn't exist. You'll never guess what she said,' to which Jack, to his credit, had come out of his window to the world and asked, 'Go on. What?'

'She said, "Of course you can't find it on the internet if it doesn't exist." I laughed, thinking she was being funny, but then realized she was being serious. I qualified my statement, "No, I mean no *figures* of it exist," I said. And she said, "but you can't expect something mythical to exist."'

'She's got a point,' Jack said, annoyingly, missing said point.

Laura frowned at him and continued. 'I said to her, "No, I mean that there are figures of mythical creatures like mermaids, and minotaurs and manticores etc. and they do exist on the internet, but there are no bunyips. And Briony believes that whatever you ask Santa for, he will provide, so is absolutely expecting beyond all doubt to get a bunyip on Christmas morning and there is no way we can make that happen.'

'What did she say to that?' Jack asked, raising his brow in query.

Laura was fairly certain that he was thinking what she was thinking, having recalled the conversation to mind. He was not so much interested in whether she had made Hildy understand that bunyips in their physical, play worthy form are nowhere to be found on the world wide web. But more whether she had any sage advice as to what they were going to do about disappointing their daughter. And potentially being responsible for bringing her dreams of Santa crashing down on the living room floor; taking the Christmas tree with them; all the fairy lights and while at it, throwing the stockings out on the street and stabbing Donner and Blitzen through the heart with a particularly prickly sprig of holly.

'She just shrugged and said that I probably didn't use the search correctly,' Laura told him. 'Oh, and she said that if they are from the "olden days", perhaps I should look on eBay, because someone might have one from the seventies that they are getting rid of.

'Anyway,' she continued. 'As you can see, no bunyip.' She raised her eyebrows in their shared dilemma regarding the missing mythical figure, like detectives finding a fault in their investigation. 'But, aside from that, we've got most of the items so that's a relief.'

Jack thought, for a moment, that the children's lists read a little like the number part of *Countdown* – One from the top and any other five, please Carol– although coincidentally, the number dealer was now someone else, he believed. He didn't know how he knew that, probably the daily onslaught of celebrity and TV news that pervaded his home screen everyday, words and pictures seeping into his brain, unbidden, like treacle coating a spoon. He hadn't watched the programme in years, having his own number problems to solve every day without having to do some for fun. And he couldn't just press a button to generate a number that they could get roughly close to, the numbers he played with were people's salaries and lives and every penny counted.

He noted that Laura had matched the items as fairly as possible, but even that had been difficult, she explained. She had also argued with her mother-in-law on this point. Max had wanted a remote-controlled boat, that he wanted to sail on the park pond. It was three times the price of the small figures that Briony wanted (that was assuming that if they ever found a bunyip, it would be the same price as the others. Although, she was slowly coming to recognise the fact that its rarity value might raise its purchase price significantly beyond the cost of the boat – even a superyacht moored in the waters of the Mediterranean). Cost aside, Laura knew that the small figure would look tiny in comparison, when they stood wrapped in paper and bows on Christmas morning, and she keenly felt the disparity. She felt that she should buy her daughter additional things to buoy up the haul. But, then Briony would have more things to open, which wouldn't be fair on Max who was too little to understand the concept of value, only quantity, and would have no clue as to why Santa had given more to his big sister.

Fiona, Jack's mother, had offered to buy Briony something else. "Just get her something else, dear. There are hundreds of toys in the shops, or books and games. Why don't you get her those? If it's a matter of affording it, I can help you out. You can't get her only that little thing. Santa brings big presents." she had said, suggesting that Laura's own miserliness was the cause of her granddaughter's prospective disappointment. It seemed to Laura that Fiona was oblivious to four facts. One, that 'that little thing' happened to be her daughter's dearest wish. Two, that Santa's role was to bring what was on the list, not what was the largest, most expensive and most impressive gift when you talked about it to others. Three, that even a child might smell a deceitful rat when they suddenly discover that Santa afforded them a plethora of other goodies that they hadn't put on their list, particularly if their sibling didn't get a booster too. Because how was that fair? And four, that purchasing the world's most unobtainable gift had nothing to do with money.

'It's a hard balance to strike, particularly with your mother,' Laura said.

'I know I know,' Jack agreed. 'I know she can be a snob and a bit clueless at times, but she loves the guys and just wants to spoil them.'

'But I don't want them to be spoilt,' Laura muttered. 'And I don't want Christmas to be all about greed and selfishness and presents, it's about more than that.' She looked at the gingerbread house and thought of the trolley. 'It's about this, thinking of others and sharing what we have. And I don't want a repeat of Max's birthday.'

Laura had the opinion that her mother-in-law's attitude to present choices had less to do with what the children actually wanted or enjoyed, and more to do with her level of comfort about sharing such information with her friends. Like on Max's fourth birthday, when she had asked what he wanted, and he had wanted a Ninky Nonk. Max had come across the *In the Night Garden* toys through the older sister of a friend and had gone on and on about *Iggle Piggle*, or some such thing. Laura had found the programme on the internet and Max had become obsessed, wanting to watch the old episodes over and over. It seemed like a load of gibberish as far as Laura could tell and she was concerned that it would have some significant long-lasting detrimental effect on her son's linguistic development, but he loved it, and she loved him. And at least it wasn't Peppa Pig, one must be grateful for small mercies. However, for the birthday, Fiona had bought him a wooden train set, instead. It was handmade and had his name on each carriage in different coloured letters. It was beautifully made, but it wasn't by any stretch a Ninky Nonk. Max giggled, every time he saw Iggle Piggle jiggle in the Ninky Nonk, as it roved about the Night Garden. And Laura loved to watch him, watching them. This obsession had led to wanting the little doll figures, which she had found on the internet, and had dragged around his little Upsy Daisy until she was filthy dirty regardless of how many times she Upsy-Daisy-danced in the washing machine. Fiona's wooden train didn't bounce the Pontipine family around, like it did in the episodes. It didn't do anything really. You could pull it along by a cord attached to the smokestack, but when that got a little boring, it was put on the shelf, and that's where it stayed. When Jack had challenged his mother as to why she hadn't got what his son had asked for, she had said, 'Well, I didn't want to get something with such a silly name, and it's a little train set just the same. Isn't it? It's much better for him to have something so personal. Which was tennis club speak for "Don't I look like a doting grandmother to get such a bespoke and unique present who won't succumb to such depravity as to buy a ridiculously-sounding thing from a programme."

'I've allocated the grandparents' presents, here, and ours, here.' Laura said as she pointed to the screen. Her eyes flicked down to the total. Despite her attempts at keeping things modest and trying to avoid child-spoiling at all costs, Christmas was adding up. She did a quick F2 just to check that the formula was correct and was picking up all the right cells. Perhaps she had included a sub-total in the total somewhere, she wondered.

'Wow,' pronounced Jack emphatically. 'I'd hate to see how much it would be if we weren't reigning ourselves in,' he said with sarcasm.

'I know,' Laura agreed checking each sub-total again. 'It's the stockings, I think. And the Night before Christmas boxes. They are adding up to more than last year. There's only a set of Christmas PJ's each, a pair of fluffy socks, a new book, some hot chocolate sachets, marshmallows and a packet of their favourite biscuits, but that adds up to fifty pounds each as well. I've been really careful, honestly,' she said defensively.

With Jack working such long hours, they had agreed that Laura would do most of the present buying herself, but she was now suddenly feeling the judgement of her selections pressing on her, giving her an accusatory stare from the cells of the worksheet 'It's hard with the stockings. I don't just want to get jokey tut that is a five-minute laugh then goes into landfill. I wanted to get something decent, but then you are into the ten to fifteen pounds range and before you know it, five stocking presents has cost upwards of fifty quid; and then you have to double it so that it is fair for both of them, and that's a hundred. That's before throwing in some fun sweets and chocolates.'

'And a satsuma and a pound coin for providence,' Jack said, inclining his head and winking 'I think you've done well, but it does all add up. But, hey, you know, it's Christmas and we want them to have a lovely time, don't we? So, if we can't indulge them a bit and show them how special they are at "the most wonderful time of the year", he said with air quotes, 'then when can we?'

Laura half agreed with her husband's sentiment but hearing him saying it made them sound superficial and shallow. She loved being a stay-at-home Mum, or homemaker as it was now officially called on forms and documents, and she believed that the value in her being at home was the sense of constancy and security that she provided. The children always knew that she was there for whatever they needed, she would participate in school activities like trips and being a parent helper in class. She had time to help her neighbour next door with her shopping and she was able to make healthy nutritional food, bake her own cakes and spend all the long holidays with them taking them to divertive and interesting places like museums and galleries, parks and swimming. She was free to ferry them to their clubs and activities and to ensure that they met all their regular health appointments. She had time and space in her heart and mind to take her time with them, to pour love over a grazed knee or a sadness, rather than rushing past it in a fury of stress, impatience and exhaustion. This is how she showed them that they were loved, they didn't need indulgent gifts. Yet, still, they did it. Moving mountains and attempting the impossible, like searching for bunyips, to prove it. Wasn't a year full of her day-to-day effort enough for them to know they were special?

Jack cast his eyes down the stocking section. As his wife had said, there wasn't much there. Not the quantities that some parents provided. Amounts that would stuff a pillow-case to bursting; deforming it with its various lumps and goitres, squat and bulging, like a hessian sack of King Edwards that tumbled over its top. He had seen those Santa Sacks in the shops, large enough to rival the big man's own; hanging on pegs, flat and flimsy, some personalized with names, like forgotten t-shirts in a locker room, just so that it was clear, on Christmas morning, which overflowing sack of gifts belonged to whom. How interesting it was, he thought, that Santa was supposed to be the one with the sack; a sack so bulging because it contained a gift for many children. Yet now, it was the child who had the sack, and the many gifts were for them alone. Where was the simple stocking of Victorian imagery, hung up on the mantelpiece to be filled with a few small treats? His mind was filled with a sudden image, strangely, about dinner parties at his mother's, where she had ladled soup into small bowls from a large tureen filled to the brim and had passed them to her guests. Then he imagined her just giving them all a huge tureen each instead. Nobody needed that much soup, even if it was his favourite tomato. No one needed Santa sacks. Why was enough never enough?

'You've done well,' he said, appraising the data. 'It's enough but not excessive. It's just expensive, that's all. You're right though, we need to keep a level head and not get all caught up in hype.'

Laura agreed, she had done well. But there was one glaring omission in the rows and columns of words and figures. The bunyip.

'So, what are we going to do if we can't find this bloody

bunyip?' he asked, suddenly more serious. 'Bri will be wrecked if she thinks Santa's let her down,' he said.

'I know,' Laura muttered, pausing the filling of the gingerbread house drawers. We've bought into the whole Santa thing to make them happy and for them to believe that Santa will fulfill their wishes. They're probably off in dreamland now imagining all sorts of wonders. I can't think what to do. If we admit that he can't get her a bunyip, it will destroy her belief that he can do anything or has a team of elves that can make all manner of magic happen.'

'What have we created?' Jack asked and poured more wine. 'Do you ever think that we should have nipped it in the bud from the beginning, when they were babies? Made it a No Santa Zone.'

Laura scoffed but half wondered whether he was right. 'No,' she protested, trying to convince herself. 'Of course not. Think of all that wonder and delight. You know what it's like on Christmas Eve. They are so excited with anticipation. And then in the morning..., that complete wonderment that this magical thing has happened overnight, that doesn't happen at any other time of the year. Well, it's just… irreplaceable, isn't it? You wouldn't want to deny them that, would you?'

Jack smiled at the memory of last Christmas, Briony, running up the narrow landing to their bedroom, followed by Max, pattering behind, his little steps, like mice feet, padding the carpet to keep up. They both in their Christmas pyjamas with smiles that reached from wall to wall and eyes sparkling, reflecting the landing light with joy, like a white screen at a photography studio.

'No, of course not,' he agreed. 'You're right. Nothing can quite match it. That delight. And letting them have that taste of a magical world where anything is possible?'

He had cut all the slips of paper and, together, they finished off putting them in the drawers. The drawer for the twenty-fourth was the largest. They squeezed in four chocolates as an extra treat, and also put in a printout of the photo of the shopping trolly.

Laura held it in her hands and studied it, reminding herself of what she had chosen. In addition to the food bank items, Laura had also bought gifts for the children's charity. It had been fun really, not having to worry about matching the gift to the desire. There was a freedom in perusing the shelves and seeing each thing on its own merit. A matchbox car, or an ugly alien creature. It didn't carry any burden or preconception, or worry as to where it would be stored, or whether it was part of a set and would lead to follow-up purchases as the collection was completed. It didn't matter whether it was gender non-comformative, or whether it had been made using ethical methods and not too much plastic or air miles. Or whether it would meet expectations or be safe and not glorify violence or war. She was just free. She allowed herself to feel like a romantic Santa figure, St Nicholas, or La Perfina. Sinterklaus or Pere Noel, just gleefully stepping among the little shoes of the children and depositing an unrequested treat to a willing and grateful recipient.

She thought of Albert Finney, leaping and skipping through the streets of London, in the redemptive form of Scrooge handing a bow and arrow to a boy, a doll with ringlets to a girl - with ringlets, (notwithstanding the Victorian lack of observance of gender normativity, or the fact that a bow and arrow should really be considered as too violent a toy, even with rubber suction arrows) but he was joyful in his giving and they were joyful in their receiving. How wonderful to be given something you hadn't asked for, rather than something you had. That was the real gift.

And so had Laura felt as she had picked up the items from the shelves. *One of those, and three of these*, she had muttered aloud, hearing in her mind the childlike voice of old Ebenezer, as she gleefully placed each item in the trolley. Her own festive version of *Supermarket Sweep*. The photo and the memory made her smile. There were toys and games; a couple of small teddy bears; two packs of gel pens and two colouring books (it had to be two, because she always bought things in twos. You couldn't leave a child out. What if these gifts were going to siblings? She had added a few card games like Uno and Happy Families. There was a cuddly unicorn with a rainbow mane and a love heart on its left rump. A plushy green dinosaur sat on its dermal plates looking out through the side bars of the trolley. Dinosaurs weren't the most festive of gifts, she acknowledged, but she knew why she had chosen it. Max had got largely into dinosaurs when he was in Reception and had got a little box from the Natural History Museum. It came with a little plastic landscape of barren earth and scrubby trees, and he had created his own prehistoric world on the playroom floor. His favourite was a stegosaurus, and he took it wherever he went, even into the bath and cuddled its hard plastic at night. Laura had been mystified as to how he found comfort in this unyielding hard shell with its pointed scutes and armoured tail. When she saw the cuddly one, she just had to get it, imagining the joy it might bring to some other five-year-old who needed the unconditional love of a Jurassic lizard. A love that could be offered without the risk of poked eyes or indented skin.

She would not know the children who would receive these gifts. She was not sure what they were expecting from Santa, if anything, or whether her decisions would even be welcome or not. Would they be disappointed that what she had deemed suitable where not the result of their imagined dreams and wishes? Was she as bad as her mother-in-law, thrusting upon them a gift that she was happy with rather than what they wanted? Gosh, she hoped not. All she wanted was for them to experience that delight. To know that someone has thought about them and had wanted to ensure that in that moment, they felt as worthy and loved and special as possible.

Standing up, Jack stretched and yawned. He opened the fridge, searching for a snack. He had told Laura that he would be having a catered lunch at the office so it wouldn't matter if they ate without him, which they did most nights. It had been a long and stressful day, and a headache was forming. He needed something to eat. Something other than the last few Celebrations at the bottom of the bag. He decided that a sandwich would do at this time of night and took out some cold chicken and salad.

Laura noticed that he looked tired and suddenly felt guilty for ambushing him with the spreadsheet without giving him a chance to decompress. 'How was it today? The meeting. Did you manage to get things sorted out?'

'Nearly' Jack said, spreading mayonnaise on the bread. 'We've still got a little way to go in the negotiations. They are reviewing the contract, but each day is a delay in getting it done and more money going to the lawyers. I'm worried that if we don't close the deal soon, the business will really struggle to support staff and we might have to make redundancies, and I can't bear to think about that. Not at Christmas.'

Laura watched him methodically layering the lettuce and cucumber, his hands building a salad, his mind building a strategy. He was never free of it, even when he was home. The worry, and burden. Guilt and stress. Sometimes, she thought it might be better to just sell up and move away. Go somewhere else, rent a cottage by the sea, or in the Scottish Highlands. Live off the land and catch fish and home-school the children. Let them have the freedoms of a life away from the trappings of modern society and functional expectations. A brief, magical childhood before they grow up and realise that it's all a struggle and you only get out what you put in, hard work, every day, until you die. What message was that to be giving them about the world and their futures? She reflected also on his worry that his work decisions would affect families at Christmas. Losing one's job was terrible at any time of year, why did it seem more significant at Christmas? Because people couldn't buy what they presumed was needed – toys and gifts and plentiful food?

Jack took a bite of his sandwich and felt himself instantly recharge, the nourishment reaching his strained nerves like busy paramedics arriving at a scene and launching into action at once. He looked at the gingerbread house, standing in its Advent readiness, its doors and windows replete with treats, and notes describing the gifts that his wife had arranged. She was kind and thoughtful. Empathetic. And he loved her for it. She had imagined what it would be like for children who would go without this year and had stepped in, discreetly, anonymously. With no fanfare or acclaim, just silent slips of paper in a box, and inert items in a trolley. She was a secret Santa. He did not know where these items would go. Heaven forbid it would be any of his own employees, should the deal fail. He couldn't bear that. But presumably they would be wrapped up and put under a tree or doled out of a sack by a man in a red suit – who had had no more to do with the sourcing of these items than that other man who was in the moon. Still, he would witness their delight as he handed out Laura's goodness. And the children would thank him and love him and reinforce their belief in the fact that Santa was the one person they could rely on in their times of darkness.

Laura edged past him at the breakfast bar and opened the dishwasher. He pulled her to him and hugged her. 'This gingerbread calendar is lovely,' he said, holding her close. 'You're lovely… for thinking of it and actioning it. You won't see who will get these things, but you have made a difference, not only to their Christmas but to their lives. Think how long, Max carried around that dinosaur for and how much joy it gave him.'

She shrugged humbly and kissed the top of his head.

It gave her pause, as she shut the lid of her laptop, sending the spreadsheet into mystical darkness; its secrets hidden, only to morph and reform from data to actuality in a month's time. Who were these children who required donations from a stranger? She imagined her own happy, privileged children in their place. There would be no bunyip for Briony in that scenario. She wondered, for a moment, whether it might do her daughter good to have such a reality check. For her to realise that, sometimes, as in the case of these faceless recipients of her charity, you can't always get exactly what you demand. That there isn't magic out there to make it all better, only the kindness of strangers and the efforts of others. Perhaps neither Fortuna, nor her festive counterpart Santa, turn their faces to smile on innocent children, giving them whatever they desire regardless of its ability to be sourced. Perhaps, instead, they turn their faces away to look upon another child, or simply not see any child at all. And she considered what she would do if she could begin again. It was too late, even for Max, the Santa ship has already cast off its mooring and is being borne away by the fast-flowing current. But, if Briony were a baby now, if Laura had the chance to change her tack? Would she steer them away from this fantasy of glitter and sparkles and snow and magic? Of elves whose industry could form dreams into being?

And would she moot, to Jack, that perhaps they had made a mistake? That, it is in fact an unreachable goal to create a world where figures based on myths are conjured into a reality? Whether they be bunyips or chimney hopping gift-givers. To give children a false belief. To come clean to Briony and admit that the bunyip was beyond them, and beyond Santa too. And, if so, what might that world look like?

Hers elf

30 NOVEMBER

There is that tipping point, when you lean over something, isn't there? Where the amount of your body in midair is disproportional to the weight in your feet, securing you to the ground. Only the merest movement in your toes can tip the balance and over you go. Hildy was experiencing that now. She knew that it would have been wiser to have got the step ladder from the garage but fixing the first part of the advent calendar had been easy. She had sat on the top step of her wide staircase, winding the cloth tab around the stairpost, and draping it artfully like bunting at a fete. The little numbered pennants filled with treats, were dangling like tantalus' peach, just far enough to be out of reach for Magnus to help himself at will, but close enough for him to discover a new wonder each day of December with her motherly guidance and suitable positioning for an Insta ready photo op.

It was only now, when the last piece needed attaching, that she was regretting her decision. She would have to leave it half done, hanging like a line of wet washing while she went to get the steps and do it properly.

Raising her torso back up from its inverted position, she felt her hip bones settle back below the banister rail, making her realise just how close she had been to falling over the top. Her mind went to those little desk toys, a duck dipping its beak into the water. Her beak had nearly smashed into the parquet flooring seven feet below.

Opening the kitchen access door to the garage, and flicking on the light, she felt the chill of the unheated room and she shivercd. 'Crap,' she said looking at the steps stuck behind the bikes and the kayak, pressed against the wall like someone avoiding a speeding train in a tunnel. There was no way she could move the kayak by herself, and Steve was away until Friday, and Maria not in until 12 tomorrow, which was seriously inconvenient. Then the car would have to be moved out and all the bikes. She was not doing that now. It would wake Magnus for one thing and the surprise would be ruined, and for another thing, it was too bloody cold and wet.

Walking back through to the hallway, she saw the advent bunting hanging limply from its centre point, the contents of chocolate bars and mini cars and toys weighing like a festive plomb bob. She couldn't let Magnus see it like this, it would spoil the whole effect. More to the point, it was not Instagrammable in the least.

She had planned no end of posts for this Advent, lining up a month's worth of fun and divertive tricks for the elf on the shelf to get up to, all of which she would post, and all the mums at school would regard her as so inventive and creative – they would say she had missed her calling, that her artistic skills were lost on simply making fun things for her son to do, she should be running classes or workshops or hosting online craft shows.

Actually, that wasn't a bad idea, she told herself. She didn't need money, Steve brought in enough of that, she could just do it to share her gifts – tell everyone how to make the perfect Christmas. She hadn't thought of it until this very minute – but why not? She had seen some ghastly excuses for decorations in her neighbourhood, they could all use a bit of help – try to minimize the tack and dial up the class.

She thought of her door wreath that she makes every year, and the stunning garland down the stairs, thick, lush greenery closely packed with hundreds of baubles. She had always posted pictures of her Christmas tree, but everyone did that, didn't they? Some of them were hideous too, poor ignorant fools, it wasn't their fault, she supposed. Not everyone had the same artistic eye that she did, some people put tinsel up, or lametta and had all sorts of hotchpotch-coloured baubles thrown together. Had these people never heard of a theme, or scheme? It was one thing, creating a beautiful home with perfect decorations, which people could envy and copy when they saw it in person, but the problem with that was that they passed the ideas off as their own. However, if she vlogged it, *she* would get the credit. They would say, "Oh I saw it on YouTube, Hildy's Christmas Home, or Santa's little helper, or something like that…. There were already loads of people doing it, it wasn't original – she was aware of that, but she would be the only one doing it in the area so that made her unique. She could establish her media presence and then who knows where it might take her?

Looking at the advent calendar, dangling in incompletion, she debated what to do. If she was going to Instagram her wonderful festive banister creations, she couldn't have the advent calendar affixed down the same stairs. That would look awful. She decided to move it, but that would mean leaning over the stairs again, the drinking duck might not be so lucky next time. She could leave it for Maria to do when she came in tomorrow, but then Magnus wouldn't have the big reveal in the morning, or anything to begin his Advent with. Perhaps this wasn't such a good idea, she thought. But he would be so excited when he got to number twenty-four and found the big Nerf gun inside. She simply had to find somewhere else to put it. Having imagined it suspended beneath the kitchen cabinets, around the picture rail in his bedroom, and everywhere else that had a twenty-four-foot-long wall space, she had come to realise that perhaps it hadn't been such a good idea. Either the banner had to go or the banister display.

Her phone beeped. It was one of the mums, Annie, posting a picture of the elf on the shelf hanging, headfirst, into a full glass of wine. The caption read, 'Me, the night before advent, trying to find things for the elf to do!! 🤪. Hildy sighed. She had been planning to do that one. It was so annoying when someone took your idea. Likes and hearts popped up affirming Annie's post and Hildy checked the comments. They were all in support of the humour and wit and there was a sense of camaraderie of shared experience which spoke of parents that were fueling themselves with alcohol in order to cope with the expectations of each Advent morning.

Everything within her wanted to ignore it, but she was a regular contributor and responder, it would seem churlish not to acknowledge it. She sent a heart and LMHO back and couldn't resist scrolling for another ten minutes because, well, it was there. Bringing her mind back to her dilemma, she suddenly felt tired. What was she thinking, trying to be a vlogger? Everyone was at it, posting something or other, some good, some meaningless, some funny, some annoying. She would be just another face, amongst the millions. Her designs, valid only to those who scrolled at that particular moment. She would have to be uploading content all the time and that would be draining. She needed a hook, something different. Something new. She went to the kitchen and chucking the elf to one side, drank the glass of wine that she had already poured for him.

The tickets to Lapland were on the shelf. A surprise for Magnus. They were leaving the next week. Hildy had been so excited but now it just felt tiring. What was she thinking, having to pack suitcases and buy warm clothes and extra boots and arrange cabs to the airport for a 3am flight when there was so much else to plan for Christmas? Then there would be all the washing when she got back – granted Maria would do that – but she would have to oversee it all, and that was exhausting.

She took a gulp of the wine and poured some more – the elf could sod off; he wasn't getting any more of her Malbec tonight. That was the only thing that got her through most nights. She reminded herself of the name of the hotel to ensure that the transfers were correct and in doing so, reminded herself of what they were doing. The snowy landscapes; the log cabins; the gingerbread houses and sleighs with reindeer, the snow-dusted pine trees and even Northern lights in the night sky. It was so magical. Magnus would love it, and she would love it because he did. And everything she did was for him. He was her whole life. And Steve would be there, when he so often wasn't, his work taking him from them so frequently. That was why they were doing it, because what child wouldn't want to look back on their early years and know how much their parents loved them?

Looking at the pictures gave her an idea and she suddenly sat up and forced her eyelids open. She could set up her posts from Lapland. They were only there for a few days, but if she did, what…? She did the maths in her head… twenty- four divided by three, that was what? Eight. She could take eight photos per day of herself in all sorts of poses and dressed as an elf, doing all things around Lapland and then post them each day but they would actually be her and not the same little figure that everyone has.

That would show Annie and all the others. That would give her the edge. Straightaway she went on to Amazon and added an Elf costume to the basket. She was wondering if she should get one for Steve and Magnus too and they could all wear them for a Christmas photo. Then she decided against it. She had already planned the options for what they would wear in her Christmas post. She had ordered matching pyjamas which they would pose in by the fireplace, with Magnus surrounded by all his toys and her with her hair and makeup done in a way that said, I know, I'm just lucky I guess that I can wake up looking like this, just pull on some fluffy socks before opening my gift from my adoring husband, while drinking bucks fizz and eating Christmas cookies. Then, there would be a quick change into matching Christmas jumpers for when they take Magnus out to the park on Christmas morning with his new electric jeep, from the real Santa – that he would have met in Lapland. Or she might wear her white coat and red scarf – TBC -They would have changed for lunch of course, Hildy was planning on a red velvet dress with a tartan apron and would get Steve to take a snap of her as she brandished the bronzed turkey on a platter surrounded by cranberry jewels and roast potatoes, that Maria would have prepared.

No, there was no space for elf costumes for the others, perhaps she would do that next year. She checked on the delivery date. It would come tomorrow. She clicked on Buy Now and drained her second glass.

Buoyed by her plans, she returned her mind to the matter in hand, a bloody, massive advent banner with no home. If only it wasn't so long. Twenty-four triangles, each the size of an A4 pad strung side by side on a binding tape that could run from here to the corner shop was hard to accommodate. Whilst she knew that Magnus would love the treats and toys that she had placed in each pocket. She wondered whether she had made a mistake – obviously the scale of it had been a mistake, but you had to go big, how else would you be noticed and how else could you be validated unless you were noticed? But when she thought about her own advent calendars as a child, the fun had been finding the door numbers in the pictures. Searching amongst the scene for the little digits and opening the concealed door. Magnus would not have that. He would just see the whole month displayed there at once, with no intrigue or seeking. Just something to be taken every day. There was no delight in that, just expectation.

Her brain was getting fuggy. She shouldn't have had that last glass, but the bottle was nearly empty. There was no point saving it. She had seen a lifestyle hack online once, about pouring leftover wine into an ice cube tray or little bags to freeze and save for soups and sauces. She had considered it an exceptional idea, until it came to it, and by the time she had so little left, her inclination to source said cube tray or freezer bag, was well beyond her capabilities. It was easier just to down it.

Tipping up the bottle, she drained the dregs. The bottle was empty. She always recycled, but not always at home. Steve might not be there very much, but when he was, he would have noticed if there were lots of empties. A couple of times she had blamed it on a night in with the girls, or a PFA meeting, but he was not silly. He knew that they were few and far between and couldn't account for the number that lolled around on top of each other like glass logs in a grate. Taking it to the back door, she put it outside, as she had used to put out the milk bottles when she was younger. If only it worked the same way that the next morning, you could open the door to find that they had been refilled with Chardonnay and placed there even before you woke up. She would add it to the others in her boot and drop them off in a bottle bank, next time she went to the dump.

What the f*** was she going to do about the bloody, sodding advent banner? Suddenly she felt tearful and alone. It was always her trying to make everything special for Magnus. Steve never bloody did anything. Why was it always down to her? She moved to the hallway again, banging her shoulder against the doorframe, which sent her into a small stagger, and she grabbed for the dangling advent calendar to steady herself.

Earlier she had been over the banister looking down, now she was under the banister looking up, whichever way you looked at the duck, its tipping point always led it to drink.

Though she was small, her stumble and wrench were too much for the little centre hook and it gave way, the bunting falling to the ground in weighty clunks, and settling about her head and shoulders as if she were a patient who had been hastily bandaged and was now unravelling. Which in fact, she was.

The noise might have woken Magnus. She couldn't let him see. It would spoil the surprise. Some of the contents had fallen out of the numbered pockets reinforcing her idea that it wasn't that exciting if you could just look inside and see what they were. She gathered them up trying to remember which pockets they went in. It didn't really matter now, but when she had filled it earlier, she had tried to alternate between chocolate and gift, so that each day was a different surprise. But that was proving too challenging now that it was just a tangled heap with the numbers all jumbled up. Plus, she was falling out of love with the whole idea. Why hadn't she just got a normal advent calendar for him, like everyone else? Why did she always have to be more, or do more? Why was she always proving herself to be exceptional? Good, was not good enough.

One of the pennants had torn from the binding, and she looked sadly at its jagged edge. She had neither the time, nor the manual dexterity to repair it now. Magnus would have nothing for the morning. She had tried to be so different, so much better than the other mums, but they were all in bed asleep now, their children eagerly awaiting tomorrow to open their little cardboard door, satisfied to see a robin or a snowman and get a little bit of chocolate, and yet here she was, sitting on her hallway floor, after midnight, a bottle worse for wear, and with nothing to give him. What would she do for him; and what would she say to everyone else? She had planned to take a photo and post it in the morning, Magnus looking so delighted with his treat and everyone else deciding whether to be envious or impressed. She would look forward to the responses, checking the comments and likes eagerly and would stand in the playground just like the other mums, only she wasn't like them. She was a mum and then some.

But now she had nothing.

Scrabbling for a solution like a hostess who has suddenly had to drum up an impromptu pudding out of a packet of digestives and a couple of citrus fruits, Hildy's mind raced. She supposed that she could just give him this one pennant with a present inside for tomorrow. That would resolve it and would buy her time to think about what to do. There! Her creative brain had returned a lemon cheesecake.

The one she held in her hand would do but it happened to

be number three, which he might find a bit strange for the
first day of December. She studied it, her left temple
beginning to throb, though whether it was from the wine, the
tears, or the fact that she had been hit on the head by a
number sixteen she couldn't be sure. It was surprising how
heavy a Milky Way could be – it was supposed to be so light
you could eat it between meals without ruining your appetite.
She was grateful it hadn't been twenty-two, that one contained
a Tonka truck. She tried to visually make the three into a one,
but couldn't. Then she had an idea. She would just cut off the
number one pennant and use that. Hauling herself up, she
went to the kitchen drawers to get the scissors. Unable to find
them and remembering that she had left them upstairs when
wrapping the Santa presents that she was hiding in the loft,
she went to the understairs cupboard to get her dressmaking
scissors instead. They were more appropriate anyway, given
her endeavour., She could use the pinking shears to give the
triangle a neat, unfraying edge.

Sitting at the kitchen table, she snipped off the number
one triangle and laid it to one side. Magnus would have
something for tomorrow. She was pleased that she had
recovered something from the disaster, but the rest lay in a
coiled lumpy pile, like a boa constrictor that had consumed
twenty- four little mice, each one belying its pre digestive state
as a bulge in its fabric throat.

She would have to hide it for now and deal with the rest
tomorrow. Gathering it up in her arms like she had seen Maria
do with the laundry, she stuffed it into the utility room. As she
made to close the door, number twenty got caught on the
door handle. Hildy tugged at it until it came loose, but then
paused. An idea was swimming through the wine and trying
to make its way to the shore of her mind.

As it landed, raking the shingle with its fingers as it tried to
resist being dragged back into the waves, it settled and caught
its breath. Hildy found it and dragged it further up the beach
to safety. Grabbing the pinkers again, she set to the snake,

chopping it into pieces, before and aft its snack-sized morsels, like a serial killer breaking down their victim, the better to fit it into a suitcase or stuff under the floorboards. Before long, Hildy had twenty-four triangles, and had cut them to leave a little piece of binding on the top edge. She used this to make a loop and checked the small pockets once more, ensuring that the gifts and chocolate bars were dispersed evenly. Then, sneaking through the house, as quietly as she could, like a little elf, she opened doors and cupboards, hanging the little pennants randomly until all of them were concealed.

Crawling into bed, Hildy let the wine fug envelop her, easing the tension away. As she drifted off, she imagined Magnus hunting through the whole house to find his treat each day and her mouth curled into a small smile. Not the wide, loud smile that she showed others, just the quiet one that only her pillow saw. This, together with the Lapland elf antics might actually make this Advent bearable, she told herself. Perhaps that is why she couldn't do the same as everyone else: the usual: the routine… because usual was not good enough. Usual was not special, and if people didn't see her as special, then who was she?

Her body relaxed but the twist in her chest remained, yet that was always there. If she had to describe it, she might say it was like a yum yum, two strands of pastry entwined and held fast with crystalised sugar: clamping to her chest like indigestion. Someone had suggested once that the yum yum might be anxiety or depression. Hildy had laughed at them. Of course not. She didn't say it to them, but the notion was ridiculous. Super mums don't get anxious, or depressed. They are the ones in control, the ones that others admire, the ones that stand out. They are the ones whose children remember and look back on as incredible mothers, the epitome of parenthood. Super mums save the day, even when they've made mistakes, like hanging stupid banister banners. They find ways to cover it up because no one can see their failings. They can never be known to err. After all, someone once said, "to err is human" but super mums are superhuman, so erring is forbidden. Super mums are the ones who make Christmas magical and memorable, and who make Santa as real as the one who lives in Lapland. Super mums are the ones whose elf, is herself.

The first mince pie

30 NOVEMBER

'Okay, yep, that's great, thank you. No problem. No, you can pay me on the day, and I take cash or Bacs, not mince pies... Ho Ho Ho,'

Dave ended the call and placed the phone back in his jeans pocket.

'Don't you ever get sick of that joke?' his wife asked as she peered over her crossword puzzle book.

'No! Ho Ho,' Dave replied holding his belly as he did a pronounced chuckle.

Margaret smiled and closed her book, marking her place with the pen. 'Something wrong?' she asked.

'Yeah, it's the primary school,' Dave replied, reaching for his mug of tea and finding it to have gone cold during his phone call. 'It was the girl from the PFA.'

The girl was forty-two, but to Dave, anyone younger than fifty was a girl. 'She was talking about what happened and why they are moving the grotto.'

'What's happened to the classroom it was in last year?'

'Apparently its ceiling flooded and they're doing some work on it. There isn't really anywhere else, so she asked if I minded being in the shed outside.'

'The shed?' his wife cried. 'You'll catch your death out there. It turns December tomorrow,' she said unnecessarily.

'I know it turns December tomorrow, my dear heart, that's why I'm discussing my Santa visits to schools,' Dave said with a twinkle. 'It's hardly the merry month of May, is it?'

'Oh, shush you,' Margaret said tapping his arm with the

crossword book. 'I just mean that you'll be cold out there in the shed for hours.'

'I'll be fine,' Dave replied, 'anyway they've got that cardboard fireplace they made last year, those paper flames belt out a great heat.' He rubbed his hands together as if warming them before a log burner.

Margaret moved to the bureau in the corner of the living room and checked the calendar. 'It's going to be busy for you.' Running her finger down the dates listed she read aloud, 'Town lights' switch on; village lights' switch on; school fayre; school; school; hospital; nursing home; school; shopping centre; chapel fayre; church fete; church; school; day centre; day centre; school; shopping centre…. That's seventeen….'

'Seventeen down…' Dave chuckled.

'What?' his wife asked.

You went down the list and said seventeen. It's like a crossword clue.

Margaret gave him a resigned look, 'I just don't think you should take any more bookings,' she said. 'I'm worried it's too much, and some of these are in the same day. You'll be exhausted, particularly if you are sitting in cold sheds and hot shopping centres.'

'Nah, I'm fine. I love it. You know I do,' Dave replied, stroking his beard. 'This is the best job in the world, getting to be Santa and hearing all the kiddies' wishes. I love it. I just wish I could actually make them come true. I see some of them and just know that they are not going to be able to get what they ask for. It breaks my heart really, but then to see their little faces with all that wonder and magic alight in their eyes, well that is just priceless.'

'Hmm, well, it's not really priceless, is it? Although you charge hardly anything. It probably costs you more than you make by the time you add up your petrol and your costume and all.'

'Stop moaning Mrs Claus and give old Santa Baby a kiss,' Dave said putting his arms around his wife's shoulders.

'Oh, yeah. You're Santa Baby when it suits you,' she said wryly. 'How many times have I asked you for the keys to a platinum mine? Forty years married and I'm still waiting. I don't want the sable under the tree, but a ring from Tiffany would be nice.' She smiled and shuffled in her carpet slippers out to the kitchen. 'Cuppa?' she called as she moved through the hallway humming the song. 'Oh, it's December first tomorrow,' she announced, suddenly processing what she had read on the calendar, before it being deemed a crossword clue. 'That means we can officially sing Christmas Songs.'

'Shall we be naughty and start early?' Dave asked, going over to the CD player and flicking through the Christmas albums.

'No. Rules is Rules,' Margaret asserted firmly. 'Remember, I had to stop you playing *White Christmas* when you were repairing the washing machine and that was in June.'

'That's because there were white bubbles everywhere and it was like snow and then I only sang a couple of bars….'

'Yes, and then that got you in the mood to watch the whole film. I came in from picking hydrangeas in the garden to the strains of Bing Crosby and it was most unsettling.'

'Well, okay, June is perhaps a little early, I grant you, but I think that nine o'clock in the evening, on the last day of November is a perfectly reasonable time to start. It maybe St Andrew's day for the Scots, but for me, it's all about St Nick from now and for the next four weeks.'

Margaret leant on the doorframe and smiled in conspiracy, hunching up her shoulders in cheeky guilt, feeling as though they were children plotting to steal buns from the tin. 'Okay fair enough Kris Kringle,' she replied. 'I was feeding the cake today, gave it a nice dousing in brandy and the smell was just amazing. It has rather got me in the mood. You put the music on, and I'll warm a couple of my fresh mince pies. I made them today for the freezer, but we could have a couple now, couldn't we? Start as we mean to go on,' she chuckled, patting her tummy.

After dusting them with icing sugar and pouring two small, sweet sherries, she joined Dave at the CD player. Their daughter Holly had bought them an Alexa speaker, but they were only just getting used to her listening and responding to their requests, or just jumping into life without any notice, so they preferred their old machine which still also played vinyl –but not cassette tapes – Holly had informed them that vinyl was retro; CD players were still functional; but cassettes… they were just vehicles to reveal one's age.

'So, what are we starting our Christmas music with? Bing? Noddy? Mariah? Just as long as it's not I saw Mommy kissing Santa Claus,' Margaret complained convivially, 'You use that old chestnut roasting on the open fire, all the time.'

'Well, you can't blame me for trying to get a kiss, can you?' Dave said as he squeezed his wife's waist.

'Yes, well, as long as you don't have any other Mommies kissing you, too,' she joked.

He took a bite of mince pie, the powdery icing sugar settling on his upper lip, which was already white with a soft moustache. 'I know,' he said, perusing the back of the album case. 'I've got just the right one, given my upcoming schedule,' he said, pressing the play button. The digital marker moved to the requested track and the beat began, its opening bars urging the listener to watch out and not cry, because Santa Claus was coming to town.

'I've dry cleaned your suit and polished the boots, but I think you should try it on, just to be sure.'

'What are you trying to say? That I've put on weight?'

'No, love,' Margaret reassured, 'but if you are going to be in a cold shed, you might want to wear some layers underneath, just to keep you warm.'

'I'll be fine,'

There was a knock at the door and Margaret chatted for a moment, returning a few minutes later with two shoeboxes. She added them to a pile in the hall.

'Looks like there's a good response to the appeal,' Dave

said as she came back into the room and resumed her mince pie.

'Yes, that should be the last few now. The deadline was today, but people always overrun a bit. Their heads aren't quite into Christmas yet, but we need time to sort them into age groups and check them for inappropriate stuff, the usual. Then we need to wrap them all up and get them off the Romania in time for the big day, so we have to cut it off now. I bet there'll still be a few filtering into next week though.'

'Oh,' Dave said, remembering, 'Did Holly like her wreath? You were dropping it round yesterday and I forgot to ask, what with the wreath workshops and the food bank and the advent donkey debacle.'

'Mm,' Margaret replied, scooping the last of her mince pie through the sugar and washing it down with a swig of sweet sherry. 'Yes. She said it was just what she wanted. I said it looked a bit plain compared to the others. I offered her pinecones and dried orange slices and cinnamon sticks and what have you, and I've got yards of florist ribbon, golds and reds and silver but she said that she wanted it plain. She wanted to put her own bows on it, make it into an advent calendar for the kiddies to work with, something to do with telling the time, or something. She was rushing, you know the way she does, had one foot out of the car and was trying to get home before the rain came but she said it was perfect, so that's all that matters.'

'Do you think she's happy at that school?' Dave asked his wife. 'It's quite a change from the last one and I worry that she's going to find it too… what's the word…provincial?'

'I don't know,' Margaret said shaking her head. 'I think she has these big ideas and wants to change the world. She always has…'

'Apple doesn't fall far from the tree,' Dave interjected with a smile.

His wife inclined her head. 'I think she will do what she always does. Give it her best shot and see if she can make a difference. That's what motivates her, well she's like you and me in that, isn't she?' If we can do one thing, no matter how small, to affect change for good in some way, then perhaps we have done right.'

Margaret placed their advent calendar on the sideboard and decorated around it with sprigs of fresh holly and fine stems of fir. It was a wooden one that Dave had made out in his workshop over the summer holidays one year when Holly was younger. She had helped him and watched him bent over the workbench, his apron pocket like the pouch of a marsupial, containing bradawls and chisels, rasps and sanding blocks. The block of wood was solid, a chucky leg of an old table that a customer had discarded. He had planed and refined until years' worth of grime and varnish and everyday life had gone and had revealed new and fresh timber, beautiful in its rawness. Over the weeks, Dave had fashioned an advent calendar of twenty-four little doors, each numbered and affixed to the block with a tiny brass hinge. On the appointed day of Advent, you would flick down the door and it would reveal a picture of a little elf behind working on a toy made of wood. Although Holly had been present for the first phase of its refashioning, she had then gone away to guide camp for a couple of weeks. Returning to find the work complete, she was mesmerized at the wondrous creation and would spend hours flicking up the little doors and then popping them down again at random, trying to test herself to see if she knew which elf stood behind which door. One had a wooden train, another a spinning top, one doll's house, and another, a cricket ball and stumps. One had made a guitar, another a violin. A set of pan pipes. A little open topped car. In each picture, hand painted by her father, a skill born and nurtured by painting models of aircraft and soldiers when he was a boy, the elf wore the ubiquitous outfit of pointed ears, with hat and toes to match. To her delight, Holly had discovered that on day twenty-four, the door flicked down to reveal a painting of Santa in a huge red sleigh, pulled by reindeer and the sack in the back, with all the toys built over the preceding weeks, crafted by the little elves, all put in the sleigh for Santa to begin his worldwide delivery. Holly had been overwhelmed when turning the tiny handle, a crank shaft for an elf itself, had sounded the delicate twinkling strains of the *Cantique de noel* to be played when the last door opened on Christmas Eve.

The doors were all up, the work of the elves not yet revealed. That would begin tomorrow.

Behind every door

30 NOVEMBER
DARCY

I am standing in the hallway of our house on the evening of 30 November. I am in my nightdress, which is a white flannelette with lilac flowers. My long brunette hair is brushed, my teeth are cleaned. It is bedtime, but I am too excited to sleep.

Our hallway is wide, a large picture window fills the wall at the foot of the stairs, and the staircase is wooden, painted in a white gloss. The space beneath the stairs is boarded with something like plywood, also glossed in white, enclosing within, the gas and electricity meters, a coat rack overloaded with winter coats, the hoover, and a wire stacked rack which stores those root vegetables that prefer cool, dark places. I can smell the musty damp of rooting potatoes, there are always one or two that seem to have been forgotten and have started to sprout, sending their pink tendrils off into the darkness, in the false promise of soil. At the opposite end of the hall to the window, stands a mahogany captain's desk. It is topped with green leather, inlaid with gold edging. Brass handles dangle from the solid drawers and hang like the moustaches of a Frenchman.

My little sister and I watch as our mother takes up a brass drawing pin and presses it firmly into the glossed wood of the stairwell. Leaning into it, with her whole body, she ensures it is securely fixed. Then she stands back, and takes my sister and I in each arm, enfolding us in an embrace. We giggle and squeeze our fists in delight. Our throats tighten with excitement, strangling our words into a squeal. After this sleep, it would begin.

The three of us look up at the printed card, held fast by the round, brass thumb tack. It is printed with an image that draws joy and wonder from my very being. My future self would look upon it as stylized and tacky, probably. I would think it dated, old fashioned in every way, the colours, composition and artwork. But not now. Now, I love it. Is it, perhaps that it is of its time, so I see nothing to fault? Or is it that it conjures such a feeling of love, security, comfort and tradition, that I am ignorant to its aesthetic qualities? I can no more comment on its artistic attributes than fly to the moon, but to me, it is perfect. Well, granted, perhaps a little tired, some of the corners a little dog-eared, and there has been a repair attempt on a line of perforation, but that adds to its appeal in a way. It feels familiar, comfortable, ours. I think if someone would offer me a brand new one, here and now, I would thank them kindly but refuse. For I am not sure that anything could hold such magic, and hope and promise for me than the picture that hangs before me on our white-glossed stairwell. Nothing else can instill the feeling of anticipation, excitement and awe, that stirs in me as I behold it. The twilight horizon blends into the darkness of a midnight sky studded with stars. One star, the most dazzling that I've ever seen, is suspended over a thatched barn. A tableau of beautiful, benign faces is centred on a baby, watched over and warmed by the breath of beasts of burden, an ox of fair fawn and a donkey of pale blue-grey. Shepherds stand around with sheep at their hips and lambs in their arms, some lift rustic flutes to the sky. There is a unique peace and stillness that emanates from the scene, even the muted colours of their clothing is quiet, and other than the wondrous star with its long tail, the only light comes from the glow of three halos of the Holy Family.

Dotted at intervals, all over the image are tiny lines of

perforations, and most incongruously, delicately printed numbers.

The image is, of course, the Nativity, the piece of A4 double-thickness card, our advent calendar.

*

It's strange, even with how I feel about things, now, I still can't let go of this image of the Holy Family.

Ours was a holy family. Of course, I would not blaspheme so much to state that we resembled the subjects of that starry night stable in any way, other than insofar as we were practicing Christians, and Christmas, in our house was certainly not just a cultural celebration, though we did enjoy all the trimmings. No, my mother was very insistent that Christmas was our special feast. It was the birth of Our Lord, Jesus Christ. Our Saviour. And woe betide anyone who overlooked that fact. For her, putting the Christ in Christmas was a fundamental part of our celebration. But that was fine by me. I thought that the whole Christmas Story was indeed the greatest story ever told and couldn't wait for the magical countdown to begin. It would be another few years before our advent calendars would become the kind to include images of snowmen and Santa, and to contain chocolate treats, and even when my sister and I did begin to ask for those, they were allowed, but only if they were affixed to our stairwell with a brass thumbtack alongside our old faithful image, there to co-exist rather than to replace.

Early, each December morning, we would hurry down the stairs, and try to beat each other to find the number. Some might think that they would sneak a peek at the next day, in advance, just to get ahead. But not me. I deliberately tried to shield my peripheral vision, blurring out all the surrounding numbers lest I inadvertently see one that would give away its location and spoil my search the next day. It's like turning to the answers of a quiz to see if you are correct but not wanting to see the solutions to those you have not yet done. My sister was little, three years my junior, and I would help her, often letting her think that she had found the number first and I would be bursting to open the little door but would have to restrain myself until she finally found it.

Behind every door, there was a quote from scripture pertaining to the stage in the story. Like a teaser campaign for a soon to be released movie. Despite the picture being of the Nativity, I think the scriptural references began at the Annunciation, the moment where the angel Gabriel first appeared to Mary, a lowly handmaid, and bestowed upon her the greatest honour ever given – to become pregnant by God and to bear and give birth to His son. It is strange to even say this, for my recent years of doubt and challenge has caused the bedrock of my Christian faith to start to crumble and what I once held dear, as the very core of my belief now sounds incredible, that is to say, as it directly translates, unbelievable. I was so certain of Mary's selection story that I actually remember saying to my mother, when I was about thirteen or fourteen, that I was worried that God might choose me for His work, (I was a very angelic child and it would have been quite possible) and concerned that if I became pregnant with God's child, people would think that I had been generous with my virtue; so much did I believe in God's power to do this and so empathized was I with Mary's position.

At no point did I question the appearance of great and beautiful angels which brought great news and hovered above their subjects with huge white wings. To me, Mary must have been indeed *most highly favoured* to have been chosen by God for such a moment of glory and her gracious and unquestioning acceptance of her role was to be envied and emulated. If I continued to be good, and kind and chaste, I might be just as favoured by God, because to be in His favour is all we should need or desire.

I don't know how you feel about faith but, I don't think I can really do this, unless I explain, you see. Christmas is so wound up together with my upbringing as a Catholic, and my more recent years as a non-Catholic, but still as a devout Christian, I'm not sure that I can separate the two.

Anyway, back to this calendar. Day one is a quote from the Annunciation and the little picture behind the door is a white, winged angel on a blue background with lines fanning out from his head to represent the dazzling rays of light in which he appeared. It is simply breathtaking. Like the Paramount Pictures lady announcing the trailer of the feature to come.

Do you know, snippets of scripture just pop in and out of my head without me even having to think. So entrenched in my mind are the words and phrases from years of church attendance, either delivered by the priest, or teachers at my Catholic school, or via the lyrics of songs or Christmas carols. Either overtly, or covertly, the words have become lodged in the Christmas filing cabinet of my brain, playing a word association game with myself. Complete this sentence, 'And you shall give birth to a son…and *will name him Jesus. He will be called Emmanuel, which means God with us,* or 'And she wrapped him in swaddling bands… *and laid him in a manger.* It is automatic response, so embedded that I don't even have to consciously think about it.

We went to church every week, without fail. My mother told us that it was a sin to miss it. God would know and we would know. If it was through sickness, that was acceptable, but when on holiday we would have to find a local church, and if we did miss it for any reason, then this would have to be confessed on Saturday afternoon before daring to assume that we were worthy enough to attend mass the following week without recognizing our fall from grace.

I didn't mind though. I was happy to go to Mass. I loved our church. It was familiar. I had been baptized there, made my First Confession and Holy Communion. I would be confirmed and later married there. It had witnessed our final farewells of those whom we had known and loved.

Christmas isn't the big thing in the church, of course. It is Easter. That is far more important. Yet other than a few chocolate eggs, we don't bother about Easter at all. As a society, I mean. We did, though. We were either in church, praying or fasting, virtually every day from Ash Wednesday.

The church was situated in a small residential road. You wouldn't know it was there from the high road. Its entrance was at the back, and as you pulled open the heavy wooden doors, by its strong wrought iron pull ring, you stepped from the ordinary atmosphere of outside into an inner chamber of complete stillness. There was a chill from the darkness created by the overhanging organ loft, and the flagstone floors. Stone columns with the girth of tree trunks added a coolness to the interior and the high ceiling was supported with vaulted oak timbers. Its smell was unmistakable. I can close my eyes and smell it now, candle wax, wood polish, flowers and old paper. I love that smell. It's funny how smells are so nostalgic and can awaken memories or feelings of years ago, as if they were yesterday.

The side altar on the left was painted blue behind a statue of Mary; the one on the right was red which brought into strong focus the statue of Jesus as The Sacred Heart. On this side was placed the tabernacle, the repository for the sacred hosts. These were communion hosts that had been consecrated (made holy with a special prayer, or as I once heard it referred to as, a magic spell) but not used during the service. If there were too many to be consumed by the priest, they would be placed there until they could be used later in the week for other services or to minister to the sick and infirm in their own homes. Then, I thought it sacrosanct, now, I can't believe I ever believed it.

Wrought iron racks stood beneath both statues, studded with votive lights which flickered with the prayers of thanksgiving or supplication uttered at their illumination. It is there that I found the most peace, I think. There is something so spiritually stirring about a candle. That single point of light in the darkness.

It may have changed now, the church, but that was what it was like twenty years ago, when I was last there. The reason I mention it is because it formed such a part of my identity, and it is difficult to think about Christmas, indeed my faith as a whole, without recognizing that it was born, nurtured and reinforced in that place. Whilst I may now consider it in a less positive light, for the first twenty-five years of my life, it, that church, was part of me. For the following twenty, I did not set foot in that Catholic church, or any other again, except for once as a guest.

When we think about Christmas, aside from Santa and the tree and the turkey, from a Christian aspect, it is about Jesus the baby, yet nowhere in my vivid recollections of my formative church were there any images of a child. Granted, some churches have statues of the Madonna and child, but ours didn't. In the pieta, Jesus was a grown man. In the stations of the cross carvings, He was a man. In the Sacred Heart statue, He was a man. Matthew, Mark, Luke and John have written what they believe to be Christ's every word and deed, in order to share with us His life and work through his ministry until his death at the age of thirty-three. How is it then, that we have chosen to make Christmas, His birth, rather than His life and death, the feast of all feasts?

Did you know that Luke is the only writer who even mentions the birth? The others launch in when Jesus is twelve years old. But what is there amongst Luke's words, we have taken and run with. The lights are down, the popcorn's warm and we are entranced by his thrilling film short. It sets the scene, introduces the characters, lays down the background, where this Jesus guy is from and what He is going to do. There is pathos, atmosphere, tension – are they going to get a room for the night? Will the shepherds and the kings find the way? Despite His humble beginnings, Jesus gets visited by kings to show that He is actually a superhero. It's thrilling, a real Marvel blockbuster. Everyone loves it. Then the lights go up, the drinks cups are crumpled on the floor with the popcorn, and everyone goes home. No one needs to know what happens in the main feature. The Christmas Story has it all. It is enough. We don't need to know what Jesus does later, or what happens in the 'end game' or how he defeats Thanos, or any other presentation of evil. No one really bothers with that bit. The Birth Story is a box office hit, people all talk about it; they make merchandise to sell and even do re-enactments of it on its anniversary, like the original Comic-Con. The Marvel origin stories might explain how Black Widow became a female assassin, or how Iron Man got his real heart. We learn how Captain America got his powers and what happened in Scarlet Witch's childhood. But none of them, as far as I am aware, start the film by referring to their conception, then draw the storyline to a close when they are twelve years old. It just wouldn't make much of a story, would it? But then, perhaps there is something different about it being the son of God and His coming foretold in the prophesies of ancient days? I don't know anymore. I think it is quite possibly as fictional as a Marvel movie.

And His coming is what advent is all about. Literally, the Latin translation is 'to come'. So, to return to the advent calendar, what better way to get everyone on board with the teaser campaign, than to have a countdown? Everyone loves a countdown; it heightens the anticipation and amps up the excitement levels. For those who like planning, it is the festive equivalent to a GANT chart, where each element of a project is specified against measurable targets and you can tick each day of, with satisfaction as you achieve another task and advance closer to your goal.

I think I was about twelve when we got our first chocolate one. My sister and I begged our mother in the shops, 'please, please, can we have one?' we pleaded. She relented but only on the proviso that our original religious calendar continued to be used. 'Of course,' I replied. I loved that one. I didn't want to lose it; I just wanted the chocolate as well. It was doubly exciting, there were four doors to open. I have heard people say that they used to eat the chocolate all at once and then close up the foil and doors again. Or parents say that they have had to put them way up high so that their children don't gorge on a whole month's worth and go and vomit it up, down the toilet. I don't understand this. I never wanted to do that. The anticipation of waiting for the next day was just too tantalizing, (I told you I was an angel!). Further, not only was there something written on the door, but there was also the picture behind the chocolate, and the chocolate was in a shape, too. So, there were three things for each of us to look forward to; add to that the scripture and the picture from the religious one and we had FIVE. It was literally thrilling.

For me, when I reflect on this, it is a very obvious example of delayed gratification, which I fear is not experienced by many children now. Everything is so immediate. Everything is downloadable, or delivered next day, or streamable. It is accessible at the click of a mouse, the touch of a button, or in a trip to the store. When do they learn to wait and watch and wonder? When do they get the thrill of expectation, dreaming of something that seems so out of reach that only a miracle could deliver it into their hands? When do they take the time to appreciate, to value, to respect, to anticipate and to feel that raw and expansive joy; that their heart will figuratively explode with satisfaction and happiness?

The church says that Advent is a time for preparation, for us to focus on literally what is 'to come'. We are to take that time to prepare ourselves spiritually. Are we in the right place to welcome the son of The Most High? If HRH The King is making a royal visit, his hosts don't all sit around in their pyjamas, having mugs of tea, wondering who was supposed to put up the ribbon, and plant the flower beds, or run about asking who was the last to use the big scissors. So, too, the church says, we must prepare ourselves.

The thing is, I don't know how to do that now. If there is no coming of the King, there is no need to get ready for it.

The light of the world

30 NOVEMBER

Opening the advent calendar pop-up book, Jen stood it on the sideboard in the hallway and studied it, anticipating the girls' excitement when they saw it tomorrow morning. It was new this year.

It had been difficult to find a religious calendar. It was all Santa and chocolate now, which Jen was fine with. She felt comfortable that there was space for two deities to share in Christmas and was the first to start planning for all the fun secular aspects of the feast. But, for her, Jesus was still the reason for the season, and she felt that it was important that the girls remember that.

The book was lovely, hard backed and of landscape orientation. The full Christmas story was laid out on each shining page, set in illustrations that drew you into the dusty road to Bethlehem under a star-studded midnight sky. One depicted Joseph and Mary, riding a donkey. The long road before them. Another showed a dazzling star with long tails, streaking across the sky and shepherds on green hills pointing, their faces in awe and wonder. Further into the book, there was a stable with a manger set in straw and an ox and ass breathing their warm breath over a baby as a doting mother and father looked down on them, halos shining over the hallowed heads of the Holy family. A later page depicted three men in long flowing robes of rich fabrics, carrying ornate boxes. They wore dark skin and elaborate headgear, jewelled turbans, the crowns of eastern royalty.

At the back, was the cardboard pop-up. The vista of the whole landscape, the hills in the background, the stable in the foreground. The adoring visitors of shepherds and kings, all in three dimensions, making you feel that you could just walk right into the tableau and be part of the greatest story ever told. Well, that and the Resurrection. Jen had always been taught that Easter was a more important feast than Christmas, as far as the church was concerned, but that didn't seem to jibe with the fact that everyone she ever knew had acted in a nativity at school, yet she knew of only about five others who had acted in a Passion play. And then there were the songs. If Easter was more important, why had early composers not directed their efforts towards carols for the Triduum, creating a repertoire of triumphant glorias and peaceful love ballads as there are for Christmas? Still, she allowed, it was perhaps a more appropriate subject matter for infants and juniors to celebrate a baby's birthday, than be witness to a torturous death on a cross. A bit more relatable. She sought not to question. She had never felt the need. Others had. There weren't many of her friends who still went to church, but her faith was her bedrock.

She had never doubted. She had studied scripture closely and whenever anyone threatened to disprove the bible, she had a piece of scripture ready to hand. Her faith had been as strong as a rock, 'you are Peter, and on this rock, I will build my church,' It was automatic, like a word association game. There were phrases that sprung up at her, even without consciously thinking, formed through the years of devout teaching, preaching and following. Her young life had been centred around the church, even through her teen years and into adulthood, running groups and courses, leading worship and outreach programmes and had never had a moment's doubt that Jesus was God, and God was love, and Jesus said to love one another. That he had died for her sins and for the sins of all. And that everyone's ultimate goal should be to live as Jesus preached and seek eternal salvation in the light of heaven.

It was Christmas, a time for prayer and hope. For charity and love and goodwill to all. A time for acceptance and to find the joy in the pain and light in the darkness. Because wasn't that what she had been taught, always? That Jesus was hope for all, and that to live in his light and love, is all she would need. He was the deliverer from pain and suffering. Why worry when you could pray?

The book was too new, the little doors never having been opened. She did not dare to peep. The girls would know, like when you open a paperback book for the first time and try to stop the cover creasing.

'Most highly-favoured lady,' Jen sang as she looked at Mary, her voice soft and low, the words of the carol coming, unbidden from somewhere in her soul. She remembered changing the words in hymn practice, her classmates giggling as they sang instead, 'most highly flavoured gravy.' It made the nuns mad. Particularly Sr. Bernadette. Jen had hated her. She knew that it was wrong to hate anyone, let alone a nun, and she knew that she should have confessed it at confession. But then the priest would know, and he was great friends with all the nuns, so she thought she would be in trouble. So, she stayed quiet. It seemed to seem the safest thing to do. It still was.

Only God knew that she hated Sr. Bernadette, but that might not be so bad, because at least then He wouldn't think she was so good that he might make her pregnant with His baby, which although considered a great honour, Jen was more than a little concerned about. Jen was particularly cross with her for making her eat semolina at lunch. She hated semolina, almost as much as Sister for making her eat it. Served with a blob of strawberry jam in the middle, it made her stomach heave at the sheer sight and smell of it. She liked the jam; the semolina made it warm. When Sister stood over her, her cane poised on the table, Jen took her spoon in mock willingness and compliance and placed it directly in the centre, then moved outwards, incising the warm conserve with a surgeon's precision until it met the insidious creamy slime on the plate. She would not go a nanometre further. Jen could almost taste it as her mind's synapses joined the words of the Magnificat with the tortuous lunchtimes of her convent days. It was strange how integral a Christmas carol could be to other areas and periods of life. Like a Venn diagram, with life experiences in one circle, and years in the other, the area where they cross containing the carols, because their annual repetition is prevalent in every stage. Festive mantras of reinforcement. The words subsumed into the consciousness.

Jen turned over her hand instinctively, the marks of Sr. Bernadette's cane were long gone, but the fear and shame remained. That never left. The humiliation of being punished before the whole dining room for not eating the disgusting semolina when, "in the name of Jesus, child, don't you know that there are little children starving in Africa," bore deep within. Jen had seen a pile driver once, its powerful screw drill turning the soil, boring way beneath the surface of the earth. From above, no one would ever see the damage inflicted on the ground, just a small flesh wound. The real destruction and displacement were hidden from view. And fear and shame were not only the preserve of the public display, but as prevalent in those private moments too, if not more so.

It was there, as clear as if it were yesterday. Jen was nine again, standing before everyone, hand outstretched, and wincing as the cane whooshed through the air. She remembered the expression on Sr. Bernadette's face, her features twisted with anger, contorted with effort, but also strangely detached. It was as though she wasn't even a person at all, let alone a child. She was just someone who needed to be punished.

She was, still.

A smile formed as she recalled it. With the remembered pain came a glimmer of joy. She had told Sr. Bernadette that she couldn't eat it, that it would make her physically sick. And it had. All over Sister's polished black shoes. Through the retching, Jen had been struck by how the vomit was a delicate shade of pink, where the jam and semolina had combined, and as she had bent double to heave the evil spawn out of her, her hand had caught the bowl, sending a spray of white splattering up the hem of her punisher's long, black habit. Jen had thought then whether that was what they had meant when they said that where Jesus was, there was always light in the darkness.

Perhaps, but if so, then where was He now?

It seemed strange to her, that Jesus told everyone to love their sister and brother, yet the sisters who taught her weren't very loving at all. At school, and church, and home, and for that matter, everywhere, Jen was taught that God was always watching. He knew what people did so everyone must be really good, all the time, everywhere and throughout their whole lives otherwise he would be cross, and they wouldn't get to heaven. And no one wanted that. When she was younger, she had found it irreconcilable that if God was watching all the time and knew whatever we did, why it was necessary to bother with confession, and that as long as we apologized and endeavoured not to repeat the sin, that should be enough. But it was explained to her in terms she could understand. It was like Santa. If you were on the naughty list and didn't make the effort to be nice, then you wouldn't find out until Christmas Eve when you got a piece of coal. So, you might as well, say sorry if you sinned, so that you got a chance to put it right as you went along. Then on your death day, which is like Christmas Eve, you would get what you were promised. She still wasn't sure that was entirely correct though, as she had come across many people who were living as though they knew they were getting a nice present on

Christmas Eve regardless of how unpleasant they happened to be.

So, Jen was always good and never naughty. She made her first confession and Holy Communion and when the time came, confirmed her faith in the belief that perhaps the older she got and the more she grew, she would understand the things that didn't quite make sense. She was still waiting, but still faithful that God would reveal the mystery of why he had determined for her to live the life she did. *'Fear not.'*

In the advent book, above the hillside, a shining angel was dressed in a long white robe. He hovered above the shepherds, with lines fanning out from his head to represent the dazzling rays of light in which he appeared; huge, feathered wings suspending him in the sky. His words didn't even need to be written for Jen to know them. *"Fear not…, I bring news of great joy"*, sounding like the other words of scripture she relied upon as her daily mantra, *"Do not be afraid…, I have called you by your name. You are mine."*

Yet, no matter how much you were told to 'fear not', it didn't stop you having something to fear.

A little candle in a brass holder stood next to the advent calendar book and Jen took a match to light it. The smell of the burning wick invoked in her the comfort and safety of the candles at church. Little votive lights, in red or blue plastic cups, warm and flickering in the dimness of a quiet chapel. It was there, where Jen felt the most safe. Where those who are the most unpleasant can't reach her. Where she finds sanctuary in the embrace of God. It is then when she allows herself to believe that there is someone who truly cares for her, who as scripture tells her, knows every hair on her head and who will walk with her through the darkness. It is in those moments that she is loved.

"And he shall be called Emmanuel, *which means God with us… Do not be afraid, I have called you by your name, Jen. You are mine*,"

He was not home yet. It was better that way. She could be asleep when he crept into the bedroom. She was practiced in breathing into the covers so that he couldn't hear that she was still awake. Not that that was always enough.

Before the tiny flickering votive, Jen prayed the prayer she always prayed at night. That God would send an angel of protection over them. She did not know whether dazzling white rays emitted from his head like in the picture in the calendar. She hadn't really thought much about what he looked like. Only his wings. Those huge, feathered wings that could enfold them, Jen and her girls, and keep them safe.

Pinching the little flame between her fingers, the light was extinguished, and darkness returned.

Baby's first Christmas

30 NOVEMBER

Will sat on the floor and looked at the shopping bags scattered at Johnny's feet as if he were standing in a crop field, the points of tissue paper grazing his legs like ears of wheat. His husband's expression was a combination of mock shame and pure delight.

'And how much did this lot cost?' Will asked said in mock admonishment.

'They were bargains,' Johnny replied, matter of factly.

'U- huh?' Will said in disbelief, looking at the brand names. 'I've been to those shops. They never have bargains,' he stated.

'Okay,' Johnny admitted reluctantly. 'Not bargains, but not too much, really and I just saw them and had to have them.'

'I thought we agreed to be sensible about this,' Will said plaintively.

'Er… Noooo… You wanted to be sensible…, as always,' Johnny levied. 'I'm not sure that I actually agreed.'

Will cast a glance to his husband and couldn't help but be infected by his energy and enthusiasm. He had to agree. Johnny wasn't sensible. That's what he loved about him, and to be fair, Will was sensible enough for the two of them. Where Will brought the pondering and planning to their marriage, Johnny bought the spontaneity and fun. It had mystified him really, both personally and professionally, that Johnny could have suffered the childhood he had, yet still face life with an optimism and joy that eluded the majority of those who had grown up in love and privilege. A coping mechanism, Will had presumed. A way of concealing the hurt and pain behind hope and laughter. How else would you get through the days? He had wondered.

Their upbringings had been so different. Will's, middle-class, financially secure, with loving parents who had supported him through university and were still active and engaged professionals. Johnny's, abusive, low-income, low-academic achievement, growing up in foster homes, some good, most bad, and who had finally found his feet when a local Estate agency was looking for staff. It was all about personality, approachability, charm and hard work. And he had those qualities in spades. But what Johnny had, in addition to those, was a huge capacity to love. It was as if he had gathered all the years' worth of love and affection that he might have received throughout his life, had his circumstances been different, and had stored them in vast containers, like a water tower, or food silo, dispensing their life-giving contents to others in the form of kindness, generosity and deep, intense care for others.

For Will, being the one to whom Johnny had pledged his life in marriage was the greatest honour that had been conferred upon him, and that included his Psychotherapy degrees. Just being in Johnny's orbit, was enriching and captivating, and Will had often wondered, as he watched him with others, whether he didn't do more for people struggling with their mental health just by his warm and loving goodness, than Will did, for all of his qualifications.

At the bereavement therapy group that he had just begun running in the church hall, Will felt that Johnny's presence, even if only to help with the tea, provided, to those who attended, a light and warmth in the otherwise chill and darkness of their grief.

'Come on then,' he relented, smiling. 'I know you're bursting to show me. What have you spent all our money on?'

116

Johnny bounced to the first bag and unwrapped some tissue carefully. 'Wait until you see this, it's soooo cute.'

Will watched as his partner of six years, and husband of one, carefully peeled back the fine white tissue revealing a delicate Christmas bauble that read, 'Baby's first Christmas,'

'Don't you just love it?' he asked, his eyes grew wider with excitement.

Will looked at the subtle pink sphere, hanging delicately from Johnny's fingers on a white, satin loop of ribbon. A clutch of mini white stars sat at the top, and the inscription was made in silver glitter.

It was tasteful, as far as labelled tack went, but he couldn't say that he was delighted at the thought of it being on their Christmas tree. He took pride in the elegance of their Christmas trees, and over the years, they had stuck to their theme of silver and white, each Yuletide, adding a new and fitting decoration to suit their minimalist style.

But this was pink. Subtle a shade as it might be (and Will had to be grateful for that. The manufacturer could have seen fit to select a hot fuchsia as a base for their gender-conforming baby bauble), it was still neither silver, nor white, and would hang incongruously from the branches of their expensive snow-covered artificial tree as if it were a beach ball in an Alpine fir.

His first thought was to ask Johnny if it came in any other colours (other than the normative blue for a boy, he supposed) but that would be churlish and spoil Johnny's excitement. Colour choice aside, part of him felt a little sad that Johnny hadn't waited until they were together. This was going to be their baby's first Christmas. The adoption was being finalised and soon, they would have a daughter.

Will would have to prepare himself for the house to not be sleek and stylish. For it to have toys and mess and food stains and for Christmas to be about something other than chilled champagne and late breakfasts in matching pyjamas, and for the tree to bear baubles that didn't meet the strict

117

uniform code.

Another thing, that he was readying himself for, was a change in attitude about the feast itself. Years of study in child development, and common sense, had told him that it was ridiculous to make a big fuss about Christmas for a baby. Their having neither any understanding, awareness, or memory of it made it a meaningless nonsense, and he had always had little patience for those parents who couldn't see that. However, as the moment approached for Will to consider what the festive season might be like with his own child; with *their* own child, he accepted that he was standing on the brink of complete ignorance. Who was he to say what parents should do for their child? All he knew of parenting and child development and human behaviour and development was from others. From books and studies and observations. From research and experiments. What would it be like when it was his own child, whom he desperately wanted, and to whom he wanted to give everything; and for whom he wanted to experience every wonderful and delightful thing?

He didn't know.

And nor did his husband. Because he had not even experienced those things himself. It was no wonder that Johnny desired to give his new daughter everything that he had been denied. Through the selfishness and neglect of his own parents, how much had he missed, that he was desperately trying to make up for now? Will could only attempt to understand. And he need only to look into the gleam of his husband's eyes, now, to see at least some of the vicarious joy that he was feeling at the prospect.

He reached for the bauble. 'It's lovely,' he said.

'No,' warned Johnny with a teasing smile, turning his body away and concealing the bauble in his palms. 'You, can't see it.'

'Why not?' Will asked.

'Because I haven't shown you the best bit yet.'

He turned back to face him, and as his fingers raised slowly, as if lifting the lid of a jewellery box, he revealed another word, embossed in silver glitter.

"Olivia."

Will's hand flew to his mouth, racing the tears that sprung to his eyes.

'It's beautiful,' he gasped.

Johnny beamed at Will's reaction. 'I just saw it in the window, and I felt like it was her, our daughter, calling out to us. We've been waiting so long for the adoption to go through and it's nearly here. This time last year, it was just the two of us and soon she will be here we will be a family.' He shrugged shyly. 'I don't know, it sounds silly but, it was as if the universe was saying that she is ready and waiting, and wanting to come to us as much as we are waiting for her. And, I know what we think about gender normativism, but the writing was already on a pink one…., and I know you are going to say that it doesn't go on our silver and white tree…, so, I don't know, maybe we can hang it in the kitchen or something, if you don't want it on the tree. But I just had to have it. Will,' he said grasping his husband's hand and searching his eyes. 'We are getting a baby,' he stated as if the bauble alone was making it real.

'*Our* baby.

Our little girl.

Our daughter.

She will be *Our* Olivia. And we will have this bauble to show her that she was so wanted, even before she was here.'

Will cradled the decoration gently in his palm and held Johnny's hand. Together, they gazed down upon it, as if it were the child, herself. His throat constricted with the sheer overwhelming joy at the prospect of what this small, pink sphere represented.

'So, I hate to ask,' he said, inhaling deeply and pressing the corner of his eyes with his fingertips. 'But what's in the rest of the bags?'

Johnny looked sheepish and worried. 'Are you sure it's not going to make you cross with me? 'cause I can take it all back.' 'Yeah, like those boots you bought a few months ago?' he teased. 'No, come on, let's have it. What did you get?'

Johnny pulled the bags toward him and said, 'Okay. Well…, first there is this… '

He withdrew a white babygrow with embroidery on the chest…,

'Baby's first Christmas,' he announced unnecessarily, as if Will couldn't read.

'Then there is this…,' he paused, reaching for another bag and unfolding what seemed to be a huge foam tablemat.

'What's that?' asked Will, his forehead a frown of confusion.

Johnny folded the object out on the carpet. A huge, quilted face smiled up at them. Santa's face, albeit most of it concealed behind snowy white facial hair. 'It's an activity mat advent calendar,' he announced proudly. 'Look! The beard is fluffy, which is one texture and then there are all these numbered flaps hidden in the beard and you open each one throughout Advent.' He demonstrated, searching through the undergrowth of Santa's hirsute chin, revealing little flaps and lifting them to find varying sounds and textures. 'There are twenty-four. It's so cool, isn't it? I just had to get it. Thought you'd like it too, as it is educational, because Olivia is going to be smart, like you.'

Will smiled, but inwardly felt the stab of injustice. He hated it when Johnny referenced his academic achievements as something that only he, Will, had accessed due to some innate intelligence. Of course, he was intelligent, and he had worked hard at school and university, and in his post-grad work. But he recognised how much of his success was down to the opportunities he was given and his comfortable start in life. Johnny was no less intelligent, and Will knew that he could have achieved the same outcomes, if he had been given the same start in life. It wasn't possible to win the 100m, when you started 300m behind the line and someone had tied your shoelaces together.

'She's going to be like both of us,' he said warmly. 'Although, I do wonder what part of your senses you took leave from, to get this,' he said gesturing to the grinning face.

'Why? What's wrong with it? I thought you'd like it. It's like a Christmassy baby encyclopedia,' said Johnny, seeming a little put out.

'Well, Advent begins the day after tomorrow…,' Will began.

'I know. That's why I got it,' Johnny explained.

'Yes, but Olivia isn't here yet, so she won't be able to use it, this Christmas.'

'She'll have it for next year then,' Johnny explained as if it was obvious.

'But she'll be older then, nearly two, and she won't need a texture activity mat. She'll be walking.'

'Oh,' Johnny said, a little crestfallen. 'Of course, What an absolute idiot. I just thought "baby" and "advent" and put them in the basket. I'll take it back then.'

'It's okay,' Will said. 'I can see why you liked it. She can still use it. It will be just as educational in March.' He said it to be supportive, but everything within him was crying out for him to stop speaking and just let Johnny take it back to the shop. There was an inherent part of him that could not tolerate Christmassy things outside of the festive season. It was actually toe-curling. He had once found a bauble that had missed being put away, having fallen behind the sideboard. It was only in August, moving it in order to refresh the paintwork, that he had discovered it, lying there in all its sparkly incongruence with the fresh, orange spears of gladioli in the vase beside it. He had immediately put it in the drawer, but even there, it struck him, whenever he opened it, as being as out of place as a boat in a car park.

He imagined Olivia, in the warmer months to come. The

grass, freshly mown; birdsong from the hedges, the pots, pregnant with bright flowers. She, beneath a shade, lying prone, savouring the sights and sounds of the natural world around her. Then his thought moves to the blanket, beneath her tummy. Not a brightly-coloured quilt, vibrantly printed with giraffes and zebras, reflecting the wonders of the savannah beyond her garden, but the ruddy, puffed cheeks of a grinning Santa, offering her little exploring fingers a world of rustles and crinkles, squeaks and ruffles little delights hidden amongst his whiskers. It was enough to make the back of Will's neck prickle with sweat. Outside the confines of the festive cornerstones of Advent, Santa seemed not only out of place, but verging on the sinister.

'Maybe we could wait until next year and then we could hide chocolates in it instead?' Will offered helpfully. Although Santa's image had already been spoiled somewhat by the wanderings of his own mind that he found it difficult to regain his footing in the conversation. He looked at the bags.

'What else did you get? Anything else that is age inappropriate like pull-up pants, or an "introduction to calculus"?' he teased.

Johnny hit him playfully in the arm, then opened another bag.

A bright red babygrow, with black "boots" sewn into the feet, hung from a little hanger, a hood, in the shape of a pointed hat, lay flat along its back, edged with a soft white fur. Another was a two piece with a green top and had stripy red and green leggings, with printed feet that looked like little elf boots.

Will shook his head, conveying, at once, a shared delight in the Christmas outfits, dismay at their tacky gaudiness, and despair at ever having to take their new, baby daughter out in them, in public.

'Cute,' Will said appreciatively, as each thing was extracted.

Johnny was in his element, Will noticed. Shoes and clothes were his favourite thing to buy. Something to do with not ever having any of his own, Will supposed. Having always been dressed and shod, through the donations of others, or in hand-me-downs kept at the various foster homes.

'Then I got this, a little pack of bibs…,' Johnny continued, tossing tissue paper left and right as if he were pulling Kleenex from a holder.

'Okay…, don't tell me, they say, "Baby's first Christmas",' Will guessed.

'Yes! You are right, sir. How did you know that?' he laughed, as he dove into another bag. 'Now… not clothes this time. But just look at this. They are soooo cute. Look! A little plastic cup, plate and spoon.'

'Baby's first Christmas Dinner,' Will announced, taking it for a closer look. 'That's so adorable. She can have a little bit of chopped up turkey and potato and sprouts,' he said, his heart swelling with the anticipation and expectation of what their first family Christmas dinner might be.

'Sprouts! Really? Bagsy not it! You're doing that nappy,' Johnny giggled.

They laughed together.

'Okay. I'm seeing a theme here,' Will said. 'Did you buy anything that doesn't say "Baby's first Christmas"?'

'I did actually,' Johnny said, his mouth twisting on one side into a wry smile, one of the first things that Will had fallen in love with. 'I got these too.'

Carefully unwrapping anther package, and holding them up to the light, Johhny showed his husband two more baubles. One was silver, the other was white. Both wore a subtle, matt finish and both were inscribed in the same glitter inscription style as Olivia's. Although, with one difference. Johnny handed him the silver one.

'Daddy's first Christmas,' Will whispered, smiling and reaching for it. He turned it over in his hand. On the reverse side was written, "Will, Olivia's Daddy #1". He glanced at his husband, who was holding the white one up to read, "Johnny, Olivia's daddy #2".

Will's eyes prickled with the sting of tears. Carefully taking the white bauble from Johnny's hands, he lay it carefully on the soft, beige carpet and placed his own, silver one beside it. Silver and white, as they had always been. The stylish and elegant bauble symbolism of their relationship with Christmas and with each other.

Johnny picked up the pink one and held it over them, hovering above the recumbent bauble like a hot air balloon in a summer sky.

Will's fingers and thumb came to greet it, and together, Olivia's daddies, #1 and #2, then landed it gently, nestling her bauble between them, where she would remain forever.

Johnny pulled his legs into the lotus position and sat up straight. 'So, do you really want the advent calendar?' he asked.

'I really do,' Will replied.

'What about taking it into your office?' Johnny suggested helpfully.

'Er, that's a no. What about yours?'

'I don't think it's really appropriate for an estate agent showroom. I'll take it back to the shop tomorrow. Don't worry about it. It was a mistake.'

'No leave it. It was a nice idea,' Will said gently, 'and you never know, if the adoption papers come through soon, she may get some use out of it this Christmas after all.'

The prospect sent a fizz through Johnny's scalp. 'Can you believe it. A baby for Christmas,'

'A baby is for life, not just for Christmas,' Will joked ironically.

He looked at Santa's cheesy grin and side eye and shuddered. How had the designers managed to make him look so creepy? Attached to the numbered, padded flaps, there were plastic crinkles and furry reindeer and woolly sheep and a donkey with a coarse texture like sandpaper. Rattles and squeakers were concealed in Santa's buttons. The depiction of a sack and toys sat behind his white, hairy head exposing a brown teddy, his curly coat making him feel more like a cockapoo than a bear; a steam train engine that blew a hoot when he pressed it; and a drum kit that gave a pleasing automatic rat-a-tat when he lifted the flap... A teething ring with coloured plastic keys hung from Santa's thick black belt. Will supposed that this was supposed to represent the magic instruments that Santa has in order to access every house without a suitable chimney, but it just gave him the appearance of a law enforcer in a red suit and black boots, like a paunchy Canadian Mountie, with keys to the country jail cell.

Will wondered whether there was a governing body that oversaw all festive manufacture and distribution. A sort of OffSanta that could set standards and ensure that every Christmas item met them and confirmed to established guidelines and could be reprimanded for falling short of them, like creating Santas that looked a cross between a leering perv on Brighton pier and a screw at a custodial facility.

Rather, if he could have his way, he would knock Christmas on its head and get rid of everything to do with it. His consulting rooms were busier than ever at this time of year. It was like balancing old scales, being with Johnny at home, and his patients at work. His husband, wanting so hard to make up for all the Christmas he had missed, his FoMO weighing the brass dish and tipping the balance. Then, to see his clients, the pain and worry and anxiety brought on by the season piling into the dish like gold ingots, pulling the side down like a heavy adult on a seesaw, sending Johnny's lightness and joy sky high like a squealing child.

Birthday of
The unconquerable sun

30 NOVEMBER

Taking a final glance around the kitchen, Emma reached for the light switch. Her fingers found it easily and pressed it gently, drawing the room into darkness. The scattering of junk on the breakfast bar formed a shapeless mound in the corner, like a skulking creature. A school jumper making its form, curved in its fullness, one arm like an extended paw, the other, like a curled haunch. Two horse chestnuts, a deep, shining mahogany, peeled from their silken beds in the crisp days of Autumn lay in the folds of the sweater, like watchful eyes.

She had been with Henry when they had got them, the chestnuts, his little hands finding them amongst the fallen leaves. He had presented them to her, a treasure found amongst the decay. Green spheres, studded with little points, which pressed painfully into his hands, like a handle-less mace for a medieval doll. 'Look,' she had said, and he came to her, the low sun streaming through the branches, his little face, all trust and curiosity. For that is what little children do; observe and discover and believe. She had inserted her thumbnail into the flesh of the soft shell, slowly easing it apart. The creamy interior was pure and untouched, and nestled at its heart was the nut, perfect in its smoothness with the rich patina of a French-polished dining table. His eyes had widened, his mouth forming a perfect 'o' in wonder and surprise. She withdrew the chestnut from the case and placed it into his upturned palm. His other hand came up to touch it, and he stroked it, gently, feeling its surface, soft as satin, so different from its outer shell. From then, he was a hunter, searching for more, finding for himself the treasures that lay within.

He had studied her, his eyes, as dark brown as the nut itself. Love had surged through her. Love and privilege. Because it is a privilege to be able to share the wonders that surround us, and to see them through young and unjaded eyes.

Since then, they had become his pets. The Tamagotchi of the natural world. Not that he pretended to feed them at appointed times, but more as one has a pet rock, or a special pebble. Emma had a friend once, who had a 'worry cross' that she kept in her pocket. It was made of smooth olive wood, its lines and nodes rounded, as if it had been carved in bubble writing. It was intended to provide comfort in times of stress or worry, to know that someone was there, presumably Jesus, to make things better. Perhaps it was like a Christian version of a fidget spinner, something to fiddle with to calm anxiety. She didn't really understand it, how people relied on their faith to sort things out. Her philosophy leant more towards personal agency. Doing what you could to help yourself and others and deriving strength from the nature itself, the lifeblood of the planet. Had she been born a few thousand years earlier, she might have called herself a pagan, in her attitude towards nature and community and the strength she derived from both... She stopped short of calling herself a druid or wiccan, as to her mind, nothing good came of putting too much store in doctrines and practices of any kind. As long as whatever you did was in love and for the good of each other, and Mother Earth, she thought that was a more fundamental foundation for life than doing whatever a supernatural being suggested, which usually required adherence to lots of rules that had been made up and addended over the years, and primarily for the financial benefit of others rather than the wisdom of the original deity.

The jumper creature guarded a clutch of letters, shielding

them as a child protects their work from a class neighbour who copies. Emma had cast them aside with a cursory glance when she extracted them from the school bags earlier. And with Matthew and Adam being twins, she always got two of everything. It was all too much to take in at once. She would need a mug of tea and her calendar to hand to address such correspondence as had spewed from the printers of the school office. The familiar letter head and font, reminding her about the Christmas Fayre and the associated donations for the raffle, or the tombola, (both chocolate and bottle); another denoting which parts Matthew and Adam would be playing in the nativity, (probably shepherds, like last year, following the understanding that the best way to cope with twins is to make them the same and as inconspicuous as possible); a third, requesting notification as to whether they want a Christmas Dinner, (even though they take packed lunches - and yes, she thought, they probably do because they get very excited about pulling the crackers), and if so, vegetarian or turkey? (Vegetarian). The most recent one, withdrawn from the bag today, announced the date that they could wear Christmas jumpers (eighteenth) and the date of the last day of term (twenty-second) and the return date for January (sixth). Epiphany, she noted with amusement. It tickled her that, for so many cultures, the epiphany was known as Little Christmas, and celebrated anew for the arrival of the three wise men and more gifts were shared. Yet, for others, by then, it was all over and in true Christian fashion, the threat of the eternal damnation of your soul for leaving your baubles up for a second past midnight was enough to get you reaching for the stepladder a little after lunchtime.

The PIR light shone through the kitchen window, flashing for a moment as the cat jumped off the shed roof, illuminating the advent calendars hanging on the wall. Five. Well, not calendars as such, in fact, not really anything other than limp lengths of string dangling from name cards. For Emma, Advent still represented a countdown, but not of twenty-four days to Christmas, instead, twenty-one days until the Winter Solstice. That is when they would have their celebration, their feast and fun and they would rejoice in the fact that the worst darkness of the winter was over and that the days would lengthen in hours and light, revealing more of its wonder and leading to the rebirth in spring.

It was a custom that she and Rob had developed. She didn't know if anyone else did it or not, but they chose to mark the advent of the Solstice by taking a little piece of autumn and securing it to the string. Henry had already collected chestnuts, not the ones he kept as pets, but others found with his brothers, and they had all said that it was these that they wanted to secure to the string to mark day one. To follow would be twigs, and large, brown leaves, acorns or berries, feathers from migrated birds, or clumps of moss and lichen. Each day marking another moment in the coming of the midwinter. Henry had suggested once that if it snowed, he could catch a snowflake and keep it in the freezer and just draw a picture of it to go on the string. Matthew and Adam had told him that that was silly, and Emma had to remind them that they had thought that they could do the same with an icicle that they had found on the barn roof one morning when they were Henry's age.

As was the custom with most advent calendars these days, Emma realised that a large part of the appeal was the daily chocolate fix. So, as each day's find was affixed to the string, she handed them a tin of homemade chocolate treats. Most days, Matthew chose a chocolate muffin with extra chocolate chips, Adam usually went for the chocolate brownie and Henry usually took a bite out of each and then settled on a chocolate covered flapjack which he called adventurer bars, because they went exploring in Advent. You couldn't fault the logic.

She knew that it was difficult for them at school sometimes, not doing the same things that the other children did, but Emma and Rob felt strongly that just because everyone does a particular thing, it doesn't make it right. That ethos had led them to move to the country, to buy the farm and work hard to run a sustainability business where all they produced was homegrown, homemade and locally distributed. Whenever Christmas came along, it upset the apple cart somewhat. In fact, far more so than when Hugh the farm hand had actually upset the apple cart during harvesting and had sent the pick of the russets and pippins rolling down the B road. Since they had had the boys, Emma and Rob had wondered whether it might not just be better and easier to let them just do what the other kids at school did and not have to stand out as being different. Everyone knew that if there was one thing that it was not advisable to do at school, it was being different.

Easier it may be, but not necessarily better, so they had agreed with each other to try to stay true to their beliefs as long as possible whilst ensuring the children never suffered because of it.

After all, when you really examined Christmas. What was it? A celebration for the birth of the light of the world? Yes, perhaps, but one diariased by the church to coincide with an established midwinter celebration, which also celebrates the light of the world. The light that is our world, the sun. Both seek to lift the spirits of those in the darkness, to revive their souls with renewed joy and expectation and to allow themselves to feast a bit. The pagans had done the same for thousands of years.

With the Romans holding their feast day celebrations for the god Saturn on the seventeenth of December and the pagans' solstice on the twenty-first, it seemed only natural for the church to schedule the birth of Jesus around the same sort of time. How better to introduce the idea that this new kid is cool, than to give him a birthday that coincides with a party that's already going on? A party that celebrates an unconquerable sun. A party that they can hijack to celebrate an unconquerable son.

She would deal with the letters from school tomorrow, when nautical twilight warmed the eastern sky, and she would arise with the sun.

The door with no key
30 NOVEMBER

The advent calendar that Sally held was a plain cardboard one. Not one of those chocolate ones. Her daughter couldn't eat chocolate and so she bought a box of sweets instead, mini packets of jelly babies and Haribo and Moam bars, chews and lollies. All ridiculously bad for their teeth, but with everything they had gone through this last year, their teeth were the least of her worries. That's not true. She was massively worried about their teeth, in fact every single bit of them. She was worried about everything these days.

But she had thought that if she kept the box of sweets to hand, she could monitor their treat and then supervise teeth brushing afterwards. It was getting easier. At least she could get out of bed now and could work, but it had been tough.

The calendar she had chosen was a picture of a snowy street. Victorian by the looks of it, cottages in the field by a little copse of trees all heavy with snow and then a line of little houses all along a lane into a village. The village street had shops with bowed windows, black leaded frames, dissecting their panes into little squares, providing convenient benches for the snow to rest on, piling up into the corners in drifts. The roof tops were higgledy piggledy and the signs swung out from the doors of the baker and the toy shop; all the windows aglow with yellow light.

Little children were peering in the toy shop window and elegant ladies moved about in long dresses. The girls had ringlets and velvet capes and boaters, and the boys had pedal pushers tucked into white hose.

It looked every bit the perfect magical Christmas scene.

There was no Santa, but Sally liked that. She liked to see the children in the street with their mother. It was an old-fashioned style of artwork, like an old painting and the artistic techniques were there in terms of perspective and shading and depth, but there was that detachment where you don't quite feel it is real. She had seen a painting of a peony in an exhibition this summer, and had leant forward instinctively almost to smell it, it had been so real. Yet this seemed like the artist saying, I'll just paint you a picture of what a Victorian street looked like at Christmas, instead of feeling that you could put on your muff and step right in.

Still, she knew the girls would love it and could imagine them searching for the numbers, not just on the doors but hidden in the snow and thatch and trees and toys, there was even one in the horse's mane and at the back of the hansom cab.

It had called to her when she was choosing a calendar. So many were cartoon drawings of penguins and snowmen on sleds all wearing woolly hats and sledging down hills. They were fine, she supposed, but so samey. She wanted something that the girls could get lost in, to let their imagination go wild. Rosie had been reading Little Women and Sally thought that she quite fancied herself as Amy March. Sally knew that beneath it all, she was more like bold and strong Jo, but being strong and resilient was hard, and lonely. It was easier sometimes to just be like the other girls and talk about which colour ribbon to wear in your hair and who you were going to marry. Since Rosie was thinking of Tom Holland, Sally did not feel the need to worry too much yet.

It was something she wanted to laugh about with Pete. To imagine them there together at their daughter's wedding. But he wasn't there to share her thoughts. Nor would he be at the wedding, or graduation, or Eighteenth birthday party, or waving them off to university. All the milestones in life, she would stand at, alone. Like the grey pieces of ancient stone that stood in ditches, the distance of the road aread, etched into her, while the rest of the world whizzed by.

There was one thing that she was grateful for, that they had had time to talk about these moments in their daughters' futures. It was not like a heart attack or car accident, here one minute gone the next. Sally didn't know how people could accept the incredulity in that situation, suddenly getting a visit from the police, or a phone call from a hospital. Pete had known that his body wasn't responding to treatment. They had had time to make preparations, to say goodbye. Yet, despite that, Sally still now felt like a boat, out at sea on her own, responsible for those who sailed with her, struggling against the force of the onslaught threatening to snap her masts.

Perhaps that's why Rosie wanted to be like Amy March, the youngest of sisters who would bridge the gap between herself and an absent father. Perhaps she could believe that he was away at war and might return. That she could remain in the ringlets and petticoats of childhood rather than having to be Meg, the biggest of the little women. To be support to her mother. This wasn't the way it should be, Sally told herself. And she tried. But Rosie was intuitive. She knew when Sally was struggling to stay afloat and when her presence was like an unfurled sail in a homeward breeze.

Where was Pete in this advent calendar scheme? She wondered as she studied it. In the baker's with the plum puddings and mince pies? In the carriage, driving the horse? In the alehouse further down the lane? He would be in the toy shop with the girls, reflecting the light of delight and wonder in their eyes, back at them like the lamp of a lighthouse.

Which is your door? Sally asked the ether. How can I get to you? Tell me the number and I will find it. There are only twenty-four. What is it like where you are? I cannot seem to conjure the image. All I can see are windows and doors, and none of them have a key.

Dear Santa,

My name is Briony Westcott and I am 10 years old. Last year, you brought me a Sylvanian car and caravan and I have loved playing with them. Thank you . If you don't remember, my house is the one at the end, near the bus stop.

I have been very good all year. I work hard at school and have been Star of the ~~Weak~~ Week for winning a badge at the swimming gala for the relay. Mrs Parsons said that I was a good team player because nobody wanted to do butterfly. I didn't either, because I'm not good at butterfly stroke but Helena, the girl who was supposed to do it, was crying. I don't know why. She wouldn't tell anyone. I sat with her in the changing rooms and shared my orange squash and my biscuit. My biscuit was actually for the coach ride home, but I thought Helena needed it more. It was a Jammie Dodger, and it made her smile ~~coz~~ because everyone loves those. I came last in the butterfly race.

I have a little brother called Max, you brought him a walkie talkie set and a marble run, and his room is the one next to the bathroom. The one with the Ninky Nonk stickers on the walls. Just in case you get confused, like you did last year, but I don't mind because you have so many children to visit, you must make some mistakes. I don't know how you don't get the wrong house, or even country, never mind the wrong room! (We have just

135

learned exclamation marks in SPaG. I'm sorry if I haven't used it right.).

I am good for Mum, and although I try to keep my room tidy, it isn't always. But I will make sure it is when you come.

My favourite book is about Myths and Monsters. There is a big foldout in the middle with pictures of all of the mythical beasts and I like to place my play figures on the pictures and then create stories and battles with them and imagine what I would do if I ever met one. I would like to fight monsters when I grow up. I have some figures but there are some I still need.

I would really, really, really, really, more than anything, love to have a Bunyip, Hydra and Gryphon figure. I have a mermaid, manticore, leviathan, werewolf and kelpie, just to let you know, but without the others, I can't match the pictures or play my game properly. I would also love a pair of green roller skates. I am size 3 but Mum said that my feet will grow. I would also like anything else to do with mythical beasts, like books or games. And please can I have a make-up set. Mum says that I am too young to start wearing make-up, so she won't get one for me.

I hope that is okay. Mum said we should not be greedy and ask for too much. Is this too much? If so, I am happy to go without the roller skates and games. Even if I only get one thing, can it please be the Bunyip, because we can't seem to find one anywhere, but you are Santa and you and your elves can make anything with your magic.

Thank you very much.

Kind regards (Miss Jennings said that we can say Kind regards or Best wishes in formal writing, but I have read Best wishes on birthday cards, so I think kind regards is probably the right thing. And is it formal writing if you are writing to a friend? Because you are a friend, aren't you Santa.

Thank you again.

Briony Westcott XXX

Ps. Whatever Helena asks for, please can you add some Jammie Dodgers. She seems to cry a lot, and these seem to be the only things that make her smile. Oh, and can you also give some to Rosie too, because she cries a lot too.

Thank you again. XXX

THE EPIPHANY

PART II

The Elves
and
the magicmaker

SECRET LABOURS

THE EPIPHANY

All's fayre

'Well, *I* think the key to a stress-free Christmas is all in the planning,' Hildy said authoritatively, waving one manicured hand while holding a decaf gingerbread latte in the other.

That's easy for you to say, thought Liz silently. A stress-free Christmas might be attainable if you didn't work, spent all day at the health club and came home to a house that Maria, your underpaid au pair and all round helper had made spotless for you, and a fridge full of high-end ready meals. Perhaps you were stress-free because your evenings were spent drinking organic red wine and listening to your husband talk about his hedge-fund clients, which while boring, reminded you that each one carried a substantial price on their heads and an investment portfolio that would pay for the swimming pool installation including the annexed two-bedroomed pool house you had commissioned. Perhaps you were stress-free because you weren't worried about how you were going to help your dyslexic child with their mocks revision, help your other child with their anxiety attacks, treat the old dears at work with patience and dignity, or meet the electricity bill, which for the whole house on blackout warnings still came to less than it would cost to heat and light said extraneous pool house.

She didn't say any of this, she just smiled and took the drink that was offered to her. It wasn't in her nature to feel envy or jealousy about Hildy, or anyone – well perhaps a little bit – it was just that sometimes it didn't feel fair that she had such comfort and ease, when for others, simply getting through a day was exhausting. And her feelings today were not being helped by her sanctimonious tone suggesting that the reason the rest of us schmucks couldn't cope with the impending rigors of Christmas was because we were poor planners. Liz had planning lists all over the place; one in the car for when a thought or task came to mind; a blackboard on the kitchen wall with hurriedly chalked reminders; and a corkboard, in the corner of the breakfast room that they called an office, overlaid with letters and forms and notes hanging at angles from drawing pins like the petals of a handkerchief tree. And they were just the visible lists. The others, like the secret gift list and the Christmas budget, were documented in an excel spreadsheet under a pseudonym filename. That was planning, wasn't it? The task continuing infinitely, like Sisyphus' stone rolling. Also, when she was grateful for finding a pair of matching socks in the laundry basket this morning, she realised that she had to be gentle with herself and acknowledge that she was doing okay. Maria wasn't there to answer to Liz's every whim as she was for Hildy, so, she agreed to cut herself some slack. She might not have all the fancy accoutrements that went along with Hildy's lifestyle, but as long as the plates were all still spinning, it didn't really matter whether they were Wedgewood, Spode or George at Asda, all it mattered was that they weren't all smashed on the floor.

'I mean, with children, it's all about Santa, isn't it?' Hildy continued, having taken a sip of her coffee. They don't care whether there is turkey or decorations or whether we are having brandy butter or brandy cream with the plum pudding, do they?' She laughed. 'That's for us adults to worry about.'

'Or for Maria to worry about,' Liz muttered under her breath and then sipped the froth off her cappuccino to disguise her lips, absolving them of being accused of speaking unkindly.

Emma glanced at her and smiled a discreet smile of complicit understanding.

Kristen arrived, to Liz's left, and placed the tray on the table. 'Er, this one is the coconut vanilla mocha, she said trying to decode the shorthand that the barista had scribbled on the lid. 'How you can drink that, I do not know,' she said grimacing, handing it to a woman with straight mousy hair and a severe fringe. The thought of four flavours in one coffee, and so sweet…, it made her teeth hurt to think of it. 'That one, was the oat-milk cappuccino for you, Emma.' She handed the large round mug to a woman with bouncy curls and a denim jacket. 'These are the lattes, and I think that is the one with caramel syrup,' she tapped it and nodded towards a woman with an orange scarf. 'And there's a couple of bags of shortbread there too.'

There was a chorus of thank yous and a moment of quiet as each of the assembled took a sip from their various concoctions. Kristen set her cup to one side and withdrew a sheaf of papers from a binder. 'So, thanks for making time to come today ladies,' she said, addressing the same few faces of the school PFA who always made the time. 'So, after all our weeks of planning, we are nearly there. The Christmasssss Fayrrreeee.' She announced it with a fanfare and did a fairy clap with her hands, looking around at the assembled to see if they were all as demonstrably excited as she. They weren't.

'We can get into the school from nine a.m.,' she began 'Kevin said that he is going to move some of the tables out of the classrooms the night before, to give us more space. Bless him. Isn't he a superstar?' Everyone nodded dutifully at the caretaker's willingness to help.

'So, we can begin setting everything up then. Obviously, as in previous years, the main stalls will be in the hall. The choir are going to sing carols at 3.30p.m. and then there'll be the raffle at 4pm. Games will be in the reception classrooms and Santa's grotto will be in the PPA room, as usual. The only…'

Emma put up her hand. 'Er, sorry to interrupt Kristen, but I didn't think we could use that room because of the flood.'

Kristen looked affronted at both the interruption and the assertion that someone had more information about the

Christmas Fayre plans than she did. 'What do you mean?' she asked.

'The flood.'

'What flood? How have I not been told about this?'

'Well, it only happened yesterday. Apparently, there was some leak or other and it flooded the classroom, hallway and the PPA room. They have stopped it, but they need to take up the carpet tiles and dry it all out. We're not going to be able to use it.'

'But where are we going to put Santa then? There's no other space.' Kristen said, hurriedly flipping through her binder as if the solution would just appear.

'It's okay,' Emma said. 'I've already done it. I called him last night.'

'Who?' Kristen asked reflexively.

'Santa,' Emma repeated. 'Well, Dave Jennings. Holly's da.., I mean, Miss Jennings' dad.'

Kristen looked put out and stared at Emma. She was thrown for a moment. Kristen made all the calls about the Fayre. Kristen was the chair of the PFA. Kristen had the binder. How was it that hippy, devil-may-care, Emma had stepped up and had taken control – and called Santa? And why didn't Emma call her, if anyone, to inform her about this, rather than her finding out here in front of everyone making her appear that she was not in control or up to speed with Fayre matters?

Emma read Kristen's look, confusion mixed with surprise and resentment. She felt she should explain.

'I was in a meeting, after school, with Miss Jennings, about Matthew and Adam, and that's when they discovered the flood. It had already flowed into the PPA room and had drenched the carpets.'

Hildy's natural nosiness wanted more information as to what the meeting could have been about. What was wrong with Matthew and Adam? she wondered. Had they been naughty or were they not doing well in their work? Hildy had

had her fair share of being called into meetings with the teacher about her own son, Magnus and his behaviour. She rather relished the idea of Emma's boys not being the angels they appeared to be. Perhaps Miss Jennings would give Magnus a break for a while; she was getting a bit fed up with the continual messages about his behaviour. There always seemed to be something that he was being blamed for; a spiteful comment; excluding someone from a game; his being mean; not taking turns or sharing. Hildy acknowledged that he could be a handful sometimes, but Magnus was a character. She couldn't help it if others couldn't see that, and she'd be damned if she was going to make him change his lively spirit just to accommodate the other wimps in the class. Yet, although she wanted to delve into this a little further, Kristen seemed to think it more interesting and relevant to explore what had happened about Santa and the flood.

Kristen gave Emma a hard stare, that would rival anything Paddington might come up with. 'Well, it might have been nice for you to tell me. I am the PFA chair, after all,' she bristled and the other women around the table shared amused glances. No one could be under any misapprehension as to who was the PFA chair, Kristen reminded everyone often enough.

'I did send you a message,' Emma explained.

'What?' Kristen said, rifling through her pages of apps until she found the Whatsapp with a little blob in the corner signifying an unopened message.

'Oh,' she said, suitably contrite and a bit put out.

Everyone sipped their coffees awkwardly while she skimmed the message.

'Right, 'she continued, regrouping. 'so what did you say to Sant… to Mr…Jen…Dave... Dave?'

'Well, everyone was bothered about the damage, obviously and they were all running around getting mops and what have you, but the first thing I thought of was Santa,' Emma replied. 'I suppose, because Liz, Laura, Sally and I did the grotto last year in that PPA room, and to me, that's what the room represents. I simply thought, 'where's Santa going to go and then because we had been talking about reading, Miss Jennings and I…,'

Hildy made a mental note. So, the meeting had been about Matthew and Adam's reading. Their education, not their behaviour. A piece of her bristled. It was the green bit. The envious bit. The monster that sat behind her eyes, watching and waiting for a glimpse of another's failure. She wasn't quite sure where the monster had come from. She didn't recall it being there when she was younger, perhaps it was since they had money? Or was it since having a child? Whatever had enticed it to lodge within her, it seemed very comfortable and reluctant to move on. She saw her green-eyed monster as a lazy cat, that curled up in a small part of her heart. It seemed hungry all the time and she fed it on moments like this. Well, earlier. When she had thought that Emma's perfect boys may not have been as perfect as everyone thought. They couldn't be likable and happy and healthy and sweet… and… high achievers at school. It wasn't fair for a person to have everything. That was, of course, unless it were her. That was the monster's favourite food. Hildy had realised. It sought other nourishment too, like objects and clothes and lifestyles. If Hildy could covet those in others, the monster was satisfied. But it was the tiny chips in the pedestals of others' achievements and wellbeing, they were what really sated its cavernous gut and got it licking its paws after every meal.

Emma continued. 'And I just thought…, the reading shed.'

Kristen gasped and burnt her tongue on the hot coffee. 'The shed!' she exclaimed. 'You want to put Santa in the shed?'

'Well, there isn't really any other space is there?' Emma asked. 'The classrooms are all filled with stall holders and games. The hall has space given over to the stage and the carol concert. The kitchen is well… the kitchen, and the only other places are the Head's office and secretary's office and well, they're just not suitable. But then I thought of the shed. I happen to think it could be really nice. We already have everything we need. We can use fairy lights and reindeer and maybe even put one of those pretend log burners out there and it would feel like a real log cabin in Lapland. It could be quite magical.'

There were nods of assent and murmurings of agreement around the table.

'I just thought that I should check it with Dave first, before I brought up the idea today, as it would be a moot point if he didn't want to go into the shed for any reason,' Emma explained.

'Right, yes, of course, quite right,' said Kristen, trying to conceal her surprise that hippy Emma had it all worked out and had even had the forethought to call Santa.

'And is he?'

'Is he what?' Emma asked simply.

'Is he happy to go in the shed?'

'Oh! Yes. He said that's fine. No problem. He said it would beat some of the places he has to go. When he visits the hospital, he has to get changed in the cleaning cupboard apparently. He got his foot stuck in a mop bucket last year.'

'But, the shed,' Kristen repeated again. 'We can't put Santa in the shed.'

'I don't see the problem with it?' Liz said. 'If it is good enough for our children to go in to do their reading all through the year, it's good enough for Santa for one afternoon, and like Emma said. We can make it look lovely. A real winter wonderland. The only problem is time. We have a bit more to do and not very long to do it.

'Ok then, the shed it is,' Kristen said, reluctantly acknowledging that a matter had been sorted without her involvement or her name on the concurrent emails. 'Now, where was I, (before I was interrupted, and my authority and responsibility usurped)?' she wanted to say.

'We still have lots of fake snow and white sheets. We'll just have to try to make it as winter wonderlandy as possible. There is a big take up to see Santa, so be prepared, you elves are going to be busy. Time to put on your stripy tights.'

Laura lifted her long corduroy skirt to show that she was wearing stripy tights anyway. 'Once an elf, always an elf,' she joked.

Liz sipped her latte and let the chatter wash over her. She was trying to concentrate, but her head was pounding a rhythmic throb, as if the Rank pictures man was striking her right temple with a gong beater. How was she here again? She had vowed that she wouldn't get caught up in another Christmas fayre. She had four children, and Grace was her last to come through the school. From the time her eldest, Lewis, was in reception, she had been involved in every school event; pouring tea; baking cakes; decorating grottos; helping on school trips; being a parent helper; listening to the children read. Sometimes she felt that she was doing more for the school than its senior management team. But, with reduced budgets and fundraising events providing much needed resources and extra-curricular equipment, she felt it was important to contribute her time, one last time, and the children loved a Christmas Fayre. It was always the same few who ever did anything for the PFA, and if she didn't do her part, the fayre would suffer; her colleagues would suffer and ultimately the children would suffer by not getting the resources they so needed.

So here she was again. Whilst she only worked three days a week, they were demanding. As a healthcare assistant, at a nursing home for the elderly, she found it, at once, both incredibly rewarding but punishingly tiring. She cared deeply for those whom she looked after but they could be rude and frustrating a lot of the time, testing her patience to the limit. They were forgetful and hard of hearing and sometimes it drained her so much, her days off might as well have been working days, such was the hangover she experienced.

This would be her last, though. Grace was in year six now Joshua and Elliot were both in secondary school and Lewis was at university. It was time for someone else to take the reins of these Christmas reindeer and get Santa to his PPA room, (or shed) on time.

Every year, it never failed to surprise her how busy the grotto was. It was the highlight of the Fayre and engendered the most excitement of all the other events and attractions. It seemed a strange juxtaposition, she thought, that children could, on the one hand, believe that Santa lived in the North Pole and only ever visited on Christmas Eve, yet the one-in-the-same could also come to their school on a regular Saturday afternoon in December. Furthermore, they never sought to question why he had not landed gently on the school rooftop, in a sleigh pulled by reindeer, but instead, had chosen to take up residence in the very room where they were sent on errands by their teachers for more sugar paper or a long arm stapler.

The latte wasn't helping her headache, so she poured a glass of water from the self-service jug and took a couple of paracetamols. She had had a particularly difficult conversation with relatives of one of the elderly residents at the nursing home yesterday and it had left her feeling a sorrowful heart, pain and tense. Perhaps she needed to eat something. Helping herself to a shortbread, she tried to paint on a bright enthusiasm as she returned her attention to the planning committee.

'Right! So, Santa's little helpers,' Kristen said holding up a sheet and passing a copy amongst the others. 'As you are our resident experts, the shed it entirely in your hands… we are relying on you to turn grotty into grotto.'

She giggled at her own witticism, and everyone smiled politely, except for Hildy who threw back her head and laughed loudly, at the same time saying how funny Kristen was.

An unveiled complement?

Perhaps the monster was replete.

The Pie Piper

It was a Tuesday. Lucy had left for work, her long commute into town requiring an early start. Darcy was glad that she didn't do that anymore. She had done, when she was younger, before having the children. She had worked in the city, travelled an hour in nose-to-tail traffic, leaving at dawn and home well after dusk. But she was at the top of her professional game and Richard was the same. The classic power-couple.

It had been exhilarating for her, knowing that she had the answers that people sought, the power to make decisions, the authority to manage staff and the vision to create something new and exciting. To innovate and strategise and develop something that didn't exist before. That was what nourished her and fed her sense of purpose. Where had that person gone? The one who wore trouser-suits and rushed from one meeting to the next with people running at her high heels just to get five minutes' audience. She felt a long way from here, Darcy thought as she placed her cleaning trug on the counter.

Lucy had put up her tree in the corner, a small artificial one, typical of Lucy, Darcy thought, neat, functional and something likely to cause minimal clearing up. A few small presents were set at the base. Darcy was impressed. It was only the first week of December. Cards were on the mantelpiece, those early despatchers who seemed to derive some satisfaction for being the first card to be received. Darcy hadn't sent any cards. Well, a few to her parent's generation, they appreciated the contact and outreach, but Darcy didn't really see the point of cards when you saw the same people every day. She had diligently bought them for the children when they were little, their class friends sending them to each other. Poorly scrawled misspelt names on little square cards with cartoon penguins on, as if penguins have got anything to do with Christmas? "To Mark, from Zara x". Thirty of those, for each child. That was sixty received and sixty sent, extrapolating that to the whole class. That was a lot of cards and a lot of trees. Two years ago, Darcy had bought four packs of charity cards, and they were still in the drawer. Hadn't been opened. Well, she had taken one out, attaching it to the box of shortbread she had wrapped for her neighbour, but the neighbour had visited a friend in Canada for Christmas and had decided to stay there for a few months. So, Darcy had eaten the shortbread and had switched the names around in the card, putting it up on her windowsill in the pretense that Mrs Landon had given her the gift instead.

For years, Darcy had watched her mother spending days doing the cards, them all at various stages of completion; this pile ready and waiting for stamps; this pile, stamped and waiting for the post office to open; this pile, the card written but the address lacking a few essential details like town and postcode. When she had queried what her mother was intending to do with those, she had replied that she would call them up the potential recipient and get their new address. Darcy knew that a conversation catch up would then ensue and there would be no actual need in the end to send the card. They would then go back in the box for next year. In each card, her mother had painstakingly hand-written the same brief precis of their lives to each great aunt and uncle and cousin and had stayed up late into the night bent over in poor light, like Bob Cratchit, summing up the ledger under Scrooge's watchful gaze.

Darcy had affirmed to herself that she would not do that and had had the idea to insert a printed epistle instead of a hand-written note, a jaunty overview of their lives over the last year. Churning out thirty copies on her work printer at lunchtimes, she felt like she had beaten the system. Folding each one in quarters, she had placed the printout into the card to be eagerly unfurled by whichever member of the family impatiently awaited news from overseas.

However, Darcy had only done that for one year. In the following January, when they had all returned to work, she had overheard a group of colleagues talking by the coffee machine about the various similar types of missives they had received. None of them were hers, fortunately, but the derision with which they were discussed left her in no doubt that such a thing was apparently not as well received as she had anticipated. "God, who wants to hear that Bella is doing grade three in ballet, and that Robert scored the winning goal at his club's end of season match?", she heard one say. "Yeah," another had rejoined, "or that they've finally got planning permission for the extension, or that Tiger's had kittens." "Oh God. The pet stuff. That's the worst," said another.

Darcy didn't think her letter stooped to quite such levels of banality, but she might have said that Coco, their old chocolate lab, had run away in the park, but they had actually found her again at the dog's home, which she actually thought was quite a miracle given the fact that so many dogs go missing and are never reunited. But suffice to say, these round-robin letters, as they were known, were robina non grata apparently and so that was the end of it. She would rather be known as a busy, active working wife and mother and too time constrained to keep in touch with geographically distant relatives, than to be ridiculed for sharing the seemingly inconsequential aspects of their lives.

In later years, that is, after the internet arrived, people resorted to emails instead, which she did too, occasionally. Then, a few years ago, she had stumbled across a remarkable solution. Her friends, formally prolific and efficient Christmas card aficionados had proclaimed that instead of sending cards, they were going to give the money to charity instead. Brilliant. No one would ever know if you didn't send the money to charity so you could get away with the whole thing and not only would no one judge you, they would actually admire you for your altruism. And, if you did give the money to charity, so much the better. You get out of having to write them and a worthy cause gets some much-needed support. And either way, the trees get saved. So, had the Christmas card finally died? Darcy wondered as she polished the mirror over Lucy's fireplace.

Not according to Aunty Pat and Uncle Ned.

Vacuuming the carpet, she moved the parcels and saw that they were tagged from Santa. Darcy resisted the urge to smell them and shake them and just carefully lifted them to one side. Secret Santa gifts for work, no doubt. Darcy remembered those days from her old office world. Christmas lunch could be booked anytime from the fourth of December to the twenty-second, and you had to have the present ready, just in case it was the earlier. The present didn't smell of anything, just that sort of wrapping paper smell, of chemicals – dye and adhesive. Lucy had wrapped them nicely though, with ribbon and bows. One was wide and flat, it sort of flapped as Darcy lifted it. The other one was square and neatly finished on the corners. Whatever was inside rattled a little as if moveable within its confines but not completely loose and rolling around. She was intrigued, yet also ambivalent at the same time. Presents were exciting to both give and receive. But carried also a burden of expectation. Would the recipient like the surprise? Would they value the hours of thought and tiring walking around shopping centres in order to procure the item? What if it was the wrong size and had to be returned in disappointment, or the wrong model? What if the requested item was out of stock and an unsuitable alternative found, instead? Once again, Darcy felt floored and exhausted at the thought of it. She had no idea what she was doing for presents this year and the familiar hibernation feeling engulfed her once again.

Rain began to lash at the windows, racing down in rivers. Darcy shivered. It was cold, cleaning people's houses in the winter. Invariably they only had the heating on in the morning and evenings, saving money by leaving it off during the day. There was no point in heating an empty house. Unless it wasn't empty, and your cleaner was there.

She busied herself with the cleaning and checked the time. Lucy kept the flat nice and there wasn't too much to do. Just the usual, polish, hoover, clean the windows and do the bathroom. Occasionally she might give the oven or fridge a deep clean and, in the better weather, would do the outside of the windows but she was not doing that today.

Giving everything a last look around, Darcy satisfied herself that she was finished and made for the front door. Pulling it closed behind her, she heard a voice call from across the road.

Turning, she saw Margaret waving at her from the shelter of her storm porch. She waved back and made for the car; head bowed against the rain that was slanting sideways. Margaret called again. Looking up, she saw the woman beckoning her over. She stood and ran, splashing through the surface water to the house across the street.

'Darcy,' Margaret said fondly. 'Come in and get a warm.'

'Oh, no. I really should get on. Thank you,' Darcy said pulling her phone out of her back pocket to check the time. 'I need to be across town by eleven and with this weather…'

'Oh, it won't take long, just a hot cuppa and a mince pie. I've just made some, they're piping hot. Look,' she said beckoning her inside, her brightly coloured dress and the lure of the smell of baking as hypnotic as the melody of the pied piper.

Darcy followed. There was something about Margaret, she had a calm authority that was difficult to ignore. Darcy may as well have been a child of Hamelin following the entrance down the streets to the Weisner, because, without knowing it, she found herself sitting at the kitchen table and watching the hot black mince blipping around the golden pastry.

'There,' Margaret said, seating herself opposite, having poured two steaming mugs of tea. 'That'll warm your bones. I bet it's cold in the houses you visit, eh?'

Darcy nodded, burning her mouth on the scalding tea. 'Yes, most people are out during the day and save on the heating,'

'That's why I love my Aga, it's hot all the time. Cosy. That's what we need in winter isn't it? To escape the cold and dark.'

'Yes,' Darcy said. She didn't really know Margaret very well. Back when she had been involved in the church, she had seen her at joint ecumenical events. Those moments when the nonsense of denomination rears its ugly head. You're a Christan, I'm a Christan. The three people down the road are Christan, yet we are all not the same type of Christian. Catholic, Protestant, Baptist, Presbyterian, Methodist… Do we all believe in God and Jesus? Yes? What else? Oh, there's a whole lot else, fences that we kind of sit on different sides of. Right, so when we do these ecumenical things, what does that mean? Well, that we can come together and hold hands across what divides us to all work for the greater good of this project – pray for peace, or the alleviation of world hunger, or whatever. Oh cool. So, why don't we do that the rest of the time? Don't know really!

The tea and warming room and pie were very welcome. Realising that the only common ground between them was church, Darcy intended to head off at the gatepost any questions in that direction and opted for small talk. 'How's the family?' she asked, not really knowing what family existed beyond the skeleton of her intelligence.

'Yes, they are fine. Holly is teaching at the primary school now. Been there a couple of months, well, since the beginning of term in September.'

'Oh really?' Darcy said. 'Does she like it? I hadn't made the connection. I don't really know anyone. I mean, I clean there, but that's not the same as being part of it day to day. Mine did go there but are grown up now,' she explained. 'It's probably all changed now. You know with how fast the world moves,'

'Some things change, others are always the same,' Margaret said wistfully, offering another mince pie. 'My Dave's in there this week for the Christmas fayre. He's Santa,' she explained, and Darcy could see the fondness she held for him in her eyes.

'Oh, I didn't know,' she said. 'That's lovely.'

'Yes, he does it all; the school fayres; church fayres; shopping centres; hospital; even the nursing home. Would you believe it? The oldies always like a visit from Santa. You should see them. I go along to help,' she explained. 'Give out the presents and whatnot. When he goes to the other places, they have elves and that, in stripy tights, but I prefer to go as Mrs Claus. I have my own red outfit and you know, handle his bookings and buy and wrap the presents and such.'

'Behind every great man…' Darcy said, wrapping her cold hands around the mug.

'Oh, no,' Margaret said dismissively. 'I'm not a great woman, I'm just helping him out a bit. He can't do it all himself so…'

Darcy smiled.

'So,' Margaret said, deflecting the conversation away from herself. 'I bet you're busy at church now, with all the services,' she said, remembering Darcy's former role and her position as worship leader. 'December is a busy time, isn't it?'

'Yes,' Darcy said again non-committally. She didn't want this conversation. She had not yet got to grips with her newest feelings about worship music herself, let alone being able to articulate it to someone else, particularly a believer. There were strict rules about keeping any faith doubts you may have to yourself, and it was a quick way to find yourself on the sharp end of judgement for being an unenlightened sad sap of a person who clearly doesn't have the mettle to call themselves a stalwart Christian (not really following the 'love one another thing' and another of the many reasons why Darcy was finding it difficult to reconcile her understanding of what Jesus meant with those of others). Also, she had no idea what this new wasteland would mean for Christmas, or what she would be without any of the involvements in the planning, rehearsing and performing of service music throughout Advent or for the celebration itself. She envisioned her musical spirituality like a big cake with a massive wedge cut out of it; the only remaining piece, mostly crumbs, held loosely together with a thinly whipped cream. A mushy, scrambled mess of thoughts, beliefs and opinions combined only by the icing of longevity and indoctrination.

She thought to steer the conversation away from her own faith and back to Margaret's. 'Are you still in the choir?'

'Oh yes,' Margaret beamed as if there was never any doubt that she would be. 'This what we are singing at the carol service,' she said presenting a sheet of A4 with a list of songs and scripture readings. A poster was presented at the same time detailing the date and time and a picture of a candle in a holly wreath. 'Then, there is carol singing at the train station. We are doing that to raise money for charity. That will have some other songs to, you know the fun ones.' Perusing another sheet, she laid it on top of the others deliberately, like someone playing their winning hand in a game of poker. 'This is our Christmas Eve candlelight service. A bit like carols from Kings,' she said with a wink as if it was naughty to compare their provincial effort to that of Cambridge masters, 'but oh we are doing some beautiful new songs for this one. More modern – the type of things that you like,' she said nodding towards Darcy. 'The church is all going to be in darkness,' she spread her hands to create the imagery, like a fortune teller clearing the air space above a crystal ball. 'And then there are going to be people, members of the choir, like,' she clarified, 'stationed all around and each one lights a candle at a different time and sings their part in the song, and then the chorus all come in together. Then the rest of the congregation will have their own thin taper candles and most of it will be held in the dark with only the little, tiny lights like stars. Then a big star light is going to go on, on the altar, and that is the star of Bethlehem. Oh, it gives me goosebumps just thinking about it. I think it is going to feel magical.' There is nothing quite like it, is there? Singing praises to God, particularly at Christmas. Well, I don't need to tell you, do I?' she laughed.

Darcy smiled a knowing smile, concealing her deception and weakness behind another bite of pie. She had sung at church, all her life, leading a youth group when she was no more than a youth herself. Playing guitar, loving all the Christian rock and ballads that had made her heart soar and pledge itself to Jesus. Her mind recalled the time that she had arranged a service years ago, very similar to what Margaret had described - typical of some churches - only slowly getting wind of what others had been innovating for ages, like someone wearing the fashion trends of two decades earlier. Still, Darcy was pleased, progress was progress. Better late than never. You had to praise the tryer. And Margaret was right to anticipate goosebumps. Although organizing the candlelight service had come with a burden of responsibility, the worry of ensuring that it all went to plan, there was something so spiritually charged about candlelight and music that Darcy felt touched you to your core. You would have to be of stone not to feel something, whether you were a believer or not.

And what was she? Was she a believer? She no longer knew for certain, but she thought, now, that she was verging on, probably not. It was hard to throw years of your life away in an instant, but it was also hard to continue when the trust had gone. It was like seeing the workings of a trick and no longer reveling in its wonder. She craved that feeling, that deep soulful immersion in the spirituality of that worship music, like being in a warm swimming pool and letting the water cnfold the top of your head, crowning you with its embrace. But it was different now. The words were empty. Once, to Darcy, the lyrics had been the word of God in her mind, taken from scripture itself. Now, she only heard the word of man, competent songwriters who knew how to take an already well-established subject and keep reworking it in innovative ways to meet the formula of success. It was no doubt that inspiring and heart-lifting tunes, belted out by worship greats that held sell out concerts in stadia around the world, were intoxicating to the spirit. Like a drug pusher, she had been high on the effects and had wanted others to feel it too. It had become her passion to take what was leading on the world worship music scene and bring it to local groups and churches. It was her mission. Her calling. To spread the word of God, through music, reaching the hearts of those who still might be untouched by His Grace.

Fuck! How deluded! Where was the line between devout and fundamentalist? And how long had she been putting on her trainers and running right over it?

Since childhood. She realised. With every word and deed, the message had been reinforced. It had shaped her.

How much had she been seeking not only her only personal salvation but the opportunity to enlighten the world; to be the one to let them see how wonderful a personal relationship with Jesus could be? And how much was she just another brainwashed victim of a cult, whose mission was to go out and be 'fishers of men'?

Darcy had led the worship at one of the ecumenical events and Margaret had been there, although from what Darcy remembered, the pie piper was more on the cassock and neck ruffs side of the pipe organ, than the 'wired for sound' side. Margaret didn't seem like she was the type to get on board with a set of drums and electric guitars, but Darcy had been surprised to see her clapping and dancing along. To some, worship was worship – it didn't matter what form it took. But not everyone was happy, nor clappy, and she had been aware of much huffing and eye rolling and shifting uncomfortably until she had finished and a more familiar hymn from 1863 was played.

How was she going to explain that in the last eight months, since that service, she had questioned every part of her faith and was raking through the shreds to see if there was anything left? That she no longer believed in the Christmas story, or even the Easter story or any other story come to that, because she had finally considered, after a lifetime of devout belief that perhaps the bible, is indeed, just that, stories. Not the divine word of God. Not the narrow path to righteousness, but just a collection of tales. An anthology of moments and miracles, just meaningful metaphors that simply purport a perspective. A point of view to which you can either subscribe or refute without being damned to eternal hell for heresy.

She couldn't.

'Erm, I don't actually play anymore,' Darcy ventured, hoping that it was the right balance between truth and vague.

'Oh,' Margaret said. 'That is a shame. 'Your beautiful voice and the way you sang that song on Maundy Thursday…' she clasped her hand to her heart and looked to heaven like the blessed virgin. 'Honestly, I felt I was in the garden of Gethsemane myself and suffering the agony with our Lord in person,'

'Thank you,' Darcy muttered humbly, feeling that Margaret's assessment of her singing talents were highly inflated. A year ago, though, that would have meant everything to her, to feel that her own delivery of a beautiful song had touched hearts and souls. That was what she was in the music ministry for. To create that feeling of adoration and devotion and share it with those assembled in the presence of the Lord. It hadn't taken long to get from that point to this, where she was struggling to imagine singing the lyrics to *Away in a manger* when she didn't believe any of it anymore; or *Silent Night* when she was 99% sure for the first time in over fifty years that 'round yon virgin,' did not apply to Mary the mother of God, if that indeed was who she was.

"They are just songs," an openly atheist friend had answered once, when Darcy had asked what they thought of when they sang Christmas carols. "What does it matter whether you believe the words or not? It's Christmas and that's what you sing at Christmas."

They didn't get it. No one could get it unless they were the same, Darcy decided. Unless, they had meant every word of praise and worship they sang before, and unless they could reconcile those lyrics now with their current belief.

'Why did you stop?' Margaret said. It was a perfectly reasonable follow up question. Darcy considered that she might say that she had work commitments, or vocal strain, or had broken her wrist and couldn't play guitar anymore. She looked at the open, kindly face of the woman before her and had to tell the truth. She had to admit that her faith was gone. The faith that had been her foundation for her whole life had pretty much gone to dust and that it was destabilizing. But that would mean admitting it to herself first and that was difficult to do after a spending lifetime on a particular path, especially if that path was supposed to lead to an eternal lifetime in heaven. And further, it was of no little concern to the salvation of her eternal soul if Jesus were to appear to her and she had to say, "Hey, thank you so much for your ultimate sacrifice. For dying for my sins and all that. And for loving me so much. That's really cool, but you know, I'm good. I think I'm just going to go my own way for now. I don't want to seem ungrateful or anything but having spent my whole life believing in something – in you– I got to a point where I had some questions and like there is literally no one around who can answer them. So, I kind of figured that perhaps it's all a bit of a sham. You sound like a great guy and all. I have really tried to be a good person and love others whenever I could, but as for you being the son of God… I don't know. Actually, speaking of God, is he around? Could I have a word with Him, because I really need to ask him some shit.'

'Ah, you know, work commitments,' Darcy said instead. 'And also,' she added, casting her eyes to the sheets on the table. 'I found that not everyone is accepting of modern worship. The emotions are too personal perhaps. Most people just like to stick to what they know. Sing the songs they are used to, preferably those dated around the 1860s, and never question the words or the meanings. Much like with Christmas carols. They're just songs to most people. What does it matter whether you believe them or not?'

She looked at Margaret's face, which was quizzical as if she was trying to look between the words to find what Darcy was really saying. Darcy checked her watch and stood to leave before she found it. 'Margaret, that was so lovely of you to give me the tea and mince pie, but I really should be going. I'll see you soon.'

'Alright, my lovely,' Margaret said. 'Well, hopefully we'll be hearing you sing again at some point. You can't waste a gift from God. Light and bushels and all that,' she said tapping the side of her nose. Escorting her to the door, she planted a kiss on her cheek and pressed a foil-wrapped parcel of mince pies in her hand. 'To keep you going,' she said. To her right, stood the advent donkey and the candle. It was their slot to have it this evening before the next person on the rota came for the prayer and get together. 'A quick prayer before you go?' Margaret asked.

'Oh, I don't know, I really need to get off,' Darcy said backing out of the door before anymore was said about church or faith or prayer.

'Right you are, dear. I'll just say one for you, instead,' Margaret said 'Well, you take care in this weather, yes? See you soon.'

'Yes, okay. Thanks again for the tea and the warm up,' Darcy said as she crossed the road.

'You are welcome anytime, sweetheart,' Margaret called after her then stopped to pick up a foundering piece of recycling that the wind had swept onto the porch. She turned to go inside and waved one last time.

Darcy looked back at her through the sheeting rain, feeling as misplaced as the bouncing empty carton. No further use for its former purpose, now hollow and aimless, blown off course and uncertain of its future.

The pied piper had gone. She had taken her magical music, the familiar, enchanting, comforting, unwavering belief, mesmerizing music of worship and faith, and had closed the door behind her.

The Hamelin child sat in the car and cried.

Shark's Den

'But it's not just about making Christmas dreams come true. Is it?' Holly said, trying to keep the quiver from her voice. She shouldn't have felt nervous, but she did, acutely aware of her rank in this space - lowly. 'It's about so many other factors; finance, fairness, equity, truth…'

She felt she was outnumbered in this particular debate and being new to the school, the staff room sofa felt like an island in a sea of sharks. She paused for a moment searching for her next word but one of the sharks saw the opportunity and took a bite.

'But we have always got the children to write their Santa letters in the first week of December and send them home. I think the parents find it very helpful actually,' pronounced Mrs Highbourne, the headteacher and stalwart leader of the "we've always done it this way" brigade. 'And it is so lovely to see their little faces and hear their excited chatter about what they want Santa to bring them for Christmas.'

'I understand that,' Holly said as diplomatically as possible, but I think we have to recognize that times and socio-economic positions are changing all the time.'

She stopped herself from saying that the collective years of the teachers surrounding her totalled in the region of three hundred and seventy-two, and whilst many of those years could count as contributing to valuable experience in the world of primary school teaching, she had noticed that some of their views and attitudes still seemed stuck in the early eighties.

Like a breeze through a clutch of bulrushes, Holly felt a

collective bristle pass around the staff room from shoulder to shoulder. Though whether it was because their tried and tested routines were being audaciously challenged by an idealistic young whippersnapper, or whether it was because they took her comment as an unintentional attack on their ages and seniority, she wasn't quite sure.

All she knew was that she was an ECT and had not been teaching long. This put her at a disadvantage and flavoured her up like a bucket of chum.   She had undertaken most of her training in inner London and this small primary school was only her second post as a fully qualified teacher. During her training, she had experienced four years of observing the Christmas celebrations in schools where, for many, English was not their first language, Christmas was not celebrated in their homes, and they had not even heard of Santa, being refugees from countries whose beliefs and practices were often widely different to those celebrated here. For those others, in the classes where she undertook her novitiate, they did speak English, they did celebrate Christmas but Santa would never be able to bring them the toys they desired even if they wrote him a thousand letters and followed them up with emails, which they couldn't because they were from such deprivation, that they struggled to eat, let alone own a computer with internet access. And it was this experience that was leading her to this discussion, in this small staff room, where she sat on low, padded modular chairs, encircled by sharks, seemingly benign until they spotted a sign of weakness.

'For instance, in my last school,' she began, 'we…

'Yes, but this isn't your last school, is it?' Mrs Coleman added. 'I'm well aware that you have worked in inner London, but our small town isn't like that. We have to do what's right for *our* pupils,' she said, inflecting the word whilst clasping her hands to her chest as if she were holding the collective school roll to her bosom. And *our* pupils like to write letters to Santa in the first week of December. And as such, we feel that you should have incorporated it into your lesson plans for this week.'

Holly squirmed and her heart palpated. She was feeling the pressure of these mature colleagues, mature in both years and teaching experience. Perhaps she was wrong to make a stand on this topic. She hadn't intended for it to be antagonistic. She had merely offered her lesson plans to her mentor, and this had come to light. Perhaps she should just tow the line and fall into the school's usual practice and make an easier life for herself. Teaching was something she had always wanted to do, since she was little. She would line up her teddies and dolls on the floor, opening books and placing them on their inert laps. Pinning large sheets of paper on the wall, she would write on them and check her students' understanding as she progressed through her lesson, correcting Blue Ted's spelling, or Barbie's simplification of fractions.

Taking up her appointment in September, she hadn't even completed one term yet. She couldn't fall out with everyone over this small matter.

But to her it wasn't a small matter; it was something she felt very strongly about. She had listened to many of her father's stories about his experiences as a Santa's Grotto Santa. He had always returned home with stories of children's expectations of the great Santa, and he had always felt proud to be the one in whom the children could confide their dearest wishes. The wonder and magic were palpable, and their dreams of the impossible had inspired in him a purpose for his retirement. To be the fortunate figurehead of this mystery, a vessel through which they could channel these dreams. Yet, despite her father's sense of pride and privilege to be the one to fulfil this role, Holly couldn't help but wonder whether perpetuating this myth didn't actually do more harm than good. She had even fallen out with her dad about it on occasion. He had argued that whilst he sometimes found it hard to listen to his little visitors asking for things that were actually impossible, the promise and hope that they held was important, as where would any of us be without hope? There was no timescale to hope. If Pandora and her jar had told us anything, it was that hope remained, even after all the misery and sorrow and bad things were let loose on the world. He had urged his daughter to understand the importance of a child knowing that an adult can make things better, and that all they need to do is ask. And more so, that some of a child's suffering can be caused by their own parents, so to know that there was someone else in whom they could confide and share their thoughts, was what made him put on that hot red suit and itchy facial hair and sit for hours in a noisy, sweaty, grotto. Just so that there was someone there to hear their hearts.

As a compromise, Holly had met him halfway to say that perhaps the notion of Santa was a good thing, and it inspired the conversation about kindness and giving and generosity; but perhaps it was just the list that could be dispensed with. She herself had grown up writing a list to Santa but she knew of friends who had got presents from him they just weren't solicited. They were surprises.

She suggested this now as she faced the circling sharks. It is said that sharks don't intend to attack, it is usually a case of mistaken identity as they test you out by taking a chunk of your thigh just to assuage their curiosity. However, she felt pretty sure that these sharks knew exactly what easy prey she was, and she may as well be a plump tasty seal, floating on her back with her head resting in her flippers, for all the intention for them to strike and take her down splashing.

'Might we not do this instead?' she ventured tentatively dipping a flipper in the water, just to see if she could extract it intact.

The sharks eyed her suspiciously.

'Could we just get the children to write to Santa saying that they know he must be very busy, and that making toys for all the children in the world must cost a lot of money, but if he happened to be passing over their house on Christmas Eve and was able to drop in a little gift to the value of about £10, they would be very happy and very grateful and thank him very much. A bit like the original St Nicholas.'

The sharks smirked and sidled; their glances shared laterally from the side of their heads.

'What you're suggesting sounds something like a Secret Santa, is that correct?' asked one shark with a box-coloured bob, who sat beneath a noticeboard studded with a dizzying number of posters.

'I suppose so, yes,' Holly answered. 'The children are still writing a letter, which is keeping with their tradition. But in this way, they are acknowledging that they are not the only one that Santa has to provide for which removes a sense of entitlement and selfishness, and…'

'But it's Christmas,' interrupted Mrs Highbourne. 'Whilst they might think about the practical aspect of Santa getting around to lots of children in one night, they are happy to accept that the magic helps him. It is not selfish for them to believe that he will come to them too. In fact, I think it encourages a wider sense of community. A belonging with the children in the rest of the world.'

Holly had to concede that she made a fair point in that respect. She had considered that too but then that argument had to be balanced with the other, cultural differences.

'Yes, I know there is that argument,' Holly agreed, turning her mug in her hand nervously, 'but actually, even that is a little more complicated, isn't it? Because, that perspective doesn't take into account the understanding that not every culture does believe in Santa Claus the way the western world does. It is a cultural and societal construct, and perhaps by letting children continue to believe that they are part of this worldwide shared community, it doesn't allow space for them to recognize uniqueness or the sheer breadth of cultural and religious beliefs.'

Miss Keene crossed her legs at the ankle and then uncrossed them again as she twiddled her necklace. As the main coordinator between the school and the local church, she always seemed visibly uncomfortable when matters of faiths or religions other than Christianity were mentioned.

'And also,' Holly continued, 'even within their own community here in this town, they can't *necessarily* share the same experience due to the economic diversity. The wealth divide is significant here. You have all the mansions on that side of the high road, and the council estates on this side. One child's experience of Santa will be very different to another's, even here in their own classroom.'

'So, what do you propose?' Mrs Highbourne asked leaning forward. 'I don't see how we can *change* Santa, but I'm interested to know what you think can be done about it.'

'I feel that it should be a parent's prerogative to decide what to do about it and that it shouldn't be reinforced through school.'

'That's an interesting point of view considering that your father is Santa for our Christmas Fayre. Does that mean that you think we shouldn't have a Santa's grotto? Or indeed, even a fayre at all?' The deputy head felt a swell of concern that their traditions were likely to be toppled like a stack of Jenga bricks if she were to start allowing opinions such as Holly's to settle. It was the thin end of the wedge, she feared. Soon, the thick edge would be forcing its way into their ethos and practices, and it won't be long before they would not even be calling it a Christmas Fayre anymore, it would be something hideous like a 'Holiday Happy Hour' instead.

'No,' Holly said gently, although she wanted to sigh audibly with exasperation and nerves. 'Like I said, if it's something that parents want to do in their own way, they can be free to, I'm just not sure that the school should endorse the list making. I think it's more important to teach children the value of money for one thing, and that they shouldn't just expect copious amounts of expensive things on Christmas morning just because they have asked for them. I think if we limit the expectation, it sends a good message, and then those parents who are struggling for money feel they don't need to find too much, and it won't create this big comparison amongst the children. If any parent wishes for their child to get extra, they can, but it doesn't have to come from Santa,' she explained.

'The main problem I have is with the list. The sense of expectation and entitlement. I get that they want the magic and all that, but believing in a mystery being, or beings - if you count all the workshop elves - leads them to thinking that someone will just provide it all. There is no space for truth and honesty. No space for a parent to say, "I'm really sorry Johnny, I know you want that XBox, but Dad has just lost his job and we can't afford the mortgage, never mind expensive toys."'

'You say that, because you are new to teaching and don't have children of your own yet,' said Mrs Highbourne. 'Truth and honesty sound like desirable qualities but children are innocent and all too soon they grow up and are faced with the harsh realities of life. Why not let them enjoy a bubble of protection and fantasy while they can? It is not fair to burden a child with the financial worries of the parent.'

Holly could see her point and asked herself if her own opinions were distorted. It was true, and her father had affirmed it, there were lots of children who needed fantasy. But a question still lingered. 'So, when do we teach them about truth and consequences and managing expectations and empathy, if not as part of their daily life?'

'You'll probably find that they *are* told about these things in their daily life Holly, every day,' asserted Mrs Highbourne. 'They are probably *always* being told that their parents can't afford something, or they see them worrying, or working hard. Christmas is the one and only time that everyone can be free of that.'

'You can't be free of it, though, can you?' Holly said, feeling her voice tighten. 'What's the point in thinking you can cast all your financial issues aside and have a blow out just because it's Christmas? It's mad that people get into debt, or buy loads of stuff they can't afford, for a great Christmas and then making life hard once it's all over. I'm sorry, I just think it is our role as teachers to break the cycle.'

There was another glance amongst the sharks that whispered, "Ah, the poor, naive ideological fool. She'll learn soon enough. It is far easier to keep the status quo, maintain the traditions that our culture is founded on and just do Christmas in the way that everyone expects".

'I just feel that it might be a good place to start, to be able to change things a little. Just because something has been done the same way for a long time, doesn't mean it should continue. Imagine if we could change Christmas just to keep the good bits but lose all the bad bits. You know, keep the delight, but lose the debt and worry.'

She was met with silence.

'I'm sorry, Holly,' began the headteacher, but what you are suggesting undoes decades of magic and fantasy.

'It doesn't have to,' Holly said, turning to meet the shark's dead, black eyes.

'It does. Of course it does. Santa's history has him living at the North pole with his elves and toymakers. That nothing is impossible with him. That hopes and dreams are kept alive with the spirit of Christmas magic. It goes back to Victorian times. You can't overturn that in a single Christmas, and even if you did, it is not going to begin in my school.' She offered a small laugh, as if she were joking, but Holly feared that she wasn't. She also wanted to pick her superior up on her belief that Santa came from the Victorian times. Whilst she accepted that it was that age which had formulated the notion of Santa as we know him, she had wanted to point out that the practice of giving a simple gift to children went back centuries earlier than that. But it was difficult to know how much of one's opinions to share with one's predators when one is being eyed up as a tasty snack.

Part of her felt disingenuous, arguing this case when she had derived such pleasure from the wooden advent calendar that her father had made for her. Spending hours before it, her small hand turning the tiny crank shaft to play the tinny carol, her heart and mind in the elves' workshop, watching them merrily labour away to create dreams of toys and gifts to delight the children of the world. The magic was certainly not lost on her, it was just the excess and inequity. In the Lapland world of her childhood, each elf made one toy for one child. That was where the magic could be found, that every child was equal.

As she had got older, the image remained of the industrious elves, quietly working away without acclaim or fanfare, the little people being the ones who changed hearts and brought joy. That is what had led her to teaching. And, for all Mrs Highbourne's insistence of the Victorian revival of Santa Claus (and notwithstanding that her father was the town's Santa too), for Holly, it was the quiet kindness of Sinterklaus, St Nicholas, which spoke to her heart. And he was there first. If they wanted to be sticklers for tradition, they could at least stick to the one that has been around the longest and do the job properly. She wondered whether she could propose that Santa only visited those who were too poor to get presents, as originally intended. Surely, that would be a way to change the multitude's perception of him.

She glanced at the clock. Lunch break was nearly over. If she didn't make her case now, she would have to accept things the way they were. Her mind flicked to the other lair of sharp-toothed predators, where hopeful entrepreneurs presented their ideas to a panel of prospective investors. In the same way, as here in this staff room, her idea was mooted, and the sharks, or dragons, or whatever threatening form they took, were weighing it up, testing it for marketability. It was sounding so far though, that it was highly likely, that her panel were all saying, "I'm out". No one was going to see any merit in her proposal and take a chance on it. Of that, she was now sure.

'Can I just say, that if we are going to change anything, I am not getting rid of the Elf on the Shelf,' Mrs Bennett added.

'I would be lost without that as a behaviour management tool.'

Mrs Hunter laughed and nodded. 'Well, I have Owl on the prowl, but yeah…, same.'

'Bear on the stair,' the year three teacher chimed in. 'How are you supposed to manage thirty kids hyped up on Christmas magic without being able to say that everything they do and say is being watched and reported back to Santa?'

'Exactly,' replied Alison, the box-coloured bob. 'And to my mind, they only behave when you threaten that they are not going to get all these wonderful things from Santa. If they only think that they are getting one small thing worth ten pounds, it doesn't quite have the same leverage.'

Holly sighed and gave a small smile. She felt tired and defeated. She would never be able to change people's attitudes when everything was wrapped up together. How had what was once a simple token of generosity become adopted into a form of carrot and stick punishment? And how would she come across if she questioned this method of classroom management. She couldn't speak up against it. They would look at her in the way that they often did, which was part pity and part patronising, as if the poor young dear didn't have a clue at what she had got herself into. In a way that mocked her idealistic notion that she was some kind of Anna Leon Owens without the crinoline, who could gather children to her will, by sitting on the floor and singing songs. Holly knew that they viewed her as nascent and inexperienced who had yet to learn the hard way that the best way to get a class of children to behave and do what you wanted them to do was through the positive reinforcement of their goodness being recognized by Santa, and their naughtiness being informed to him via a silent, classroom spy, whether it take the form of owl, bear or elf.

Still, the sharks were circling anyway, might as well be hung for a sheep as a lamb, she told herself, wondering why so many proverbs and fables involved animals. Probably because they often described the same behaviour that humans recognized in themselves, yet they didn't have words that they could hide behind. The bell was going to go in ten minutes. However, Holly thought that she was unlikely to have another chance to state her views, given the fact that they seemed so at odds with the consensus in the room. She decided to brave it.

'Well actually,' she ventured, 'that is an area I have a bit of a problem with. Using the threat of these bears, owls or elves, to make children do what we want them to and purely with the prospect of them not getting toys. I feel it gives the wrong message if we say…,' she searched her mind for an example, ''Johnny, it's not nice to hit Mark. If you do, the elf will see and tell Santa and you won't get any toys.' If anything is Victorian, surely it is an approach to teaching that is like that. Don't we need to say, Johnny, it's not nice to hit Mark, full stop. Why not say sorry and be friends?'

The sharks all turned to look, the hammerhead, the tiger, and the one with the box-coloured bob. Holly knew that sharks didn't have lips, but if she had, she felt that they would be licking them now, in anticipation of their attack.

'Also,' she continued, 'I have actually met children who are scared of the fact that these figures watch them all the time and might play pranks in their houses. Those children can't cope with change or disorder, or invasiveness into their homes.

'Well, those parents don't need to buy into it, do they?' said Miss Leeming defensively.

'True,' Holly replied. 'But even if the child is not on the spectrum and wants all the fun and intrigue of a naughty 'being', that's another thing. If one child's parent does and another doesn't, the child will wonder why they have been left out. Even if they don't want their toothpaste squeezed out and left all over the bathroom sink by the naughty elf prank, they still might notice that they were not deemed as worthy as another child to be visited by a magical creature.'

'I rather think that undoes your earlier argument,' Josie

Hawkins said. 'You are proposing that parents have the right to choose whether they buy into elves and Santa, but now you have just said that if one parent does and the other doesn't the child will feel left out.'

Holly had to admit that Josie had a point, it did seem as though she had contradicted herself. She tried to recover her direction. Only five minutes left before the bell. She might have to forget this one and accept that at least she had tried.

She was saved from responding by a knock at the door, the mealtime supervisor needed the accident book and first aid kit. It was nothing serious but enough to disturb the conversation and it gave her a moment to refocus.

'I don't know. I haven't got all the answers,' Holly replied. 'Perhaps it's something we could think about together, see if we can't find something that works. It doesn't have to be perfect…, just better. I know that it feels too big a thing to change… Christmas. But what if the Suffragettes didn't change anything? What if Racism wasn't being changed? What if attitudes to the LGBT community weren't changed? These are big things that needed to change, and it didn't seem possible. They were *too* big. But it is happening. Why can't we change the Santa thing? It can be really hurtful for the children and really stressful for the parents.'

The sharks were silent. Holly thought for a moment that they might, in fact, not decide to take an arm off, but instead to swim away to ruminate on her words. She smiled at them and exhaled quietly, letting ten minutes of tension ease out through her lips, her lungs like an inflatable bed, slowly collapsing in on itself.

There was a sound from the sharks. They hadn't swum away.

'My mother was actually given a piece of coal you know,' said one, breaking the silence. It was Anne Ferguson, whose outfits comprised such quantities of nylon and polyester that

Holly wondered that she wasn't PAT tested on a regular basis for electrical safety.

'Really? No,' said Miss Leeming incredulously.

'Yep,' asserted Anne. 'Told her that she was on Santa's naughty list.'

'And was she?' Miss Leeming asked, 'Naughty, I mean.'

'I've no idea, I presume so, otherwise they wouldn't have done it.'

'Awww, that's cruel,' said Alison, the box-coloured bob. 'But I can see that it is a great way to keep you from being naughty. I've got one or two in my class that I'd like to use that trick with.'

'Me too,' agreed Miss Hawkins with a laugh, giving voice to the shared head-nodding going on around the room, "There have been many occasions when I have been very grateful to Santa for helping me to get thirty-two children to sit down and be quiet.'

Holly stood and moved to the sink to wash up her cup. She suddenly didn't want to be here listening to these women. They were supposed to be people for her to look up to and learn from. But, if this lunchtime was anything to go by, she didn't want to learn what they had to teach.

By no means would Holly have claimed to be an expert in educational psychology, and she acknowledged that she was inexperienced. But surely, these teachers couldn't approve of such forms of mind control. She wondered what Vygotsky or Piaget might have thought about Santa and how he fit within the realms of child development. She also asked herself whether she was the one who had it all wrong. What was the difference between being an inspired and enlightened leader, swimming against the tide, and a delusional fanatic who can't get on board with everyone else who was going with the flow?

'Miss Keene looked at the clock. 'I'll go and get them in from lunch,' She stood and picked up the whistle from the

176

hook. 'So, what have we decided then? Are we all doing this thing or just Holly or what? I don't mind either way, I just want to know what to put in my own lesson plan.'

'Well, we need to have consistency across the classes,' Mrs Highbourne said. 'Holly makes some interesting points, but I can't see them taking off. I think we should stick to what we have always done for now. It might be possible to carry out a parent consultation, and we can cross reference that against our demographic information and see where we end up. We should probably run it past the governors as well. I could bring it to the next board meeting.'

'Oh, okay,' said Holly, turning to face the headteacher, both surprised and grateful. Grateful that her thoughts had been heeded, and surprised that she still had all her limbs. 'Great,'

'Er…' Mrs Highbourne flicked through her black leather diary, 'That will be on January 28th.'

'But that's next year,' Holly protested.

'Yes, but it will give us plenty of time to canvas opinion before next December, won't it? Not that I think that there is any point. Silly notion. Who would want to change Santa?'

She turned on her heel and pulled the door towards her with all the authority of someone who controlled everything. Which, of course, she did.

Holly felt a pressure in her chest which was forcing her mouth to quiver, and tears pricked behind her eyes as she stood and filled her water bottle from the tap. She moved to the door and stopped to pick up the post that was in her pigeon-hole. A plastic wrapped resources publication lay on the top of the stack.

It was the Christmas issue, with templates for snowflakes and cut outs for a nativity scene. A mass-produced reminder that her attempt to change the world was going to have to go bigger than one letter at a time. These printed resources were numerous, and even then, still only a tiny proportion of similar sorts of things on the internet.

As she opened it and cast it onto her desk when she got back to her classroom, it fell to the floor. A sheet fell out and skittered across the carpet, carried on a draught caused by the opening door. The children returning from lunch.

Yvonne, Holly's teaching assistant, was following the children and supervising the hanging up of coats and hats in the cloakroom. She crouched down and picked it up. It had a picture of Santa in one corner and a post bag full of letters in the other. A row of lines filled the page, following the words "Dear Santa," and a space was left beyond the words "Love from….".

'Oh, a Santa list. Did you want me to do some copies of this?' she asked Holly. 'I was wondering if you were going to do them this week. We've always done them first week of December.'

'Yes, so I understand,' Holly replied quietly as she searched her laptop for the afternoon's topic lesson. 'Heaven forbid that should change.'

'Hm?' the teaching assistant asked as she placed the Santa list in her tray for copying.

'Nothing,' Holly smiled weakly. She exhaled slowly trying to ready herself to greet the children. Her heart was still racing, and she had felt a little raw and hurt from the staff room Santa exchange.

'I'll get these done later,' Yvonne said, tapping the sheet in the tray. 'Oo, it's so exciting. I love this time of year. It's so magical, isn't it? What about you?' she asked.

Yvonne had been at the school for five years, but they had only been working together for a couple months and were still finding their way around each other. It was a strange dynamic. Holly was the teacher and therefore notionally in charge in the classroom, but Yvonne was so competent and confident, and at one with the ways of the school and its individual idiosyncrasies that Holly often felt sidelined by her and found it difficult to assert her authority. It didn't help that Yvonne was formerly a paralegal who had suddenly decided to create a different work-life balance. She was smart and efficient and great with the children. Having been there for a while, she knew all the children who had come through the school and had since left. And, in following their school journey, she also knew their younger siblings who were not only in this year five class but also the lower infant classes and reception. This, together with knowing all the parents too, made her an integral part of the school.

'Yeah,' Holly replied, answering Yvonne's question 'I do love Christmas. Well, certain parts of it. I just struggle with the excesses, I think. I feel it can just be a bit too over the top.' She smiled apologetically, not knowing how her views would be taken by Yvonne who was clearly already poised on the starting blocks, ready to take Christmas at a sprint. Holly always felt like someone was going to call her a miserable old humbug or Scrooge if she didn't bounce into Christmas rituals like Tigger on Redbull.

'You wanna see excesses? You should have been at some of the Christmas parties we had at the law firms I used to work at,' Yvonne said raising her eyebrows in a knowing way. 'Corporate hospitality, fancy bars and restaurants, always a new little black dress to wear, or a red one, or a silver one…' she counted her previous wardrobe features on her fingers. 'And there was always a Secret Santa – with a really high limit – the bosses got something for us on the paralegal team. And then at the parties, we'd always have a not-so-secret Santa come to visit…' she lowered her voice and whispered behind her hand, 'well let's just say that the stockings he filled weren't the type you hang up on the fireplace, if you get my meaning.'

Holly grimaced and thought of her own lovely father dressed up in his Santa outfit, purely there to perpetuate the magic of the season. She realised that not everyone's Santa was the same. If there was a real Santa, she would feel sure that he would be furious at having his name and branding exploited in such ways. Although she wasn't religious, she felt that God must feel rather the same way, when fervent bible bashers extol their interpretations of His Word through their own prejudiced filters. She could imagine Jesus saying, "Whoah! Wait! Hang on a minute, that's not what I meant at all. You guys have twisted my name and branding to suit your own twisted agendas. All I wanted was to teach everyone to love one another. That's it! Bottom line." It would be like St Nicholas saying, "All I wanted was to share my family's wealth with the poor, and to leave tiny little treats and gifts for the children and now look what's happened. You've blown it all out of control. Children are writing me lists a yard long of all of these extortionately expensive presents they want, which I now have to employ a workshop full of elves to help me fulfil, and if that wasn't bad enough, now there are lecherous pervs going around office parties making rude jokes about their sacks; and girls in sexy Santa outfits thinking that a bit of red satin and a fur trim makes them worthy of the Santa name that stands for goodness and charity."

Then Holly had an idea. She didn't know if it would work, or what Mrs Highbourne and the sharks would think about it, but she felt it was worth a try. She would need Yvonne's help, but even Emmeline had an army to get her movement off the ground, and what Holly planned wasn't exactly a movement, just merely a shift of perspective.

'Yvonne?' she asked. 'Would you be free for a drink one evening, after school? There's something I want to discuss with you. A little bit of Christmas planning for the class. I might want to do something a little different this year.'

Old St Nick

'Cheers!' Holly said as she clinked glasses with Yvonne.

'Happy Friday!' her classroom assistant replied.

'We made it,' Holly said as she took a sip of her beer.

'Blimey, that's not a good sign,' Yvonne smirked 'You've only been in the class for ten weeks.'

Holly laughed. 'Yeah, I know.'

'Is everything alright? I mean I know teaching often isn't quite what people expect. I've seen them, just like you, coming in all excited to make a difference and inspire the youth of today, then they realise it's all Ofsted expectations and paperwork. I mean I know I've only been at our school for five years, but my aunt is a teacher, and has been for twenty years. She loves it and would never give it up, but she does say that it's changed for the worse.'

'I suppose that's like lots of jobs though, isn't it? Rising costs, falling staff numbers, it's just pressurized, but as hard as it is, it doesn't remove our basic desire to want to make a difference though. I still feel that.'

'Great,' Yvonne said. 'I thought you were just in it for the twelve-week holidays. I know I am,' she cheered Holly again and sipped her lager.

'No, I'm really loving it and I love our class. They're adorable and I love them all already. I just had a bit of a thing with the other teachers, and it left me feeling a bit, I dunno, patronised I suppose. I mean I know I'm new to the industry and young comparatively, but I'm not a child and I am qualified.'

'Why what happened? That's if you can say. I mean. I get it if it's confidential and you can't share.'

'No, it's nothing like that, it's not about a child. It was about Santa.'

'Santa?' Yvonne queried.

'Yeah, well, more specifically, about the letters.'

'What about them?' Yvonne asked. 'I have copied them, if that's what you are worried about. Were they hassling you that they weren't done yet? They can get a bit like that. Especially Janice. We can get them done first thing on Monday. Don't worry about it.'

'Well, actually,' Holly said. 'It's just the opposite. I don't want to do them at all. And I said so. I told them that I didn't think it was right to get children to write lists and that it breeds a culture of expectation and unrealistic assumption that all parents can provide what they want but within the current cost of living crisis it might just not be possible. I mean not just now, I have thought this for a while now and I've even fallen out with my dad about it.'

'Well, he is Santa, isn't he? Yvonne laughed.

'Exactly. It makes it a bit harder,'

'So, what did they say, the other staff? I can't imagine they were up for it. You've got a couple of traditionalists in that crowd. Don't like much in the way of change round these parts,' Yvonne drawled in a West Country brogue.

'I know, I gathered that,' Holly said. 'They said about getting a parent consultation and going to the board of governors.'

'That's more than I expected, to be fair. You must have made a convincing argument.'

'Obviously, not too persuasive,' Holly replied. 'The board meeting is at the end of January and Linda did say that she might consider it in time for next year once the consultation has come back.'

'So, if you don't do the letters, what *are* you going to do?'

'Well, I was thinking that the main thing is to just allow a little space for discussion first. I'm aware that this is likely to be a long haul and I can't overturn centuries' worth of tradition, and nor do I want to, really. I'm not saying that we need to throw the Santa Baby out with the bathwater. I think I just want a little more thought and equity and just not the assumed excesses. I feel that children need to have a little redress and a reminder of where Santa came from.'

Yvonne reached into the packet for a crisp, 'Sooo?' she asked. 'How are you going to do that?'

'Well, the thing is, it came to me when Linda was talking about the Victorians. She said that Santa has been around since then, which of course is wrong, and it just made me think that perhaps it might be a good idea to revisit the origins of Santa. Let the children see the roots of the tradition. Where it all began. We can make it a class project, I know we can't vary the learning objectives for the week too much, we still have the curriculum to meet but I thought we could build it into our non-core subject time; the art, the history, our IT and playtime and storytime.

'I'm listening,' Yvonne said. 'And this is where I come in?'

'Yes, please. I can't do it by myself, but you are so brilliant at all that stuff and so great with the children, past, present and future, and I feel that if we could create this big thing about the origins of Santa it might help refocus everyone's idea.'

Yvonne drained her glass and withdrew a leatherbound notepad and pen from her bag. 'Right. Let's make a list. What we want to include and what we need to do. I'm thinking Odin, Sinterklaus, St Nicholas, Father Christmas, all that, right? Is that what you were thinking?'

'Well, not Odin, perhaps,' she smiled. 'I know that's probably where the whole reindeer thing came from, with his Sleipnir and the Winter Hunt across the sky. But, if we mention those origins, the kids are likely to question a little too much and then the parents would really have our heads. But, yes, the other things. The idea of St Nicholas originally sharing his wealth with the poor. I'd love it if society pushed the notion that Santa only still brought presents to the poor kids. That would soon reduce the whole consumerist thing, wouldn't it? It bothers me on a number of levels…,' Holly continued. 'Firstly, the greed. Some children already have so much and yet Christmas is a free for all, a time, when it is okay to ask for more and more, no matter how extravagant.'

Yvonne nodded and was about to open the other packet of crisps but was worried that Holly would think that greedy too.

'Secondly,' Holly continued, ticking off her fingers, 'there is the inequity. Not everyone in the class is going to be able to receive the same things. That's not fair, why should one child get more than another based purely on their parent's levels of disposable income? Thirdly, there is the behaviour thing wrapped up in it. How some naughty pain in the neck who behaves badly, gets more than a nice, kind well-meaning child. What would they think about themselves if Santa rewards in that way? It's just all wrong. The whole original notion of giving has been malformed into receiving. Where, once, the thought was about giving to and sharing with others, as the original St Nicholas. Father Christmas was all about Christmas cheer, spreading joy to others and the festivity of bringing light and sharing food and drink and warmth with others. All we are teaching our children now is excessive spending and thoughts of what to get and what they want. And the other thing is this ridiculous belief that he is infallible and with him everything is possible. It's like God, only when God doesn't answer your prayers people say, 'Oh well, it's not His plan, or He works in mysterious ways, or He will reveal things in his own time… With Santa there is no such cop out. What happens if Santa doesn't answer your prayers, or your toy list wishes? It is crushing for the child, and/or crippling for the parent. I just feel the whole thing has become so distorted and I hate to be part of perpetuating the status quo.'

'Woah,' Yvonne said, exhaling. 'I hear you. You're right, but what can you do?'

'Well, I'm thinking that we try to let the children see the

joy in giving as well as getting. You never know, it might change their perspective to see what others have in line with what they need.'

Yvonne felt excitement stir in her stomach and she sat forward with her elbows on the table. 'Uhum?' she agreed, urging Holly to continue.

'So, this is what I'm thinking… we have a few weeks of Advent. And I'm not saying we need to make it churchy or religious or anything. I'm just saying that we could take each week to do something, something with the kids for them to have a proper think about things. Like, we could go to the nursing home and sing to the pensioners in one week, then we could go to the shopping centre or railway station and sing to the shoppers or commuters, spread a bit of Christmas joy, not for any money – just to bring a smile – but we could make some mince pies and hand them out. Then I was thinking we could have a toy donation, where the kids choose something to donate and then we take them to a children's charity. We could go to a hospital perhaps, the children's wards and obviously if it is safe to do so, our guys could play with the other children, read them a story or play a board game or something like that.'

'The shoe boxes,' Yvonne suggested, warming to the idea, her brain trying to think of other things. 'I remember doing that,'

'Yes, I did think of that,' Holly said, 'but it is too late now. Mum organises it at church and the deadline has already passed. They need to get them sent abroad. And also, if we have families who can't afford Santa presents for their own children, they're not going to be able to send things to others.'

'True,' Yvonne agreed, feeling deflated. 'I think you're right though. This would be a great way to help them to really feel the joy of giving. They could all be little Santas or a bunch of little elves. The elves of 5C.'

Holly took another sip of beer and was lost in thought for a moment. 'We're going to need permission slips and agreement from the parents and from school to take them out to places, and to make their donations. And back to the inequity point, if children don't have many toys, we can't expect them to give any away. Perhaps we could get them to make something instead?'

'We could do both. We could arrange a donation box, in which no one needs to know whether you have given anything or not. So, the children who can afford to give something do, and the others, we could make Christmas cookies, gingerbread, and cuddly toys.

'You absolute legend,' Holly said excited to see Yvonne's enthusiasm. 'That is exactly what I was thinking.'

'No,' Yvonne said raising a finger to stay Holly's words. 'Santa is the legend, and it is our job to make everyone remember exactly that. He is a legend, and only a legend.'

Lights out

Despite being in a bag, the pot had left a little trail of soil on the floor of the bus. The driver had taken the roundabout at a lean, casting a scattering of fine compost onto the lino.

Kayleigh had thought to kick it to one side with her boot, but her sole was wet, so it had left an ugly smear. Serves her right for trying to be lazy, she thought, and she rummaged in her pocket for a tissue, withdrawing a scrumpled napkin that she had picked up from the coffee stand. Rubbing the mark away, she was reminded of that fateful morning in the bathroom. Something about the same type of flooring, she supposed. The practical, wipe-clean surface, suitable for bathrooms and buses. Not that she needed reminding, really. Finding your partner dead on the floor was the sort of thing that never left you. An indelible mark on your mind that no amount of rubbing could erase.

Pressing the bell, she gathered her things and stood in readiness for her stop, clutching the plant pot to her chest, lest it break like the last one. That would be all she needed. She couldn't afford the replacement in the first place, never mind a replacement for the replacement. The bus lurched again, sending her body sideways, in enmity with her legs as if they had had a disagreement. She reached for Liam's hood to steady him.

The doors opened and the gas exchange lowered the floor, level with the kerb. Her body and legs reconciled, and she stepped out. It was a short walk to the flats and the rain had stopped. It was starting to feel colder, and her mind tried to recall how much credit was left on the electricity key. A December night in with no power was sodding miserable. But having bought the pot and an unanticipated bus ride, she wasn't sure where the credit was going to come from. The food allowance, perhaps.

Liam was chattering about a jeep that he had seen in a magazine. It was made for kids but was nearly as big as a real car.

'You should see it. It's black, yeah?' his tone checking that she was listening and had understood. 'And it has no roof, but a windscreen like this. Then it has normal headlights, but also two other ones that stick up on the bonnet like big eyes. It is sooo cool.'

Kayleigh smiled and made the appropriate reallys? and wows!

'And you should see the tyres. They're like tractors. I think they could go off road. Imagine taking it to the BMX track. Nnneee, nneeee,' he said, mimicking his driving through the mud and changing gear. She couldn't imagine how he even knew about changing gear as she couldn't recall the last time he had even been in a car. They walked and bussed everywhere. And the only time he had seen the BMX track was when a boy at school had held his birthday party there and the club had loaned Liam a bike to be able to participate.

'That sounds amazing,' she said and widened her eyes to share in his excitement.

'If I had one of those, I could drive us to the garden centre and we wouldn't have to get the bus, and you wouldn't have to carry the heavy pot. I could get our shopping and drive you around like the queen.'

'You said it had no roof,' Kayleigh said. 'What about my hair?' she joked, though her coiffure wasn't likely to suffer too much damage since it was always either rough ponytail or a messy bun. She kept her showers to a strict minimum time limit and if she could eek out another day here or there without washing her hair she would. Besides, shampoo and conditioner were expensive.

'I don't think you'd fit in it anyway,' Liam said practically.

'It's just for kids. I could take the plant pot though and you could just walk alongside.'

'Right,' Kayleigh agreed. 'We'll do that.'

'I'm going to put it on my list for Santa,' he said decidedly.

'Oh,' said his mother, the heavy plant pot suddenly weighing less than her heart. Her mind scrambled to find the appropriate response. To be too dismissive would sound suspicious. She still had to make it seem feasible that Santa could meet this request. But, if she didn't head this idea off at the pass now, it would be much harder to resolve later. Which magazine had he seen? She thought getting rid of the Argos catalogue had been enough. The adverts on TV were avoidable to a certain extent because she could distract him with other things between his programmes, but this wasn't always possible, and she knew that advertising was too big an opponent to take on by herself.

'How is Santa going to fit that in his sack?' she asked.

'He's magic. He can make it small and then make it bigger.'

'Right,' Kayleigh said. 'And when it is bigger, where are we going to keep it?'

'Well, we could keep it on the balcony,' Liam said confidently as if he had already predicted this line of questioning.

'But we would have to carry it up and down the stairs every time you want to use it,' she said hoping that mentioning the stairs would put him off. They would run up and down those steps as quickly as they could with their breath held so as not to smell the ever-present odours of urine and vomit. Anything that was likely to protract the time they spent in that stairwell was likely to be a powerful argument against it.

'We could put it in our garage,' Liam said suddenly.

'We haven't got a garage,' Kayleigh explained thinking that if they had, Liam could have kicked the football against their own door, and not the one near Flat One, and might have prevented them having to spend what little money they had on replacing the sodding pot.

'But we must have,' Liam said. 'There is a garage for every flat.'

'Yes, but you have to pay extra rent for the garages, and we can't afford that so Flat six has two, his own and ours which he uses to keep all his work tools in.'

'Oh,' Liam said looking at his feet.

Kayleigh wondered whether he would hear his shoes speaking to him, in the way she did, telling him that if there was any spare money going around here, they took priority over a toy jeep and a garage in which to house it.

'What about asking Santa for something else?' she said. 'Or I have an idea. I've been thinking about this. Why don't you just ask Santa for a surprise? You could wake up on Christmas morning and find something you'd never even thought of, and it would be the best present ever.' She put as much enthusiasm into her voice as she could. Though whether this was for Liam or herself, she wasn't sure. Above all, she wanted to protect him from disappointment by finding that Santa couldn't provide what he wanted, but she knew that there was no way he would be getting a jeep, or anything remotely like it. There was no spare money and the only way that she would be able to provide anything for Christmas was by not paying her rent and then trying to get more work in the new year to pay off the arrears. It would take a while for the housing association to find out, if she avoided their letters and phone calls for a while. It was either that or go to Tag, the loan shark who lived upstairs. If she could seal this 'surprise' notion, it would enable her to at least get him some of the essentials he needed, like the new shoes, and his school trousers did look a bit short now, as did the sleeves on his winter coat, as well as a few surprises from Santa.

'But we are doing our letters at school,' Liam said looking up at her. 'What would I write? Miss Jennings said to write about five things. Should I just write, Dear Santa, I would like five surprises?'

'Yeah,' Kayleigh said. 'Imagine that! You make up on

Christmas morning to find five great new things, just for you.'

'But what if they are things that I don't like? Like a cricket set, or a chemistry set, something like that?'

Kayleigh shifted the heavy pot onto her right hip, as if it were a toddler, like she used to when Liam was little. She put her other arm around his shoulders.

'Listen,' she began. 'I think Santa's elves are all around us, watching all the time? They know the sorts of things you like and what you might wish for. And they are probably telling him what a good, kind and thoughtful, caring boy you are. And they also know where we live, so, Santa will know to bring you something that you would like, and something that we don't have to have a garage for, won't he?'

Liam looked up at her and studied her face. Kayleigh feared that talking about being watched by elves might have creeped him out and cause him nightmares tonight.

'Maybe I could write one thing I'd like, like the jeep, and then four other surprises?' Liam said, clearly trying to find some compromise between the conflicting thoughts of his mother and his teacher.

They turned the corner into the courtyard by the garages and planned what to do about the plant pot. The broken remains of the previous attempt at horticultural landscaping had been cleared away, but the void that remained shouted vociferously that it had once been one of a pair, its life partner suddenly bereft and left to nurture the young plant in its care, alone. Kayleigh could relate to that.

There was no light from within Flat One, and although the light was gloomy, it was not yet three o'clock. Everyone in the flats left it as long as possible before putting on the lights. Lights cost.

Clutching the pot to her chest, she nodded to Liam, and he stepped towards the door, pressing the bell under the number one. A faint ring could be heard inside, and Kayleigh raised her eyebrows at her son in readiness for the reception they might expect.

They had rehearsed it on the bus. If there was no answer, they would take it home with them. Neither of them could afford to leave it there unannounced for it to be stolen or damaged before the owner of Flat One had even known that they had made good on their word.

If the grumpy man did answer the door, Liam would apologise for breaking the old one, explain that he had put some of his pocket money towards buying the replacement and would be more careful when playing football in the garages. Kayleigh would then hand it over and explain that they were just going to replace the empty pot, but in seeing the potted mini Christmas trees in the garden centre, they had thought flat one might like it, as it wasn't really a good time to plant anything else.

It had physically hurt Kayleigh to watch Liam count out his coins at the cash desk. They referred to it as pocket money, because it came from his piggy bank. But it was not pocket money in the way that other children got, a little weekly allowance for sweets and comics and small toys, earned just by the passing of days, or for doing small chores. For Liam, this was money so rarely added to, (or withdrawn from) that Kayleigh was dismayed to find that a couple were euros that her cousin had given to him when she came to visit, and that was two years since. Although the garden centre couldn't accept them, there was no doubt that she was intending to take them to the post office and see what the exchange rate was.

There was no answer.

'Oh well' Kayleigh said shrugging. 'We tried. Let's go up. We'll try again another time.' Liam nodded and ran ahead of her. 'Deep breath,' he said, as they always did as they climbed the concrete stairs.

The mini screen read that they were in emergency credit. She didn't know how long the electricity would last; it was like playing a game of comfort roulette. Prioritising, she put on the kettle. If they were suddenly going to be plunged into darkness, she wanted Liam fed and a cup of hot tea. She could go out and walk to the corner shop, but sometimes their machine was broken and that would mean a much farther walk to the other estate. She was going to play it safe and feed him first. 'Beans or spaghetti hoops?' she asked, placing the pot on the floor in the corner of the room. The Christmas tree looked nice and filled the room instantly with a fresh fragrance.

'Hoops!' Liam said, his fists clenched with excitement as if he had just been promised tickets to the World Cup. Kayleigh gave him a thumbs up from the kitchen door. 'You got it, dude,' she said popping a slice of bread in the toaster. Even with a simple life, you still needed power for hoops on toast.

She opened Liam's school bag and took out his reading book and homework diary. If the lights were going to go out, she at least wanted the homework done. Then the rest of the evening could be spent snuggled up in bed together and her reading stories to him by the light of her phone.

There was a letter from school, a reminder about bringing in clothes for the nativity. Liam was to be a sheep. Parents were urged not to worry about buying expensive costumes online, anything from home would do, all he would need would be some white tights or leggings, a long white T–shirt, (plain – no logos) and some cotton wool balls. Not to worry about a mask. They were making those in school as part of their art project. The other letter was an additional reminder about Christmas lunch and to make a turkey or vegetarian selection, even if you were on free school meals; and the date that they were wearing Christmas jumpers.

Kayleigh's stomach turned. Liam didn't have a Christmas jumper. He didn't even have any jumpers at all. A couple of hoodies, but no jumpers. Nor did he have white tights or leggings? She asked herself who would have those just lying around in the drawers at home. No one, unless you were an understudy for the lead in Swan Lake or the entourage of Paris Hilton. And cotton wool balls? Were they joking? She would have to have a word with the school tomorrow and explain that she wasn't able to provide what he needed. They might make him a shepherd instead, where he could wear a couple of brown towels and a tea towel on his head.

She looked at him, eating his hoops, watching cartoons, laughing at their antics, like any other child. But he wasn't like them. He didn't have what others had. He noticed; she knew that. He was aware that the uppers of his shoes flapped in animated conversation with the soles, and that not everyone's did that. That his classmates spoke of holidays they had enjoyed, or new games and computers they had. Their weekends were spent at bowling alleys and cinemas, they ate milk shakes and burgers. Their parents drove them to match fixtures in warm cars, and they went to each other's birthday parties. He chatted about it all. Never whining and complaining, merely observation and the wonderment of a life like that. He relayed their lives like someone observing people in an entirely different era than someone in the same school class. Her heart swelled for the innocence of him. Liam, a sweet-natured, loving, affectionate little boy who didn't ask for his drug-assed dad to OD in the bathroom and who had just spent three of his own pounds, which might as well have been three-hundred, to pay for damage to a crappy pot, that was probably old and brittle and broken anyway, all because he had nothing else to play with than a ball against a garage.

If she were to cast him in a play, he would be the fucking angel.

They hadn't put up their tree yet. It was only a small little thing, a scrappy artificial one with wires that stuck out like the arms of a Dalek. Whenever she looked at it, she felt as though it was pointing to her, its Christmassy arms and mechanical voice saying, "we will exterminate you". The festive season, threatening to take her down once more. She visualised the natural one in its place. This lovely little piece of life in their home. It didn't even need decorating. To do so, would spoil its beauty. Their other one needed to be draped in so much tinsel and lametta to bridge the voids between the sparse branches, yet this was dense and lush. She touched the needles, soft and fresh, and she bent forward, to inhale its perfume.

There were no trees nearby. The park, of course and some plane trees own the avenue, which were nice in summer, but they were bare now. Yet, this little pot of outdoors made her feel at home. A time before she had met Sean and moved here. A time before drugs had sung their siren's song, luring him to his death. She knew what the other people in the flats thought of them. Half of them weren't any better. She knew what went on in the top floor flats. Misery loved company, and birds of a feather, shoot up together. But those in the lower flats were mostly elderly and infirm, who strained with every grumpy word and sought to make it known that they did not belong there. That they were better than this. That they were good, decent people who had just happened to fall on hard times and needed assistance from public services, not ne'er do wells who dwelt in the world of immorality.

But you didn't have to actually do drugs to be tarred with the same brush. The stigma attached itself to you like a bad smell to your clothes. You didn't have to fry a kipper to stink of fried fish. You merely had to stand in the kitchen.

'Do you like the tree, Liam?' Kayleigh asked as she ran her fingers through the branches as if they were feathers.

'IIIII love it,' Liam said standing up and falling back into the sofa. 'It's like the one in the town square.'

'Yeah,' Kayleigh acknowledged. 'Maybe just a tad smaller than that one,' she said, envisioning the huge specimen outside the town hall, for which six paving slabs had been removed to erect it and which was held in place by steel cables on three sides.

'Yeah, obviously,' Liam said, which was his new word. 'Just, that one is real and this one is real, and we've never had a real before and I like its smell. It makes me think of the park.'

From the corner of her eye, all Kayleigh could see were

corners. Straight lines, the walls meeting the ceiling, the windows looking out onto other flats, other straight lines, other edges. All manufactured, planned, built. The visions of architects, designers, town planners. Nothing organic, free or grown. Their lives in a box of boxes.

Here was something that represented outdoors, life, growth, and she was about to give it away, to that miserable bugger downstairs who did nothing but cast her scathing looks and shout at her sweet son.

'Do you think Flat One will be home yet?' Liam asked. 'Shall we take it to him? I want to see his face when he sees it. I think he's going to like it much better than the dead twigs he had before.'

'Do you know what?' Kayleigh said as she sat on the sofa and pulled him towards her. 'I think you're right. It *is* much better than a few dead twigs. And that is what our old Christmas tree is like, a few dead Dalek arms. How about we keep this one?'

'What?' Liam said, his eyes searching the room as if he was expecting to be on a surprise reveal show and he was looking for the host. 'Can we really? But what about Flat One?' he asked. 'We still owe him a replacement pot.'

'And we'll get him one,' Kayleigh said. 'I'll get it. You can just know that your three pounds went towards our very first ever real Christmas tree. And if we look after it, we could keep it on the balcony and have it for next year and the next year and it will grow so big, that soon, they will have to plant it in the car park out front and we will have to put the star on from the top floor flat.'

'Yesssss,' Liam said, making a fist of delight for the second time that evening. 'And Spiderman can come and put on the lights because it will be too far to reach from side to side.'

'Okay. That's decided,' Kayleigh said. 'We'll get out the decorations tomorrow. Yeah?'

'Yeah, but not all the tinsel and shiny stuff,' Liam said. 'We need to still be able to see the tree, coz that's the best part.'

'Maybe just some lights and a few baubles then,' Kayleigh suggested.

'And the star.'

'Or an angel,' Kayleigh said pretending to lift Liam up and stick him on the top of the tree, which actually only reached as far as his mid-thigh.

Taking a string of fairy lights, that she had in a bowl on the counter, she draped them over the tree and flicked the switch. She barely used them, batteries were too expensive, but this was a special occasion, and it would only be for a moment to get the effect.

'Embracing the zeitgeist, Liam ran to his room, returning with a laminated star that he had been given by school for moving up a reading stage. He placed it on the top, balancing it in the crown of tiny branches.

Switching out the lights, and flicking the television to standby, Kayleigh and Liam knelt before the little tree in silent appreciation of its natural quiet beauty.

There were no Daleks here.

'Love you,' Kayleigh said planting a kiss on top of her son's head.

'Love you too, Mum,' Liam replied. 'And I love our tree.'

Kayleigh nodded and sat on the floor with her back to the sofa. 'Me too,'

'Do you think that Flat One will mind… not getting the tree?'

'Nah,' Kayleigh replied. 'He didn't know he was going to get it. He's just expecting an empty pot.'

It was easier to accept having nothing when you didn't know what else was available. It only hurt more when what others had was put right before your eyes. For once, they would have something that others didn't. For once, someone else could have a pot full of nothing. A smile formed at her lips. In a world where she was feeling particularly flush, she could get another one to put in the stairwell. Perhaps if there was a pot to piss in, it wouldn't be pooling in the corners of the communal hallway.

'Do you know how the Christmas tree came about?' she whispered, as if she were sharing a secret.

Liam shook his head. 'No, because, obviously, it is very strange. I have heard of a tree house but not a house tree. Whoever thought of putting a tree in a house?'

Kayleigh giggled and pulled him to the ground to lay on their backs. 'Look,' she said pointing up through the branches overhead at all the little battery lights.

Liam turned his face from hers and peered towards the ceiling, the lower branches tickling his nose.

Kayleigh held his hand and spoke in her "once upon a time voice" 'Well, apparently, many, many years ago, a man was walking through the forest one night. His feet crunched in thick snow, and above him, the dark branches of the pine trees met overhead. It was wintertime and the sky was perfectly clear, no clouds and no moonlight. All he could see through the branches of the trees were millions and millions of tiny, perfect stars. Just like this.' She was aware that her little strand of twenty lights didn't adequately convey the scale of the universe, but she hoped that Liam could picture it.

'The man thought that it was the most beautiful sight he had ever seen. The smell of the pine, the crisp coldness of the night and the beautiful stars. And do you know what?'

Liam's dark eyes turned to her in query and she enfolded him in her arms.

'He wanted to share it with the person he loved most in the world. His wife. Of course, he could have just got her and taken her back out into the forest, so that she could see, but he didn't, because she was sick and couldn't leave the house. So, he found a tree that had fallen in a storm, but was still very lovely, and he took it back to their little house. He stood it in the house and covered the branches with little candles, so that they would be just like the stars. Then they lay on the floor beneath it, just like we are now, and they looked up through the branches, each one like a ladder leading up to the stars, to a world where everything is possible.'

The television standby light disappeared, as did the clock on the oven. The heating would be gone too, and Kayleigh knew it would be cold soon. They would go to bed in a minute, clean their teeth by the light of her phone and wish the evening away until sleep came. But they were lying together in a forest full of trees and a sky full of stars, and the promise of a world where everything is possible. Just a few minutes more.

Just a few.

O Tannenbaum

DARCY

I know some people, particularly those who have an artificial tree, who like to put it up and decorate it sometime around the last week of November, the better to enjoy it for a full month before Christmas Day, and then of course the twelve days beyond. But for our family, it has always been the first Saturday in December. Probably because we have always had a fresh tree and that seemed the optimum time to get it.

When I was younger, I lived in a nice suburban area and our house was a four-bed semi. My journey to and from school took three buses and a half hour walk. In the winter, I left home in the dark, and returned home in the dark. As I trudged down the long road, on the last leg of my school run, and on my last legs of fatigue, I would glance into the lit windows of the homes I passed.

I know that sounds a bit stalkerish, I mean, I didn't stand in their flower beds with my nose pressed up against the window, I simply glanced. But there is something so comforting about a light in the darkness, and a sense of company within reach, when you feel alone. I read somewhere that in the wilds of Scotland, people always leave a light on through the night and their front doors open, in case any wanderers or lost travellers need shelter. Or suche lit windows act as waymarkers…, I like that. I mean, there are a lot of people who wouldn't do that in case they woke up to find their telly stolen, but it is a nice idea, I think. Like a little sanctuary light on the side of an altar, always burning, even though there is no one around, just to let you know that there is a custodian somewhere who might provide help and assistance.

In my early years, I would do this walk with my mother and sister, it would be lighter as our primary school was closer and would come into a warm house and my mother would make us hot blackcurrant juice and crumpets for afternoon tea. Five years later, things had changed. Our financial situation had worsened, my mother now had to work full-time, the boiler had broken, and we had no money to repair it, so there was no heating. By the time I let myself in at five-thirty, the house was dark, damp, cold and empty. Those meters, that I told you about, in the understairs cupboard, had been changed to coin meters to manage our usage and bills, and the wooden frame of the big window in the hallway had begun to rot, letting the rain in around the sides.

That is why I loved to see the yellow glow from cosy sitting rooms as I passed by in the dark light. I imagined the radiators hot to the touch, not stone cold like ours. I imagined that there would be an inviting aroma of stew or something hearty and tasty, like the meals we used to have when Mum was home. Sometimes there was the flicker of a blue light, and I imagined people stretched out on a comfy sofa watching TV, not huddled around a two bar electric fire, fighting for space with the dog. Sometimes, when I glanced in, in my twilight ambles, I would see someone approach the window and draw the curtains. I know it wasn't because they were aware of some schoolgirl looking into their lounge each evening, but because it made it even more cosy to block out the night, the harsh reflective blackness on their double-glazed windows, it was because it further softened the already enveloping comfort of the living room.

I didn't know the people who lived in these houses, too far up the long road, were they to be considered neighbours, so I didn't know for sure that any of the things I had imagined about them were true. It was just how it appeared from the outside. Perhaps they had terrible sadness, or grief, or loneliness. I hadn't considered that at the time. Perhaps the warm, inviting windows were a façade to a coldness within, that wasn't of the making of a broken boiler. I just thought that they seemed perfect. It may have been real; it may have been fake. We never really know what goes on behind every door, do we?

Still, in these houses, in the last week of November, a new light appeared. In addition to the warm glow of a lamp, and the blue atmosphere from the television, there was the twinkle of coloured fairy lights, either dancing from the branches of a Christmas tree, or marching in an endless, fruitless chase of each other, around the window frame. If the pull of cosy perfection was too much to resist before, I was now undone. There is nothing more uplifting to the spirit, I think, than fairy lights. Are they named for their size? I wonder, because they are tiny, like miniature lights from a fairy world, or is it because they are magical?

There exist two preferences, it seems, when it comes to fairy lights and they separate people into two camps, multi-coloured, or white. When I was little, they only made multi-coloured, and they were those ones with large lamps with filaments and thick green wire. There weren't many on each set, and by the end of Christmas there were even fewer. In later years, we moved to warm white, and quite frankly, I have never looked back. Even now, I have them on everything; in the bedrooms; in the living room; in the garden in the summer; in my conservatory. But my earliest memories, and as the photos we have from my younger days attest, the fairy lights were always red, blue, green, and pink; and my heart soared with excitement as soon as they were plugged in, and stayed on, of course. There was always the untangling to deal with before any illumination could take place, and despite however neatly they had been put away the previous year, they always emerged in a twist to rival the Gordian knot. Then, if they didn't work, so began the tortuous test of each individual bulb to see which one was letting the whole side down. With that lazy and unproductive member of the team, removed and replaced with one from the subs bench, they would then blink into life, to the exclamation of huzzahs. For me, a tightness would form in my chest which seemed directly connected to my tear ducts and the overwhelming joy would spark in my heart in the way the filament had sparked in the electrical circuit.

The lights were working. It was time for the tree.

I can divide my memories of tree purchasing and erection into four distinct categories. The first, until I was about twelve, the second, until I was about twenty-nine, the third in my thirties and the fourth in the last seven years. That is a lot of trees, more than fifty, because some years we bought two. I am an environmentalist, and every piece of cardboard or paper I buy has to be from sustainable forests. I reuse scraps of paper all the time and I recycle whatever I can't re-use. So, that said, it has always been a dilemma of mine, when it comes to a Christmas tree, whether to go for real or fake. Can I, in all conscience, justify a beautiful living thing to be cut down, in its prime, to merely exist for a few weeks before dying a miserable death, purely for my gratification? No, I can't justify it, but when it comes to a Christmas tree, it has to be a real one. I have considered the fake ones, telling myself that although it is plastic, it will last forever and will mean I don't have to struggle with my conscience every year. But then, I have seen a few fake ones over the years, in offices mostly, where bits have broken off, or it loses its stand, or the wonky top can't be straightened, and it goes in the bin. Surely, a compostable tree, fed back into the earth and another one planted in its place is preferable to another thing chucked into landfill. I have come to terms with feeling happier that Christmas trees are evergreen, until they die, rather than green, actually, for... ever. So, for us, it has always been a real one and always at least six feet tall.

Having a real tree means that you can't get it too early, for fear that it would be a brown, naked stick by Christmas Day, with all the presents lying under a blanket of dun needles.

Hence electing the first Saturday of December as the optimum time. However, even then, depending on the weather, we might keep it outside for a few days, giving it a deep drink of water before actually bringing it in and putting it up.

Off the hall, in our family home when I was younger, there was a large dining room with a bay window. It looked out onto the front garden and therefore, the road. For any other schoolgirls, happening to pass by our house, they might look in and see our tree and envy the style and elegance that it portrayed. Because, in those early years, the ones that form phase one of my tree memories, there really was style and elegance and plenty. My father was doing well, financially. We mixed with other families who had done well for themselves, and, at Christmas, there was always a round of elegant cocktail parties at each other's houses. I remember my sister and I sitting on the stairs, in our pyjamas, looking through those white glossed stair rods, above the advent calendar, and watching with excitement as our guests would arrive. My mother would have spent days crystalising fruit for a stunning centrepiece, glazing huge hams and studding them with cloves, making salads and gateaux. My father would set up the breakfast table with all sorts of wines and spirits and glasses, making a bar that would rival the drinks lounge at The Savoy. This was before the large window in the hallway rotted. This was when everyone would come in evening dress, with jewels and fur wraps and bring with them a waft of cold, December air on the wave of their perfume and cologne. In later years, we would be allowed to go to the parties, and I would wear my best outfit and feel so grown up to be amongst these stylish and friendly people, sipping lemonade from crystal glasses.

In one grand house, the Christmas tree took up the whole corner of the drawing room, in its natural finery, reaching high up to the high Victorian ceilings, but in another, the only tree in the house was a table-top plastic one with a few baubles that were too big and out of proportion for its size. Both wealthy families, both elegant, fine houses, two very different trees. It struck me as disappointing that not every home gave the same weight of importance to the tree. How could you raise a glass of eggnog to this little tinsel laden plastic collection of wiry twigs and serenade it with a verse of *O Tenenbaum*? You simply couldn't.

To ours, however, you could. In these plentiful times, we had a greengrocer on a little parade of shops at the end of the road. It was always cold in that little shop, as it would have to be, to keep everything fresh. The front bore displays of seasonal fruit and vegetables in open boxes, and everything was put into little brown paper bags. Oh, how I wish for that now. When I am battling in the supermarket to find something that isn't wrapped in ten folds of plastic wrapping, I just want to be able to stand before those wooden boxes of clementines, still with their green stalks and leaves, and count them into the bags, hearing them snap with the weight of each fruit, or carrot, or parsnip. The smell was always so fresh, and the potatoes always had a covering of earth. I loved it there. Well, the reason I am telling you this is because this greengrocer used to choose our Christmas tree and deliver it with our veg order. His name was Reg, I don't know if that was his real name, or whether he made it up because it was funny to call him Reg the Veg. It seems incredible to me to think that my mother trusted this man to choose our tree every year, because in all my later memories of tree selection, she would never trust anyone to meet her strict, festively arboreal standards. When coming face to face with the tree that she would eventually deem worthy of being erected in our home, she would follow an exacting routine. She would ask someone to hold it up for her, study it from all angles and distances. Ask said person to twirl it around so that she could check the straightness of the trunk, check the top that it wasn't straggly; check that no branches were broken; that there were no gaps or holes between branches; check for vertical spacing between levels to allow for maximum ornament drop or twirl ability; ensure that the base branches should allow for space to be secured in the pot; it had to be the right type of pine…, a Norway spruce, and had to look new and healthy. So, with this ritual in place, every year since 1978, it mystifies me how she could just place her usual weekly order with Reg the Veg and say, Oh and a Christmas tree please… you know the type I like.' And he did. Reg never failed to get a beauty of a specimen. It was always perfect. We would have to wait for him to close up the shop and make his deliveries, so it would be dark by the time he arrived. It would be too late to put it up then, so it would stay down the side passage of the house until the next morning, and we would wait the few agonizing hours until daybreak, when we could bring it in.

Putting it up was a feat, in those days. We did not have the fancy stands then that we have now. We had a bucket, which I would decorate with Christmas wrapping paper, to conceal its true identity, and my father would get some builders' sand from one of his cronies. Never one for doing anything around the house, as there was always something more pressing at the pub to see to, he reluctantly accepted his role as tree erector and would grudgingly huff and puff it into place, with his strong biceps, packing the trunk with sand and old bricks to secure it, under the supervision of my mother who would be orchestrating it into pride of place in the large bay window of the dining room. As I said, its front aspect looked out over the garden onto the road, and although the huge tree with its wide branches blocked out most of the natural light, it did look very impressive from outside.

There was one year, when Reg had left the tree in the side passage, as normal, but my father had not left his business at the pub for long enough to come home and see to it. My mother had berated him for not caring enough about his home life to put up the tree for the children, citing our repeated requests and disappointment that the tree was still lying on the wet ground nearly a week since its delivery. It was the normal cycle of things that we wouldn't see him for days, then whenever our paths did cross, such as at his hungover reveille at midday, my mother would take the opportunity to raise whatever series of pressing matters were bothering her such as unpaid bills, unpaid mortgage, why he didn't want to spend time at home with his family or do anything towards the Christmas effort.

For the most part, such words of admonishment could be easily avoided by finding something pressing to do and leaving the house before any plan of action could be pinned upon him, but it would seem that this particular year, her words had struck a chord. And, in the early hours of the morning after a lock-in at a local dive club, he sought to make remonstrance for his desertion and dereliction in festive duties.

We awoke and ran downstairs, eager to open the advent calendar. My mother was standing in the hall just staring into the dining room with her head in her hands. She was crying.

Leaving the calendar, I approached her asking what was wrong.

'He's gone mad,' she said in a soft voice.

I looked to the bay window. There was the tree. It was up, and for a split second, I was excited. After church, we could come home and spend the day dressing it, and playing Christmas music and it would be wonderful. What I had failed to notice was that the tree was up alright, but it wasn't in a pot or a stand, or anything. Its trunk stood on the carpet, the top of the tree, slightly too tall for the room was bent over and clung to the ceiling like a collection of green geckos. It had a lean to rival a Pisan tower and strangling its neck, like a medieval captive villain was a thick rope, pulled a little more to the left than the right, causing its unequal posture. Both ends of the rope were tied to the curtain track, crossing the window bay like a tightrope across Niagara Falls. A further web of narrow-gauge string bound the ankle of the tree, fastening it to the pipes of the radiator.

It is an emotional dichotomy to be both grateful and

cross at the same time. He had at least heeded my mother's request and tried to make amends, but what was he thinking? He went to the pub. She and I, as far as my nine-year-old efforts could execute, managed to right it and when it was dressed and lit up in all its glory, no one would have known how it had begun its Christmas season. I wonder if there were any schoolgirls passing, thinking how grand and beautiful and perfect that dining room looked from the outside, with its splendid tree. Would they think, as I did when I passed those other houses that everything within was to be envied and desired? Was the proverbial grass greener on the other side of the window-pane, or was it just astroturf, giving the impression of lush, verdant blades? And, I wonder, would they be able to tell what was real and what was fake?

In later years, when my father was even more absent, my mother and I would do the tree. My sister would join in later, when it was already up. But to begin with, I would fill the bucket with the sand, which always made my hands itch, and I would root around outside for a few broken bricks too, as wedges to hold the trunk. Mum and I would wrestle the huge tree into a prone position across the porch step, half in and half out of the house and, if necessary, any lower branches trimmed off with secateurs. Then we would drag it in, and heave and ho it into place, packing the sand and bricks around it. At Christmas time, the large desk would be moved into the back area of the house, leaving the whole wall free to accommodate this piece of vegetation that we had seen to uproot from the ground and welcome into our home, and we would step backwards along the hall, checking from all angles that it was straight and ready for dressing. They were very happy times. My mother would play her Johnny Mathis Christmas LP and have a sherry or two and warm mince pies. We would rummage through the boxes of decorations and find our favourites. My sister would tease us, each time we went to put on an ornament, to race to our intended branch and put hers there, instead.

Our angel was quite a tacky thing, really, which always surprised me because my mother did not 'do' tacky. Everything was tasteful, so why we had this ugly plastic doll, which we put up every year, I don't know. Even when her white, nylon dress became snagged on the pine needles, and her wings had fallen off, I gave her emergency surgery by affixing new wings made of gold card and saw to her wardrobe malfunction by fashioning a couture gown made from a gold doily. It was really ghastly, but for my mother, loyalty to tradition is important. She is not one for 'out with the old, in with the new'. Perhaps it is from growing up in a post war period where things were scarce, and waste was inconceivable, or perhaps it was that certain Christmas items carry with them a nostalgia, a memory of a happier time, a hope that by holding on to the item, you hold on to the feeling they once engendered. I have never asked her, but I wonder now, whether that ugly angel might have once adorned their first Christmas tree as a young married couple. Perhaps that's why she resurrected it every year. Perhaps, from her pine-top vantage point, that little seraph had silently watched the annual dissolution of a young woman's dreams. Perhaps her torn dress and broken wings were the manifestation of my mother's spirit.

It seems strange that when our financial stability lessened, our tree purchasing doubled. In my late teens and twenties, we would still get a tree for the hallway, but we could never really enjoy it there. The hall had become so freezing with no heating, and with the rotten window frames that it became something we ran through, rather than spent any time in. My father had locked himself out one night, and Mum, refusing to let him in, since she was in no mind to admit him in such a state of inebriation, had let him stay out in the porch. At some point in the early hours, he had obviously considered it too uncomfortable, and had put his strong shoulder to the door, repeatedly, until it finally gave way and splintered off the hinges. A cheaper, ill-fitting, poor-quality, temporary replacement had to be hurriedly sought and hung there (which it did for the next thirty-five years), but the draught excluder in the shape of a sausage dog was no match for the biting wind that seeped under and chilled the hallway to an arctic tundra. One benefit to the temperature of the hallway, was that the Christmas tree felt very at home there, thinking it had travelled not far from its natural habitat of a Norwegian forest. It thrived, and was as healthy by the time it was taken outside on the night of the Epiphany, as it was on the day it was brought in. Given the sub-zero temperatures our hallway reached, we should have put it up in June and enjoyed it for longer. So, anyway, because it was so cold and we never spent anytime actually looking at the tree ourselves, (it being all for the benefit of people who could see through the dining room window) we would get a little tree that we would put in the back area of the house, where we had the sofas and the television. This was a lovely place in the summer, with two huge windows that overlooked a mature garden of tall trees. It was a flat-roofed extension with a door down steep steps to the patio. The living area was large and open plan, with two long sofas and a mahogany coffee table, which was actually a canteen of silver cutlery. I used to spend hours polishing the silver and putting each piece back in its custom shaped polythene bag, then stack them in their velvet lined sections. But in the winters of our discontent, in my late teens and early twenties, the living area was only marginally warmer than the hallway, thanks to the aforementioned two-bar electric fire. This thing was very unattractive, and it smelled of burnt dust, but a friend had given it to us, and we were very grateful. It was a bizarre juxtaposition that the expensive G-Plan sofas, elegant table lamps and silver laden coffee table shared the same space as this cumbersome faux fireplace. What was real and what was fake?

The bitumen on the flat roof extension had failed, allowing heavy rain to seep through. This bowed the ceiling until, like a full bladder, it could contain it no longer, and relieved itself of its liquid burden through cracks, then later, through the holes which it had made in the plasterboard and onto the carpet. The lighting strips which ran along that part of the ceiling were too dangerous to have on with it being so wet, so they had to be removed for safety. The whole area spent sixteen hours of each day in complete darkness, and us with it. So really, the lights of the little Christmas tree that we put up on the corner did more than just lift our spirits for the festive period; they actually provided much needed light along the whole back wall of the house. They say that it is bad luck if you *don't* take your Christmas decorations down on January 6. I felt that it was bad luck if you *did*, because without the additional light from the tree, it was quite likely that you would trip over one of the many receptacles that were catching the drips from the leaking ceiling and end up face down in a wet bucket.

One Christmas tree memory that I have was in my late twenties. I was married and had been out at work. From work, I had gone to the shopping centre to get the last items on my Christmas gift list and didn't return home until quite late. As usual, I had been well prepared and had begun quite early, ensuring that the majority of my gifts had been sought, purchased and wrapped and I only had one or two more things to get. I had met my husband at the shops, and we returned home together at about 9pm. He put the key in the front door, while I got the shopping out of the boot and as I stood behind him with the bags, I wondered what was taking him so long to open the door. He said that it was stuck, the key was turning but the door wouldn't open. I tried it, thinking that he was doing something silly. But it was the same. The key turned freely but we couldn't open the door. Then he said something that made my blood run cold. 'It's as if the catch is on from the inside,' he said. 'Someone could be in there.'

We opened the side gate and went round to the back garden. All seemed quiet until we saw something glinting on the patio. It was broken glass. The back window had been smashed.

The Christmas tree lay sprawled across the floor, the ornaments crushed and scattered in splintered shards. Of course, the presents had all gone. The whole house had been searched, drawers opened and turned out, wardrobe doors left open. Certain items had been stolen such as our camera, and a watch and some jewellery but I think what hurt the most, aside from that awful feeling of violation, was the loss of the presents and the damage to the tree. It had stood in front of the window that they had chosen to smash. They could have broken the large window in the back door, or the kitchen window and climbed onto the countertop, but for some reason, hurling a brick through the window against which a six feet tall tree stood was more appealing. A three-seater sofa lay along the wall beneath their chosen entry point, why didn't they drop onto that, and commando roll to the floor? I don't know. There was simply no need to destroy the tree, unless they kicked it over on their hurried exit when they heard our key in the door. Still, I suppose, if you are the type of person to break in and steal, in order to feed your drug habit, your modi operandi are not going to necessarily be well thought through and open to logical scrutiny. And, if a few baubles are wrecked in the process, it is of no consequence, nor is the quantity of sentimental value they possess.

My mother had always had a fear, despite living in a very nice neighbourhood, that our presents would be stolen while we were out at Midnight Mass, so she never put them under the tree until she came back in the early hours of Christmas morning. She would hide them, all wrapped and ribboned behind the sofas, or under beds. I used to look at adverts or films where presents of all shapes and colours surrounded the base of the tree and wish that ours could be like that, but she wouldn't hear of it. As I said, you could see through our dining room window to the tree in the hall; we had a crappy front door that didn't fit properly; and we had scrimped and saved for Christmas presents, there was no way that we were going to put them on display for burglars, with a sign that read, please come in and help yourselves. Even though I had hidden my presents in my first marital home, it didn't matter. Even though we had a strong front door, it didn't matter. They still came in and helped themselves.

What I can't fathom, when I think about it now, is how I went back out and replaced every single present. I don't know why. Surely, it would have been acceptable to say to people, you know what? We suffered this terrible thing, a burglary, a violation and all our things are gone or broken, and so I'm sorry, but I don't have a present for you. But I didn't. I remember trying to find the same coat in the same size and colour that I had bought my mother weeks earlier, when the stocks were fuller and the choices wider. I had also been tasked by my in-laws to buy for the rest of the family. "Oh, you know what everyone likes," my mother-in-law had said, "I'll give you the money and you get all the gifts." And so, I did. Twice.

Since then, tree shopping has been a delight, and it is still one of the things I am most excited about in the run up to Christmas. In my phases two and three of tree shopping, they broadly followed the same pattern. Phase two was always at the same garden centre where I used to live, phase three, always at another one having moved. In both, it was always a family event, we would all go and choose it together, one for my home, and one – or two – for my mother's.

It is a funny concept, isn't it? Having a tree in one's house. Whilst it is often accredited to Prince Albert, bringing his German traditions to Britain, and establishing the idyllic Victorian Christmas, it apparently goes back farther to Martin Luther in the sixteenth century, who was returning home through the forest one night and saw the stars of the night sky twinkling through the branches of the pine trees overhead. He thought it so beautiful that he tried to re-create it for his family by bringing in a tree and fixing lighted candles on it. I wonder if he had to rope it to the curtain track, too. Worldwide, and over the centuries, the meaning and practices behind Christmas trees are many and varied, and worth a Google, but of course, like much of our tradition, we have adopted pagan ways from our forebears. I am a bit pagan now, I think. Now. But given what I've told you about our Catholic upbringing, it's hard to believe that we would even have a tree, isn't it? Catholics and Pagans don't really see eye to eye, though the amount of superstition and rituals they both follow, you'd think they'd get along famously.

Of course, adorning the house with greenery is a pagan practice and it is no coincidence that Christian and Pagan rites and rituals were merged in an attempt to combine ancient traditions and beliefs back when the Roman church was taking Europe battle by battle. Yet, despite their co-existence over many hundreds of years, having a Christmas tree in church was where the two belief systems obstinately refused to coalesce. I remember my mother being at once, both gladdened and stunned to see a tree go up in our church, before Our Lady's statue in the latter days of December. 'Never allowed,' she would say. 'I can't believe it, a tree was never allowed in church, in my day.' Perhaps it was just one of the ways that the church has been forced to relax its views on things in the vain attempt to retain its faithful and to keep Christmas for itself rather than losing it to the mass wave of cultural commercialism that threatens to draw its believers to a new and shiny God of the material.

Interestingly, on that note, when I was in my late teens, a new family moved into the house next door. They were Jewish. Lovely parents and three young children. I used to babysit for them sometimes. It was my first awareness of a faith different to my own and I was fascinated to learn of their traditions and practices; to see the different brands of foods in their cupboards and the paraphernalia they had in their dining room for their Friday Shabbat. They were quite progressive and somewhat lax with some of the stricter observances, compared to other Jewish friends who I met later in life, but it still surprised me, when just after celebrating Hanukkah, with the Menorah still lit, I went in to babysit and was met by a Christmas tree standing in the living room, fully lit and adorned with all sorts of Christmas themed baubles and surrounded by presents. I was only sixteen and didn't know much about the Jewish faith. I knew that broadly, their Torah was pretty much the same as our Old Testament, and that Jesus was a faithful Jew. I knew that He was observant to Jewish law and practices and that His Passover meal had also been His Last Supper. But I also knew that Jesus was a pretty divisive factor when it came to our beliefs, so it seemed very strange to me that this pine-needled monument to His birthday was occupying most of the floor space of the lounge. I was nervous to ask them about it, in case I showed my ignorance, but I ventured the question anyway.

"Oh," the mum replied with a casual wave of her hand. "The kids wanted one. All their friends at school have Christmas trees and they wanted one too. We do the whole Christmas thing for them, otherwise they feel out of it. It's just a cultural thing, anyway, isn't it?"

Good point, well made. There were no Christmas trees around, that night in Bethlehem. Olive trees perhaps, but I doubt that there were any Norway spruces. And I'm pretty sure that when the Three Kings bought their gifts of gold, frankincense and myrrh, they didn't say to Mary with fingers on their lips, 'Shh, we won't wake the baby, we'll just slip the prezzies under the tree, shall we?'

It's just another tradition that we have made an essential part of Christmas preparation, that we feel the celebration just wouldn't be complete without. Although, I do know of some people who, uncomfortable with the thought of hacking bits of evergreen off a living tree for no reason (other than it being midwinter), choose, instead, to have naturally fallen branches of trees that have no greenery, but who still like to have the festivity of fairy lights and natural ornaments. I admire that, but also can't help thinking of Phoebe in that episode of

Friends, dragging a barren stick back to Monica's apartment to save it from the voracious chipper.

Despite her many, many years of making the case for real over fake, and the exacting standards to which my mother has held every single tree ever to set trunk into her home, my mother did at one point some years ago, accept that a very nice quality plastic one will do just as well. True, it doesn't have that unmistakable fragrance of Alpine air, or cold Christmases. It doesn't tinge your fingertips with sap when you touch it, the fake needles don't accidentally catch beneath your nails, stabbing the soft skin. It doesn't fill the room overnight with the natural pine scent, that no amount of disinfectant or air freshener could ever emulate. The branches don't droop at the end if you put on the wrong sized ornament, nor do they bounce back up suddenly, like Tom Daly on a diving board, when a bauble slips off. The trunk doesn't feel damp and dark when you bury your head underneath, writhing on your tummy, to fill up the container with water each week; and the dog doesn't wee on it when you first bring it home, thinking that you are the best owner ever to erect a bespoke peeing post for him to use without having to go out for a walk. It may not fulfill any of these things, but as a repository for a string of warm white fairy lights, and a lifetime's collection of Christmas ornaments, each pregnant with a wealth of meaning and memory and nostalgia, it does the job perfectly well.

Three years ago, we passed the responsibility of choosing the tree to our son. It wasn't so much a rite of passage, as though we now deemed him worthy, or manly, or mature enough to choose the tree. It wasn't like the festive equivalent of a Bar Mitzvah, or a tribal coming of age ceremony where he had to go out and find the tallest tree in the wood, chop it down with a hand- made axe and return it to the village single-handedly to prove his manhood.

He merely asked, 'Is it okay if I choose the tree, this year?'

'Of course,' I replied. I only agreed because I knew that

my years of tutelage in tree selection, handed down from my mother to me, and from me to my children, would mean that he was equipped enough to make a good decision. I felt it was a safe bet to take. He did us proud and found a wonderful tree, as did my daughter, when it was her turn, a year later. Ah, yes, young Jedi, the students have become the masters.

Our local garden centre now makes up all the years of phase four. They have a Christmas market, Santa's grotto, a brass band, local artisan stalls, street food vendors, warm chestnuts, mulled wine… the whole lot. We dress up in our Christmas jumpers and put on scarves and woolly hats. We mooch about the stalls, sing along to the carols and each choose a new tree ornament. Moment by moment, we generally allow Christmas magic to be absorbed through our skin. We find the tree, they net it up in sustainable netting, we strap it to the top of the car and head home to dress it with our own baubles and ornaments. Every year, we have added to our collection, and the children ask for the stories of where and when we got certain ones. They each hang their respective Baby's First Christmas baubles and none of us can believe that there was a time when our Christmases didn't include them.

Of course, there were the years of nursery and infant school when every ornament shared a common design feature, the carboard tube from a toilet roll. Nooooo! Please… not on my beautiful, themed tree of silver and white, or gold and cream. I don't want a cotton wool snowman, complete with orange nose, or crackers, made out of hot pink crepe paper and covered with purple glitter, dangled from the frontmost branches in pride of place.

There is a little mark on the ceiling from when it scraped, it was too tall, last year. I've been meaning to paint it, but it's quite nice to leave it really. Reminds me of the joy the tree brings each time I look at it. All that sparkling beauty.

We each take our new ornament and with ceremonial synchronicity determine our intended location and place them on, ensuring that we have done the first one together. After that, we progress through the box, drinking sherry and eating mince pies, as I did with Mum for so many years. Well, I have the sherry and mince pies, they have lemonade and crisps, which you have to admit, just isn't the same, but I suppose every tradition has to evolve with the times. When the Christmas music has finished and the tree is done, it is late in the afternoon. We step back and turn off the main lights. The room is in darkness. I stoop to the plug socket and flick on the fairy lights. The glass ornaments shimmer, the gold reflects, the lights twinkle. Is there anything more magical? I know it is magical, and when I talk about it, I can recall those feelings, but for some reason, this year, it just feels all too much. The garden centre will be full of people wanting to sell their homemade crafts, which I don't want. The food vendors will be selling overpriced street food. The effort of sorting through all the trees, examining each one and trying to do so without eight other pairs of eyes claiming it as their own the moment you put it down, feels comparable to climbing a mountain, and moving all the furniture and finding the stand and getting it stood up straight, before even contemplating getting into the loft to get the decorations and untangling all the lights. And what do you do with an angel, when you don't even know whether to believe in angels anymore? It just feels too much.

There are green, fake trees with fake snow on, there are fake white trees, that don't even pretend to be green. There are even fake black trees. There are baubles and ornaments to suit every type of taste and décor. There are traditional themes, red and green, there are modern, pink and orange. There are fairy lights that look like lanterns, or even mini trees themselves, there are lights that look like holly berries. There are stars and angels to sit on the topmost branch. There are natural ornaments like dried orange slices and cinnamon sticks tied with twine, that can adorn a fake tree, and there are decorations of plastic and glitter, and all things fake that can adorn a natural, real tree.

Do I get a real one, or a fake one, or not even bother at all? I don't know.

When we walk down the road, as darkness falls and look at all the trees in all the windows. There are those homes that look cosy but might be bleak. And those that look bleak but are filled with love. Who is to say what is real and what is fake? And how can you know which is which? Or which is better?

Just another Tuesday

Dragging the vacuum cleaner through the corridor, like a reluctant dog on a walk, Darcy made her way to the office. 'Come on, Henry,' she said, smiling to an old man walking with a frame.

He looked up quizzically at her impertinence for hurrying him.

'Oh, sorry, not you,' she explained. 'The hoover.'

He stared at her, then refocused on the floor before him, placing the frame carefully and shuffling his slippered feet in its wake. Place the frame, (one) step, step, (two, three). Frame – step, step. Frame – step, step, as if he were dancing a waltz.

The office door was open as Darcy approached and yanking on the hose, Henry raced up behind her like an excited terrier. She could hear Liz on a telephone call and waited a moment to see if she was bringing the call to a close. It was her scheduled time to clean the offices, but life in a care home didn't always run to schedule. The early morning rounds of pills and breakfasts and getting the residents up and dressed were scheduled, certainly, as were the mealtimes and the activities. But the unexpected events; the falls and personal hygiene accidents; the disagreements over the remote control and the frightened responses to visions, both real and imagined were the non-routine events that threw the day off kilter and made a laughing-stock of the clocks on the walls.

Time meant something different there. To the staff, it was a framework, like scaffolding around a house. It gave them something to climb onto, to aid their getting from one level to the next. But there were days when time was so irrelevant, it was as though the floorboards had been removed, the ladder taken away and the whole scaffold dismantled into a pile of metal poles. To the residents, time was nothing. Day was night, Sunday was Thursday, and the only way they knew it was lunchtime was because the dining room smelt of mashed potato.

Not wanting to disturb, Darcy raised a finger to Liz that she would come back later and turned to walk into Henry's body, whose enthusiastic approach had set himself obediently and unexpectedly at her feet. Tripping over him, she dropped the handle and her cleaning trug, causing a crash.

'I'm so sorry,' she mouthed to Liz who smiled and beckoned her in.

'Don't worry. Nearly finished,' she mouthed back and pointed to the chair for Darcy to sit.

Darcy smiled and accepted. She still had the bathrooms to do and was grateful for a break.

Returning her attention to her call, Liz resumed her conversation. 'Yes, that would be the twenty-third,' she said flicking her eyes to her calendar.

Darcy could hear the indistinct words of the voice on the other end of the call.

'Yes, that's fine. No problem. Great. Okay, yes, I'll tell him, thank you. Okay. Thank you, yep, speak soon. Bye then Graham. Bye. Bye.'

Returning the phone to the cradle, she turned to Darcy and stood.

'So sorry about the disturbance,' Darcy began.

'No, it's fine. Don't worry. I was finishing up anyway. The room's all yours.'

Liz stooped to log out of the computer but left it on for the night shift.

'Christmas!' she stated simply, shaking her head.

'Hmm?' Darcy asked, unsure of whether Liz was making a statement to herself or was requiring a response.

'Christmas. It's so hard. That was a relative,' she said nodding to the phone. 'I've had them calling all day, turning themselves in knots trying to organise the family. They can't bear the thought of their dad in here on Christmas, so the daughter wants them all to come and visit and bring the grandchildren, but the other daughter said that it was too far to travel and her kids would rather stay at home and play with their new toys than sit in the car for an hour to come and visit a smelly old nursing home. So, she's suggesting that they collect their dad on the twenty-third and take him home so that he can spend Christmas with them, but I was trying to advise against that as his needs are quite extensive now and I'm not sure they fully appreciate how difficult it will be for them.'

Darcy nodded and her face showed the sympathy she felt for both sides of the family.

'You know, we make Christmas nice for the residents here. They have Christmas dinner and Santa brings presents and they have carols around the piano in the afternoon and a mince pie. They are happy. I hate to think of the relatives all falling out over it.'

Darcy wondered if Santa was Margaret's Dave, and the presents were the ones that Margaret sourced and wrapped. She rather supposed they were, and that she probably provided the mince pies too. Some people were too good.

'What about the father?' Darcy wanted to ask but was not sure whether that crossed propriety bounds of patient confidentiality rules, but they hadn't discussed names and there were many men in the home, it could have been any of them. Or all of them. She was sure it was a problem that affected most families. Her own father had passed away years earlier and her mother was on her own. She was well, thankfully, and able to live independently, but throughout her whole married life, Christmas had been an ongoing source of disagreement and competition between parents and in-laws, grandchildren and geography. 'How about we do Christmas Day at yours and Boxing Day at ours?' Or 'But we came to you last year?' or 'Just be honest, you prefer Jan's kids to mine.' Or 'We simply haven't got the space, that's why it's better if we come to you.' She couldn't imagine what additional layers of complication existed when care homes were involved.

As if reading her thoughts, Liz expanded. 'I mean, I have tried to explain what they would need, a specially adapted car that can take a wheelchair, or someone strong enough to carry him. A ramp, from the path up to the house steps. A bed made up on the ground floor if he is to stay overnight, but even if not, they would need to be able to get him to the toilet, or at least be able to change his pads. It would spoil their day, and his. I personally and professionally feel that he would be happier here. But people are so reluctant to see Christmas as anything other than the ideal that they all expect. The irony being, it so rarely is.'

Darcy decided to ask. 'What about the father? What do you think he would want?'

'It's impossible to know, sadly,' Liz said. 'His dementia is advancing so rapidly. Some days he wants to go home, others, he seems quite content. When we put up the Christmas tree, he said that he had done it, because, we learned, that it had always been his job to go and cut the tree from the wood and put it up. Ours is artificial, and he's in a wheelchair so…,' Liz shrugged as if to say, what can you do? 'Then the other day he said that we must all be stupid for having a Christmas tree up in July because didn't we know that keep decorations up beyond the Epiphany would bring bad luck?' And earlier on, he was crying, looking everywhere for his money. I calmed him, asking what he wanted his money for, and he said that it was Christmas tomorrow and he hadn't bought his wife a present yet. He wanted to buy her a silver necklace. But, of course, it's not Christmas for weeks yet and his wife died eleven years ago.'

Darcy felt her heart might break. The tears which had been presenting themselves to her on a daily basis, appeared again.

Liz patted her hand. 'It's awful, isn't it? They have this

fragmented mish mash of duties and memories, all stirred up and out of linear order. Some are so vivid, others are vague, and for the most part, they have nearly eighty years' worth of Christmases in their minds, from all different parts of their lives. Their childhood, adulthood and old age. It's like trying to do a jigsaw with pieces from loads of different Christmas puzzles and attempting to make one image of Christmas. It's impossible. This is why it's so difficult to speak to the relatives. I know they feel that they are doing the right thing, but I just worry that it will hurt all involved, and for what? For one day. I would rather that the families have their own Christmas, let our residents have theirs, and then just have another visit whenever they can. Christmas just comes with too many expectations for all involved.'

Darcy's mother loved doing puzzles and it was a given, that she would receive a new one every Christmas. Her eyesight wasn't so good now, so Darcy wasn't sure whether to maintain the tradition this year or not. Last year, the puzzle had featured the twelve days of Christmas and there were lords- a- leaping and ladies dancing around a pond in the snow where swans swam, and numerically assorted birds sat in the frosty trees. The year before, it had been people ice skating on a frozen lake, all wrapped up in scarves and hats, a huge Christmas tree in the background. Darcy imagined the boxes falling to the floor and the pieces getting mixed. Two thousand little fragments of pictures needing to be sorted when the colours were so indiscernible. And that was only two. She couldn't imagine the broken, disordered minds of these elderly residents, eighty years' worth, sometimes more, of Christmas pieces, jumbled together with no frame to contain them, and no box lid to guide them to what the finished picture is even supposed to look like.

Trinity

There were twenty-three on one home page, and twenty-five on another. Darcy felt jaded before she even began.

Her A4 pad sat beneath her coffee mug, a pen laying diagonally, like a dead body at a crime scene. Which is sort of was. Darcy felt like drawing around it in white chalk, silhouetting where a once vibrant life, full of purpose and promise had once existed, before its life was cut short, replaced by the screen and keyboard.

She was no Luddite. She was technical in a professional sense. She could handle complex spreadsheets and had created powerful and inspirational PowerPoint presentations. Her typing was fast and efficient, and she was not one to stand in the way of change. Indeed, most of her professional life had been exacting change; responsible for capital works, policy and procedural improvements, innovative and creative strategies. She had done it all, but there was something about the online world that just drained her. It was so huge. So unlimited, so boundless. And instead of seeing this through the eyes of her younger self, the person who encouraged others to look beyond the walls, she now found it too much.

Darcy had recognized in herself recently, that in order to make a decision, she needed those walls, and it stunned her. Was this age? Did getting older, and losing your self-confidence mean that things needed to become smaller? When had she become someone who needed to know the boundaries before being able to know where she fit within them? When did she start to scale down instead of up? Is this why Christmas was feeling so daunting this year? Not too many years ago, ten in fact, she had decorated fifteen

225

Christmas trees in one week. Three were for one of her new build projects (a shop, a restaurant, a hair salon); two for another of her projects. Two were for the church, one in the Sunday school room, the other in the vestibule. Two were for home, (the main one and the children's one). Two were for her mother, one in the hall, one in the breakfast room, because her mother had sprained her wrist and couldn't do it. Two were for the school Santa's grotto, and the last was one in her office. In addition to that she had created a Christmas menu for one of her projects; arranged a Christmas farmer's market for another; helped her mother with her Christmas food shopping; baked not only her own Christmas cake and mince pies and cookies, but also some for the school and church fayres. Had served in the grotto, two thereof, and had manned the tombola at the church fayre. Had musically created and sung in all the services; bought all the presents for the whole family, everything for the children from themselves, and sodding Santa, including in-laws; had put on a Christmas nativity at church; had gone out on a soup run for the homeless in the city, had done carol singing at the supermarket, and had personally ensured that every single person, young and old, whose Christmas she touched, was drenched from head to foot in magical elf dust.

So, how was it, that she sat before her computer, with her handwritten list to her left, and her deceased stylus, that she couldn't pick a bloody turkey?

Two tabs were open at the top of the screen. One supermarket, she hadn't even looked at, relying on the theory that if their cornflakes were made of real gold throughout the rest of the year, she was fairly certain that, at Christmas, when supermarkets believed everyone's purse strings were not just eased apart a little further, but ripped off and cast into the rubbish with the Quality Street wrappers, the cost would be too rich for her taste.

The supermarket she did usually shop at throughout the

year didn't provide such a service as Christmas food ordering, so that was out too. Which left her with two. Of which, one had twenty-three turkeys, the other twenty-five. Each promised a similar range of characteristics, which Darcy began to assimilate. Both offered whole turkeys in small, medium or large sizes. One was measured in kilos, the other in kilos and servings, which she used to find quite funny because, as a child, her mother had always bought a huge turkey. There were only four of them, six if her grandparents came to visit and yet the butcher's estimate that it would feed seventeen saw it stripped to the bone within two days.

There were crowns for those who didn't want legs. Darcy found them a bit macabre to look at. She struggled to cope with the idea of the mass extinction of turkeys at the best of times but seeing it already missing its wings and legs seemed an unnecessarily premature mutilation.

Then there were the free range – ah, yes, Darcy thought, it was bad enough eating a poor turkey without feeling that it had led a miserable fattening factory existence. Her conscience could cope a little better if she imagined it gamboling across verdant fields in its former life. But could you be sure they had really been free range? What about avian flu, weren't they all locked up for fear of a poultry pandemic? Perhaps she should go for organic, just to be sure. She scrolled to the price. How much? No, she was sure free range would be fine. There were farm assured standards, surely, they wouldn't get approved if they didn't meet the required standards. She would ensure that it was British. British and Free range. Now, what size? She scrolled for more advice on kilos and servings, then felt squeamish again that the poor creature was being marketed in servings. Her mind flicked back to the movie she had seen about the plane crash in the mountains and them all eating Jim, or whoever. Eying up his carcass according to how many servings they could get out of him. Bronze or Gold? What was this now? Was this their colour? Or their medal winning achievements? If the latter, then gold certainly. If the former, perhaps bronze. Advertising pictures always showed a glistening bronzed turkey, so bronze would be better, no? But then her daughter had shown her something online about advertising trickery. They soaked a tampon in boiling water and put it behind the turkey to show how piping hot and juicy and delicious it would be, and had inserted a balloon inside it, pumping up the chest cavity like a pair of fancy dress breasts and had slathered it all in boot polish to give it the bronze glow every Christmas dinner maker attempts to achieve, so perhaps imagining which turkey of the forty five here listed, was going to be able to offer that might be a moot point.

Oh, but here was black. A black turkey? Weren't they all black? Darcy wondered. She had to google it, just to see. But did black relate to the colour of the feathers, or the colour of the bird once plucked? Would that go bronze or gold, when cooked, or just black? She had been at her in-laws' one Christmas and one too many Proseccos were had, and the turkey was in fact, black. Burned black. How much was a black one, she wondered? £101.42?

Right.

Scrolling down the rest of the page, the food options just kept coming. The extra joints of beef and venison and clove-studded hams. Whole salmons and trout en croute. Buffet food, party food, desserts, cakes, cheesecakes, puddings. Then there were the vegetarian options and the vegan treats and the wines and champagnes and cocktail spirits. Aperitifs and digestifs. Where were the walls? There was too much choice.

The ordering had been open for a month already. It closed in five days. If she didn't decide now, there would be no turkey for Christmas Day. It would be like the year her mother had run all over town from shop to shop, trying to find one to find the deep, wide, fridges empty. She had been distraught, and relief had overwhelmed her when she finally found one. Was that so that tradition could be maintained, was it so that they could have all enjoyed the turkey? Was it because Christmas couldn't be Christmas without it? Was it because it shamed her to feel that she had failed as the Christmas domestician? For so many years, she had ordered from the butcher weeks in advance. Fresh fruit and veg from the greengrocers on the corner, who delivered it all in wooden crates standing on the cold doorstep with the freshness of winter on his heavy herringbone coat, handing over the crates in fingerless gloves. Placing them on the step of the kitchen door. The clementines in paper bags, their green leaves still attached. The citrus zest making Darcy's mouth water at the mere thought of peeling them, the freshness amongst the sugar and richness of all the other food. Her mother would arrange them in a crystal bowl, the Christmas lights refracting in dazzling prisms, the bright, deep orange incongruous with all the red and green but the embodiment of Christmas, nevertheless. A few years later, times had changed, there had been no money for the butcher, no personal service from the greengrocer. Yet it was still possible to get the clementines, not in the crinkle of the paper bag, but the orange nylon net. Still the crystal was the same. Once you had nice things, you always had them, that was the nature of material possessions, it made you feel that you were something, even if you weren't. Even if the money was now gone and the wallpaper peeled from the damp walls, the crystal bowl of clementines still remained. A reminder of a wealthier past, a sleight to a comfortable present. At the toes of her Christmas stocking, she and her sister had always found a coin and a clementine. The coin for providence, the clementine, a symbol of a promise that they would never go hungry. What cruel superstition was this? She wondered. Such talismans had held no such power. The money had gone, and they had gone hungry.

There was a picture of a clementine cheesecake, its centre decorated with some sort of glittering gold sugar dust in a star shape. Darcy scrolled straight past it, it was no match for the clementines in the paper bag, nor in the crystal bowl. It promised pounds, perhaps, but that was more in the respect of expenditure and weight gain, not the coins of financial wellbeing.

Scrolling down the pages of images was like scrolling through the photograph albums of Darcy's past. Each one transporting her to a time or place. This one, of the yule log, the kitchen at her family home, carving lifelike ridges and groves into the chocolate icing and dusting it with icing sugar snow. The fruit cake, made in October half term, the brown paper standing up at the side like walls of a prison, so much higher than the side of the tin, to keep the cake straight and regular, its top singed and the uppermost currants crisped to black bombs where they had caught in the heat of the gas flame. She had helped her mother to make it, pricking the dense fruit with holes, feeding it over the later months with brandy, like veins carrying liquor to the valves of fruit. When it was ready, the week before Christmas, she would inhale the heady aroma of alcohol, brush it with warm apricot jam and seal it within a tomb of marzipan. Golden slabs of sweet almond paste that she would eat the offcuts of. The covering would always be snow. A royal icing, softened with drops of clear glycerin and lifted to peaks with a fork. That was Darcy's favourite bit, how best to make it seem like real snow. Little plastic pine trees and reindeer stood on the top alongside a Merry Christmas plaque in gold lettering.

Every year, they did this, Darcy and her mother. No one else even ate it. But Darcy's mother said you had to have one, for when people dropped in. And they did, in those days. People were passing and they popped in. Why did that not happen anymore? Darcy wondered. Something to do with texting, and personal space and busy lives and the twenty-four hour nature of existence, she presumed. You could never know when anyone would be at home. But in those days, you did, because where else would anybody be?

How many years? How many cakes? How many turkeys? Who said that this is what Christmas had to be?

Television mostly, Darcy realised, and Tradition. The Tand T, that packed more explosive than dynamite and was just as destructive. The years of traditions and practices passed down from her mother, who had brought her own expectations from her own past. Together with television cooks and makeover shows and movies showing you how Christmas should be done and suggesting new ways to be traditional. Have a tree but dress it this new way... have a turkey but cook it this new way...bake a cake but do it this new way... Add a third T – turkey and there was the trinity of Ts. Three, in one body of Christ... mas.

When newly married, Darcy had opened her Christmas present from her mother-in-law, unwrapping it in front of everyone, to find a Christmas cookbook. Since the lunch was already in the oven at that point of the day, and she had already spent the previous six weeks planning the menus for the whole Christmas season, Darcy rather thought it had a dash of tardiness in the proceedings and an aroma of insensitivity about it. The woman hadn't even tried the food yet, that Darcy had slaved on for so many weeks and most of the previous day, so it seemed a little premature to suggest that she needed further tuition in the form of a step-by-step guide. Kneeling up from her position of lowly filial subjugation, she thanked the woman and leaned to give her a kiss, humiliation burning her cheeks. "You're welcome, dear," the woman had replied. "Well. You will be making Christmas meals for the rest of your life. I find it helps to have a little support in your corner. Look, here you can make notes on your recipes and build your own Christmas food bible. You will find it invaluable; I guarantee it."

The memory rose in her stomach, bringing the same feelings of anxiety, duty and obligation that she had felt that Christmas morning. But her mother-in-law had been right. She had needed it and had used it religiously as if it had indeed been a holy book. The pages were stained with grease splatters and gravy and the brown sticky juice from mincemeat. But like the bible, if the same set of traditions, expectations and behaviour are going to be passed down through the generations, there has to be a set of guidelines. There was no room for diversity or difference in faith. There was only doctrine. There was no room for diversity or difference at Christmas. There was only doctrine.

Would it matter if they didn't have turkey? Darcy asked herself as her finger hovered over the mouse. Could she deviate from the expectations just once? What if she went to the family and said, 'How do you all feel about chicken, this year?' They would probably whine and say that it wasn't Christmas without turkey. Because it wasn't. Scrolling down, she had left the turkeys, the beef wellington, venison, gammons and whole salmon and had got to the vegetarian section, the pastry rings of butternut squash and cranberries. It looked lovely actually. She could imagine herself quite happy with that. But her parents-in-law? There was no way Richard's father would eat that. That's if they were coming, she still had to work that out, too. She dared not imagine what they might say if she suggested that they were going to try something different. Perhaps not contribute to the mass slaughter of poultry and propose that as turkeys were actually quite expensive, this year she had decided to do something else.

She could anticipate it. Richard's father would ask were they really so poor that they couldn't even have turkey for Christmas? His mother would ask Darcy whether she had misplaced her Christmas cooking bible, but wouldn't miss the opportunity to have a dig that she had been doing Christmas for so many years by now she should be able to manage most of it without the book, or heaven forfend, had she got a vegetarian book, and was she running away to join a commune rather than sticking to the doctrine of her forebears? She would explain... No, they weren't poor. They could afford a turkey and if something was going to give its life up for you it should at least be valued highly. It wasn't the money per se, if that's all you spent at Christmas it wouldn't be too bad, it was just that on top of everything else. It was hundreds of pounds. For what? One day? They would then argue that it wasn't 'One day,' it was Christmas Day and people expected turkey on Christmas Day. Darcy could then say, well, no people actually expect turkey on Thanksgiving in the US because that actually had some historical and cultural significance for them regarding the early settlers, and that Britain has just adopted it, so you know, they really were free to think outside the roasting tin. She would say that vegetarianism was a good and healthy and sustainable lifestyle and what was wrong with a vegetarian Christmas? They would retort that not only was it inconceivable to have a Christmas feast sans bird, but there would also be no turkey sandwiches, or bubble and squeak or turkey soup and curry the following days and that would be unacceptable. Then Rich's mother would probably voice her concerns that Darcy was clearly losing it, that if it was too much for Darcy to cope with a proper Christmas dinner, she would be delighted to 'do' Christmas at their house, just to ensure that there were all the trimmings, and that nothing could good come from listening to anything said by Hugh Fernley Wittingstall because Christmas was no place for vegetarians.

Three. Of the forty-five turkey options, she had whittled them down to three. Common amongst them were their qualities of size and former lifestyle – large and free range. The colour, she was still undecided. Bronze probably. Should she ask Richard? She didn't know. How did she find it so difficult to make a decision? Food was so difficult these days. Every single shop required a careful study of labels to discern amount of food miles, sustainability, plastic packing, fair trade, palm oil for the orangutans, too much water used in its production, insecticides, carbon footprint, conservation standards, budget. Having a social conscience was time-consuming, expensive and exhausting, and that was just picking up a few bits of Saturday night supper. There were thousands of items on this Christmas page. Was it feasible to be able to carry out the same extent of due diligence for the ethical bottom line of each pig in a blanket or prawn in a cocktail?

She glanced at her handwritten list. Turkey was at the top. She wanted to be able to pick up the ink-filled cadaver, apply a few chest compressions and revive it with purpose by ticking an item off the list. But she had been looking at the screen for forty-five minutes, and spending time in her memories for twenty. Over an hour and still no turkey. Turkey tin, turkey foil, gravy browning, bacon, pigs in blankets, sprouts, carrots, parsnips, maple syrup, potatoes, stuffing, cranberry sauce, melon, pate, cheese platter, savoury biscuits, sweet biscuits, yule log(buy/make?) Christmas cake (buy, too late to make!), mince pies (pastry, mincemeat) gingerbread cookies, stollen, plum pudding, brandy butter, brandy cream, chocolate dessert, after dinner mints, liquors, wine. Party food and snacks (in case someone pops in), shortbread, box of chocs (Quality Street/ Celebrations etc.), clementines. The same things that had been on her list for over forty years and chronicled in the Christmas cooking bible for twenty.

They were the foods that made Christmas, but they were also the foods that had been made *by* Christmas. Reinforced by Television and Tradition. Turkey and the rest were the doctrine of the Christmas food religion.

Darcy felt the burden of the sinner.

Believer, deviate from the path of festive food righteousness if you will. Seek what exists outside the walls of this faith. But prepare ye for an eternity of retribution, for there is no salvation for the pilgrim who defies the holy Trinity.

Sleigh ride together with two

The consulting room was downstairs, and Sally had left Will in there, writing up some notes while she excused herself to the bathroom. As she crossed the landing, the door to the airing cupboard was ajar. She automatically went to close it, the occupational hazard of a disordered mind whose limit of control was the small things like wonky forks on a table, or unclosed doors. She saw the bibs, folded, and lying on top of the clean laundry. She knew she ought not to, but something drew her in. She wanted that enveloping comfort that can only be found in warm, fluffy towels. Will and Johnny's towels were thick, like marshmallows, their pile dense, like a lush carpet. She allowed herself the indulgence of holding them up to her face and burying herself in their warmth. Then suddenly remembering that she had been crying, lowered them, checking for traces of giveaway mascara.

In the bathroom, she stared at her reflection in the mirror as she let the steaming water run over her hands, not knowing who she was but grateful that the pain from her chest-hurt was being outrun by the scalding of her fingers.

Moving back through the house, she let her eyes glance around. It was their private space, she knew that, but she couldn't help but notice the elegant furnishings. All style and class. Everything was new and tasteful and shouted quality. Pieces stylishly curated and displayed. She smiled to herself, sometimes the pain allowed a smile to still show itself. It had to, for the sake of the girls. Will had shared with her their exciting news, the long-awaited arrival of their adopted baby

Olivia, but Sally didn't think that they had fully comprehended what having a baby would do to the house.

The door to the nursery was open. Not even ajar. It was almost announcing itself to the passer by, like a market hawker, "Come, please, come and have a look", so she did. It was tastefully furnished in muted tones of beige and oatmeal. Sally liked it. It was restful and calming. The perfect place for a baby. She didn't like the bold, monochrome patterned mobile and geometric wall art that hung over the changing table. In her opinion, it jarred with the overall aesthetic, and she was surprised because the rest of the house seemed so well put together, but Will had explained to her once, some weeks ago, that that neutral colours were no good for babies because they needed bold, clearly defined shapes to focus on that helped to promote early cognition and mental stimulation. Sally understood, but she still didn't like them.

Next to the cuddly toys on the shelf, a speaker had been placed that would pipe classical music, again for neuro-acuity. And a nursing chair sat in the corner, draped in a cosy blanket for nighttime feeds. A few fabric books and early learning toys sat in the wicker toy-box, too advanced for a new baby, but Sally recognised the classical trait found amongst all new parents; their always anticipating the next stage of development, before the current one had been fully enjoyed. There was something so hushed about the nursery, just waiting in its quiet readiness, that it felt as if there was a baby already there, swaddled and sleeping soundly in the walnut wood crib. Two babygrows hung on their little hangers on the handle of the wardrobe, a Santa and an elf. Hope and expectation oozed from everything in this room. The fruition, after the waiting. The gratification after the longing.

It was Advent, the countdown, or count up, whichever way you looked at it. The waiting had commenced. For the coming of a baby. No rocking chair or changing mat awaited the Christchild. No stimulating mobile, nor plush teddies. Yet, Sally thought, from the little she remembered from school,

Jesus' birth was supposed to be the fulfilment of ancient prophesies; the salvation of mankind and Living Water to all those who followed Him. She could tell as she looked around that that even Jesus could not have been more wanted and anticipated than the child who would soon call this room her home.

She made to turn away from the room but paused. Standing before the changing table, she took in the shelf above. There was nothing surprising. Indeed, it was its normalcy that was the most beguiling. It was neatly arranged, the shelf, with nappies, one above the other in rows, like wood cladding. Clear jars were filled to their brims with cotton wool balls and buds. Packets of wipes were stacked on the shelf below, for easy access, and next to them, were two bottles, baby oil and lotion. Without even having to open them, she knew their smell. Another of those powerful nostalgic portals to the past that reminded her of her life before this one.

The bewilderment of how her life had come to this was an ever-present condition. Her future had seemed so fixed and certain, mundane even in its stability. It had never occurred to her that it could all change in an instant.

Checking her phone, she checked the time. Nearly school pick up. When it came to school time, Sally found herself at a precipice. Her child-free time, the edge; and the evening routine, the wide-open sky ahead, continuing on to the horizon. Some days, it simply felt too exhausting to take the step. The after-school clubs, dinner, homework, reading, clearing up, bath time, bedtime… all feeling as unavoidable as free-falling off the cliff. Some days, she just wanted to stay on the edge, feeling the wind in her face. A wind that was passing through. That had come from one land and was moving on to another. Reminding her that there was a world that existed beyond routines, beyond this village, and beyond this small, little life. Sometimes, she wished the wind would take her.

But for now, this small, little life was what she had, and it was what her daughters had. *She* was all their daughters had. So, she had to press on. The wind would have to move on without her.

*

Emma was there collecting the boys. Sally waved and pushed the gate to enter the playground. Perhaps she could have them round for tea, Sally wondered. The twins and Rosie got on well and Hannah loved to mother little Henry – despite being only a year older than him. It would be good for them, Sally told herself. But she knew that if she were being truthful, it would be good for her too. The evenings were long and lonely, and having the house full of laughter and chatter took some of the pain away. Usually, after the girls had gone to bed, she would collapse into the chair with a glass of wine and allow herself a little television time. But watching a crime drama wasn't the same if you couldn't discuss whodunnit. It wasn't the same without someone to chat to about it. She had taken to watching cooking shows instead, thinking that she might inject some new creativeness into her suppertimes but neither of her girls had much of an appetite for proper mealtimes. There was nothing like an empty seat at the table for someone's absence to be felt more keenly. Crediting herself with too many brain cells to watch reality shows where participants had to do little more than wear bikinis and sleep with each other, she had found that documentaries were her viewing feature of choice. Often, they covered topics that exposed people's loss and suffering, and it gave her some twisted solace that many carried crosses that were too burdensome to bear, not only she.

Rosie had taken to waking sometimes and would come downstairs. She would kneel on the floor next to Sally's legs and rest her head on her knee. Sally would change the channel to something less thought-provoking and cover her with a blanket, stroking her daughter's long, brown hair until her eyelids closed. She would take her back upstairs. But on those nights, found that she settled more easily with her in her own bed than in the bottom bunk of her own room. Each found comfort in the other, both filling the absence left by the former occupant of the space.

In Rosie's own bedroom, her little sister slept deeply, never noticing, until morning, the patch of warmth, seeping through the mattress like honey, or the stinging urea soaking her pyjamas and giving a rash to her legs.

These night times spoke a thousand words.

Yet, though none were spoken, Sally heard.

'Hi,' she said, giving Emma a light kiss. 'Alright?'

'Yeah, good thanks,' Emma replied brightly. 'You? Was it therapy today?' she asked with a smile of compassion.

Sally nodded.

'Aww,' Emma said, giving her a hug. Sometimes, there were no words.

'How about you? Good day?' Sally asked, feeling it less painful to ask about others than dwelling on herself.

'Checking on the sprouts,' Emma replied. 'Len Williams said that his have got some sort of blight and it has taken out part of his crop. So, I'm on it. I'm a sprout scout,' she said with a laugh.

'I was wondering if your guys would like to come over for tea tonight? It's only pizza,' Sally ventured.

'Sounds lovely. Thanks.'

Sally smiled and felt a weight drop from her shoulders. She felt she could take a step into the afternoon abyss, with Emma there.

The phone pinged. It was Emma's.

'Oh crap! Sorry, that's a reminder... the boys have the dentist. I completely forgot with all this sprout business. I'm so sorry. Can we do it another day?'

She turned and flashed a beaming smile at her twins that were barrelling towards her, their coats on their heads, pretending to be superheroes.

'Oh, yeah… sure,' Sally smiled weakly. She felt her tiptoes teetering over the cliff edge again.

The boys were closely followed by Rosie who handed her school bag and pe kit into her mother's waiting hands. Sally kissed her on the top of her head and looked around for Hannah. 'Where's your sister?' she asked, seeing the rest of her class milling out to the waiting parents.

Eventually, she saw her, still at the classroom door, standing next to her teacher who was waving and trying to attract her attention.

'Oh no, what's this about?' she muttered to Emma. 'Miss Leeming wants me. Gotta go. I'll see you soon, yeah?'

'Okay. Hope everything's alright. I would stay, but I've really got to get to the dentist. Sorry,' she said apologetically, shepherding her boys out of the gated space.

'Hi baby cakes,' Sally said looking at her daughter's sad face. Hannah ran to her and clung to her legs, burying her face in her jeans.

'Heeey. What's this?' Sally asked, in an open way, which she hoped addressed both her daughter and the teacher.

'We've had some tears, I'm afraid Mrs Rimmer,' the teacher began. 'I can't quite get to the bottom of what happened. I think it may have been something to do with Christmas. The children were talking about their advent calendars, and that got them to talking about Christmas songs and decorations and…' Sally didn't need to hear anymore. She knew what had provoked the tears and the thought of it had formed tears of her own and a golf ball of emotion strangled her throat. She nodded, folding her lips in on themselves to stop them quivering.

'That's okay,' she managed. 'We'll have a talk about it at home,' Sally said and began to lead Hannah away and back to Rosie who was playing hopscotch on the markings on the ground.

'If there's anything we can do?' Miss Leeming began. 'I

know this must be a difficult time for you all. Perhaps, if we knew what had happened specifically, we would be able to manage it in class, or at playtimes. Just so that we can be aware. I can inform the mealtime supervisors too.'

Sally nodded. Peeling her daughter from her legs, she crouched down to look into her face, sweeping her damp hair from her face and tucking it behind her ears. 'Look,' she said, trying to put a lightness in her voice that she didn't feel. 'Rosie's playing hopscotch. Why don't you go and play with her and let Mummy speak to Miss Leeming for a minute. Okay?'

Hannah glanced over at Rosie and weighed up the suggestion. Her sister caught her eye and beckoned her over. Sally turned her face back to the teacher.

'Was it *When Santa got stuck up the chimney*?' she asked.

A flash of confusion burrowed the teacher's brow, 'Sorry, was what… when… what?'

'The Christmas song,' Sally explained. 'Her dad used to sing it to her and do the actions. He used to pretend that he was stuck and ask the girls to pull his legs to get him 'out'. He would lie on the floor and huff and puff as if he were Santa, and they would pull and drag him around, sliding on the wooden floor. They loved it.'

Something pressed on her chest and squeezed it, like a balloon that's nearly deflated and can be squished at one end and bulge at the other. The bulge forced her throat to close up at the base of her neck, while her brain struggled to decide whether this was a happy memory to be enjoyed, or a painful one to be avoided. There had been many of those. And despite their frequency, her brain hadn't got any better at decision-making.

Miss Leeming smiled. 'What a happy memory to have,' she said, making a decision on Sally's brain's behalf. She fondled a piece of paper, uncertainly, folding and unfolding it, the activity allowing her mind time to work out what to say.

Sally glanced at the girls, in the way mothers do. Eyes

flicking automatically every couple of seconds to check that they are still there.

'So,' Sally continued. 'It may have been that. Or it might have been *Sleigh Ride*... the song – Sleigh ride together with you. You know... that one.' Her lip trembled into a wobbly line. 'The girls would pile up the sofa cushions on the floor to make a sleigh and use their skipping ropes to put around Peter's waist. He would pretend to be a horse – or reindeer and pull them along as they sang the song. They would sing "giddy-up let's go".' Her voice sounded strange, strangled, and about an octave higher. She reached into her pocket for a tissue to stem the dribble from her nose. There was usually a reliable pack of them, but her fingers only found a wrinkled rag. She squished it against her nostrils and sniffed. 'They asked him to do it again and again in the run up to Christmas. The song would come on and the cushions would come off. Last year...,' she smiled at the memory (her brain deciding that it was happier enough to cause her to smile), 'he even put them on the office chair – because it had wheels – and pulled them behind him all through the kitchen and dining room.' She turned the tissue around between her fingers to try to find a dry bit. She sniffed again and took a breath.

'Would you like to come in and sit down?' the teacher asked, reaching for a little chair and placing it by the door.

'No, I'm fine, really. Thank you,' Sally replied, allowing herself a restorative sigh. 'I don't know what to say Miss Leeming...,'

'Claire, please,' said the teacher, feeling that sharing this family's ghosts of Christmas past, was too personal for school formality.

'Claire...' Sally repeated, smiling weakly. 'The problem is that Peter loved Christmas, we all did. But he was something else. He went all out and as soon as it was the last day of November, he was up in the loft, getting down the decorations, and buying more... Whatever new gadget or gimmick was around, like the outside projectors and the light up reindeers and the Santa climbing on the roof. He wanted it all and wanted to create that magic for the children. He dressed up as Santa on Christmas Eve– made me do it too, just in case they awoke at night. And he always brought fun and life to every Christmas song. He even got the barbeque out, so that he could roast chestnuts on an open fire – because we don't have a fireplace. If you could bottle Peter's zest for Christmas, it would solve all the world's ills, because he felt, and radiated, complete and utter joy and delight.'

'It sounds wonderful,' the teacher said kindly. 'And I think I can understand now why Hannah found it so difficult today.'

Sally felt fresh tears spring to her eyes at the thought of her daughter's pain. 'The problem is that I can't think of any song, or any Christmassy thing that the other children say or do that won't remind her of her dad. He was, and is, in everything. It is not a case that there is one particular thing that the school can be aware of and prepare for. It is the whole of Christmas. Unless you can cancel it altogether,' she offered with a small laugh.

She said it flippantly but part of her was wondering whether that actually might be easier on the girls, to just go somewhere else, where Christmas wasn't celebrated, and just avoid the whole thing. To spend the next month in some far away country, playing on the beach, in a tropical paradise that has palm trees instead of pine trees; tofu instead of turkey; sail rides instead of sleigh rides, and pineapple mocktails with little umbrellas in, instead of the mugs of hot chocolates and marshmallows that Peter used to make them all as they cuddled together on the sofa and watched Christmas movies. Why should she perpetuate their pain, and hers, doing nothing, as every day of Advent scrapes off the scab and opens the wounds once more?

It would be the first Christmas without him, and Sally just didn't know what to do for the best. Should she keep things the same? Not that she could inject the same joy into it, as she used to, or as her husband used to - he was next level. But imagining that the girls might find some solace, constancy and reassurance in the familiar traditions, and feel close to him in their shared memories, Sally had planned to do as much as she could to keep things 'normal'. But then she had to accept that Christmas, by its very essence, wasn't 'normal' for most people; never mind, for two little girls whose 'normal' was gone forever.

Perhaps taking them out of school and going away would be the best thing. Not that she had the money to do that. But it was the only way to avoid it. Christmas. She suddenly had some understanding of what it must be like for people of other faiths and cultures living in the Western world. Your whole environment suddenly transformed into a collective expression of attitudes and practices that you might not subscribe to yet are thrust in your face through every form of media. What if you just wanted to avoid it? You couldn't. Christmas wasn't just something that you could opt into or out of. It was pervasive. It came with its own rules and expectations, behaviour and tropes. It was not enough to simply be aware of it and let it happen around you, you became part of 'It'.

When she reflected on it, she realised that it was all their own doing. Hers and Peter's. They could have chosen to opt out many years ago. To "do" Christmas in a way that was more measured. To not go all-in. Why hadn't they? Why had they conformed to what their society had led them to believe was the right way to do Christmas? They had had a choice yet hadn't taken it. Somehow, being indoctrinated to think that if you didn't celebrate the festival with all the trimmings, you were a heard-hearted, scrimping, stingy Ebeneezer Scrooge. If you didn't lavish your children with presents, or your table with plenty, you were miserly and miserable.

It struck her now, that, if Dickens was trying to say that we forge our own chains, link by link, through our actions in life; and – as his Christmas story suggests, strive to leave a legacy of charity and equity between rich and poor– then why have we, as a culture, chosen to disregard that bit of the lesson and seek to just purchase and own and consume more ourselves at Christmas-time?

She felt sick and sorry that the joy and delight she, and her wonderful husband, had forged in the creation of their own Christmas, was now the heavy chain of sorrow that their daughters wore. Stumbling and struggling under the burden of it, like the repentant Jacob Marley. They could now not see, or hear, or taste, or experience anything to do with Christmas without it hurting so much more than it would have done, had it not carried as much emphasis. However, unlike Marley, they had not forged their own chain, theirs had been bestowed upon them, stocking by stocking, bauble, by bauble. Any joy and delight they may glean, buried beneath a great, heavy garland of tinsel.

'I'll talk to her,' Sally said. 'I don't really know what to do about it, but maybe we'll talk about how they want this Christmas to be.'

'Alright,' Miss Leeming agreed gently. 'Did you want me to mention it to the school bereavement therapist?'

'Yes,' Sally replied. 'The girls like her. And I know that I'm grateful for any professional help. It's not like I know to cope with all this.'

'I'm sure,' the teacher agreed. 'It's a terrible time, for all of you. If there is anything I can do, or any way that you can think of that will help the girls. Please do not hesitate to talk to me. Okay?' she said warmly, squeezing the top of Sally's hand.

As Claire Leeming pulled the classroom door closed, she shut behind it the mini Christmas world that it had become over the past week. Therein, the children chatter in words and spirit of expectation and anticipation. Christmas was coming. Their classroom was decorated with paper chains and a little tree with sparkling lights in the corner. The post box for

Christmas cards stood at the front, its mouth open at the ready to consume the season's greetings in the malformed glyphs of Year 2 pupils. Rehearsals for the nativity play would commence, followed by Christmas jumper day and Christmas lunch day. To opt out wasn't an option. It was all expected and all there to be embraced, encouraged and enjoyed.

A sickness formed in Sally's throat at the thought of her little girl in this world of her father's creation. Could she ever say, "No, Please Miss Leeming, don't play that music, or sing that song, because my daddy used to sing that and now, he is gone"?

As her teacher, what could Miss Leeming do? Try to balance a child's grief and loss, and painful sensitivity to Christmas with the fulfilment of the hopes and anticipation of the other twenty-nine? No scales could equalize that disparity.

Flicking off the tree lights, her mind flashed back to the discussion with Holly in the staff room. Holly was right. She could see it now. Christmas was experienced differently by children, not just from a financial perspective, but through family experiences. It couldn't be right to treat the whole class the same, and it couldn't be right to do the same thing every year, when every year could be so altered.

A playground at playtime, by its very nature, is a space for play. For laughter and games, fun and freedom. A place to chase and be chased, to squeal and shout and laugh. A place to climb monkey bars and skip with ropes.

A playground, after all the children have gone, is an empty yard. Quiet. Soulless. Its equipment, inert, its markings, void of little feet. It's tarmac, hard and unyielding. Skipping ropes stowed, used neither for skipping, nor sleigh -ride reins. It was just a space where life used to be.

Straightening the blind, Miss Leeming watched Hannah take her mother's hand and cross the playground, her sister leading the way. The gates closed behind them. Tomorrow they would walk into another day of Advent.

A word which means, to come. But how could anyone ever know what was, to come?

Deck the Halls

DARCY

For us, once the tree was up, it was open season for the rest of the decorations to be released from their long incarceration. We keep ours in the loft, but in my childhood, they were kept in the uppermost part of the built-in wardrobe in my parents' bedroom. It was too high to reach on a daily basis, so you had to properly mean it, if you wanted to gain access. The most appropriate thing would be to get a step ladder, but as we didn't have one of those, my mother would stand on a dining room chair and hand the boxes down to me. I would take them carefully and place them on the bed, getting increasingly excited as a top leaf would flip open, revealing its contents. It was a strange feeling to experience both the new and the familiar at the same time. Being out of sight and mind, for a year, meant that when I opened the boxes, it was like seeing everything anew; carefully turning over each item, appreciating it, yet at once wanting to move onto another, eagerly searching the trove of treasures for the next wonder. Yet, they are also not new. The faint smell of dust from the tinsel, or the rustle of it as it slips through my fingers, and the memories triggered from each ornament, makes the novelty merge with nostalgia. "I made this in Reception," I would say fondly as I held a star made out of lollysticks. "And look at this", finding another thing we had done at school, a picture of Santa whose legs and toy sack were affixed with paper fasteners, which you could move independently to his body. It had a little piece of red string, with which to hang it on the tree. Ah, then there is the ubiquitous cardboard tube, to which

I have referred before, omnipresent in various guises, serving as a body to some once festive character or other, dressed in tissue paper, which was scruffily adhered at the time of its creation, and got increasingly the worse for wear as the years passed. I even still have the old dress of the angel, before it was upgraded, by me, to the classic statement piece of Chanel's doily collection that she continued to wear for the rest of her days. I suppose my mother found it too difficult to discard. Having said that, in my younger days, most of our baubles were glass so, if they broke, we would have to replace them. But now, so many are just plastic. Even so, I still find myself wincing in shattering anticipation if a bauble is dropped today, only to find that it bounces along the floor with nothing to show for its ordeal, except in extreme cases, perhaps a small dent.

I have some decorations that never make it on to the tree, either because they are now a bit old fashioned, or don't suit my current theme, or actually, because they carry memories that are just too painful to have dangling next to your face while you are trying to watch a Christmas special. They stay in the box. I know they are there; I meet them, greet them, quietly acknowledge their place in my history, then decide that staying locked away in the loft, year upon year, is exactly where they should be. Yes, I know. I hear it. I know it sounds as though I need therapy. "Let's unpack that box, shall we?" I hear you say, "No," I reply, "because it is it's full of tinsel and lametta and heartache!" All joking aside, I might put a tiny sprinkling of lammetta on, if a particular branch warrants it, but never heartache, and never tinsel.

For all those who don't make it onto the hallowed branches, there are some without which the tree would not be complete. The Baby's First Christmas ones, of course. I have a select collection of very sentimental ornaments. I won't bore you with each one. They might be pretty, or fancy, or even plain to your eyes, but you won't affiliate them with any additional significance more than that. They are merely festive trinkets. We have some beautiful decorations that boast fine detailing, that are delicate and eye catching, tasteful and elegant. They bring a sophistication and classical finesse to the tree which is echoed by the judicious placement of ornaments of many shapes. 'Not just round balls,' my mother would say. 'I don't like a tree that just has balls.' We have many ornaments that were gifts, or that we bought while on holiday, or carry lots of personal significance. Not least, Christmas pig.

Christmas pig has to be present at every tree dressing. It is, of course, a teddy bear. A very small, little wooden figure sitting on a toy drum. The drum is blue and white (yes tell me about it, it has never coordinated with any of my colour schemes), and it sits, legs splayed out as teddies do. It is so sweet, with its small ears and a well stuffed tummy. Its cute face has two little black eyes, but, the muzzle, that has been stuck on as a separate piece, is an unfortunate shape and renders the darling little bear's face a smidge porcine. It goes back to the first Christmas that my husband, then boyfriend, joined the family for the tree dressing rigmarole, which as you know by now, is quite a big deal for us. He was on his best behaviour and trying to impress upon his future mother in-law that not only would he promise to love, care for, inspire as an equal partner in life, protect her daughter and all that stuff, but more importantly, he would learn how to do a good tree. "Ah, this is sweet," he had said as he held up the wooden ornament, "a Christmas pig".

Goodness, the very notion! She was mortified. As if, with all you know of my mother's tree tastes, any of her ornaments would feature a pig of all creatures. He was nearly escorted off the premises. Still, fortunately, she decided not to banish him from the kingdom. She forgave him, we married a few years later, and Christmas pig lives on.

I'm sure that my mother's resistance to a tree that is all balls, if you'll pardon the expression, is because they don't carry these sentimental suitcases. A box of twelve plain, round, silver baubles from Tesco's can't invoke a thought, or a memory, whether it is positive or negative, joyful or painful. They are just featureless and undistinctive. But decorations, can be like the humble paper chain, something that links past Christmases with those of the present and future, from generation to generation. Even if the ornament itself does not survive, its story does.

Do you know…, returning to the pagans, for a moment, and thinking about decorations that are unrelated to the tree itself, I think they were onto something good with the idea of bringing fresh greenery into the home in midwinter. Aside from the fact that it looks spectacularly good in candlelight, there is something so spiritually uplifting about a piece of the outside bringing life and nature inside. In the way that a simple jug of wildflowers can lift the mood of a room with their colour and scent and beauty, so too can boughs of deep, glossy green. They catch the light and imbue the atmosphere with notes of wood and sap and fresh air, much in the way a clump of grass can do in the summer.

When I was little, our centrepiece, on the Christmas table was always made from fresh greenery. Its creation began with a circle of soaked oasis in a shallow flower arranging dish. I would watch as Mum would transform it from a bare clump of green, spongy foam, adding a sprig here and there, at different lengths and angles, until it became something resembling an evergreen Titanic, with three long, white dinner candles rising from its lush depths like smokestacks on a deck. She would begin with offcuts from the base of the Christmas tree, if there were any. But the majority would be long springs of laurel, then trails of ivy would be added, and finally holly. I wanted to go to the holly tree in our garden in a waxed jacket and Hunter wellies, with my secateurs in a willow trug, and snip off some sprigs, feeling like someone in a photo from *Country Life* magazine, imagining myself saying, 'just nipping out to the grounds, to gather greenery from the hedgerow once planted by Capability Brown'. Unfortunately, however, our holly didn't produce the distinctive red berries for which it had gained such notoriety, nor did we have acres of parkland, so, instead, we would wait until it got dark and go out and nick some from the park that backed on to our house.

Mum had a couple of pictures in the living room, and she would put a sprig of holly along the top of each one, and I would make a little arrangement of my own for along the top of the upright piano, but that was wear our nod to paganism ended, at that time. It being hedonistic and all that was evil, and all that. I always wanted one of those Victorian fireplaces, with a white Adams mantelpiece, from which would hang heavy swathes of holly, adorned with red velvet bows, and would meet in the centre with a fabulous wreath. However, we didn't have a fireplace of any kind. When times were good, our only heat source came from our functioning radiators which didn't lend themselves aesthetically to wreathes and bows; and then when the boiler failed, we had the electric fire that I told you about (and for one winter, a Calor gas heater); over neither of which it would have been wise to drape anything lest the whole house go up in flames.

I wanted to deck all our halls with boughs of holly and have one of those grand front doors with a wreath on it, like the ones on all the Christmas cards. In fact, we did have a wreath, it was just not on a grand front door. We put it on the porch door. It would have looked better on the inner door, but no one could see that from the outside, so we hung it on the outermost door instead. The problem was that it was glass, so we couldn't fix it on with a nail or anything like that. We had to suspend it from a piece of ribbon. In bad weather, it would swing and sway, the sharp points of holly scratching the glass as it moved to and fro, like a pirate ship on high seas. The long tails of the ribbon would tap like little fingers begging to be let in, and now and again, the whole wreath would lift up and bang against the door. Instead of producing the effect of a classically festive aesthetic, it scared me to bits.

Some of my friends had those decorations that were made of foil and could concertina in and out. When fully extended, they could cross a room from corner to corner, or droop from the coving in shallow scallops. I always found them to be very jolly. They were reflective and colourful and big. In one of my friend's houses, they were suspended overhead in the living room, crossing at the centre, and they moved imperceptibly, in languid waves as the heat rose in the room. It felt, to me, as though I were beneath a magical net at the bottom of the sea, with shoals of coloured fish darting about overhead. To complete the festive decoration ensemble, these friends also had a small, fake tree with multicoloured lights that was suffocated in tinsel and dripping with lametta. I know that I would not have liked to decorate our house in that way, and that I have always leaned more towards the elegance of a classic Victorian Christmas, but when I was in their homes, it is the warmth, love and hospitality that are the things I remember. The welcome, the generosity and the sense of lively fun, noise and laughter. The cosy carpets, curtains and sofas, none of which matched, but all of which engendered a feeling of squashy comfort, safety and happiness. I was not just looking through the window of the room that I craved, I was actually in it. I had seen behind the door. When I look back on it now, I knew that room was not perfect, by any means, and I knew that we were blessed with a lot that those friends weren't, but what is clear is that Christmas decoration is individual and personal, and that's what makes it so wonderful.

The closest I got to decking the *halls* during those early years was to deck the *hallway*. You recall that there was the white glossed staircase? Well, its decorous treatment was, in our early days, a few lengths of horrific tinsel. I felt that it was time for an upgrade and leaned towards the style of the desirable staircases, as seen in American movies, where a lushly thick garland, punctuated with luxuriant red velvet bows, entwines itself down the stair rods like a festive boa constrictor wearing a tuxedo tie. Suffice it to say that we couldn't really afford that, when it came to it. But the next best thing were the cheaper types of garlands which now I think about it, were really just lengths of matt, green tinsel. Flimsy, flat, and in a shade that was just a Pantone number lighter than mushy peas. My luxuriant American red bows, the size of two cottage loaves, were not within budget either, but I was able to get a card of twenty, ready-made bows that had little gold twist ties on the back. They were less the scale of wholesome, rustic loaves and more the size of cocktail sausage rolls. Still, it was all a welcome recovery from the severe bout of tinselitis, with which we had suffered since the seventies, and a move towards the US exports of how a well-decorated Christmas home should be in the eighties. And, of course, where America goes, we follow, and to give credit where it's due, they can 'do' Christmas decorations. So, in an attempt to really elevate my garland to Hollywood proportions, I was delighted when I came across a pack of fake apple decorations at my local garden centre. They were small, red and shiny and looked good enough to eat, and with all the willpower of Snow White, I seized upon them.

I hadn't really considered how those stupendous boughs of greenery in the movies had been affixed. It certainly wasn't Sellotape, I can tell you that, because that doesn't work. I suppose it helps to have a whole props department and set directors to make the designer's vision come to life and I imagine they have all of the appropriate tools to hand (unless they really do use a festively vested boa constrictor who deploys its bone-crushingly strong reticulations to hold on to the stair rods, itself).

Putting up decorations is hard. You can't use tape in case it pulls off the paint or wallpaper when you remove it. You can't use Blu tack, because things are usually too heavy, and sometime throughout the night, it finally gives up the effort of holding on, and your chosen festoon is found collapsed on the floor in the morning. Thumb tacks aren't too bad, but you can't put them directly into a wall. They need to be pressed into the coving, or into the back of the bookcase. Although caution must be used here as no one wants the antique armoire to be so studded with discreetly inserted drawing pin holes that it looks as though it is suffering from a bad case of woodworm.

You remember I told you that my father had dutifully tried to contribute to the tree erection efforts that one time? Well, in fairness, he may have done it three times, but that's not much over the space of my twenty-five years of living in the family home. Well, at that same time, he had also attempted to put up the tinsel in the dining room. He had done quite well, considering that he had probably stood on a chair to reach the high walls, even being, undoubtedly, too inebriated to do so (Health & Safety alarm bells sounding loud and clear). And, as with the tree, you couldn't fault him for being results-focused. He did achieve what he had set out to do, it's just that his methods were questionable. The tinsel did hang from the coving, all around the room. It did swoop, albeit in slightly unequal parabola, so, we couldn't really complain. It's just that, of all the methods of adhesion that he could have chosen; the tacks; the tape; the putty etc., he (or it might have been the whiskey) had elected, instead, to go to the First Aid kit and hang the tinsel from the walls with sticking plasters. The shiny lengths looked like they had injured themselves at repeated intervals and as if it wasn't bad enough to have secured the festive festoons with sterile dressings, they were children's ones and printed with little images of Mr. Bump.

As I struggled with my pea green tinsel garland, I wondered if he might have had the right idea. The Sellotape hadn't worked, so perhaps the First Aid kit held the answer, I could use a bandage, or a triangular arm sling, just tie it round the handrail and job done. No, they don't have bandages in the movies, there must be another way. I did find another way, I used florist wire, and it was all fine, except I just couldn't get the droop right. It wasn't quite the same as the thick swathes of the films, with the beautiful, large bows. But with a bit of readjustment, it was as close as I could get it. I tied on the little, red bows which instantly elevated it from its dull raiment of mushy peas, and the rosy apples were a triumph.

It was a shame that our carpet was brown and beige wool, in a geometric design that was all the rage when it was very expensively laid, some years earlier, but did nothing for the aesthetic in my pursuit of the perfect American Christmas staircase. Theirs were either marble, or polished wood, or carpeted in a deep burgundy. Right, that could have been why it didn't look quite the same. Still, my garland was all we could afford; it had not turned out too badly, and it was definitely more on trend than tinsel, so I went to bed tired, but satisfied.

Overnight, there had been an inexplicable engineering malfunction with the florist wire. The two side fixings had come undone leaving it only secured to the top and bottom of the handrail, and at one position in the centre. Most of the apples had scattered to the hall floor.

I stood in the hallway and looked up with a sigh of despondency. After all my efforts, my movie-style garland now hung forlornly, dangling like a pair of post-menopausal breasts, inadequately supported by a dull bra of mushy pea green. Whilst the only upside I could find was that not *all* of the little, red apples had fallen off, the garland gods were still using me for their amusement. Those deities of decoration had ensured that two tiny apples were retained in the chest of despair. I don't need to tell you where they were.

Suffice it to say, the pea garland went into the charity box, but I did save one little apple, just as a reminder. A reminder of what? My constant need to dress our house for Christmas in a way that alleviated the drab, hues of lack and struggle? My wish for a bright and sumptuous home that I saw in the movies, regardless of how unrepresentative it was, of the majority of people? My aim to reclaim the bright, sumptuous home we once had that would rival any of those in the films, before it decayed with the mould of financial ruin? For the small, shiny apple, a nipple to a drooping breast, to represent the only one of mine that remains after the cancer? A reminder that anything you have for one Christmas can be gone the next, and to value it, however ordinary it may be.

I have a little box. It is shaped like a treasure chest and covered in an ornate gold damask, hinged with a matching gold tassel opening. It used to hold bottles of Frankincense and Myrrh, the fragrances of kings. A little card came inside it, explaining the significance of each one, the representation of the gifts brought by the Three Wise Men. The gold: Royalty. Frankincense: Divinity, and Myrrh: Humanity. Gifts from the mysterious Orient, carried from afar. Just the very notion of it, the idea that I could hold, in my hands, the same things that the kings had brought in the Christmas story. It wasn't every day that one came across gold, frankincense, and myrrh. Well, granted you came across gold quite often, in terms of wedding rings, or crosses, indeed, I actually wore a gold crucifix every day at that time. Incense: the only incense I had come across was at the midday mass on Sundays, and holy days of obligation. That's funny, I think, that they called Mass an obligation. Why would you actually bill something as a holy day of obligation? Surely the holy day would be significant enough in itself for you to want to go to mass willingly, as a sign of acknowledgement and respect for whatever amazing thing it was such as the Assumption, or the Ascension of Our Lord, or the Asencion of Mary, or the Transfiguration or feast days, or whatever. I rather think now that the devoted should not *feel* obliged to go, nor should *be* obliged to go. But there you have it; they were days of obligation and days for incense. Bells and smells, as they say. The thurible would be wafted around by the altar servers, as they processed around the church. Now, I burn incense lots of the time, particularly if a room needs a freshen up. I open the windows and let the old air out, the fresh air in and light an incense of lemon or citrus to clean the air. I know some people don't like it. They find it gives them a headache. I was like that with the frankincense and myrrh that came in this box. I liked the idea of it, but it used to give me a headache and nausea, I had to get rid of it in the end.

In my late teens, a new shop opened on our local high street. It was run by a sweet Indian couple. I only went once or twice. My mother didn't really approve of it because there were images of elephant gods on the walls (I know). Well, that's slightly unfair, it's not that she didn't want me to go in and she never stopped me, in fact a couple of times she came in too, but she always seemed uncomfortable, as if being surrounding by things that were exotic and unfamiliar, and watched by the array of Hindu religious art and statuary, would stain her Christian soul. It was these very things that made me want to go. I loved the unusual; browsing the items made of mango wood and sari fabrics, the garishly coloured posters of Ganesh and seeing little ornaments like jewelled bangles and woven handbags and blankets. There was always a haze of incense, rising up in thin grey tendrils, searching inside me for the spirit of adventure and curiosity that I was never encouraged to pursue. The Indian couple were lovely, they welcomed me warmly and would quietly watch as I meandered around this intriguing world, which despite being only at the bottom of my road, gave me a glimpse of another continent and life. I might have asked them questions. Who was this god? What does that goddess represent? I might have done, I should have done, But I never did. To do so, would be to recognize that were other faiths, other beliefs, other gods. But I was told that there wasn't. There was only One True God. Repeatedly, my whole life, from home, school, church, friends. Only through belief in Him and no other would lead to everlasting life.

I had wondered what would happen to the nice Indian

couple when they died, if they had chosen to believe in their elephant gods and their blue demon gods, and such like. What was to happen to their souls if they did not come to know Jesus in time? Surely this was the need for all those early missionaries, for missionary priests still, to go out and convert these people lest their souls not be saved. Really? Is this really what I believed then? How could I have the arrogance to think that my God was the only one? How could I have little to no understanding of other faiths and religions? It was never taught in those days; I was raised in a bubble. A Catholic bubble that kept the outside out, and inside in. A bubble, into which you were born and baptised, within days of your arrival into the world, lest you might wander as an infant into a little Indian shop and think for yourself, I think I'll try this. Then once you are in the bubble, you accept all the rites and rituals until you confirm them in public to the whole of your inside community that you are going to stay in this faith forever, because it is the right one, the true one. And then you dare not ever leave it, because you will be sinful and then die and your soul will be lost.

So, at Christmas, as I have found, one must not be distracted by the shimmering gold of boxes with tassels on, because they take you to a world of the Orient. To a world where Jesus is not recognized as the Saviour, to people who believe in other things and do not perform our Christmas rituals, because to them they are meaningless. The poor, unenlightened souls, that I once considered them. It is no wonder that we grew up believing in our supremacy, when we had been told from childhood that only the Far East's three most learned scholars were the ones wise enough to know the truth!

I think that our endless search for the perfect Christmas is fed by the need to make our homes as we see them in adverts, movies and in the stores, hence my droopy garland. Do my hot chocolates taste better because they are in a

Christmassy mug…? Yes. Does it feel more festive putting my children to bed on Christmas Eve, in Christmas duvets…? Well, I imagine it would. I didn't used to because I thought that was an extra expense that I couldn't justify, but I sort of get why people do. Do I have to change the towels and tea towels into red ones with Santa on…? No, of course not… but I do on Christmas Day. It's ridiculous, but we do it. I wanted fairy lights in the kitchen, (not just because I love fairy lights, as you well know), but because when I was watching all the Christmas cooking shows on television, they were always there. Behind Nigella, or Mary Berry, as they wove their cinnamon-spiced spell of a recipe, the lights would be gently glowing. They would casually drape themselves across a shelf adorned with red milk jugs, or a white biscuit tin with holly on it, reflecting off a strategically placed bauble, and drawing everything into a dreamily soft focus. I had to have that because, everyone knows, that there is no way that you can make a yule log without having the fairy lights on, that's the magic of Christmas home-baking.

It's like outside lights. When I was younger, it was an exception rather than a rule to see any form of external decoration on houses in the street. There was the odd one, who would throw a length of multi-coloured bulbs over the privet bush or stick a sign on the front lawn that read 'Santa Stop Here!' but it was all fairly minimal. Yet in the American movies, every house along the wide avenues has their rooflines covered with rows and rows of lights. Every tree is bedazzled, not only with a few lights scattered through their branches, like Martin Luther had seen on his wander home in the sixteenth century, but wound tightly around every trunk and branch, studded with so many hundreds of densely packed lights that it was as if they were each wearing illuminated fishnet stockings.

Have you noticed how many more houses now extend their decoration to the outside of their property? I have done it myself. Richard and I have stood outside in a cold

December wind, he up a ladder, me holding the base to stop him falling as the gale whipping over the valley threatens to knock him into the agapanthus. Why do it? Because it is festive and Christmassy and welcoming when you come home in the dark. It is welcoming to visitors, or to those who pass by. Here, in the village at night, it is very, very dark. We have no streetlights, and on the night of a new moon, or when the cloud obliterates the stars, it is possible to not even see our house from the road. The Christmas lights are almost a way marker, acting like the candle in the Scottish crofter's cottage. From inside the house, other than when the lights come loose and tap against the window, you forget that they are there. They are of no benefit to us, inside. We cannot see or enjoy them once we are in the house. So, what is their purpose? Why do we decorate the outside of our homes? It is mostly for the enjoyment of others.

Indeed, when the children were little, where we used to live, there was a house which began preparing their Christmas lights display at the beginning of September. The man worked so hard, up on the roof in all weathers to install the spectacle, but I'm sure he got as much joy from seeing people enjoy them as they did from looking at them. Of course, there are those, for whom the effort is not so altruistic and is more for show and one-up-man-ship. Like in that film, *Deck the Halls*, have you seen it? No? Well, Matthew Broderick and Danny DeVito are in it, and they are neighbours, each one going to extreme lengths to outdo the other's decorating efforts, even trying to ensure that all the lights become visible from space. Or like in that other one, *Christmas with the Kranks*, the couple are ostracized by their neighbours for not putting up house lights nor fastening their model snowman on the roof. If you don't join in, people want to know why, there must be something wrong with you. Never mind that perhaps you can't physically put them up or can't afford it (or that there aren't any more left in the shops because Joyce has bought them all to communicate with Will. Ha! Have you seen that?

Stranger things? No? Really? I thought everyone had seen it. It's a bit of a phenomenon. This boy goes into a parallel space called 'the upside down' and no one can find him, but his mum feels that he is still in the house and can communicate through the lights, as they flicker and flash on and off. She then gets out all her Christmas lights, and all the others in the whole town, and writes an alphabet on the wall. Each light corresponds to a letter and that way, he can talk to her and send her messages. Life is like that sometimes, isn't it? Even though someone is there, they're just beyond reach.

Mind you, I wouldn't like to have seen Joyce's energy bill, lighting every light in the town. There didn't appear to be any energy crisis in Hawkins, Indiana. Have you heard the news recently? They're talking about an energy crisis. where bills are predicted to treble, if not quadruple over the coming year. There is talk that low-income families will have to choose between eating and heating. I mean, that's not exactly a new thing for some, but a new wave of frugality and economy will be experienced, and people might have to face the reality of being more careful with the ready power supply they have enjoyed up to now. I wonder where Christmas lights will feature on the priority list. There may be fewer illuminated reindeer nibbling the front lawns; fewer rooftops lit up like the landing strip of terminal four at Heathrow; fewer projectors beaming dancing festive patterns on the walls, and fewer neon Santas climbing into chimneys. Perhaps after all our seasonal decorative advancement, our Christmas preparation will see us sitting at the kitchen table once more, with a newspaper, a toilet roll and a pot of PVA clue.

Or what of those who have no kitchen table? There is a housing crisis, and refugees displaced by war and natural disaster. What shallow, incomprehensible nonsense and disparity is it to be wasting money on decorating a home, when some have no homes? This is just another question that I ask myself. It all seems so excessive and blinkered to reality.

We had our soffits and gutters repaired this year. Our old

lights can't be fixed to the frames. We could get something else, different fixings, a wall projector perhaps. But that is more decision, more cost, and I seem incapable of making Christmas decisions at the moment, because how can one, in all conscience, bother about decking one's halls, when others have no halls, walls or even a roof?

Away in a manger

The three of them stood back and admired their work, the children pointing out the decorations that they had made in former years. Jen smiled and nodded appreciatively, though secretly wished she could tuck them around the back. Whilst she appreciated that getting the children to make decorations was a fun and worthwhile activity, she had rather hoped that the teachers would scale them appropriately. Making angels from toilet roll cardboard tubes and snowflakes the size of a dinner plate might have looked proportionately correct on the tree in Trafalgar square, but on their eight-foot artificial tree with barely the space for a cinnamon stick between one branch and the next, they looked more like villains hanging from a noose than festive decorations. Still the fairy lights and baubles provided much needed cheer in the corner of the room.

The advent calendars stood on the sideboard, a week's worth of doors open, a visible documentary of the journey to Christmas. The 'elf on the shelf', was on the shelf and Jen made a mental note to remember to stage whatever misdemeanour he was next up to. She had vowed not to get sucked into this commercial con, but the children had begged her when they saw it in the shop saying that all their friends were doing it. Jen had heard the mothers complain about it in the playground, always plotting things to do, planning in advance, spending more money on various props and outfits like some pixie Barbie. She had enough to worry about without this nonsense, but the girls' lives were already different to their friends' so the last thing she wanted to do was add yet another way for them to feel excluded from normal childhood, particularly Helena. The whole notion of it seemed ironic to her. If the idea of the elf was to watch the children's behaviour and report back to Santa, why then were the elves encouraged to be made to do naughty things?

It was their tradition when the tree was finished to turn off all the other lights and then have a count down and switch on the fairy lights to collective sighs of contentment and excitement. Jen felt as though Christmas was well on its way when the tree was up.

And the crib, of course.

Slowly withdrawing it from the box, she took care not to get splinters in her fingers. It was big but crudely made. Just rough offcuts of two by two, to make the vertical supports, a top and bottom of single ply and it was filled with packing straw from a fragile ornament that had once been shipped to her. The children liked to spread out the straw, untangling its curls that had been formed by a year of inattention, like a patient hairdresser.

She placed it on the sideboard next to the calendars and reiterated to the girls that the crib pieces were very old and very delicate.

They nodded sagely, appreciating the gravitas, and watched as she began to take out each figurine.

***

This is the ox. A large beast, laying down, its hooves tucked beneath it. She strokes its soft muzzle. It is not soft, of course, it is made of some sort of pottery. It is delicately painted in muted matt tones, but its blaze looks soft. She places it at the back, because they are always shown at the back, and it is where her mother used to place it too. It feels heavy in her hand. They are large, these figures, it fills her palm comfortably like a mango, though she had never held any mangoes when she was Helena's age, nor for many years since. They had not come across such exotic things.

The next is a shepherd. She places him to one side. She is

not ready for him yet, preferring to add those at the end. He is tall and has slim legs and wears some sort of tunic and leather boots, like a medieval minstrel. He wears a deep red cloth hat. Helena picks him up and looks at him. Jen tenses. She knows that they are only things and that she shouldn't place such value on them, but she does. Sometimes, it is only in the tangible, that we can feel that we are real. She worries Helena will drop it and it will break, or even just chip. If the paint chips, Jen would not be able to recreate the colour or the finish. There is something too ethereal about it, like a faded masterpiece.

Reaching her hand into the box of packing curls, her fingers surround a shape, almost triangular. It is Our Lady. Mary. She wears a long white robe and a pale blue veil that falls from her hairline and folds delicately down her back. She is kneeling with her hands clasped at her heart and her head is tilted to one side and her gaze falls at somewhere before her. Jen places her in the middle, but slightly to the right and scoops the straw away so that her base nestles in.

She is followed by Joseph, who also kneels, and whose head is also slightly turned, this time, to the right. He has a kindly face and a gentle smile. Jen knows of course, that when the tableau is complete, he will be looking at his son in the manger. She wonders, not for the first time, how he can look so kindly upon a child who is not even his, when her husband cannot look at his own children with kindness. Although they may not be the child of God, as Joseph was led to believe, they are children of God still. Good, sweet, kind girls and do not deserve the impatient ire that their own father issues, or to witness the mark of his hands on their mother.

Another two shepherds follow, dressed in a similar style to the first, one plays a rustic instrument such as a wooden flute, the other wears a sheepskin gilet, which whilst fitting for a shepherd in those times, did always make her, a child of the seventies, think that he was just missing, a pair of flares and tinted sunglasses and a shoulder bag with a peace sign on. She had said the same to her mother, who had admonished her for blasphemy. This was a visitor who had come to worship the child, Jesus. Jen doesn't see that as she holds him today. Perhaps it is because she feels that that child of the seventies is long gone. And that the promise of a future of peace and love that she imagined, purported by the sheepskin shepherd, has not only *not* come to pass, but has been replaced by violence and anger.

The soft, grey hues of a recumbent donkey reflect the warm browns of the ox as he takes his place beside it; behind the manger, the most fitting place for these beasts to be, the warmth from their bodies and breath warming the Christchild.

Three kings follow, in robes and headdresses decorated with painted gold and colours of jewels. One has a smooth black face; the others are bearded. All are tall and thin and walk with a slight stoop, perhaps to signify their age, and therefore their wisdom, or the burden of their long journey. Jen checks her own posture reflexively and finds that she too is stooped. She rolls back her shoulders to ease the knots of tension and stands a little straighter, but that awakens a bruise at the base of her neck. She has neither travelled from a distant land – in fact she has never even been to a distant land – nor is she old enough to be wise. In fact, if anything, she is stupid.

The kings bring their gifts of gold, frankincense, and myrrh. She glances at her gold wedding band. A ring, a circle, a symbol of eternity. It sparkles in the fairy lights of the Christmas tree, teasing her. All that glitters is not gold. The incense, taken from a tree, an expensive fragrance to represent sovereignty. She too had been given gifts of perfume. Perhaps not a king, but one who has given himself that same authority. And myrrh, an embalming fluid used in death, a prophecy of Christ's death to come. How many nights had she prophesied her own, when the force of his hand might strike her that bit too hard. What would become of the girls then?

Gifts of significance and meaning, but also gifts of wealth. Jen wondered whether Mary and Joseph ever thought of turning to the kings and saying, 'we do not need your gold, we can manage by ourselves. Because if we are beholden to you, we can never be free.'

She sets the manger in the centre, its placement drawing the outlying figures together and bringing to life the vision of the composer of this tableau. The person who has moulded and painted these figures; who has designed their bodies, and postures and attitudes; who has shaped their faces and painted their expressions; who has produced this manger scene to be replicated and established in homes, far from the little town of Bethlehem. Who were they? Jen wondered. And did they know how their work would pass on through generations and for the Holy Family that they created to be a symbol of hope to those in need?

The baby Jesus figure, she gives to Helena, and Freya moans. She wants to hold him. She wants to be the one to place him in the manger. Helena turns to look at her and advises her that that's not the way. It is too early. He has not been born yet. He must lie under the straw on top of the roof until Christmas Eve. Freya snatches him and stamps her little foot in tantrum. Jen fears that he will break, and speaks softly, soothing Freya and calmly explaining that Helena is right, he should be put in the hayloft roof until Christmas Eve, when Mary has the baby. As her own mother had said to her.

Freya points out that the Mary figure doesn't have a fat tummy, so she must have already had the baby so she should be able to put him in the crib already. Jen agrees with her child's logic but explains that the crib stays up a long time, even after Christmas, so it makes more sense if Mary looks like she has had the baby. Freya says that they should put the crib up at Christmas then, and not now. Again, Jen is both surprised and challenged by a little girl's logic. Where was her own challenge? She had always accepted everything willingly. She had never challenged. Is that why she was here now? A weak and frightened shell, with no more autonomy and strength than the sheep before her. She knew that she should ask whether it was worth staying for the gold. Not that there was gold in its raw form, but that which gilded the roof over her head. Without which, she too would need to seek the sanctuary of a stable. She knew that it was necessary to reposition the figures in her own crib. For too long, the hierarchy and authority of the king had gone unchallenged, but she cannot. She is not strong enough. Her place was here, the mother, kneeling, her gaze set before her, unaware of how to reach that which exists around and about her.

Helena asks if she can place the angel. Jen nods. But instead, she hands it to her sister, explaining that even if they can't put the baby Jesus in yet, the angel can be present, because he had already appeared to the shepherds. How well she already knows the order of things.

The angel is not part of the original set. He comes from somewhere else; another crib scene, a much smaller one. In his former life, he was glued on to the apex of the stable, but now he has no personal adhesion properties. Helena runs to the desk and comes back with a small ball of BluTack. She offers it to Freya who takes the little angel in her little hands. It looks incongruous with the large stable and figurines. What should be the imposing and authoritative figure of the messenger of God, who incites fear and wonder to the shepherds on the hills, looks rather diminutive here in Freya's small hands. Still, she proudly plays her part in this tradition and affixes him to the top of the ply roof. He is slightly askew and looks like he is pointing to something on the top of the Welsh dresser rather than the birth of the Saviour of the world, below him.

Helena suggests that he looks as though he could be pointing to the star. There is no star. The girls ask for a cereal packet and some tin foil. Helena cuts a star shape, and they giggle as they fix it over the crib.

The star has made the crib theirs. Why had she not thought to make one, in all the years when she was a child? Jen wonders, setting it up with her mother, and even throughout all the following years as an adult and mother herself? It must be true what they say, that after a while, your eyes get accustomed to the darkness.

***

Later, the girls were in bed and Jen was struggling to think what to do with the elf. It was only a few days into Advent and already she was tired of having to find creative ways for him to misbehave, or indeed copy someone else's. Flicking through Pinterest for some ideas, she scrolled through the images. Squeezed out toothpaste…, messed up lipstick…, spilt milk. Funny for some, perhaps, but not for her. The king would not tolerate that, and it would be her lipstick that was messed up, by the back of his hand.

She looks at the crib and wonders about laying the elf in the manger. It is vacant after all and will be for the next few weeks. He was about nine inches too long for the little bed, but she could curl him up on a pillow and cover him with a blanket from Freya's doll's house. Her mother would have a fit. If she had thought the groovy shepherd was blasphemous, putting a naughty elf in the birthplace of the Light of the world would strike her down on the spot. But then, that wasn't altogether a possibility that could be ruled out anyway, so she might as well give the girls a giggle in the morning.

His long, bendy legs didn't obey Jen's attempts at encouraging him into a foetal position, they stuck out at an angle as if he was dreaming himself in mid hurdle in the 400m. He is bigger than the ox and ass combined and in relation to the tiny angel, he is gargantuan.

Jen couldn't help wondering whether it wasn't a case of art imitating life with the elf a bigger prospect in the story of

Christmas than a tiny angel, and Jesus missing from the picture altogether. Maybe it was blasphemous after all?

The proportional imbalances in the crib reminded her of the huge cardboard angel on the Christmas tree, hanging on its bit of ribbon, at odds with the scale of everything else, to her chagrin. Taking some Blu Tack from the ball, she wrapped the arms of the elf around the angel, in something of a waltz hold, and moved a faceted silver bauble to the branch above them. Their very own disco ball.

'Beautiful top line,' she said. 'It's a ten from Jen,'

***

Dinner was cold when he came in. Jen had hurried to heat it, explaining their busy evening with the tree decoration and the crib setting. But he was in no mood for excuses.

The girls were in bed, Jen would look in on them in a moment, when the bleeding stopped, just to check. The blood dripped on to her shirt. Deliberate, crimson drops like tears. She would wash the shirt in cold water, once he had gone to sleep.

The crib, with the tinfoil star and the tiny angel stand on the sideboard. The figures, silent within. Jen glances over at Mary, but she looks away. Her face is only ever turned away. Jospeh too. The shepherds and the animals, the wise men, all look to the manger. None to her.

Still, she prays her nightly prayer for their protection.

From the branches of the tree, a light shines. In its beams, an elf, and an angel waltz, dancing the dance of love.

They watch two others dance. It is not a dance of love.

A baby watches from the hayloft. A child who is a king. At once, both meekness and majesty.

A girl watches from the staircase. A child who is a child. Her parents, at once, both majesty and meekness.

Christmas penguin

'I'd hate to see how long we'd be waiting if we *hadn't* booked online,' Johnny complained as he handed Olivia another packet of mini rice cakes.

'I don't even know what we are doing here,' Will replied. 'It's ridiculous. She's a baby. She's not going to remember it anyway.'

'You don't know that,' Johnny replied defensively.

'Er, I do actually, research shows that our earliest memories form at about three years of age. She is not even one yet.'

'Yes, well, she's extra smart and is going to be an early developer,' Johnny said. 'I can just feel it, and when the psychologists of the future realise that our earlier memories are from aged eight months and thirteen days, they will be able to prove that she did remember it,' he answered with a knowing nod.

'No, what you are confusing that with is your projection,' Will countered. 'You are projecting a reality on her, that will be supported by a photo, when we actually get there – if we actually get there– of her with Santa, and this, together with the stories we tell her will reinforce the idea until she actually believes that she remembers the occasion. Such is the power of the mind and the power of suggestion.'

He looked at the queue of people snaking around the huge Christmas tree in the heart of the shopping centre. It usually sported a huge fountain which infused the air with its fine spray and soothed tired shoppers as they sat around and rested their aching feet. But at Christmas, the fountains were replaced by a Christmas tree equal in height to the cascading water and sporting baubles the size of watermelons. At its foot, stood mechanical figures, snowmen or polar bears, and huge wrapped boxes, stacked, with large bows, lit with a thousand stars. Johnny was pleased to see that there weren't any penguins. He could not abide the ubiquitous Christmas penguin, sledding and ice-skating, wrapped up in scarves and bobble hats. Did the marketing people not know that penguins were only found in Antarctica and not the Arctic, from whence Santa hailed? There was no likelihood that penguins would ever frolic with polar bears or elves and actually inhabited the other side of the planet from the Jolly Old Elf.

In the boughs of the tree on the snowy wasteland, was a little log cabin with snowy edges, and sat within was the man himself, attended by his elfin minions who corralled while they carolled, and herded the thousands of children and their fraught parents through the Santa drive – in.

With all the magic and charm of a drive through take-away, buggies essentially pulled up to the window, placed their order, had their registration snapped on the parking system, collected their order, and then moved on to allow space for the next child hungry for fast and immediate Santa satisfaction. And much like a fast-food burger, it was unsatisfying, unfulfilling and left you wanting more Santa Christmas half an hour later.

Olivia was getting restless. Despite rigorous planning, Will and Johnny were edging dangerously close to a full meltdown and having to remove Olivia from the queue even before she had seen the first polar bear.

Suddenly finding oneself with a baby, no matter how long-awaited she had been, was disconcerting for both of them, particularly when the paperwork had suddenly found itself efficiently processed and the agency had contacted them three weeks early. The two new fathers had hurriedly had to make arrangements at work to take leave, Johnny's being the least flexible, given how Will could work from home and simply rearrange his clients to suit. Johnny had to book the adoption leave and hand over his portfolio of property sales in their various stage of completion to other colleagues and to train the intern to cover some of the more basic admin elements like the photos and listing of the properties online. Adjusting to this new life in their midst was delightful and terrifying in equal measure, with each day bringing a new set of questions. Was she sleeping too much or too little? Should they swaddle or not? Was her poo supposed to be that colour? Was that just a little cough, or the beginnings of croup? Why wouldn't she stop crying when she was fed, dry, comforted, entertained, and loved more than anything in the world? What else could she want? Could it be colic? When did they start teething? The health visitor had encouraged them to go to the parents and tots group, but Will and Johhny had found little in common with the other parents, predominantly mums, who preferred to share stories of mastitis and the healing progress of stitches than whether their babies should be crawling yet, although many of them seemed confident that their child was developing at a much faster rate than the others, and declared the fact with modest boastfulness.

At least the Santa train had chuffed a couple of feet and they were closer to the main winter wonderland tableau. Now, Will and Johnny had more to point out and exclaim over than they had in the wasteland of the tundra, stuck at the back of the queue between the shoe shop and the iPhone cases kiosk. Stimulating chat had been a struggle, and they had already gone through Olivia's favourite textile book three times. She seemed rather to prefer to chew the book now. They suspected that she might be teething, or hungry, or perhaps it was boredom of sitting in the buggy for so long. Although, probably not hungry. They had fed her repeatedly, with each new food item being a welcome diversion from the tedious wait. When they had first arrived, she had been asleep, and they had discussed whether to wake her. No. Never wake a sleeping baby, had been one school of advice. Make the most of it to get your chores done and take the opportunity for a rest yourself, another had been. Still another…, yes, you must wake them to get them in a routine, otherwise you'll have no life of your own and everything will be constructed around the infant's timetable. How was one to know what to do when the advice was so conflicting? Will had thought that with several millennia of people having children, it seemed fair to assume that a general consensus of understanding about such things might have been reached by this point in the evolutionary development of the world, rather than diametrically opposed opinions which sought not to advise, but merely to obfuscate and confuse.

They reasoned that if she woke up when she was good and ready, she would be her brightest and best self by the time she got to the grotto, and the resulting photo would be a triumph. Yet, if she awoke too soon, the infinitely long queue would be too much for her to endure peaceably and she would no doubt launch into a bout of anti-social wailing, forcing them to abandon the project altogether, which Will was okay with, but Johhny would not hear of. The worst outcome, that Will could foresee was the prospect that she would remain asleep throughout the whole interminable wait, until their reached the little log house, and the two grown men would have to go in to see Santa by themselves.

Fortunately, that wasn't necessary. She had awoken. Relief enveloped Will as he no longer felt it necessary to busy himself in deep conversation and intent study of their phones to avoid the empathetic stares from fellow queue parents. Johnny was unaffected. What other people thought about him was a consideration he had had to dispatch early in his life, otherwise he may never have got out of bed in the morning. He was all the better for it. For Will, on the other hand, meeting the expectations of his parents were paramount, and meeting those of society, as much, if not more so. After all, it was society which determined not only whether your life was respectable, but whether it was acceptable. Being with Johnny allowed him to glimpse the freedom that came with not caring so much. His husband would say, "imagine that there was no one here. What would you do? If there was no one who could see or judge you, how free would you feel?" Will could grasp the concept and felt ashamed that he had to have the mechanism pointed out to him. He was the psychologist. He should be the one offering such empowerment. But he also knew how much human behaviour was determined by upbringing, nature and nurture, environmental factors. And even though he was aware that the power of the individual resided in the self, and was free to reinvent itself at any time, it was always constrained by its baggage. It was always weighed down by the fear, concern, guilt and the burden of others' expectations. In reality, it begged the question, how could one ever really fly, when one's wings were clipped by the opinions of others?

Olivia needed changing.

Will and Johnny argued about who was going to do it. Not because they didn't want to change the nappy. That, they accepted as part of fatherhood and were equally willing to deal with the business end of the whole baby business. The reason they were arguing was because whichever of them went, they would need to take the baby bag, and possibly the buggy too as the toilets were half an acre away and on the third floor, which in the pre-Christmas crowds would be much simpler in a buggy than carrying her all that way. That would leave the other one standing in a queue for Santa all by themselves with no child, no buggy and no excuse for being a grown man standing in line to see another grown man sitting on a throne wearing in a red suit and black boots (Although Will had reminded Johnny of the time he had joined many others in a queue outside a nightclub in East London waiting to see someone of just that description, though on that occasion, the throne was for a drag queen, the red suit, sequined and the black boots were patent leather stilettoes).

Johnny had lost the coin toss and was the one who had to remain while Will went away to deal with the nappy situation, although it was on the condition that Johnny could keep the buggy for validation purposes.

'Hurry,' Johnny pleaded. 'Do not leave me here for too long on my own. No getting sidetracked by other shops or anything. Okay? You need to be back as soon as you can.'

'Don't worry about it,' his husband replied. 'The rate this line is going, you'll still be here on Valentine's Day.' He laughed and hoisted Oliva onto his hip and the nappy bag over his shoulder. 'Won't be long,' he said and gave Johnny a peck on the cheek. 'Now be a good boy and wait patiently okay? Otherwise, all these elves will notice, and they'll tell Santa.'

'Just be quick,' Johnny replied.

He stood with the empty buggy and watched Will leave. As he glanced down at the pushchair, he realised that Olivia's stuffed penguin (the creature who couldn't leave their daughter's side without triggering severe separation anxiety) had been left behind. Johnny called after him, knowing that it would be much easier to change Olivia's nappy if she had Pedro to cuddle. But it was too late, Will had disappeared into the crowd and the general hubbub was too loud to hear the calls from his husband.

He glanced around conspicuously and caught the eye of the woman behind him. She smiled and he nodded then pretended to be immersed in his phone to avoid any awkward conversation. He wasn't a rude person as such, it was just that in a slow-moving queue, as on a train on a long journey, you had to be mindful as to when to engage in conversation with someone. Too late, it would seem as though you had been deliberately rude and distant, and then if you found that you really liked them and found them interesting, you didn't have enough time left to enjoy them. However, if you started too early, you could be stuck with the passenger from hell and unable to escape. That had happened to him with the railway enthusiast on his last trip. Mistaking his companion in the next seat as a fellow commuter, he had mentioned the delay announcement. That began a litany of railway pros and cons, the best lines, the best trains, the best engines, the worst engines, the history of the branch lines in the Northeast and how the Scottish rail service differed from the Midlands, and so on.

There were still a lot of people in front of him. If he got chatting now, he would be stuck for a long time. And then when Will came back, it might be awkward, having to integrate him into the conversation, or detaching himself politely from any more dialogue with the stranger.

Plus, the woman's child seemed to be a bit of a brat, running around, and trying to open the bows on the fake presents. Johnny peered out beneath his lashes to see if the mother was telling him off. But she had disappeared. He looked all around, wondering why she had just left the buggy in the queue. He supposed that perhaps the younger child had needed the toilet, but surely, she wouldn't leave the older one there unattended. He acknowledged that he was new to parenting, but he was pretty certain that leaving them alone wasn't really acceptable. That sent him into a quandary. Was she hoping that he would keep her place, in which case why didn't she ask him? Or perhaps he was supposed to edge her empty buggy along to keep pace with his own advancement. Maybe he was supposed to do that. But what if he did so and then when she returned, she would admonish him for touching her property? He didn't know what to do. Also, if he didn't do anything, would the person behind her in the queue just bypass the buggy and move it out of the way releasing her place in the line? If so, was it his responsibility to mention it, so that they would be aware of the woman's possible return? Queueing was fraught with risks and difficulties. No wonder certain cultures didn't do it. He had been in some places where people just turned up, stuck out their elbows and leant forward, pushing like mincemeat through a funnel. Everyone came out as a line of sausages at the end, it wasn't necessary to go in as a straight line too. Johnny was usually cool about matters of this kind, trusting in serendipity to work things out for the best. You couldn't sweat the small stuff. There was often too much huge stuff to sweat; and over the years, his stuff had made him as hyperthermic as if he were wearing an Aran sweater, three woolly jumpers and a fur hat whilst adding more water to the coals in a Swedish sauna. Perhaps it was having Olivia now. It was a depth of responsibility that he could not have anticipated. Suddenly, everything he thought and did, he did so through her eyes. She would learn about the world from him, yet he wasn't altogether sure that he understood it well enough himself yet. Will had always been the sensible one, constrained by his fear of what people might say or think, before he took a step. He called Johnny the wind beneath his wings, the one who helped him to feel free, to remove the shackles and fly. Yet, Johnny felt a new sympathy with his husband's parents. Granted, their attitudes were perhaps a little too extreme, but he had no example of parenting to draw on from his own life. He had made his own decisions and his own mistakes, that's what happened when you had no one to rely on or to guide you. But he was now the guide. He would be Olivia's guide. What if he did it wrong? How much of what he wanted for her was to make up for what he hadn't had? Was this why they were here in this queue? And, if this was always to be his benchmark, to relive his childhood through her, would that steer her wrong? He felt he heard learned somewhere, that that was a common parenting mistake. He wondered whether it just applied to Christmas or whether it was found in every aspect of the child's ambitions and goals.

His eyes found the empty-buggy woman, and the younger child. She was putting the boy on the back of one of the display reindeer and had stepped back to take a photo.

Johnny was sure that the animated creatures were for display purposes only and not play equipment to be clambered over and sat upon. He turned back to his phone to shield his demeanor in case it belied judgement and disapproval. Not that he was the type of person who judged others on the choices they made. Unless he was now?

Willing his husband and daughter to come back, he inched forward in the queue as another child exited the drive-through excitedly holding their gift from Santa and tearing off the paper. Something about it seemed a bit distasteful to Johnny. The nature of it, too greedy and grabbing.

God, what had happened to him? He might have been that same boy, years ago. So forgotten and overlooked, that the prospect of receiving a gift would have seen him behave the same way; tearing off the paper, careless of its disposal, carelessly tossing it to the floor in the wonder of an unsolicited present. Provided through the kindness of some unknown benefactor. It was not greed. It was disbelief. It was all-encompassing amazement that this item, this thing, this gift was his alone.

Johnny then frowned. The boy didn't appear to be experiencing the moment in quite the way Johnny had allowed and seemingly unimpressed by the gift, thrust it into the stomach of his mother. Glancing at it, she shook her head, and then threw it in the nearby litter bin. The child folded his arms and pouted. She stroked his head with a hand whose fingernails were painted a glossy pink with small diamonds on the tips. A large handbag with gold chains hung from her shoulder and she mouthed words which Johnny made out to be something like, Disney Store. Johnny raised his eyebrows, thinking that apparently, in direct contravention of the song lyrics, it is still acceptable to pout and cry if Santa Claus comes to town. Olivia wouldn't be like that, he promised himself. He and Will would raise her to be polite and respectful and grateful. They had waited too long and had fought too many battles to waste their chance of parenting by raising a spoilt brat.

Oh, he realised. This is what it meant to worry about what people thought.

His mind had been wandering while he watched the exit door of the grotto, and he hadn't noticed that a spoilt brat closer to home had removed Olivia's Pedro from the buggy and was now pushing it through the fake snow.

'Ryan! Ryan, here. Let's have a photo with the penguin,' Johnny heard.

'Penguin? he wondered, looking around. There weren't any penguins in the display, He had verified that earlier, as they had arrived. So where had this kid got a penguin from?'

The line inched forward again and the woman behind nudged the buggy with her hip. The shopping bags hanging on the back overbalanced and it tipped up; the wheels, scraping up Johnny's calves. He looked around instinctively.

'Sor-ray,' the woman said stressing the suffix of the word unnecessarily. 'It's these bags.' She shifted the baby on her hip.

'It's fine,' Johnny smiled politely and helped her to right the carriage and remove the bags so that it didn't happen again.

The women picked the bags up and slipped them back over the handles. 'Cheers,' she said to Johnny. 'Waiting to see Santa?' she asked unnecessarily, with no hint of sarcasm. It seemed like a genuine question, although quite what else she expected him to be doing was beyond him.

'Well, my daughter, yes,' Johnny clarified.

'My Ryan wants to see Santa, don't you Ry?' she called across to the child who was kneeling on the floor moving the fake snow in dredges piling it all up into tall drifts.

The child ignored her, but she was nonplussed, clearly used to one-way conversations.

'What are you asking Santa for?' she said, possibly to remind him of what to say when he got to meet the benefactor that was going to make it happen.

'Mega cyborg hand, smart ball, night vision goggles and slime' he mumbled, omitting a definite article and with no hint of joy or excitement.

'Oh,' Johnny replied, 'I haven't heard of that. What's a mega cyborg hand?'

The child ignored him too.

'It's a mechanical hand that you can build and use to pick things up,' the mother replied on his behalf, evidently used to the protocols of dealing with both rhetorical and unanswered questions.

Johnny was waiting for her to tell her son to stop pushing the snow around like that, as it was revealing the bare tiles beneath lending a sense of the 'not so wonderful' to the wonderland winter scene.

She exhaled visibly, puffing her cheeks out and putting her free hand on her hips. Johnny was reminded of a cartoon wind cloud blowing leaves off trees.

'God, this is taking for bloody ever, innit?'

Johnny nodded.

'Did you book online?' She didn't wait for an answer, it clearly was an unnecessary protocol in her line of communication. 'I did but what's the bloody point? There's still a million kids here. How do they expect kids to sit quietly and behave when they've got to wait in the queue for so long? He'd better be worth it,' she warned, her eyebrows asserting her caution. 'I went to Santa at the Grange Centre last week and he was a right grumpy bugger. Kept telling Ryan that he had to be a good boy and behave nicely otherwise he'd get nuffing on Christmas. I mean, that's awful innit? Imagine Santa saying that he'd get nuffing. I couldn't believe it. I mean. I tell Ryan that. It's the only way to get him to do what I say, sometimes. I tell 'im that he better be good or else. But Santa can't say it, can he?'

'Well, I suppose…,' Johnny wasn't quite sure what to say. He felt pretty sure that that was supposed to be the whole quid pro quo about the arrangement. Child is good and on nice list: child gets present. Child on naughty list: gets nuffing; although he had always got nothing, and it had little to do with his behaviour. Indeed, sometimes it had even seemed to be the opposite. He had known plenty of naughty children in his younger years whose behaviour had seemed inversely proportional to the rewards by Santa. It seemed as though you could raise all kinds of merry hell, abuse someone, even kick the shit out of them and still get your dearest wish in the toy department. Santa didn't seem to give a figgy pudding about it. Johnny had never been able to work that out.

'I'm thirsty,' Ryan whined running back over and fishing into the bag on the handlebars, he pulled the bag down to see inside and in doing so flipped it up again, scraping Johnny's shins this time.

He stooped to pick it up again.

'Why don't you sit down in the buggy to drink that? And here, do you want some Haribo?' Placing the other child on the floor, the mother opened a packet of sweets and gave them both a fizzy drink. They stood looking up at her, like featherless birds in a nest.

'Great,' Johnny thought, that's just what he needs, to be more hyped up. Then he felt bad. Perhaps the child had behavioural difficulties. Will often talked about how difficult it was for children to conform to societal expectations when they couldn't understand social conventions. Perhaps the poor child was suffering with the noise and the unnaturally loud volume and brightness of the surroundings. He shouldn't judge the child or the parenting. He tried to think of something positive to say as they edged forward a bit more.

'How old are you?' he said to Ryan as he watched him tearing off the head of a jelly baby.

'Six,' the boy replied.

'Six?' Johnny repeated sounding impressed, because he imagined that's what children liked.

The boy nodded then made to run off again. The mother sighed. 'Stay here, Ryan, we're nearly there. Look. We are nearly at Santa's house.'

Come on Will. Hurry up, Johnny thought. How long can it take?

Just then, he saw him approaching through the crowds. Olivia wailing and wriggling in his arms.

'Here,' Will said, handing his daughter back to Johnny. 'I definitely drew the short straw there.'

'Huh? You think? Try standing here with Maleficent and Voldemort's love child,' he said nodding his head behind him. He took Olivia from Will's arms and kissed her on the nose, trying to calm her down. 'What's the matter with her?' he asked.

'Forgot bloody Pedro, didn't I?'

'Oh yeah, I called after you, but you didn't hear.'

'There was a queue for the toilet with the baby change. I nearly just lay her down on the concourse floor and changed her there. Why do they not have enough of those toilets?' he asked. 'If you look around here and see the hundreds of kids, why have they only got two in each toilet block? It's mad. I finally got in there, wiped it all down from the kid before and then laid her down and then I realized I didn't have the sodding penguin. She kicked off and then screamed all the way through the changing and in the lift back down. The looks I got. The usual judgement.' He made air quotes with his fingers, '"Dad doesn't know how to change the baby", or "Single dad only has the child at weekends, doesn't know what to do," or worse still, "gay dad, adopting baby – what an affront to all that is right and holy". I saw them all between here and Primark.'

Johnny kissed the side of his head and suddenly felt that he had come off better out of the bet. Ryan and his mother had been annoying, but she had just spoken to him as another parent. That was something. He tried to put Olivia in the buggy, but she arched her back. It was clear that the buggy was filled with sharp spikes that she had to avoid, why could her dads not see that?

Johnny was rummaging through the bags, a frown forming on his forehead. 'Where is it?' he was muttering.

'What's the matter,' Will asked taking a sip from his water bottle and combing his hand through his hair.

'Pedro, I can't find him.'

'What?' Will asked, understanding the gravitas of the statement, recapping his bottle, and joining in the search at once.

'He was here, and I held it up for you when you left, but you didn't see, so I put him back in the buggy, I'm sure of it. Now he isn't.'

He looked all around. The woman behind him had begun talking to the woman behind her. He interrupted.

'I'm sorry to interrupt,' he said to their glares, 'but, have you seen a penguin? A stuffed one. I think I heard you mention one earlier. It's my daughter's.'

'What?' she said, in the way that people do when they have actually heard what you've said but they need some response-processing time. 'A penguin? Er, well Ryan had one earlier, but it was a display thing... like the polar bears and reindeers.'

'I don't think it is a display,' Johnny said looking around. 'There aren't any others anywhere and penguins aren't Chrsitmassy, anyway,' he had to add. 'I think it might have been my daughter's.'

'Have you seen the Christmas penguin?' the woman asked her son.

'Well, it's not really a Christmas penguin,' Will added. Penguins are from the Antarctic and Santa is from the Arctic, so you know, you'd never see penguins with Santa,' This he realized sounded ridiculous and if not a little xenophobic. Not only was it an unnecessary qualification, given the seriousness of the situation, but because he was trying to explain the reasons why the two things couldn't be seen together due to the geography of their habitats, never mind the fact that one of them actually didn't even exist.

He turned to Ryan and crouched down to his level. His psychology training had taught him that this was a calming and cooperative position to adopt when speaking to children. Although, he might have read somewhere that it was the worst thing to do when confronting a temperamental dog and that you should remain standing to assert your authority. So, unsure of which to go with, he did a lean forward stance, aiming for somewhere in between authoritative and approachable. 'Do you know where the penguin is that you were playing with earlier?' he said in his most encouraging tone.

The boy looked up and shook his head defiantly.

'Oh, well you see. It is Olivia's here. And she is just a little baby. So, she doesn't understand why she doesn't have it. And it's her favourite. She feels happy when she has it,' Will explained, then went for the empathetic approach. 'I'm sure you have a favourite toy at home, that you wouldn't like anyone else to take away from you, is that right?'

Ryan looked sullen and glared at him from beneath menacing eyebrows. He remained silent.

Will stood up straight and glanced at Johhny as if to say. Oh, I thought that would work. I don't know what to do now. Reason, empathy and understanding perspective is my modus operandi. I'm not sure where to go next. He looked at the mother for some assistance.

'Ryan. Do you have this baby's toy or what?' she shouted. 'I'm telling you. If you don't tell me right now. We are going right home and there will be no Santa today or any other day, get it? And you will get nuffing on Christmas Eve.'

'It's over there,' Ryan said pointing to the drift of snow.

Will waited for him to go and retrieve it. He didn't.

'There's my good boy,' she said ruffling his head. 'Santa will be very pleased with you. I bet those elves will tell him what a good boy you are,' she said, nodding to the grotto assistants.

Give me strength, Will thought to himself as he waited for her to pause in her positive reinforcement long enough for him to ask if the good boy would kindly go and get it back.

'Do you think you could go and get it for me?' Will asked. 'Since you know where you put it.'

Ryan stared at him. 'I don't know where it is, just over

there under all that snow somewhere.'

Johnny smiled at the mother, recognizing Will's patience to be wearing thin and with his expectation of social norms more finely attuned than his own, made for a timely intervention. Olivia was still screaming, her cries tearing the already fraught nerves of the waiting populus to their last thread. 'Hey mate,' he said to Ryan, 'any chance you could help us find it? I'll come with you, yeah?'

Shrugging, Ryan led him over to the deep drifts. Will stayed with Olivia, cuddling, rocking, and bouncing her to the judgmental stares of the people in the queue while he internalized their unspoken thoughts. "Gay dad, adopted baby – what an affront to all that is right and holy…" the usual. He didn't know if they were thinking that, but that's what years of persecution can do to you.

There was no sign of Pedro. Johnny had at least expected to see two upturned flippers beneath the snow, like the feet of the Wicked Witch of the West, crushed by Dorothy's crashed farmhouse. Digging around in the fake, fluffy flakes, he tried not to notice the stares of those with nothing better to do in their slow pilgrim's progress than cast their disapproval upon him. He imagined that he and Ryan looked like father and son, playing in the fake, display snow, flaunting all the rules of propriety, disrespecting property, behaving badly like two naughty elves. Then he caught sight of the actual elves, eyeing him disdainfully. One was on their way over. Oh God, Johnny thought. He was going to be told off, in front of everyone, for something he hadn't done. Some things never changed.

Where was the bloody thing?' he thought as she swished the snow from side to side, wishing that Christmas had come early and brought Ryan his cyborg hand. It would come in useful, round about now. Just then, his own hands found Pedro and he withdrew it and held it aloft, kneeling in the snow and beaming at Will, as if he had won gold in the winter Olympics.

He handed it to Olivia whose eyes lit up immediately. The tears stopped and her body went soft and pliable, like proven dough. Suddenly the spikes in the buggy retracted and she allowed herself to be lowered in and snuggled in her sheepskin liner, clutching Pedro to her heart.

'Thank bloody God and all his angels for that,' Will said releasing a deep sigh. They each took a breath, relishing the quiet calm.

The mother returned to her chat with the person behind and Ryan went to see if he could wrestle the large bauble off the tree.

He could.

The queue moved and, contrary to their shackled shuffles up to now, Johnny and Will were able to take a proper stride forward. Last year in Spain, they had each bought a pair of cheap espadrilles in the market. They were tied together with elastic, with enough allowance for you to be able to see if they fitted without being able to take a proper step. Then, after the purchase was made, the elastic was snipped, and they were free to walk normally. It was very emancipating.

'God, what a bloody nightmare this has turned out to be?' Will said. 'I hate to say I told you so, but…'

Johnny gave him a side eye. 'We are talking our daughter to see Santa Claus for her first ever Christmas. It may be a bit fraught, and I may now be under some sort of elvish subpoena for criminal damage, but she will never have another first Christmas. We will never get this time back again. That's why we came and however difficult it has been, waiting in line with flippin' Chucky back there, it will be worth it when we have that photo with Santa to look back on forever.'

Will rolled his eyes. 'But she's so young. She's not going to remember any of it. She's still in nappies for goodness' sake. And believe me I know, as I have just changed one at great personal trauma.'

Johnny made a face.

'It is mad, taking a baby to see Santa. Ivan the Terrible

there is six. He's a bit of a monster, but at least he knows what it's all about. Livvy hasn't got a clue. What's the point?'

'The point is... my love, that she will have a photo with Santa for her first Christmas and we will send it to your parents...,' he paused, letting Will visualize the happy moment. 'And we will put one in her first-year album, and it will be amazing. And then every year after that, we will bring her to see Santa and she will have a photo with us to show her that we will do anything and give her everything and show her every wondrous experience in the whole world. Because we are two gay guys and we never thought, with all the hate and prejudice that we have had to fight, that we would be able to share our lives with each other, never mind with a baby and to make our family complete. And she had no one, given up and left by a mother who couldn't cope with her. She is ours and we will give her everything to show her what she means to us and to give her the wonderful life she deserves. And if that means waiting for hours in the heat, with Jingle Bells on repeat, screaming kids and sore feet to see bloody, sodding Santa Claus because that's what kids do, then that is what we'll do. So, that, at least for me, is the point.'

'You might have just made a very convincing argument there,' Will conceded. 'She is worth everything and deserves everything. And so do you.'

An elf approached, the bells jingling on his toes and his cheeks were painted with a pinkish red grease paint. He smiled at them and checked his iPad.

'Name please,' he said in a Glaswegian accent smiling a wide comic grin.

'Kendall, Olivia Kendall' Will said.

The elf scrolled, his finger swiping up as rows of names sped by.

'J..., K... Ah... Kendall. Here we are, Thank you, excellent. 'Now just a bit of '*elf* and safety,' he smiled and docked his head in irony.

'God, how many times a day do you have to say that?' Will

asked.

'Ach too many,' the elf replied. 'And it's only the first week of December. I can see me being the cause of any risks to health by Christmas Eve,' he joked, 'coz, I'd have lost my jingling mind,'

Johnny laughed. There wasn't anything that could take the shine off the moment. In fact, the elf's attitude was simply adding to the magic.

'So, if you can leave the buggy outside when you go in, that would be great please,' the elf said. 'There's not much room in there and if you could just sign here to say that you won't take any of your own photos inside that would also be great.' He presented the tablet and pointed to a box for a signature. 'Some of our elves haven't given consent, so… Also, if you could just sign here, just use your finger… That's great, just need an electronic signature to say that you will adhere to this policy.'

Wary of signing documents without reading them fully, Will leaned in to take a closer look. 'I haven't got my glasses. Sorry, what does it say?' he asked the elf. 'What's the general gist?'

'It's about sitting on Santa's lap,' the elf explained.

'Oh of course,' Johnny nodded. 'Child protection. Can't have children sitting on his lap, these days. I get it.'

The elf looked at him. 'Well, yes, for the children, obviously, but it is also to protect Santa, both in the respect that he can't be wrongly accused of anything, and also, it is an infringement of his personal space, so he would have to give consent to for any child to sit on his lap without asking first.'

Will and Johnny looked at each other.

'It's policy,' the elf said.

'Right, yes of course,' Will said.

'And just one final one here too, please,' the elf said gesturing to another space for Will's fingertip signature.

When had Santa become so wrapped up in litigation? he wondered. In the meantime, Johhny was secretly worrying whether any of these forms and signatures were in fact the wonderland grotto seeking damages for trespassing on the display; unpermitted distribution of fake snow fluff; disturbance of the peace in respect of Olivia's screaming; and intimidation and coercion of a minor, in getting Ryan, the devil spawn to hunt for an interred animal, presumed dead; and the introduction of a non-native species from the Antarctic into the delicate ecosystem of the Arctic.

'What's this for?' Will asked.

Hmm, Johnny mused. Will was obviously secretly concerned about these things too.

'Staff abuse,' the elf replied. 'It's a reiteration of that sign, over there.'

The men turned to face where the elf was pointing. A large red sign, surrounded by a border that resembled candy canes read "Please treat our staff with respect. Abuse of any kind will not be tolerated".

'Abuse?' Johnny scoffed. 'Who'd abuse Santa and his elves for God's sake.'

'You'd be surprised,' the elf replied.

'No, really?' Will asked.

'Yep. He gets his beard pulled, his shins kicked, and that's just the parents,' the elf laughed. 'No, I'm joking. The parents don't usually do anything physical, but they do shout. They have a go at him if he doesn't say the right thing, and some kids have been known to punch and kick if he doesn't agree with what they've asked for – like a puppy or a pet rabbit, or something like that. Or if they ask for something impossible and he tries to help out the parents by saying that his elves might have trouble making that particular thing. The kids then go crazy saying that he is Santa, and he can make anything happen and that if he doesn't, he is rubbish.'

'Wow!' Johnny said shaking his head. 'That's a lot. I had no idea being Santa was so risky. I get the elf and safety thing now is more about the safety of the elf.'

The elf laughed. 'Yeah' he said, sharing a look with a girl

elf who was guarding the door, and she gave the nod of the shared experience.

'Right, you're up,' the elf said, evidently satisfied that all legal requirements had been met to his satisfaction 'There you go Olivia,' he said, bending into a low bow and gesturing the way forward. 'Have fun meeting Santa. May all your Christmas wishes come true.'

Will and Johnny smiled and parked the buggy to one side. Will lifted Olivia out and she looked wide eyed at the fairy lights twinkling above her. She made excitable cooing noises and pointed at them and bounced up and down in Wills arms, rocking over his forearm as he held her. She put her head back and gazed up as they walked into the grotto area, which was all black with a starry lit sky.

The girl elf smiled at them, checked her iPad, and opened the door. 'Santa, here we have Olivia to see you,' she said and ushered them through.

Will and Johnny smiled at Santa and went to sit on the bench opposite him, suddenly feeling very silly. Two grown men sitting opposite a legendary figure which was really a man dressed up in a suit. How much of the shared pretense were they supposed to acknowledge?

*

Olivia took in the small room and studied the man in the corner. There were eyes, that much she recognized. The two men who loved her had those. But they had more to their faces that could help to create expression. This person did not. His, was all covered with white hair. Was he smiling or cross, or worse, impassive? She couldn't read it at all. Didn't he know that she was a baby and needed to be able to study these features? How would she know whether he was kindly, or to be feared? What emotion should his face stir in her? She had so little understanding of the world yet, her only cues were in the faces of others.

Her own eyes glanced upwards at her own people. Perhaps she could glean from them whether this experience was to be enjoyed or feared? They looked a little uncomfortable, but also smiling. They stared down at her, willing her to be… What? Excitable and happy about this situation? But she wasn't. This was a small dark place, hot and stuffy with strange lights and sounds. They were stimulating, certainly, like the mobile that hung above her changing table at home. She felt sparks in her mind, like bright lights as she tried to make sense of it all. The colouring was different to what she was used to at home, and outside, where the air brushed her face and entered her nose, soothing her to sleep. What was this place?

The man with the white furry face leant in close. She recoiled backwards to retreat. Then he reached his finger out for her to hold. Perhaps grasping it would help her sense what this was all about. Her people were smiling. Their faces seemed more relaxed now, encouraging even. Their sounds seemed excited. Perhaps this was a safe place after all? She wondered what her plushy was making of the whole thing. If Pedro were confident, then she might be too. She was suddenly aware of his absence. Without even thinking about it, her bottom lip seemed to be being dragged down at the corners, and a well of sadness filled her like the milk in her bottle. She glanced at the eyes of her people, who seemed to read her thoughts, understanding, present in them.

'She wants Pedro,' Will said looking all around. 'Crap! Sorry Santa,' he said, covering his mouth and looking contrite as if he were seven and worried about being put on the naughty list. 'It's her favourite toy. It's in the buggy outside. I didn't… er, we, didn't think she'd need it in here. Thought she'd be alright without it for a few minutes, with all the lights and everything.'

'Oh, dear,' Santa said kindly. 'Poor Olivia. What are we going to do?'

He looked to the men before him. 'Shall we do a quick

photo before she really gets into it?' he suggested.

'Might be too late for that,' Will said.

'Livvy…, Livvy…,' Johnny sang trying to coax her back from the edge of the abyss. 'Olivia… Let's have a smile with Santa, shall we?' he said, bouncing her on his knee. 'Because this is your first Christmas and we will never get this chance back again,' he whispered.

Will touched his husband's arm, recognizing that longing for what has been lost was as painful as longing for what was to come. He knew that Johnny yearned for a whole album full of childhood Santa pictures for Olivia, because he wanted her to be able to look back on them and understand what she meant to them. But he also knew that this represented Johnny's grieving for his own lost childhood Christmases. For the years when he was neither on Santa's nice nor naughty list. When he was on no list at all. 'We can come back another time,' he said gently. 'I'll have a word with the elf, and we'll book again. There are still weeks before Christmas. We've got plenty of time.'

Johnny turned to him and smiled.

'We have got plenty of time,' Will repeated deliberately. 'And I will stand out there again for hours for you to have this,' he said.

Olivia threw her head back and screamed.

Santa winced. He was no stranger to screaming children in the grotto. Many a photo over the years had captured a child's misery at meeting Santa for the first time. But something with this family felt different.

'Why don't we get the penguin? Santa asked. He shared a look with the girl elf and called her over. 'Can we get the stuffed toy from the buggy, please?'

'Sure,' she said, and she popped outside, her toe bells, jingling as she did so.

'Really Santa?' Johnny said, speaking to him with all the incredulous wonder of a child. 'But what about your queue?

Have you got time?'

'Dave, please,' Santa said, pulling down his beard and shaking hands with them both. 'It's no trouble. I know the queue piles up, but these moments with Santa are defining and carry lots of significance for families. Let's see if we can't calm her down. The queue can wait a bit. Besides, my elves tell me, there's a couple out there who are definitely on the naughty list, have been pulling the baubles of the tree and riding the reindeer display. They can wait.'

The girl elf returned with Pedro and although she had ceased crying, Johnny noticed that Olivia was eying her warily, seemingly doubtful as to whether the girl with the pointed ears was going to hand her her favourite comforter or keep it to herself. Still, she seemed content. He noted that he might have to admit that penguins did have something to do with Santa after all.

*

In the end, the man with eyes but no face was not to be feared. My people were very happy with him, and I had Pedro, so I could afford to go along with the situation. The lights were actually quite startling, and I called out to them. This made my people laugh. They like it when I make my own sounds, particularly when I make the sound that is like da. They kiss me and say clever girl and clap their hands. So, I will keep doing that. I smile and clap my hands and they like that too. I am not sure why. I suppose I will keep doing what they seem to enjoy. This is how I will learn to do and say things, to behave in a way that suits people's expectations.

I have two people. They are both Da Da. My person, Johnny, looks very happy that we are here with the man with the furry face (I touched it, it feels soft, like Pedro). My person, Will, looks very happy that my person, Johnny looks happy. I think this is what love might be.

There is a lot to learn, being a baby. People think you sleep all the time, but you don't. You spend all the time trying to understand what is going on around you. And you are taught to do and like the things that other people do or like. My people talk to me. Usually in the rocking chair, at bedtime. I am sleepy, but that is the time they feel most able to share their thoughts and wishes and dreams for me.

It is a lot of responsibility, trying to bridge the gaps lost in their own worlds. It would seem that both of them feel that they are missing something.

Maybe, when I am bigger, I will be able do the things that I want to do or like, myself. Or maybe not. I am not sure yet how everything works.

Perhaps that is what it means to be in the world. That you can't ever just be you because you are always part of someone else and their thoughts and hopes and dreams.

*

Johnny placed the photo in a frame and set another into a Christmas album. Olivia looked more wary than content, as if she were trying to make sense of the whole Santa thing and finding it an imbalanced equation. But he had done it. He had given her something that he had never had. And isn't that what parents did at Christmas? Being made a parent only recently, he didn't know, and had regretfully had precious little personal experience to draw upon. However, he was fairly sure that indulging them in every trope and Christmas experience, most specifically those to do with Santa, whether they understood it or not, was the ultimate way of showing them you love them.

Cave

There is a small robin. It gathers twigs and moss to
make its home in the hawthorn hedge.
For is it not a basic need for all life to feel safe from
the harsh realities of the outside?
For many though, it was not enough that the harsh
world existed outside, it existed within also.
A home can be a cage.
A castle can be a prison.
A cave can be a crypt.
But a crypt can be a cavern.
And a cavern, a grotto.
And a grotto, a dwelling place for Gods.

Grotto

Nudging the internal glass door with her shoulder, reluctant to put down the bags that were balanced in her hands, Laura stepped from the foyer and into the school. Kristen rushed forward and opened it from within with a broad smile that revealed her large, white teeth. An expensive watch slid over her knuckles.

'Thanks,' Laura said, 'I was wondering how I was going to manage that,'

'You're over this way,' Kristen said, beckoning Laura to follow her before she was fully through the door. It began to close on her handbag and Laura had to skip through before she was trapped.

Kristen had marched ahead and was halfway across the gym hall before she stopped and turned with an air of impatience that Laura wasn't walking to heel.

'Sorry,' Laura said unnecessarily as she followed her.

'The shed is obviously through that door, but you can prep things in the year five classroom if you want. Emma texted, she and Sally are on the way but caught up in roadworks on Kenbar hill, and Liz is coming in about half an hour.'

Laura deposited her armful of supplies: Wonderland in a box. There was more in the car, it would take at least four trips. Although she had planned the thematic design in her mind, it wasn't the same as feeling the space. She took the key and let herself out of the classroom. There was a small piece of grass with stepping-stones that led to the cabin. Her pre-lit reindeer from home were destined in her design to graze here, nibbling the carrots she would scatter on the ground, after spraying it with fake snow first of course. She would chew a couple and spit them out, her mastication lending credence to the notion that real reindeer had been here to eat carrot snacks. It was a practice they did at home too, for the children. It made it more realistic to show that reindeer had landed from their transit across the rooftops.

She thought she had anticipated the practical issues there might be to resolve such as extension cables, and wall fixings. and had prepared herself for all, hammer and nails, Blu Tack, gaffer tape, masking tape, cables, batteries, screwdriver. Staple gun, paper clips. It didn't take long to learn the tricks.

It was her happy space though, being creative and artistic, fashioning wonder out of everyday items, sheets were snowy landscapes, chairs could become a train, windows covered with schoolwork could become a starlight night sky, a bench could be a sofa. A plain wall could be a chimney breast. A cardboard box, a fireplace. A dining chair… a throne. A grotto was a home for gods, and gods needed a throne.

Hildy broke her reverie.

'Knock knock, cooeee. Only me,' she called. 'Lots to do, eh?' she said looking around and picking up the stacks of reading books. 'How they think we can make something of this place, I don't know,' she said, 'and it's freezing out here.' She rubbed her arms to reinforce the point.

Laura's nose was red, and it did have a chill, but she knew that within a few hours it would be transformed by her hand.'I think it will be lovely,' she said. 'It's nicer than the PPA room. It has far more character and is in keeping with Santa's own house. I haven't seen any picture books that show a photocopier, guillotine, shelves full of sugar paper and a letter from Ofsted in Santa's workshop.' She smiled wryly.

'Well, I'll just see if Kristen needs any help and then I'll be back, okay?' Hildy said brightly. 'Many hands make light work, and all that. We'll all chip in to help.'

'Take your time,' Laura said as genuinely as she could. She did actually mean it. Hildy's help could be counted upon no further than to warm the room with the amount of hot air she expelled, through all her chatting. When it came to physically achieving anything tangible, it was better to resource other hands to make the work light. Her skills and interest were more suited to using her local contacts and schmoozing the local businesses for the raffle prizes than mucking in with the real work. But Laura had to concede that there was a place for that too. Asking people to part with their money didn't come naturally to Laura but it was a necessary part of the fayre. She, however, much preferred her efforts to be directed behind the scenes; making the magic happen for the children. Fundraising was all well and good, but for her, imbuing the world with Christmas spirit and making the impossible possible was the real reason for the season. Whilst she sought no credit or acclaim in her endeavours, there was some small part of her that felt a twinge of hurt when she opened the local newspaper after the event to see Hildy's grinning face between those of some local business dignitary and the Headteacher, the caption lauding her participation in the festive event. Not even Kristen ever made it into the halls of fame, and she was the head of the PFA. It was like most things, Laura reflected. No one ever saw the humble workers when they were gazing at the Queen Bee.

And no one ever saw her up late at night, sourcing the wonders for the winterland, or snapped the person sweeping up the mince pie crumbs that had got trodden into the carpet of the Year 3 classroom.

'I've provided tea and coffee and biscuits in the staff room,' Kristen said magnanimously, which Laura knew from past events meant that she had signed off the petty cash slip from the PFA money they had all helped to raise, and that some other poor minion, probably Hayley, as she lived next to Tesco Express, was commissioned to bring them in.

'Lovely, thanks,' Laura said.

'Is there something wrong?' Kristen asked.

'No,' Laura replied, her hands on her hips, still in her

reverie at how to realise her design.

'Oh,' Kristen said. 'It's just that you haven't made a start yet. Chop! Chop! What are you waiting for? Christmas?' she laughed loudly at her joke and spun on her heel.

'I've actually got to bring in more stuff from the car,' she explained. 'I'll pop out and then might make a coffee when I come back in. Emma, Sal, and Liz will probably be here by then.'

'Well, they'd better be,' Kristen said impatiently, checking her watch. 'I haven't heard anything to the contrary and I explicitly told everyone to inform me if there were any problems. You remember me saying that, don't you?' She stared at Laura as if daring her to deny her words. 'Honestly. Sometimes, I think people just think I am head of the PFA for the good of my health, rather than trying to make a difference for the educational wellbeing of our children. It is a heavy cross to bear and I need commitment.'

Laura nodded and muttered something about the roadworks and the team's repeated demonstrations of loyalty to the cause at all the previous events like the summer carnival, Halloween parties, Junior discos, Sports' Day refreshments and so on. She also wanted to point out that said team were not employees on a thirty-five hour a week contract, they were volunteers, because they *all* wanted to support the school and their children. It was not Kristen's personal mission. Also, and most importantly, somewhere between the last Christmas Fayre and this one, Sally had lost her husband in a battle that he was too infirm to fight. Even finding the strength to get out of bed and keep going, not least, honouring her former grotto responsibilities, made her a goddess in Laura's eyes.

Laura had her head in the boot when Emma and Sally approached. They reached in and took bags and rolls of white fabric and an electric reindeer. A throne back made of gold cardboard with a red satin padded seat back stood on the back seat and Sally picked it up. 'Oh, I love this,' she said. 'Did you make it?'

'Yeah, I use it for the kids' birthdays. I tie it to the dining room chair, makes them feel like royalty for the day.' She smirked. 'It's got their initials drawn here,' she gestured to a filigree font in which there was a curly B and M entwined, but I don't think anyone will notice. It just occurred to me that we needed to give the chair more grandeur. We have the big rocking chair for Santa, but we don't have anything for the children. I thought it might make them feel a bit more special if they have their own throne.'

'You think of everything,' Emma said hoisting one of three electric reindeer under her arm. 'Who's this guy?' she asked, 'Rudolf? And have I broken his neck?' She looked alarmed. 'Why's it dangling like this?'

Laura giggled, 'That is Comet and he's not broken, I just had to detach the latch pin to get him in the boot. It's adjustable, so you can have them in different attitudes, either looking up to the sky, or grazing, nose to the ground.'

'Speaking of standing around with your head in the air, where's Kristen?' Emma asked.

Laura laughed. 'Ah, she's busying herself with her clipboards and wearing out her pointing finger, directing people to places.'

'Well,' Emma said defensively, 'She'd better not direct Sally anywhere or she'll find herself and her clipboard, stapled to the top of the Christmas tree.'

They laughed and entered the school, following Laura across the gym where Hildy was rearranging all the bottles on the tombola as fast as Jemma Gaffrey was putting them out. 'No. Aesthetics, Jemma. Think of Aesthetics. You can't put Lidl shampoo next to my bottle of Irish Whiskey. I donated that. It should be on the top shelf to attract people. It's single malt, for goodness' sake.'

'Sorry guys,' Liz said as she came into the reading shed. 'Grace had swimming this morning and Karl's car is in the garage, so I had to drop her back first. What have I missed?'

'Nothing yet. We've just been unloading Laura's car,' Emma said. 'We haven't come across the industrial snow machine, or the Zamboni for the ice-skating rink, but I think they are in there beneath the sleigh and the five other reindeer.'

Laura smirked. 'Let's get coffees from the staff room, then we can begin,' she said, moving towards the door. 'Kristen has provided provisions,'

'Hayley, you mean,' Liz smiled.

As the morning advanced, the reading shed retreated, like an animal threatened with thrown stones, skulking back into the trees. With the passing of an hour, the small cabin had undergone the most extreme cosmetic surgical procedures permissible at one time. Its façade had been clad in slabs of plywood gingerbread, the mortar, voluptuous bulges of white icing, and painted jelly tots framed its windows. Standing to attention on either side of the door were life-size guards, two dimensional sentinels, in the parade uniform of a Nutcracker. Snowflakes lay on the ground, reindeer nibbling pieces of crunched carrot hidden amongst the blades of grass. The path, an avenue of candy canes, as tall as broomsticks, from which hung black-framed lanterns with candles within. Between them stood huge lollipops, the size of the ones that cross children safely across the road, their round heads swirled in red and green. Hypnotic and entreating. Inside, a small log burner filled the otherwise fabric darkened room with a warm orange glow and a basket of chopped logs sat at its feet, like a loyal dog. The windows, though not yet noon, looked out onto a starlight night sky.

Beside the mantelpiece, its fibreboard body, chiselled and tanned to the shape and colour of ancient oak, a tall tree stood, adorned with trinkets of red and green that shone in the firelight. Red velvet cushions, sat on the rocking chair, like the robe of a king. Lush garlands of dark green foliage looped across the top of the low walls and tartan bows of green and red fixed them to the roofline. Gift boxes, wrapped in shiny paper and dressed with blousy bows sat around the tree, like children listening to a storyteller.

A smell of mulled spice filled the air, ginger and cinnamon, nutmeg and pine and a plate of mince pies sat on a small table, a glass of milk beside them and a sprig of holly on top. Candles flicked on every sill and surface, their flames a clever facsimile of fire.

'I think you should do the honours,' Emma said handing the power cable to Laura. 'It was all your work, the planning and resourcing and everything.'

'No, we're a team,' Laura said determinedly. 'We'll all do it.'

She counted them in and together they pressed the switch. The fairy lights filled the room with stars.

'It's breathtaking,' Sally said, tears spring to her eyes. 'My girls will love this.'

Her friends encircled her in an embrace, which at any other time would be recognizable as a group hug, here it served to be the words they didn't have.

'I wanted to do sherry because that's what we have at home for Santa,' Laura said, reading Sally's heart and trying to lighten it with banality. 'But I didn't think it was very PC with the kids around.'

'It's okay, Dave probably has some in a hip flask,' Emma joked. 'I know I would, if I had to do nothing but sit in a shed and listen to kids asking for stuff for three hours.'

'He should see if he could win that bottle of Hildy's single malt,' Liz added with a smile. 'Where is she, by the way? I thought she was supposed to be helping.'

'Typical Hildy,' Emma said. 'Everywhere and nowhere.'

Sally felt her ears deafen to the banter, as if someone had wrapped them in felt. She looked at the wrapped gifts. Stacked artfully around each other, they appeared like a little village, each one, a little house with a world of wonder within. Of course, she knew that they were just for show. That they were just empty shells that looked presentable on the outside but hid the void inside. She knew that feeling.

Whilst she appreciated Laura's work, part of her wondered whether perhaps it was irresponsible, surrounding a tree with so many gifts. What message did this give to the children? That it wasn't really Christmas, unless you could create a small urban development beneath the branches of the evergreen tree? Would every child, who entered this cave of wonders, expect the same plethora of presents under their own respective trees on Christmas morning? Would hers? The girls had put bikes on their list to Santa, and she had got them. She had chosen them, had arranged them to be stored in one of Emma's barns until Christmas Eve, their own small house not having anywhere suitable for concealment. But funds were short, and with most of them allocated to the bicycles, and some retained for filling the requisite stockings, there wasn't much left. Certainly not nearly enough to create a gift village at the base of their small tree.

'Are you alright, Sal?' Emma asked, tapping her knee. 'You looked miles away there. We were talking about the snow.'

'Sorry,' Sally smiled, 'snow, yes.'

'Well,' Laura explained as they closed the portal to the fantastical world and made their way back to the classroom. 'In the past, we have made the corridor like a winter wonderland, haven't we? But as we don't have that now, I was thinking that it seems a bit strange to not have any transition space. It might be hard for the kids, who use the shed every day at school, to imagine that it is Santa's real house. It is a bit of an imagination stretch to be standing here by the year four toilets, reading phonic displays and multiplication tables and then in a few short steps, feel transported to the North Pole.'

Sally caught up. 'Oh, yes, so what shall we do?'

'Well, I was thinking that we could dress this bit up a bit too. That's why I have all this white fabric for the floor. We can pile it up and I've got these white polystyrene balls. I thought we could make snowmen, look with hats, and black buttons and carrot noses.'

'Jeez, Lor. How long did it take to get this stuff sorted?' Emma asked.

'Well, I've been planning it for a while and picking up bits and pieces from charity shops now and then. Then, I've got this midnight blue starry fabric for the sky, and we can put more fairy lights through.'

'I don't mean to be a buzzkill, but have we got enough time for all of this?' Liz asked. 'The fayre is in a few hours, not *Christmas yet to come.*'

Hayley appeared with a tray of mugs. 'How's it going, guys?'

It seemed a rhetorical question as she looked too harried to wait for the answer. 'Just collecting the empties,' she said. 'We haven't got many, so I'm trying to wash them up as we go along.' She glanced at the biscuit plate. 'Sorry, the biscuits aren't more interesting, Tesco Express didn't have a great selection today.'

The friends shared a look of understanding.

'Do you ever think that we've been doing this for too long?' Emma laughed after Hayley had gone.

Laura smiled. 'Anyway,' she continued, putting the top hat on Emma's head. 'It seems like a lot, but it shouldn't take long. Oh and look at this, I've got this projector that makes it look like it's snowing, and I thought we could play Christmas music through these speakers.'

Liz was handling a box of fairy lights. 'Are these new?' she asked.

'Someone donated them apparently,' Laura said. 'Hildy just popped them in, but they haven't been PAT tested so I don't think we should use them. Don't want the whole school blowing up.'

'Don't think we should be singlehandedly responsible for the destruction of the planet either,' Emma scoffed. 'Look at all this stuff, the fairy lights, the reindeer, the snow projector, the fake log burner, the sound system… Energy crisis? What energy crisis?'

'I know,' Laura said, her face a grimace of guilt. 'I was thinking that too. It's not great, is it? We teach the children to turn off lights when they leave a room and switch the TV off standby to save the planet, and then say that it is okay to go wild at Christmas, lighting up the kitchen to the chimney top and everything in between. But it's Christmas. Can't we just go mad for one day and then be good for the rest of the year? Throw caution to the winter wind?'

'That's what I'm going with,' Sally added. 'Life is hard. You need to take the fun when you can get it.'

The others nodded in silent agreement.

Laura thought about their words. She had been mindful to source everything as responsibly as she could, finding things in charity shops or making them herself out of wood and cardboard. The fairy lights were LED and had such a low energy draw, surely, they would be okay, and it could be argued that the fireplace was actually functional heating, to keep Dave from going hypothermic, not just a frivolous aesthetic. The tartan curtains she had added would insulate the usually single-glazed windows, and the snow was simply a load of old sheets that would have otherwise gone to the dump. She felt that she had done well to meet the Christmas demands without a rape of the planet. Granted, perhaps they could have done without the snow projector and the music, but then, would those things for just three hours make that much difference when the skylines of Tokyo, Hong Kong and New York blaze their lights, night in and night out, so distinctively they are visible from space?   But then, she thought, if everyone decided that their little bit didn't count because other huge conglomerates continued to belch out their energy-guzzling products, then no one would make a change and we would remain in homeostasis.

'I think it is all great,' Sally began, not wanting the Climate

Crisis to diminish the expectant joy for her daughters. 'My girls really need this, and there may be other children who do too. We can promise to save energy for the whole rest of the year. But just for today, could they have a little glimpse of joy and wonder? They really need it.'

Putting her arm around her shoulder, Laura gave her a squeeze.

'The only thing I was wondering.' Sally added, 'was whether we could just have fewer presents under the tree? I know they look amazing, but I worry that children will expect to have more if they see lots here.'

Laura's first thought was one of disappointment, that reducing the collection of presents would be detrimental to the display effect, but she could see Sally's point. 'I hadn't thought about that,' she admitted. I think you're right. Let's up the wonder and dial down the commerciality.'

'I'm all over that,' Emma agreed. 'What's the beauty of a Christmas celebration…, twinkling lights, nice food with friends, cosy rooms, natural beauty like snow and pine trees. The rest is just too …extra.'

'Thanks,' Sally said, smiling at her friends.

'Do you ever wonder whether it is right to do a grotto at all?' Liz said thoughtfully.

The others looked at her as she stood on a chair pinning lights to the ceiling tiles. 'I mean, perhaps we shouldn't be perpetuating this whole Santa thing at all.'

'It's interesting you say that,' Emma said. 'The boys came home with a letter from Miss Jennings. Did you get one from Grace's teacher?'

Liz shook her head in confusion. 'No, what letter?'

'It was about Santa, saying that they were still going to do their letters as per tradition, but in addition, she wanted to take them out to the hospital and the train station and your nursing home, in fact.'

'Oh, yeah, Holly did ask me whether she could bring the

children in to sing one day, which I agreed to. The residents will love it, but I didn't realise it was alongside anything else. Grace's teacher didn't send one. I wonder if they just didn't put it in the bag.'

'No, I think it was only Miss Jennings,' Laura said, 'because none of the younger ones got it either. I think she just wants to promote the notion of giving and sharing as per the original St Nicholas, rather than just getting, and receiving through letters.'

'Oh,' Liz said, 'That's cool.'

'It's nice,' Sally said. 'I think it's a good idea. Rosie did mention it. She said that they did a maths problem about how half of them had Monopoly, and the other half didn't, and if the ones who didn't want theirs anymore gave it to those who did, they wouldn't need to buy new ones.'

'I know,' Emma agreed. 'The boys mentioned it too. I think it's great. It's exactly what Rob and I have thought. There's already so much stuff out there, yet people buy more. Why not just share what we have when we no longer want it?'

'Rosie said that Miss Jennings told them to think very carefully about what to put on their list, because if it was just something they could already get from a friend or the charity shop, they don't need to ask Santa for it.'

'I like that,' Emma said. 'We don't believe in lists anyway. Rob and I did lists when we were children, but when we had the twins, we agreed that we would still give them a present from Santa, but it would be surprises, just so they wouldn't ask for a whole load of on trend presents that you had to fight people to get, or that are impossible to find.'

'I wish we'd done that,' Laura said. 'We've gone mad trying to find that bloody bunyip for Briony.'

'Oh yeah. How's that going?' asked Liz, 'Any luck?'

'No, I think we are going to have to get her some Fimo and write a note from Santa to say that she needs to make it herself.'

The others laughed. 'Oh no. Do you think she might guess

then that Santa's not real?'

'Quite possibly,' Laura said. 'Though I can't say I'd be devastated. I love all the magic and stuff and their little faces when they get so excited, but it is all such a hassle for parents, and they think he can work bloody miracles. I can't bear the disappointment if she wakes on Christmas morning and it's not what she expects.'

'And she's not of the age when the cardboard box is more fun to play with than the actual toy, is she?' Liz said. 'I've had that one. We spent a fortune on this sand digger thing that Elliot wanted when he was little and Karl went down to Hamleys in October to make sure we got it, and then on Christmas morning, he looked for it for five minutes then just sat in the box with his construction helmet on, pretending he was down a hole, like a still-closeted member of the Village People.'

Emma laughed. 'What about if you get the Fimo and make it for her?' Emma suggested.

'I did think of that,' Laura admitted, 'but what if it's crap? Then she'll think that Santa won't believe she's been a good girl and got her something nice. The elves in the workshop are supposed to be master craftsmen, able to make everything perfectly, and even if they can't, they can use magic to make it. If I create what is essentially something from the Playdoh Little Shop of Horrors, that's going to be her hopes dashed. At least by giving her the opportunity to do it herself, it keeps some of the magic alive.'

'God, there's so much wrong with that statement isn't there?' Emma said. 'We teach the kids that Santa is infallible, like some sort of Christmas pope. This amazing guy who can make all their wishes come true. A fur-trimmed Pharoh. Then we encourage our already commercialised children to be greedy and ask for loads of stuff with no clue of the economic cost to us. Then we control their behaviour with a carrot and stick approach... literally, reindeer carrots,' she smirked. 'And we let them think they are being watched and reported about by a creepy elf, which is just another way to make money and add more stress to already knackered parents at this time of year…, and hypocrisy of hypocrisies, he's encouraged to do all these naughty things and then has the audacity to report back to Santa that the child's been naughty.'

Reaching into the corner, Liz fixed the last of the lights up in the night sky uncertainly, unsure whether Emma was suggesting they just dismantle the whole grotto on the spot and dump the entire contents of the North Pole in Kristen's lap.

Emma wasn't finished. 'Then, as if that's not bad enough, parents get into loads of debt to meet all these expectations and demands, and the kids wake up Christmas morning with all their dreams having come true and think Santa's flipping God, while the only credit the parents get, is the balance on their Barclaycard with twenty-three percent interest on it.'

Liz smirked, 'So remind me why we're doing this grotto then and making it meet every traditional requirement of a Dickensian Victorian Christmas?'

'Probably because the kids love it, and we love our kids, and we'll do anything so that they won't feel sad or disappointed,' Sally said quietly.

Emma held her hand. 'It is that, Sal. I know it is. And I know that it will probably never change. Rob and I will keep doing things the way we do, so it doesn't even affect me. And I know that doesn't suit everyone, I just don't like to see the bad side of Christmas, when it should all be for good.'

'So, are we allowed to carry on making snowmen?' Laura teased.

Emma made a face. 'Yes,' she relented. 'I suppose.'

'Good,' Laura said. 'I thought we were going to be carrying everything back to the car for a minute there.'

Liz laughed. 'Could you imagine Kristen's face if we downed tools and refused to do a grotto this year?'

'She would have apoplexy,' Emma said. 'Anyway, we would never leave the fayre without a grotto. It is our thing.

We're like the Vestal Virgins, never letting the fire going out.'

'Well, not the virgin bit,' Laura smirked.'

'Yeah,' Emma laughed. 'But no, really. I may not approve of Santa, per se, but the principles of joy and comfort and wellbeing transcend the two mythologies. Deities are deities, whoever they are. Believed to be able to offer all sorts; worshipped and offered sacrifices; attended to by minions who do their bidding, or disciples that perpetuate their tropes; accommodated in elabourate throne rooms and given chariots to ride in. Whether you are Osiris, Zeus, or Santa, your home is your temple. Your grotto, the domicile of deities.

'And this grotto might be for Father Christmas, but we are the women to keep the flame burning. We are like acolytes of Hestia, our goddess being the ruler of the hearth, of family and we, are her chosen ones who will never let it go out.'

'So, the electric log burner I got for the shed isn't just to keep Dave warm?' Laura commented, inclining herself to the notion that she was a significant part in the tropes of a deity. 'It represents an eternal flame, keeping the joy going.'

'Yeah,' Emma agreed with an affirming nod. 'Because without the hearth, there is no centre to the home. It feeds and warms and gathers people to its heart. And where people gather, there is shared identity and the support of community.'

'I like that. I am the goddess, Hestia,' Liz pronounced, wrapping herself in one of the white sheets and balancing a polystyrene ball on her shoulder in the attitude of a Greek goddess. Her still being up on the chair adding an impressive air of statuary.

Emma laughed.

'Did you know that Hestia didn't have many temples to herself in the ancient world, like other gods and goddesses? But she was welcome in every single one. Why? Because life is difficult, and if there is anyone whose warmth can offer love and wellbeing, then their flame should never be allowed to go out.'

The door opened. It was Hildy. 'Ladies. How's it going?'

she asked, cleverly having selected a safe time to ask, when the work was mostly done. She took in Liz's garb and her lofty pedestal. 'What are you supposed to be, a snow angel, or something? Because if so, we could use a miracle. There is all sorts going on out there,' she gestured to the school hall, which may as well have been a distant galaxy, so ensconced they had been in their world of winter and wonder. 'Kristen asked me to tell you that this is your list of children who have already paid to see Santa,' Hildy continued. 'The man himself will be arriving in about twenty minutes. Mags and Debs are going to be his elf helpers, they are the only ones who have been DBS checked. That's unless any of you wanted to do it?' She looked at them in turn.

Liz laughed. 'I'm six foot,' she said. 'I don't think I'm really elf material.'

'And I think elf shoes aren't very good for my Achilles tendonitis,' Laura said. 'No arch support.'

'You can't, actually anyway,' Hildy said, consulting her clipboard. 'Because you are on the refreshment stall, now.

'Right. Lovely. Well. It all looks excellent,' she said, popping her head around the cabin door, like a sergeant on bunk inspection. 'I shall have to see if it matches up with the real thing and then I can report back for next year.'

She relished the confused glances of her audience.

'The real thing?' Emma asked.

'Oh, didn't I tell you? We're taking Magnus to Lapland. We're going tomorrow actually.'

'How lovely,' Laura said. 'That's amazing. Jack and I have talked about taking the children but it's just so expensive.'

'Yes, it is,' Hildy agreed, 'But they are only young once and it's nice to spoil them. And, this is all very nice,' she said waving her hand to encompass their work, 'but it's nothing like the real thing, is it? The snow, the roaring log fires, the reindeer rides and sleigh rides and ice skating and of course, the "real Santa",' she air quoted, 'not Dave from down the road.' She laughed loudly.

The friends shared a glance.

'HO HO HO!' boomed a voice as the door opened. 'Afternoon everyone. I'm a little early.' The face that went with the voice looked at them warmly and smiled. 'I'm Santa, but you can call me Dave.'

'Pleased to meet you, Dave,' Emma said shaking his hand. 'I'm Emma. I was the one who phoned you about the flood.' She introduced the others and led him outside, down the candy cane and lollipop path, the lampposts of confectionary, and opened the door to the shed.

'Your new grotto,' she announced proudly. 'We all helped but it is Laura's inspiration really.'

Laura smiled modestly.

'It's magnificent,' Dave said. 'So cozy. 'My wife made me wear my long johns and layers of thermal vests when she heard that I was going to be in the shed. But this is lovely. It's fit for a king, nicer than my living room at home. You may never get me to leave,' he joked.

Saying their farewells and assuring him that they were not his elves but would be soon attended to by some suitably qualified assistants, they left Dave to get changed.

In his cabin, he would transform himself from man to deity. He would assume the robes of office and take his place on his throne. He would await the visitation of his adoring subjects and enjoy the comforts of his status. He would sit by the hearth, before a flame that never went out.

He would consume the offerings of milk and mince pies, and the mothers of Christmas, who were also the daughters of Vesta, would ensure that the eternal fire of tradition and perpetuity continued to burn.

This was his grotto, and a grotto was the dwelling place for gods.

Ginger 19

Darcy had arrived just as the last sheet of snow was being folded and packed away. An assortment of adult-sized lollipops and candy canes stood around her, lounging against the wall like bored bouncers outside a nightclub. Two nutcrackers lay on the ground as if they had tried to get in without the appropriate ID and had come off worse in a physical altercation.

She stepped carefully around the boxes of fairy lights and smiled as she saw Laura and Liz.

'How did it go?' she asked. 'Looks like it was quite the spectacular.'

Laura smiled. 'It went really well, I think,' she said. 'The kids seemed to love it, Santa survived and it's all over for another year.'

'Laura was amazing,' Emma ventured. 'I think it was the best one yet. A grotto fit for a god; it was. Or a goddess.' She shared a wry smile with her friends.

Darcy didn't get the reference but smiled anyway.

'Sorry, Darcy, do you know Emma?' Laura asked.

'We haven't met,' Emma said extending her hand. 'I'm Emma, and this is Liz and Sally. We are Santa's little helpers. The grotto's kind of our thing, but props have to go to Laura. She sourced so much stuff. Mostly recycled,' she added, gesturing the boxes full of grotto building materials.'

'Hi,' Darcy said, smiling. She put down her cleaning trug. 'I clean the school,' she explained 'Oh and Laura's house and the nursing home,' she added nodding to the women she knew. 'I used to do this sort of stuff, too,' she explained, gesturing to the room. 'My kids are older now, but I know what goes into it. A lot of work and little reward.'

'We've tried to leave it as clean as possible,' Liz explained. 'Sally has been picking up the flakes of fake snow virtually piece by piece.'

Sally smiled meekly and uncurled her palm, releasing its contents into the bin. 'It's biodegradable,' she said, but I'm still not sure Mrs Highbourne will want it being trodden throughout the school, I've tried to get up as much as I can.'

'I'll leave no flake unturned,' Darcy replied. 'What we can't get, Henry will,' she said, nodding towards the vacuum cleaner.

She asked herself how many years she had done the same thing as these women, as her children had moved through the primary school. Part of her was glad to not have to be involved in the grottos and baking and service to the school and church any longer. It had been stressful, with her children young and the demands made upon her time and efforts, those both paid, and unpaid. But, now without it, whilst she relished the freedom, it had made her rudderless, seeking a purpose to Christmas. What was it all for if not to create magical worlds for others?

Emma broke her reverie. 'Darcy?' she began, a question in her voice. 'Do you do cleaning, other than houses and schools?'

'Er, yes. I do the nursing home, like I said, and some offices..., the church, the pub. Anything really. It's all money,' she explained with a shrug.

'Only, I was wondering…, we have a farm, and one of our farm hands has had to go back to Scotland, to visit a sick relative, and we could use a bit of help.'

Darcy frowned and didn't know what to say. 'I don't think… I mean, I don't know anything about farming.'

Emma laughed. 'Oh sorry, no… No, I didn't mean… Ha, no you don't need to drive a tractor or lift the sprouts or anything like that,' she snorted. 'No. You see. We are having a bit of a celebration in our barn, and we just need to spruce it up a bit. It's not terrible, like it hasn't got sileage in or anything. Just cobwebs, and a dusty floor and we need to wash down some furniture and get it ready. I would have asked Dylan, but he had to go and then the sprout problem has put us back a bit and I've still got some chutneys and jams to label for the farmers' market. It would be really great to have an extra pair of hands. But don't worry if you don't want to. Just thought I'd ask. Obviously, you can tell us how much you would charge for that sort of thing. I know you might want danger money for mud and spiders.'

'Oh,' Darcy said, relieved that she didn't have to milk the cows or shear the sheep. 'No, that sounds fine. I'd be happy to. It would make a change from emptying wastepaper bins and wiping coffee mug stains. When is it? I would just have to check that I can fit it around my other clients.'

'The celebration is the twenty-first, but cleaning would have to be about nineteenth, really, to allow time for getting the rest of it set up.'

Darcy checked the calendar on her phone, swiping it up and down and frowning. 'Yes, I can jiggle some things around. That's no problem.'

'Not that I want to take work away from you, Darcy,' Laura added and turned to face her, then Emma, 'but Ems, if you needed help, you could have asked me.'

'You are joking,' Emma replied. 'After you doing all of this and everything else you are doing, and having to make or find a flipping bunyip, you have got enough on without having to help clean my barn,'

Did she just say bunyip? Darcy asked herself. What the hell was that? Repressing her curiosity while the friends talked, she remained quiet.

Laura smiled.

'She's right though,' Liz said. 'We would have helped. You and Rob can't manage Sprout-Covid by yourselves and still get everything else done.'

Bunyips and Sprout-Covid? What were they on about?

Darcy wondered.

'Sprout-Covid?' she asked, choosing the one question that she might have a hope of understanding the answer to, given the fact that there were at least normal words.

'The next farm over has had problems with their crop over recent weeks,' Emma explained. We thought we were going to get it too, some sort of airborne parasite. It's okay, we didn't, and the sprouts were fine, it just put us behind because we had to monitor them so much more closely,' Emma said simply to answer Darcy's question. Then she squeezed Liz's hand. 'You're one to talk. You've got more infections than you can shake a stick at, at the nursing home. And you are keeping actual people safe, not just a few acres of sprouts.

'Honestly guys, thank you, but if Darcy is happy to help then we will be fine,' Emma added gratefully. The two exchanged numbers and arranged to meet.

'Do you need a hand getting this lot back to the car?' Darcy asked, looking around. 'Looks like clearing up might take until next Christmas.'

As the school emptied and all traces of the fayre were erased for another year, Darcy felt buoyed. A lightness that she hadn't felt in a long time unrounded her shoulders from their natural stoop. As Henry moved along, consuming the snowflakes like a festive Pacman, she even found herself humming the tune to *A Winter Wonderland*.

What was this? She had neither found anything worth humming about for a long time, nor had discovered anything wonderful about winter, or autumn, or even summer. When she thought about it, she might have been in a non-humming, wonder-free- state for some time now.

She emptied the wastepaper baskets and wiped down the coffee stains in the staff room; worse today, given the swelled numbers of caffeine imbibers, brought into create Christmas. But she didn't mind as much for some reason. Perhaps it was the thought of the work at the farm. That would make a nice change. Or, it might have been spending time with those women, their friendship and care for each other tangible in their words and attitudes. Yes, it might have been that. Come to think of it, when had she last spent time with people who made her feel good? When had she last spent time with anyone other than Richard? Laura and Liz, she knew from cleaning, and they were always very welcoming and friendly, but that was a professional arrangement. They didn't socialize. But she found herself very drawn to the others, bright and bubbly Emma, her blonde curls as bouncy as herself, and Sally, quiet and thoughtful. She was pleasant and kind, but Darcy could sense a fragility, a delicacy which she felt had less to do with her fine features and diminutive frame, and more to do with a brokenness within.

It had stimulated her, being in their presence and she found herself wanting more of them and their easy company. And the prospect of cleaning a barn for a celebration, that was new. For a while now, new had felt daunting, fear-inducing. That happened when you lost your self-confidence. New was to be avoided, rather than welcomed. Same, was where you stayed. Same and safe and usual. But where Same dwelt, so did Ordinary, Unremarkable, Uninteresting and their roommate, Dull. With Anxious, Afraid and Uncertain right next door.

Having dragged Henry around, his stomach replete with glitter, fake snow, torn raffle tickets, mince pie crumbs, Haribo (which he vomited back up) and strands of fake Christmas tree needles, Darcy returned him to the cupboard and closed the door. It stuck, requiring a firm shove for the catch to go home. The vibration, causing some sort of earth tremor that destablised the items on the top of the cupboard, sent a top hat tumbling down from above, and with all the natural weight rebalancing of a leaping cat, came out of its rotations, landing squarely on her head. She deduced that a snowman had probably been relieved of it earlier by the mischief of a pupil or an elf and had not returned with the rest of him to Laura's car. She checked inside to find that it had Laura's name on it though Darcy imagined this was more as a practical way to recover her property than proof that Laura was given to regularly wear a top hat as part of her daily wardrobe. In the way that clothes maketh the man, millinery maketh the snowman and Darcy avowed to reunite the two when she visited the house on Monday. A scarf and a few coal buttons would do, but only a top hat could ever really pronounce you as a bona fide snowman. What was the phrase? If you want to get ahead, get a hat.

She only had the year three boys' toilets to mop and then she was done. She lifted the hat off her head and placed it on the teacher's chair. It made her smile because it looked like the class was being taken by a very small man, who couldn't see over the top of the desk.

The smile found the muscles that had been awakened earlier. After a time of misuse, and the anxiety of Christmas approaching, Darcy's facial contours had settled into a topography of droops and frowns. It felt strange for the apples of her cheeks to be blushed Braeburns as opposed to wrinkled windfalls.

The caretaker was around somewhere, but something in her new lightness of mood disregarded the fact that he might come in at any moment, jangling his keys and checking his watch; and in an uncharacteristic moment of whimsy, she placed the hat on her head. Catching sight of herself in the reflection of the wide, class windows, the darkness beyond, she laughed. The flush of mirth reminded her of an old advert for engine oil, where a graphic image reconstructed the path of the oleaginous fluid smoothly filling the pipes and powering the pistons or cogs, or whatever it was that engine oil did. Her laugh, although small, did the same to her veins, albeit with serotonin, rather than Castrol GTX.

A previous version of her, the one that used to laugh more readily, more frequently, might have read her image in the top hat as redolent of Fred Astaire, and she would have set to the cleaning of the year three boys' toilets, by holding out the slender mop to one side, bouncing it onto the wet tiles, splashing its loopy feet while she provided the soundtrack with the rubber soles of her own Ugg boots. It would be more of a slap dance, than a tap dance, but it would have delighted her just the same. As mad as a hatter, without the poisoning of any toxic mercury, just crazy on life.

She wasn't quite sure where that person had gone, buried somewhere under the routines of endless cleaning, money worries and missing her children she supposed. Her young parenting life gone, her middle-aged one undefined. Well, those together with the fact that there was now a massive hole where her faith used to be. Her social life was non-existent and she had not seen her waist for four years. Added to that, Christmas was coming, and she simply did not have the energy for the planning, decision-making and delivery of festive perfection that everyone expected.

Not a few hours earlier, the school had been filled with Christmas Spirit from the fayre. Its essence, permeating the school air, infecting all present with its air borne protists, like a virulent strain of Emma's Sprout Covid. They had stood nose to nose as they played Christmas games, visited the grotto, and clutched their raffle prizes. Then, they had taken it with them, back to their homes, sharing the infection with others who willingly let it seep through their skin and into their hearts.

Only Darcy seemed immune, as if she was in quarantine. The sole person in the bubble who had not yet succumbed. A mask, gloves, and healthy squirt of sanitizer away from contracting the full impact of a fun-filled, lighthearted *joie de Christmas Eve*. Darcy relished this particular form of isolation though, hiding away from the regular routines of society. Feeling overwhelmed, anxious, and worn by the fast and frantic frenzy of modern life and annual celebration, she wanted to just opt out, remain socially distanced and locked down in a private world. Apparently though, according to experts, isolation wasn't very good for one's wellbeing, negatively affecting both mental and emotional health.

Considering this, Darcy wondered whether her earlier thoughts of dancing with the mop were more indicative of madness or wellness.

Her work was complete. Returning to her bag, she found a Tupperware box lying on top, labelled with a yellow post it note. Probably someone's home-baked offering for the fayre, returned to her bag by mistake, she assumed. To her surprise, the note was not in fact a marker to ensure the property was returned to the baker, but was addressed to Darcy, herself.

A bit of sugar power to help with the cleaning! Love L, L, E and S. xx

Opening the box, she was instantly met with the aroma of warming spice. A smiling gingerbread lady lay supine, in the base of the tub, looking like a happier version of Millais' Ophelia. Her dress, trimmed with white icing and fastened with three buttons of green jelly tots. Lifting the box to her face, Darcy allowed herself a deep inhale of Christmas past, her chest expanding as if the fragrances of ginger, nutmeg and cloves were pillars propping up the walls. At once, she was a child making gingerbread biscuits with her mother, and she was also a mother, making them with her own children. A dizziness whizzed in small circles to the top of her head, like the spirals from the tip of a magic wand. There it met with a frisson of joy, and they danced for a moment in the sparkles of the wand's enchantment. Christmas found her stomach, and the places beneath her tongue, when she imagined taking a bite. Tasting the sweet warmth. Closing her eyes, her feet left the carpet tiles of the school foyer and stood, instead, in the kitchen. The heat from the oven warmed the fronts of her thighs and she stepped back, pulling down the door and reaching in, her hands inserted into padded gloves, like a baking boxer. The gingerbread rested for a moment and was then removed carefully with the fish slice and eased onto the metal rack. While they cooled, icing was mixed and scooped into piping bags, while carols played, and children laughed. Little fingers placed little sweets as buttons and bows, or eyes and nose. A house was built, roof tiles of smarties, and decorations for the tree, each pierced with a bamboo skewer and threaded with ribbon. The piping drew outlines; baubles on branches; boots and belts; bobbles and beards. The icing was art, the ginger was heart. The icing didn't stick, the house fell down. They all laughed, made mugs of hot chocolate, and ate the walls.

Tears sprang to Darcy eyes, but these felt different to the others. Happy tears, they call them. She was reminded of the paper chains she had made when she was little, the ones they used in school whenever a project called for unity or togetherness, such as children across the world. Each, cut out of folded paper, like a little gingerbread person, their rounded hands touching, linking them in all their wonderful unique diversity. But at the same time, in their uniformity, the type that says we are all the same, we love, we hurt, we cry, we laugh.

The little cookie in the box was socially distanced, not linked to others, like unproven dough on a baking sheet, or cut from folded paper. Yet it had the same powers of connection. She was not Ophelia, lying alone in tragedy and sadness. This was Darcy, the gingerbread transcending time, not only threading her to her past with fine lengths of ribbon, to the precious times of the past, spent with her children in Christmas preparation. But also taking her by the hand and connecting her to Christmas present.

The spices in her nostrils made her sneeze.

Darcy wondered if she was coming down with something.

Some strains were strong, mutating and adapting, their strength finding your weakness. You could take precautions, but sometimes, infection was unavoidable. Especially if the pathogen was Christmas kindness.

It's illogical, Captain!

'How was the fayre?' Rob asked as the boys bundled in, a puffball of padded jackets, cold air and energy.

'We got sweets,' Matthew said as he held up a cellophane cone of pick and mix.'

'Greeat,' Rob said with sarcasm. 'Just what we need for a relaxing Saturday evening, three kids hyped up on sugar.' He smiled and kissed Emma as she placed a canvas shopping bag on the breakfast bar.

'Did you get much work done?' she asked.

'Yeah, thanks. It was great, just having a couple of hours to clear some emails. So was the fayre okay? How was the grotto?'

'It looked amazing actually, even though I do say so myself,' she said with a hand placed to her chest in mock grace. 'Although it was all Laura really. We helped, but she really pulled out the stops.'

Her husband smiled and began emptying the bags and putting away the produce. 'Yeah?'

'She was outstanding. She had accumulated all this stuff over the months from second-hand places and things from home and it really did look magical. I almost believed in Santa myself. Look!' She showed him the photos on her phone and played a little video with the projector and the music and the little fire burning.

'Very Eco,' he said smiling.

'I know,' she said. 'We had that discussion and Liz thought for a minute that we were going to scrap it all,' she laughed. 'But then Sal said something about really wanting it to be magical for the girls and all the children who need a bit of wonder in their lives, and we thought, aaah, just go for it, the whole hog – or the whole falafel, for the vegetarians amongst us,' she smiled. 'Speaking of which, I thought bean and beetroot burgers for tonight?'

'Perfect,' Rob said, 'I'll get chopping the beets.'

He moved to the sink to wash his hands. 'I bet the kids loved it. What did our guys think?'

'Well,' began Emma as she rinsed the kidney beans and began slightly mashing them in a clear bowl, 'Henry loved the whole winter wonderland bit and did enjoy seeing Santa. He was beside himself with excitement. Ask him later. He said that he saw a real reindeer who was eating a carrot and there was snow by his house, even though there wasn't any snow in the playground so Santa must be "really, really magic" to be able to make it snow in just one place. And that it was good that we left out mince pies and milk, because that's what Santa had there, so he was happy that we got it right. Apparently, Santa asked him if he had been a good boy and Henry said no, because he had peed on the veg patch one time – which was news to me,'

'Good job the kidney beans have come from a tin,' Rob joked.

Emma continued, 'And he also told him about the time that he hid in the washing machine which had made Mummy cross because she was worried.'

Rob sniggered, 'Oh God, remember that? And what did Santa say?'

'According to Debs, one of the elves, who couldn't stop laughing, Santa said that it sounded as though Henry was really a very good boy, and that as long as he was kind and never did anything that hurt other people, that that was what mattered.'

'God, it sounds like confession,' Rob laughed. 'Did he give him three Hail Marys and a Glory Be?'

Emma laughed. 'Get this though,' she added. 'When Santa

asked him what he wanted for Christmas, he said he didn't really mind because he liked surprises, but he would really like it if Santa to use his magic to get rid of all the broccoli in the world so that he never had to eat it again.'

'That's hilarious,' Rob said.

'I know, that's why I let them get the pick and mix. I know some of the sweets aren't vegetarian, but I felt bad. Imagine, of all the things in the world that he could ask for, it was for no more broccoli.'

Rob made the bean mixture into patties and placed them on a tray in the fridge. 'So, was everything else okay? Same old Christmas things at the fayre?'

'Yeah, everything you would expect. All the usual. It really is so superficial and tacky – the foil and plastic decorations, the cardboard cups for the mulled wine, which whilst cardboard, were still not recycled but put in the black bags at the end of the day. The processed foods, the hampers, you should see all the packaging in all of the hampers. And do you know what one of the raffle prizes was? A twenty pound turkey, from the butcher on the high street. It was very kind that he donated it, but everyone was buying raffle tickets to get it because it was worth about a hundred quid. The hall was crammed, so that's hundreds of people who want turkeys and hams and bacon and sausages and fancy trout and salmon and it just seemed all so gross.'

Rob nodded.

Emma continued. 'But then I realized that I was being judgy and self- righteous about everything. All I could see was excess and waste and more trash for landfill and more commitment to climate change and I thought my God, when did I become such a bloody fun sucker? I've lost all sense of fun and occasion and specialness. All I could see was everything wrong with it all, and nothing right with it. Other than Sal's point of view about making magic for the girls, it was just all a bit much, to be honest. But it was good for the school, good for the community and fun for all the children.

Does it matter that I just see it as a money-making rape of the planet, when I'm the only one? I wondered whether being a salmon and swimming up the Eco stream on your own isn't a bit bloody lonely and whether I've just lost balance and got all out of proportion. Then I saw the crappy sweet cones and thought – yes, please. I'll have three, here's my money – let my kids feel like kids for five minutes instead of my six-year-old worrying about peeing in the veg patch and hating broccoli.

'Life is short,' Emma said, 'as we know too well from poor Sal and Pete and there can be so much hardship. Why not just enjoy whatever we want and hang the consequences? Take the easy road. Do what everyone else does and just follow the rest of the salmon.'

He bent forward and rested his elbows on the counter and took her hands in his.

'Hey? What's brought all this on? You don't usually have so much self-doubt. Where's my fierce eco warrior, eh? Where's that young campaigning student gone, the one who fought for a different social cause every week?'

Emma met his gaze. 'I don't know, really. I think Christmas is just too big a beast to take on, I'll just focus on something easier, instead, like human rights and global warming.'

Rob stood and took a glass from the cupboard. 'A glass of peapod burgundy?' he asked, their private joke about the organic wine they'd made, an allusion to their attempt at self-sustainability.

'To Tom and Babs,' he said clinking her glass in cheers, a familiar salute to those who had inspired them.

'Tom and Babs,' she said and took a sip.

'Anyway, remember Margot and Jerry?' Rob said. 'They got all the fancy stuff from Fortnum's, or Harrods or wherever it was, and they had much more fun with crackers that they had to make their own bang.'

She smirked.

'I know,' she relented allowing herself to be drawn back to the vision she shared with her husband.

'I'm just worried, you know, about the future. I'm worried that this sustainability thing will be too hard to manage. If Christmas proves anything, it is that people like the idea of saving the planet until it comes to them having to make changes to their comfortable lifestyles and traditions. If they don't ever change then where does that leave us and our livelihood? Might it be easier to... you know... do what everyone else does.'

'Well. Since when have we done what everyone else does?' Rob asked, placing his hand over hers. 'We believe in our values, and they are the right ones. We can't give up now. The ship is turning. Just think, we were doing anti-plastic demonstrations years ago and now everything is being made from recycled plastic. True we have a way to go to stop it being manufactured at all, but it is getting there. There's a massive move to reductarianism, and veggie and veganism. It used to just be attributed to hippies, but people know it makes sense and is becoming more mainstream.'

Emma smiled, 'Oh, talking about vegetarians, guess what Mags said? She was one of the other elves. She said, "You know that thing you say to people about pigs being as intelligent as four-year-old kids, and you wouldn't eat a four-year-old child would you?", I said, "Yeah", she said, "Well, having been in a whole room full of them this afternoon, I think I would say, "yes please, load me up with a full portion and I'll have a dab of mustard on the side"'.

Rob laughed and they both took a swig of wine.

'Ooh, something else,' she added. 'I met a friend of Laura's today. She's called Darcy and she's her cleaner and she also cleans the school. And I asked her if she would help us get the barn ready, you know, since Dylan's away, and she said she would. She's going to come around and we'll have a cuppa and she'll give us a price. Oh, she's so nice. She seemed a bit quiet at first. A bit withdrawn, you know? I don't know, shy or something. But she chatted with us for a while, and we had a laugh and then she helped take down the whole grotto and get everything back in the car, and that was before she did the actual rest of her cleaning job.'

'That's great,' Rob agreed. 'That will be a great help.'

'Yeah, Liz and Laura offered as well, but they have enough going on themselves.'

'How was Sal?' Rob asked.

'Not bad. She made the best of it. She asked if we could take some of the presents away from under the tree, in case the children thought that such a huge amount was to be expected on Christmas morning. She's worried that she can't give the girls more. All the money has gone on the bikes and a few stocking gifts. I just don't think she can even conceive how to get through the day.'

'You did tell her to come here, didn't you?' Rob asked, topping up Emma's glass.

'Yes, and she's grateful. I don't think she knows what to do for the best. To try and keep Christmas the same as it was with Pete, so that the girls feel that he's still here, or to do something completely different to prevent them from the pain and just gloss past the whole thing.'

'The second one, if you ask me,' Rob said. 'She could come here, and we can do our thing and she can just try to relax and let us spoil her. The girls could play with our guys, and it might remove some of the sense of loss.'

Emma nodded, feeling the anguish of incapacity anew.

Rob gave her a kiss. 'Do you think the guys are going to be able to even eat dinner after all those sweets?' he asked, placing the frying pan on the hob.

'Maybe it's like alcohol,' Emma said. 'You need to fill up on decent food to absorb all the refined sugar and E-numbers. They'll be hungry soon, Matty and Adam can always eat.'

'True dat,' Rob agreed. 'Oh, you didn't say. What did the twins think of Santa? Did they want a worldwide ban on broccoli too?'

Emma smiled. 'Well, here's the thing. They were queuing up, with all the other kids, and were all excited and everything and then Magnus walked by and said that they were stupid for wanting to see Santa.'

'What?' Rob cried indignantly, 'Why? Don't tell me, he told them he wasn't real?'

'No, well… yes… of a fashion, but not in the way you mean,' Emma explained.

'He did say he wasn't real, but not that he didn't exist. Just that he – the Santa in the grotto – Dave – wasn't the real Santa. The real Santa was in Lapland, because that is where he lives and he is never anywhere else until Christmas Eve, so therefore he, Dave, couldn't be Santa so there was no point telling him what you wanted, because he didn't have the power to make it happen.'

'What?' Rob cried.

'Yeah,' Emma nodded, 'And what's more, he, Magnus, was going to see the actual, real live Santa tomorrow, so he was the only one who was going to get what he asked for.'

'What?' Rob cried again. 'The little lying snotrag.' He took another swig of wine as he shook his head in disbelief. 'Low blow,' he said. 'the depths some kids will go to. God.'

'Well, yeah, but he's not actually lying. Hildy told us that they are leaving tomorrow to go to Lapland. She said she'd check it out and report back as to whether our winter wonderland and Santa's cabin were authentic.'

'Oh my god, you've got to be kidding. Can she hear how ridiculous that sounds? She's going from one made up place to another made up place and is going to compare them against a set of made-up criteria to see if the first made up place is as good as the real made-up place. What a bloody idiot. God some people have more money than sense. You wouldn't find any pigs around who are that stupid,' he said. Wow, this sort of stuff does get me. It's commercialism gone mad.'

Emma nodded and began to lay the table.

'So, what did the boys say to that?' Rob asked.

'Here they come, you can ask them,' Emma replied.

'So, Mummy was telling me about the fayre,' Rob said leaving it open to see which part the boys chose to mention. 'Did you have a good time?'

Henry began. 'I got sweets,' he said proudly.

'Yes, you showed me,' Rob said aware that this was clearly the highlight of the day, so good, he named it twice. 'Anything else?'

'I got this from Santa,' he said showing a sticky Alien man whom he was making climb down the pepper grinder. 'Look, he climbs down.'

'Do we have to have him at the table?' Emma chided. 'Can we play with him later perhaps?' Or chuck him away, she wanted to say, only that would be more unnecessary junk in landfill. (There she goes again, she told herself. Let the boy have some fun for a minute. She had brainwashed herself so that she couldn't see fun in anything anymore).

'Oh, he's cool,' Rob said. 'He's a bit like Spiderman, clinging on and climbing down walls.'

Henry took him from the pepper grinder and threw it at the wall, where it crept down falling over itself as each point of contact peeled and stuck in turn. The boys all giggled.

Rob shared a glance with Emma, seeking forgiveness for his unwitting suggestion.

'And I don't need to eat broccoli anymore,' he added, 'Santa is going to magic it all away.'

'Oh, is he?' Rob asked. 'Did he say that?' He thought might have to have a word with Dave the next time he saw him at the farmers' market.

'Yep!' Henry said, convinced that as his request had gone to the highest authority, it was so to be.

'How about you Matt, Ads? What did Santa say to you?'

The boys looked at each other and then back to their burgers.

Matty began, 'Magnus said that it wasn't the real Santa and that the real one is still at the North pole, and that everyone was silly for believing that the one in the fayre was the right one. He said he is just a man dressed up and he knows because his mum runs the fayre.'

(Hildy runs the fayre? Really? Runs the no work, maximum acclaim racket, perhaps, Emma thought to herself.)

What should she do about Santa? She considered her options.

a) She could take this opportunity to say here and now, yes, Magnus is right. He is not the real Santa. He is one of his helpers. He has lots of helpers who meet all the children just to put faces to names. Or…

b) That Magnus is right, he is just a man dressed up. He is Dave who comes to the farmers' market for his favourite red onion chutney. The real Santa is in Lapland, waiting to see only the children whose parents are well off enough to go there. Or…

c) Magnus is actually wrong, and this is the real Santa, and because he is magic, he can be here at school and can also magic himself home by tomorrow to be there for when Magnus gets there. Because the reindeer and the sleigh are magic; or he has a time portal, or both; because otherwise – how else does he get around the whole world in one night? And if he can get to every child between Canada and Puerto Rico in one night, he can certainly get from Heathrow to Greenland which is only a few hours even by easyJet. Or…

d) You know what, the whole thing is one great big lie. There is no Santa, the parents give the presents. So, let's stop making a whole big thing about it and enjoy our dinner in peace.'

Obviously, she wanted to go with (d). Their decision, when the twins were born was to allow the Santa charade, as long as it was kept in perspective. He would only bring small stocking presents. And the main present, which was still not too extravagant, would be from them which the boys had been very happy with.

'What do think about that boys?' Rob asked. 'Matty? How did you feel when Magnus said that? Do you think he was right?'

The little boy shrugged.

'Adam? What about you?'

Emma knew that, of the two, Adam was usually more likely to share his thoughts and then Matty would follow.

'He could be right. His mum does run the fayre,' Adam replied.

Emma inwardly bristled and outwardly smiled at the logic. Children were so trusting of authority, The bearing and weight they gave to teachers and parents. In their little worlds that was all they had to go on. That and what they saw on television and movies. If there was anything that contradicted what they perceived to be real, it was destablising.

'But he does have a magic reindeer,' Henry said. 'I saw him. I saw Comet, and there were two others too.'

'Don't be silly, Henry,' Adam said. 'Santa has eight reindeer to pull the sleigh, not three.'

'Be nice Adam, don't call Henry silly,' Emma said gently.

She couldn't blame Adam though. He was right. It was in every cultural reference around. Songs and poems and pictures and movies. Santa had eight reindeer, nine if you included Rudolf. As with any form of brainwashing. You didn't know that the unique thoughts you held were considered in need of a biological cycle at 60 degrees. They simply got rinsed a little bit every day until the stains of original thought were washed clean.

It was all so illogical. She wondered for a fleeting moment whether parents in the age of the Ancient Greeks had a similar problem with their kids. She herself had quoted Hestia earlier, based on her understanding of what the goddess stood for, and the particular tropes attributed to her. But could there have been a time, in earlier millennia, when little Archimedes and Alexander bickered at the dinner table that Cerberus, watchdog of the underworld, had three or eight heads? Or maybe even nine, if one of them had a red nose?

'As I see it,' Emma ventured, 'Like Miss Jennings said, Christmas is a time of sharing, giving and happiness. So, you are going to have your trips to the hospital and the train station and the nursing home. You are giving them your time and your lovely singing and your cookies that you are going to make. And you know that Santa is going to bring you some little things on Christmas morning. Also, you have each pledged to give something else away to another child, which is lovely. Isn't that what the first Santa did? St Nicholas? He gave things to the good children who didn't have anything. So, in a way, you are like Santa too, when you do that. Perhaps everyone who helps another child by giving or sharing is a Santa which is why there can be one in Lapland and one in school and one in every house and school in the country, or even the world.'

'So, there are lots of Santas?' Adam asked
.

'Quite possibly,' Emma said.

'It would explain how he could be seen flying over the skies all around the world at the same time,' Rob said. 'I want you boys to believe in whatever you want to. Whatever makes you happy and to trust in the wonder and magic that exists in our amazing world. So, don't let Magnus or anyone else tell you that what you believe in is wrong. Maybe just try to find where you can be good and kind, and if it is every within your power to share magic and wonder with others, take the opportunity to do it. All Santa does is try to make others happy, it's other people who spoil it. We can't know for sure who the real Santa is, because nobody has seen him in real life on Christmas Eve, so how does Magnus even know whether the one he is seeing tomorrow is the right one. It's not

Christmas Eve yet. No one knows for sure.'

The little rubber Alien fell down the wall and into a pair of Henry's trainers, one little bendy rubber leg in each, looking like Mr. Potato Head in his big shoes. It made the children laugh and gave them the idea to go and dress him up in different things. They asked to leave the table and Emma pondered the poignancy. A gift from St Nicholas being placed in a shoe. The gesture transcending centuries and cultures.

'Nicely done,' Rob said finishing the last of his meal.

'I don't know,' Emma said. 'I was confusing myself by the end. It's all such a load of nonsense, I don't know if it helped or not. They either think Dave is the real broccoli-busting Santa, or not because everyone is Santa... But then if they think that, they will realise that there isn't one actual Father Christmas, and that will be all the magic gone. I told them that there was magic and wonder everywhere and to share it with others. But if that be the case, they'll be wondering what the guy in Lapland is all about. They probably haven't got the foggiest. But that makes all of us.'

'I wouldn't worry about it,' Rob added. 'Parents have always had to make crap up. They try to answer the questions put to them, but the answers vary from household to household, adding a greater sense of confusion. They put bits and pieces together like how Santa will get down the chimney if they live in a block of flats – he can make himself small..., or he can come out of a radiator pipe instead..., or that he has a magic key. We're not the first and we won't be the last,' he assured with his eyebrows raised in a knowing way. 'And how he can be called Kris Kringle, and Sinterklaus and Father Christmas, like some dodgy villain with fake passports, or someone in a witness protection programme.'

Emma laughed.

'And what about his wife? Is there a Mrs Klaus or not? Does he get the letters by post or email? Does he have a portal or magic dust? And is Rudolf actually one of his reindeer or not, because according to Nash's poem, he only had eight so who on earth is bloody Rudolf?

'It's all deflection. You've managed to deflect the immediate problem, made them think about the real St Nicholas, the Santa origins and concentrate on giving and sharing rather than receiving and whoever does the giving is less important… whilst still, I think, managing to retain a vagueness for other kids that the gift giver isn't the parents, even though that's not what we do. I think you've covered all the bases.'

'Don't you think it's funny that they were more swayed by the fact that Hildy organises the fayre that she knew more about the grotto than me who gave up four hours of my Saturday to preparing it?' Emma said as she washed the dishes. 'Typical Santa situation, credit is given to the most visible figurehead, not the ones who actually do the work and make the sacrifices…. Not that I want any credit,' she added, 'None of us wanted thanks for it, I just wonder whether that is the right message to be giving children. They see enough of it on social media, that those who have the most to say are usually doing the least, whilst the quiet multitude support them.'

'You take on social media, tomorrow,' Rob said putting the dry plates away. 'Let's go and chill out, I could do with a sit down, my back's aching a bit.'

Emma followed him into the lounge, where logs crackled in the fireplace and he stretched out on one sofa, while she curled her legs under her on the other. She looked into the fire then stood to go and check on the boys.

'Where are you going?' he asked, 'not to put the kettle on by any chance?'

'If we were the types to do Santa lists, a Teasmade should be on the top of yours,' she joked. 'I'll make a cuppa in a minute; I just had an idea about that Alien.'

'What?' Rob asked.

'Santa gave me this at the fayre today,' she said brandishing a little round Sherbert lollipop that had a cloth elf hat with ears and pixie boots. She had put it in her back pocket and had only just remembered as the stick dug into her back. 'The last thing the guys need is more sugar, besides there's only one so there'd be war, but I thought as the boys were dressing up the alien, I could put these hat and pointy ears on it and see if his little boots fit his little rubbery feet.'

Rob smiled. 'Okaaay,' he said drawing out the word in suspicion. 'I thought you were against the little creature, that it was just another piece of crap destined for landfill.'

'Yeah, well I did think that at first. But I just want the boys to see that I have a sense of fun and that I'm not an old Grinch that just makes them eat broccoli while we save the planet.'

'You are anything but a Grinch,' Rob chided. 'Don't be nuts.'

'You wanna see nuts?' Emma said. 'You know I don't believe if the whole elf on the shelf thing, but I'm going to create my own.'

'What do you mean?' Rob said in alarm. 'You're not going to put nuts on the alien, are you?' he called after her as she skipped up the stairs. 'Keep it PG, Emz!'

Minutes later, the boys came running down the stairs and ran towards the fireplace. Emma followed.

'Do it Mummy. Do it!' Henry shouted gleefully as he jumped up and down.

'Do what?' Rob asked, pulling himself up to a seat amid the excitement.

'Well,' Emma said standing before the mantelpiece, 'We don't have an elf who does naughty things and tells Santa if we have been bad or mean. Instead, we have a very clever elf who watches when we do kind and fun and caring things.'

Emma raised her hands to her mouth making a trumpet shape and sounded a fanfare through her pursed lips as though she was playing a kazoo.

'Bumbububummm! May I present to you, the Bancroft family's version of the famed elf on the shelf… the not so famous… but, in my opinion, distinctly superior… Spock on the Clock.'

She sat the rubbery alien, complete with elf hat and pointy ears (which could be quite easily mistaken as Vulcan) on top of the mantel clock. His legs dangled easily and terminated in tiny turned-up boots on his tinier feet. 'He's going to sit up there and watch us all be kind to each other and go and tell all the people who live on other planets in deep space, how nice the people of Earth are.'

She stood back and gave him a Vulcan salute. Matthew and Adam followed, adjoining their index and middle fingers together and separating them in a V shape from the other two. Henry tried it too, but couldn't quite make it, simply holding up three fingers, as though he was a Brownie greeting Tawny Owl.

They giggled. 'Come on Daddy, you have to do it too.' Henry said dragging his dad to join the guard of honour.

'You do know that Spock didn't have any emotions, don't you?' he said to Emma wryly. 'He operated on logic and fact and data, not on feelings and touchy-feely kindness. Have you ever even watched Star Trek?'

'I did, a little bit,' Emma countered, 'But, he was the only Alien I knew who had pointy ears and a name that could rhyme with a household object.'

'Good point, well made,' Rob agreed, 'I've thought of another one, though… He doesn't have pointy ears, but you could have had Data on the radiata,' he laughed. The boys bent double laughing, not knowing who Data was but feeling the mood of the room and the festivity around the fireplace.

'Who was that empath in Guardians of the Galaxy?' he asked.

'You're asking me?' Emma asked incredulously.

'No. Boys. Adam, who was it? The one with the black eyes, what was her name? Ah what was it…?'

It came back to him as Adam spoke at the same time. 'Mantis. That's it. She had pointy ears, didn't she?'

'She had antennae, dad,' Matthew said tiredly.

'Oh yeah, that's it. She would have been a better one for feelings though.'

'Uhuh?' Emma retorted, and what household object does she rhyme with then?'

'Oh yeah,' Rob said realizing that he had skewed the moment.

'Empath on the bath?' he joked suddenly. His finger raised like Einstein having a eureka moment. Then he spied the laundry basket at the end of the sofa with the washing all neatly folded ready to be put away. He picked up a pair of Henry's underwear and held them aloft. 'Or, no, no, wait. What about Mantis on the pant-ies,' he said proudly.

Emma groaned. The boys giggled and bundled him on the sofa.

Spock watched.

Emma watched.

The boys, her husband, her whole world right there, in that moment, laughing as they tickled Rob and he turned, tickling them back. Her heart wrenched for Sally, her friend, grieving for the same.

Whilst she regarded Santa, and everything to do with the whole charade, illogical, she could not escape the fact that the notion of him brought joy and love, hope and happiness to children whose lives could otherwise be filled with fear and lack and sadness.

Who was she to spoil it?

The plum pudding model

Liz cradled the phone in the crook of her neck while she scrolled through the diary in her outlook calendar with one hand and flicked the pages of her paper desk diary with the other. Although she had to maintain the shared calendar for the nursing home, she was old-school and only felt that she could think and plan clearly if she had the paper calendar to hand.

The voice on the other end was speaking not only to her, but also to a third person, in a hallway or living room somewhere on the east coast.

'So, what about the twenty-first?' he asked. 'Jill is asking about the twenty-first, now, because we have our son and his girlfriend coming on the eighteenth and we need to have some time with them before Mum arrives.'

Liz cast her eye over the page, and sighed. This was the fifteenth similar call of the day, and about the thirtieth over the last week 'Yes, the twenty-first would be fine.'

'So, we could come and get her on the Friday, bring her back with us and then, bring her back to you on Boxing Day, would that be okay?'

Liz took a breath and delivered her well-practised speech as if it was the first time, which for many, it was. A nursing home was a bit like an all-inclusive hotel, with guests checking in and out all the time. Granted, the stay was invariably longer than a fortnight and there were immeasurably fewer discos and Tequila nights, but the principles of hospitality were the same. Staff had to make everyone feel valued and welcome, at all times, and never was it permissible to reveal tiredness or frustration. Where it differed to a hotel was that, in most cases, the guests didn't elect to be there, and the arrangement of admission and excursions was left to anxious relatives. She made a mental note to herself to contact the marketing team. Perhaps they could put some information in the brochure or something about arrangements for Christmas.

'You could,' Liz offered gently, 'but honestly, she really is quite confused. Christmas doesn't really mean the same thing to Mum.' She always said Mum, or Dad, omitting the pronoun. She felt that it gave the impression that they were in this situation together, as if she were a sibling, sharing the care of the client's family as if they were her own parents. 'She won't know the exact date of when Christmas is, so if you want to come any other day, it really won't matter to her if that's more convenient to you.'

'But the rest of the family are coming for Christmas Day,' the voice explained. 'Well, some are coming Christmas Eve, and of course my son, Liam is coming on the twenty-first. He has been working abroad. We haven't seen him for nearly two years. It will be so amazing to have him back. And to have the whole family together again.'

Liz could hear the excitement in his voice and the image of a united multi-generational Christmas that they were planning. 'Look Harry, Can I call you Harry? Is that okay?'

'Yes of course, please,' the man replied.

'Harry,' Liz repeated. 'Mum is very forgetful as you know and as much as you want her to be with you to have the family all together, I am worried that having her home will be difficult for you at such a stressful time. Particularly with your son coming home. You will want to spend your time with him and looking after Mum is a full-time job.'

'But it's Christmas,' Harry replied. 'She has never missed a Christmas with us.'

'I know, but…'

'No, really,' he interrupted. 'Always. I can't bear the thought of her being alone in that place on Christmas Day… no offence, I mean I know it's a nice place.'

Liz smiled. 'None taken. And it is a nice place, and we do make a special effort to make Christmas as nice as possible for our residents. We have our lovely tree and carols… In fact, I have just been on the phone with a teacher from the local school, the children are coming to sing. Isn't that nice? And we will have Christmas dinner with turkey and all the trimmings, and we even have Santa who comes and brings some little gifts. We have got a Panto group coming in to do a little fun show and there will be Christmas cake and mince pies and mulled punch – we can't do wine because most of them are on too much medication. Honestly. It will be a very festive time. We put up little trees in each room and play Christmas songs. We are even having a tea dance. You do not need to worry. We will look after Mum, and you can have a nice family time together.'

'But Mum *is* our family,' he stressed. 'We can't have a Christmas without her. It wouldn't be right. I promised my dad when he was ill. I promised that I would look after her, and then I couldn't and look what's happened. She's in a home. I never said I would put her in a home. But since the fire, I just couldn't…'

'Harry,' Liz soothed,' I know. But you must not blame yourself. It is absolutely the right thing for Mum to be here, safe, and warm and with company. I know that Christmas won't feel complete without her there, but she really will not know the difference. She understands that Christmas is coming and has memories of it, but she could have Christmas any day and it won't make any difference to her, really. You do not need to make the long journey here to get her, take her back and then bring her back again. It's a lot for you when you have other commitments too. Please just bear it in mind. Christmas is stressful enough without having to manage your mum as well.'

'My mum isn't something to be managed,' Harry said defensively.

'I'm sorry,' Liz said. 'Poor choice of words. I was simply

thinking of you and your wife and the rest of your family. You know getting her there is one thing, but she will need a lot of personal care if she is with you for that many days. Are you sure you are equipped for that, both practically and emotionally? You also have to consider whether it is right for Mum to make the journey and be in a different place. She has only just settled here and to move her again could be very distressing. She will be confused and might get upset or frustrated.'

'I don't know about all that, to be honest,' Harry replied. 'I just feel that it would be wrong to have Christmas without her.'

'Well, I'll pencil the twenty-first in. If it will help, I'll send you a list of all the things she will need for her care based on what we do here and you and your wife can have a think about whether you are feasibly going to be able to do that, particularly if you have other family staying with you. Is that okay?'

'Yes, thank you, Liz. We'll say twenty-first and we'll be in touch nearer the time.'

Liz put the phone down and wrote it in the book and entered into Outlook. She made a note to send off the details and then completed some more filing, liking to leave a tidy desk on Thursdays for her Friday's off. She would go and see Maureen as part of her rounds.

Walking into the woman's room, she found Maureen in the chair. The television was on, but she was staring at the wall.

'Afternoon Maureen. How are you today?' she asked as she went over to open the window a little. 'It's a bit stuffy in here, do you want a little air?' she asked.

'No, it's cold,' Maureen said rubbing the tops of her arms.

'You need your shawl on,' Liz said picking it up from the back of the chair and wrapping it around her shoulders.

'Ooh that's better,' the lady said and shrugged, smiling up

at Liz. 'Thank you, dear.'

'Is the wrist feeling any better?' she asked, picking up the sling that was on the floor. She placed it gently over the woman's neck and cradled the cast within it. Maureen winced. 'You have to keep the sling on, Maureen,' Liz advised. 'It will keep the arm at the correct angle to heal properly.'

'Oh,' Maureen replied absently, looking down at her forearm in surprise as though it had suddenly appeared. 'I don't know what's going on with this thing,' she said raising the plastered limb. 'I can't get it off.'

'You're not supposed to get it off, lovely. You have to keep it on. You've broken your wrist, and you need to support it.'

'I haven't broken anything,' the woman replied indignantly. 'I would know if I had broken my wrist,' she said with a scoff. 'Someone has just put this thing on me, and I don't know why, and I can't get it off.' She began pulling at the soft inside threads with her other hand.

She hadn't remembered the break, or the fall, or the circumstances leading up to the fall, or much of past two years. Maureen didn't remember much past the previous five minutes. Liz thought to deflect her attention to something else.

'What were you watching?' she asked looking at the screen. It was a house renovation programme with images of befores and afters in each room, with people ooing and aahing at the transformations.

'Gosh, look at that, that kitchen looks nice now, doesn't it?' Liz said directing Maureen's gaze to the reimagined space which was all gleaming surfaces and bowls of shiny green apples and open shelves with artfully placed jars of muesli and dried fruit.

'Is it raining?' the woman said instead.

Liz glanced at the window. 'No. It's dry and mild.'

'I need to go shopping,' Maureen said looking thoughtful.

'Do you? What do you need?' Liz asked.

'I've got nothing in. I need to go to the shops.'

She began looking around, a frown of concern crossing her forehead. 'Where's my purse?' She made to push herself up, but the effort hurt her hand and she fell back down into the seat.

Liz placed a steadying arm on her shoulder. This was a common theme amongst the residents, a sudden flash of memory from before, when they had duties to fulfil and obligations to meet; domestic responsibilities to see to. The time before now, when such duties had been replaced with sitting in a chair for hours, possibly partaking in group activities, probably not.

'Well, it's getting dark soon. It's dinner time. Perhaps you could go shopping tomorrow?' Liz said, inflecting her voice with the optimism of potential.

'I can't go tomorrow,' Maureen said impatiently. 'I need to go now. I've only got green apples and Harry doesn't like them. They are too sour and too big for his little hands. He likes the small, sweet, red ones. And strawberries. I must go and get him some, for when he comes home from school.'

The television had moved on to the built-in wardrobes in the master bedroom, yet Maureen's mind was still in a kitchen that wasn't hers, and the need to replace the aesthetic apples with the fruits of her son's childhood.

Liz patted her hand. 'We'll get the apples in the morning, okay? When your hand feels better.'

Maureen acquiesced. 'It does hurt, you know. I can't think what I've done to it.' She gazed at it, again as if seeing it for the first time.

'You had a fall, Maureen. You broke your wrist. That's why you have to wear your cast and sling, to help it to heal.'

The woman nodded, and then looked to the window. 'Is it raining?'

'No,' Liz repeated patiently. 'Just getting dark. It's dusk, dinner time. Shall we get you down to dinner?'

'I'm not hungry,' Maureen said. 'I've just had lunch.'

'Well, perhaps just try a little bit,' Liz ventured. 'You had lunch at twelve thirty, and it's five o' clock now.'

'Five o'clock?' Maureen said surprised. 'What did you get me up so early for? Look how dark it is. It's not even dawn yet.' She gestured to the window to prove her point, that the sun was nowhere near atmospheric twilight yet, never mind its nautical and civil counterparts. 'That sky looks like rain,' she said. 'Is it raining?'

Liz nodded quietly. 'Yes,' she said. 'It looks like it might rain.' An answer that she hoped was ambiguous enough to bridge the gap between truth and falsehood. She heard the trolley being wheeled along the corridor outside, food being brought to the rooms of the bedridden.

Maureen's impairment was of the mind and the wrist. The rest of her, Liz tried to get down to the dining room on a daily basis. Hearing Maureen's mouth dry, the syllables of her words clinging to the roof of her mouth, she refilled the water glass with fresh water and offered it to her.

Maureen shook her head, looking away as if it had a bad smell.

'I know you don't like it, but it's good to keep hydrated and it is warm in here, and it will get you going for the trip downstairs,' Liz explained.

Maureen obligingly took a sip and then placed the glass back down again. Hearing the trolley outside, she looked to the door.

'That's my Harry,' she said.

'Is it?' Liz began, not certain which incarnation of her son she meant. The fruit-loving child, or the semi-centenarian whom she had just spoken to on the phone.

'Yes. He's coming to visit today,' Maureen said assuredly. 'Can you find my shoes? I don't want him to see me in my slippers.'

It was always difficult to know how much to engage in a discussion about family. In some respects, it brought a smile, a reminder of a connection to another life and time, the familiar comfort. The reassurance that they were still within reach. At others, it stirred a feeling of loss and separation. Having spoken to Harry not yet an hour earlier and being fairly certain that he had been calling from his home two hundred and fifty miles away, Liz was reasonably confident that he wasn't, in fact, standing outside in the corridor.

'It's nearly dinner time,' she said instead. 'It smells delicious. It's making me hungry. I think it is cottage pie. You like cottage pie, don't you?'

'I don't really like the cottage pie here,' Maureen replied. 'I don't think they cook the mince for long enough. Not like when I make it. I like to cook it for two hours at least in a nice stock, that really makes a rich flavour. Do you know…,' she said pausing as if a moment of inspiration had just struck her. 'I should make one for you. There's nothing stopping me. I could do one for you tomorrow. Shall I?'

There were too many things wrong with this statement for Liz to know how to respond. Firstly, the woman was mostly confined to this bedroom, whose cooking facilities extended to no more than a radiator and a hot bathroom tap. Secondly, the last time Maureen had cooked anything was four years ago. Meals on wheels had taken care of her culinary requirements prior to her being admitted to the home. Before that, she was not able to get to the shops, handle her money, know when to use food by or how to follow a recipe or even cook an old favourite. Food had rotted, new fresh food, piled on top of old, blackened food. Fruit flies congregated around the bags of onions and potatoes which were composting down to a foul-smelling mulch. Ironically, it was cooking her famed cottage pie that had awakened her family to her need for care. The mince had burned to black in the pan, sending acrid smoke curling throughout the house. The alarm had saved her but not the kitchen. Perhaps that was why she thought the makeover kitchen was hers because there was nothing left of her own to remember.

'Yes, that would be lovely,' Liz replied taking the woman's hand and folding it into the crook of her own. 'You can make me a nice cottage pie and I'll bring the pudding. What shall we have?'

'Rhubarb crumble and custard,' Maureen said, her eyes alight. 'Or No, No, Christmas pudding and brandy butter.'

'Ooh, lovely,' Liz said, and she meant it. She enjoyed the dark richness of plum pudding and the sweet, liquored butter.

'Have you got space on the hob?' she asked, looking Liz squarely in the eye. 'It is always hard because you have to use up one of the hobs for that. It is bubbling away when you want to get on with the vegetables and the gravy.' She shook her head and looked into the distance, searching her mind for the memory of making family Christmas dinners.

'Did you set fire to it?' Liz asked.

'Hmm?' Maureen asked.

'Did you set fire to the pudding?'

'What pudding?

'The Christmas pudding. You were talking about Christmas dinner and steaming the pudding?' Liz reminded her gently.

'Was I? Oh,' she smiled a slight shake of the head which Liz had come to recognize as an apology, an awareness that she was supposed to respond in a particular way and that she had fallen short of expectations.

'Not to worry,' Liz added. 'But you made me think about Christmas puddings and I fancy one now. I love putting the bit of holly on the top and pouring the brandy over it and setting it on fire.' She bit her bottom lip. The memory had spoken to her mouth and had made her mention the ritualistic arson of the pudding. But she heard it as it was said, too insensitive, possibly igniting Maureen's memory of the culinary carbonization of her kitchen?

The inconsistent reliability of the woman's mind had chosen to keep this cabinet locked up and she was happy instead to reminisce about the pudding ritual herself. 'Oh yes, we did that and made a wish. You have to make a Christmas wish'.

'Yes,' Liz nodded. 'We do that too. There is a lovely blue flame for just a moment, it's almost transparent, like a ghost, and you try to think of your wish quickly before it goes out. It's not like a birthday candle which will burn until you blow it out yourself. The flame flickers and then disappears, as if someone had just turned the gas jets off.'

God! What was wrong with her? Once you became aware of something, it seemed that every word referenced it, hammering all tact and delicacy into oblivion. Like once you hear a double-entendre, everything afterwards sounds saucy and rude. Had she really just used the words candle, burn, flame, flicker and gas jets to someone who had set fire to her home?

Liz hadn't meant to be inconsiderate. She had simply allowed herself to remember a special part of Christmas that she loved. And, in the spirit of shared cultural understanding, such as we have with other Christmas celebrants, wanted to invoke the recollection. It had been Maureen who brought up the matter of making a wish, so Liz couldn't be blamed for insensitivity on that count, but she was wondering whether she should have answered no, that she didn't make a wish. Because what does a person with dementia wish for if they had a pudding flame before them now? Agency over their life? Regaining their independence? The ability to read and follow a story in a good book, or to remember characters in movies so as to enjoy a film? Would they wish to be able to understand the news, to recognize what is going on in the wider world, or even what was going on in her own world within these four walls? Would the silent desire of their heart be to be able to go outside, wherever and whenever they wanted? To buy apples and strawberries and feel, once more, the sense of purpose that their lives had in being providers to their children? To be able to remember how many grandchildren she had and what their names were? Would Maureen wish to be back in her own kitchen, the one she had, before it turned to ash, making cottage pie, passing on her recipe as a legacy, advising to cook the mince for longer, the better to make a good stock? Would she wish that she could remember her own love story with her husband, or recent events? Might she wish that she could remember yesterday or what was asked of her five minutes ago, before they flickered away like the blue flame on the pudding?

Or was that what Liz wished on her behalf?

Perhaps Maureen was in her little goldfish world, where time didn't matter, and that all you required was for your needs to be met with kindness and dignity. Or where your thoughts were so transient, you were not even aware of what you wished for, because the moment you had wished it, it was gone.

Liz tapped her hand. 'You know, I could get us a little one. You can cook them in the microwave now, you don't need to boil them. And they come in different sizes, tiny, like this.' She made upturned her palm and covered it with the curled fingers of her other hand, as if she were concealing a tennis ball. It will be just for us, and we can light it and I'll even find some holly.'

Maureen's face lit up like a child's.

Liz knew that Maureen wouldn't remember it tomorrow. She wouldn't even remember by the time they got to the dining room. But Liz had found this to be the best way to cope with dementia, keeping the hope alive in the moment. Sometimes doubt gnawed at her stomach, as though she was being deceitful, promising something that couldn't really happen, that didn't exist. Like Maureen being able to make a meal in her own kitchen. But what else did they have in their lives? When everything else had gone, if they could at least trust that there was both something to look forward to in their future, and that someone had heard them recall their past. Because there was not much else in between.

'When I was little, we had a range,' Maureen said as Liz helped her stand and put on a cardigan for her sojourn beyond the bedroom. 'A huge, black one it was, and my grandfather used to blacken it and polish it. He scrubbed it with a wire brush too. My grandmother used to sit beside it all day. I remember she wore all black lace, like Queen Victoria. I don't know why. I loved her, though. She was deaf and so rarely spoke, but it was as though we didn't need to. In those days, children had to sit down and be quiet. You could only speak if you were spoken to, which wasn't often in a house full of adults. I mostly sat at her feet. The two of us in a world of silence.'

Those kitchen memories were there, always. Liz realised. The hearth of the home, the source of food and warmth, light, and life; or at least, a warm place to wait out the days.

'She always hid a sixpence in the pudding, though,' Maureen recalled with a smile. 'For good luck. I used to worry that I would swallow it by mistake and spend the rest of the Christmas holidays in hospital. She may not have spoken much, but she let us know she was there, by little things like this.'

Liz turned to face the woman. She watched the mind behind her eyes wandering away, meandering down a garden of her brain, kicking aside the dried torn up roots of memories and searching amongst the overgrown brambles for a green shoot; a living thought, like a weed that was fertile but growing in the wrong place, a thought unconnected to others.

'They gave me coal once,'

'Coal?' Liz remarked, surprised at the sudden turnabout.

'Father Christmas. My uncles. You know the saying that if you were naughty, you would get coal? Well, they did that. They thought it incredibly funny. There was a big box with a bow from Father Christmas and I was so excited, and I unwrapped it with them all watching me. I was the only child, so Christmas was always a fun time for me and there was a box, inside a box, inside a box and so on and then right in the last one was a lump of coal. I felt my heart would break. I had always been such a good child, well you didn't dare be anything but, in those days, and then with my mother's temper, well I didn't want to ever be naughty and there was God of course, he knew what you did and between God and Father Christmas, if you were naughty, you got nothing. I was so humiliated. They all laughed. I'm surprised I ever liked Father Christmas after that.'

'But was that just a joke? Did you get a proper present as well?' Liz asked.

'Oh yes, I got a nice pair of roller skates.'

'Oh good,' Liz said feeling relieved on Maureen's seventy-five earlier years' behalf.

Liz wasn't sure whether this was a positive or negative memory. It contained so much. Maureen had only just retraced her mental footsteps back forty years to Harry's childhood, yet she had just zoomed further back in time to her own. She had recalled her uncles, none of whom were still part of Maureen's life, as far as her records showed. The range was present in her mind, as was her grandmother, all dressed in black sitting beside it all day, as life came and went. The black range and black clothes, in a black kitchen. There was a moment in time when that had been both, at once, a recollection and a premonition. The set, the same; the cast of characters, different. And to recall the feeling of humiliation at being the butt of her uncles' trick, that had stayed over the years. It is funny how deep emotional scars are usually tied to the memory with strong cords. It is rare to have one without the other. But also, the fondness of the memory of the roller skates and Father Christmas. The coal had just been a cruel joke. It didn't mean that Santa had labelled her as naughty and unworthy after all. She was loved.

'Sounds fascinating,' Liz said. Her patients often surprised her like this. They couldn't keep anything in their heads for five minutes, but certain memories and knowledge were still there, locked in, ready to be withdrawn at just the right moment. It didn't happen often, but when it did it was disarming. It was easy to treat them child children, to speak to them in simple sentences and keep their thoughts as small as their worlds. It was sometimes distressing for them if they couldn't recall something, their brains like mashed potato or candy floss; their minds, a clouded mass, an untended garden with weeds and ivy strangling out the normal functions until they were covered, buried beneath the foliage, fighting for light and air.

They passed the cross on the wall. Maureen's family had placed it there when she first moved in. They said that she had been a faithful Catholic all her life, but Liz hadn't seen any sign of it in the months she had been there, until just now when she mentioned God judging her actions. She never mentioned wanting to go to church, or to see the priest or pray. But this was how it was. Things that were once so much part of one's identity and beliefs were now gone. Not through any deliberate defining moment of not believing, nor in a gradual fade of belief, just that it was no longer relevant. When a person lives second by second, they no longer have the need to examine who they are, what they once stood for, what they once knew and enjoyed, or what visions they have for their future. There is only now.

Maureen wouldn't remember the offer of the pudding. Liz knew that, and the kitchens would serve Christmas pudding on Christmas Day anyway, so what did it matter? It did occur to her though that it wouldn't be the same as they remembered. Many of the patients couldn't leave their rooms and would have the Christmas dinner on their trays. The rest were served in the way of mass catering, *mis en place*, with the food already on the plate, usually cut up into small pieces, the better to serve ingestion and digestion. Liz knew that there would be no crowning of the plum pudding and ceremonial lighting of it in a dress of blue flame. And for the first time, she wondered whether, despite their best efforts, the home couldn't really 'do' Christmas sufficiently. She had gently suggested and persuaded so many families this week, that Christmas wasn't valued by the residents in the same way as the relatives believed, and that the nursing home was adapted and motivated to make Christmas as enjoyable and meaningful as possible to the residents. But perhaps it wasn't. So deep-rooted were these thoughts and feelings and rites and rituals. Where were these in the mass catering, one size fits all approach?

Liz often tried to do little extra things like bring in some fresh wildflowers, or herbs from the garden in the warmer months, or sometimes she would make some shortbread and share it out. If she found something personal, that she thought the residents might like, she would bring it in. Like the time she brought a newspaper feature about an air show to Kevin, who had once been a pilot. Arthur shared stories about the allotment he used to have, so she showed him clippings from the horticultural show, and he explained with pride that his marrows and tomatoes had one first prize for ten years. Bill, formerly known as Professor William Marsden, had been a brilliant astrophysicist. Much of what he knew had now gone, but Liz would show him discovery articles on her tablet, and his hand would scribble formulae. She would ask him what they meant but he didn't know. The cat cushion that she found in the charity shop was hideous, and Liz wouldn't give it house room, even in the litter box, but Betty loved it, because it reminded her of Socks, who she had had to leave behind.

It was as though parts of them were locked behind mirrored glass. They could see out, but you couldn't see in. You didn't know that they were inside, until they shared something, unbidden and unrelated to anything current or topical. As if there was a scratch in the silvering and through a jagged sliver, you could see the person they once were.

Liz decided that she would keep her promise to Maureen, and to anyone else who wanted to partake in the ritual burning of the plum pudding. She wondered whether Bill, the scientist might be interested, although she reasoned that a plum pudding to him might only mean the negatively charged electrons or neutrons, or whatever they were in an atomic model. She would bring in a couple of small ones from home and heat them up in the microwave in the staff break room. Then, crowning it with holly and offering it a liberal libation of brandy, she would light it and they would all make a wish before the blue flame flickered out. It probably broke endless procedural rules with regard to diet restrictions, food hygiene standards, fire safety regulations etc. and she would definitely not conceal a silver coin within. Choking was unlikely to bring you luck. But to be able to see a moment of joy on their faces, and to be able to explain to anxious relatives that their loved ones were still given access to such rituals that embodied these happy memories, would be worth it.

'We'll have our own little Christmas pudding ceremony,' she said as she walked Maureen slowly to the lift. 'We'll have Christmas even before Santa comes,' she winked.

'Santa is really Odin, you know?' Maureen said. 'And his reindeer is the Sleipnir from the winter hunt.'

'No. Really?' Liz affected surprise. 'I didn't know that.'

'It is Norse mythology,' Maureen explained. 'I used to be very good at mythologies. I used to be good at lots of things. I could do my catechism and mental arithmetic… You had to say the answer quickly when the teacher banged the desk with the ruler. If you didn't know it, you got a whack. And you should have seen my ledgers. I was a very good bookkeeper at the shipping office. Never made a single mistake, you know.'

Liz pressed the button for the ground floor.

The doors closed, meeting silently, a quiet kiss. Maureen gripped Liz's arm like a child does, their first time in a lift, when the floor feels that it is slipping away from you. The firm foundations beneath your feet, no longer there, instead a vague floating feeling. Everything that was strong and secure, now just a mist where you can only rely on the support of another to keep you upright, to stop you from falling entirely into the abyss.

She tapped the woman's frail hand in reassurance as if to say. I am here. You are not alone. I will guide you through the fog and you can walk where I walk.

'You are very clever,' Liz said. 'Nowadays, no one needs to remember anything. The answer to everything is just a click away on the computer.' She led the woman slowly down the carpeted hallway, the sound of cutlery growing louder and the smell of dinner becoming an amorphous scent of meat, stewed apples, and disinfectant.

She wondered, not for the first time that if the once acute and lively minds of her patients, bred on a routine of mental acuity, rapid fire arithmetic and catechism could end up in this obfuscating fug of confusion, then what hope did following generations have when their brains were trained for no more than two minutes of content retention and access to a global web of knowledge at the touch of a button?

She settled Maureen at a table with three other ladies. They had a table by the window, overlooking the garden. Liz knew that Maureen liked it there. Even if the woman didn't much enjoy the company of the other ladies, they often talked about the changing flowers of the garden beyond. Sometimes she would remember all the flowers. At other times, the names would escape her. She might remember that she had a particular shrub in her garden, or wonder where another had gone, not realizing that she wasn't at her own home. Liz had observed her sometimes, getting worried that the slugs would be at the hostas, or that she hadn't watered her begonias. Liz would explain that the gardeners would see to all that and that she didn't need to worry. Maureen would accept it but wonder why, or how, since she didn't have a gardener and looked after the borders herself. Her mind, as always, struggling to fight back against the ivy climbing up the walls outside the window, its strong tendrils inserting their feeders into the stone like tiny grappling hooks and shrouding out everything else that had thrived before.

Liz did notice one thing though as she tucked the napkin

into the top of Maureen's collar, there was a holly bush, complete with red berries. She would nip out and get a little bit for the top of the pudding next time she was on duty.

'Look,' she said to the ladies. 'The holly and the ivy.'

Humming the common refrain, Liz began the song, but faltered after the first line. The other ladies joined in and continued where Liz had stopped, the words flowing mellifluously, honey off a spoon. There were no interruptions, no halting pauses. No searching for the right thought, or appropriate response. No fear of judgement or admonition. No impatient response from listeners. Just fluency and melody.

Of all the trees in the wood, these women bore the crown.

In music we are lost and found.

In ritual, we are bound.

The sun will rise, the deer will run,

and when we are full grown,

we are more childlike than ever.

Crisis for Christmas

The woman smiled as she packed the toys and board games in the bag.

'Someone's going to be happy with this lot,' she said. Her eyes crinkled at the edges as she spoke, and she peered over the half spectacles at the end of her nose. She was all woolly jumpers and bangles. A pair of fuzzy Christmas stockings hung from her ears, and she wore light-up reindeer antlers on her head.

Kayleigh smiled in return and reached for the bag, handing over a twenty-pound note. People didn't use cash very much these days. Even here, in the charity shop, they had a card machine, but Tag didn't deal in money that was traceable. His financial transactions were less credits and debits, and more, credit and credit.

Leaving the warm shop, she stepped out into the grey street. People milled around happily, their large bags knocking against their legs. The cafes looked cosy, their warm glow and smell of coffee, stabbing her stomach as she walked past. A small brass band played on the corner and their acolytes shook plastic buckets up and down. The proceeds, intended for a homeless charity. She ducked her head and crossed the road to avoid making eye contact and hated herself for it. She wanted to be able to contribute to ease the suffering of others, but she was having trouble easing her own suffering at the moment and couldn't spare anything of her own meagre wealth. The only money in her pocket had been given to her by Tag. Fifty pounds, which may as well have been a thousand for all her ability to pay it back. She would though. She had affirmed to herself. She would get extra work. It would mean leaving Liam on his own for a while, but at least he would be able to have the things he needed and even a couple of things that he wanted. Not the jeep, of course, but a few games and toys.

She prayed a silent prayer that the games had all their pieces. The boxes appeared to be in good condition. Slightly worn at the corners and the covers a bit faded, but she felt sure that Liam wouldn't mind. It would just be nice for him to have something new – well not new – but new to him. His shoes had become resistant to the continual seam of Gorilla glue, and the upper and sole had decided to part company as part of a more permanent arrangement. Kayleigh had hammered a nail through the top, but it didn't stop the sides lifting as if they were sly mouths whispering insults to passers-by, and it didn't stop the rain wetting his socks. There was simply no choice but to get him some more, and to find a warmer jacket for him since the frosty wind of midwinter had made moan over the last week, his thin waterproof was no match for it.

Knocking at Tag's door had been a new low. One of his minions had answered. She knew him from the old days when Sean had hung around with these lords of the top floor flats. It didn't matter that they were all in social housing; a home for everyone. There was nothing equitable about them. The ones on the ground floor were for those who required disabled access and adaptions. The middle floor were others, like her, those for whom life had given lemons, not with which to make lemonade, but the human equivalent of a defunct car, useless and pretending to be something it wasn't. The top floor seemed to be the equivalent of the penthouse, where the parties were held – well raves with loud garage music – and where the barons held their courts. Tag had given her a month to repay the fifty, and she would. She couldn't not. His interest rates were calculated less by percentage APR and more by GBR.

Over the years, she had heard about those who had been

unable to meet the repayment terms. It began with a bit of a bruising, then threats, usually against loved ones, then action, or hospitalization, whichever came first. That was if you were a guy. For women, other agreements could be reached. And there was no way she was doing that.

It would be okay. She would give Liam a nice Christmas because the guilt was too overwhelming not to. It would not be extravagant, or wasteful. He didn't ask for that. He didn't ask for anything to be fair. But that's what made it all the more important for her to be able to make it nice for him. Because he never moaned or complained, yet he noticed that for some reason, Christmas was different for him.

She had kept back some money for the electricity. Of all things, she wanted to ensure that they would have warmth and light, the basic human needs. She had even bought a small string of fairy lights that ran on the mains power because the batteries were too expensive to replace, and the little tree was bringing them so much joy.

It was better when Liam was at school, he was warm and fed at lunch-time and they only had to fill the evenings. Although she loved him being at home over the holidays, the flat was like an icebox most of the day. Being outside was often warmer, particularly if he could be playing football.

With no heating to protect the pipes against the cold, they had frozen. The water solid inside them, like ice pops that needed to be eased out of their tubes. The repairs team had logged the call but were under pressure seeing to all of their residents. All they could do was wait. The other basic human requirement, water, not available.

A lowness came over her. Daily life was hard, and fitting Christmas around it was impossible. It drew disparity into a stark, fairy-lit focus. The thought of going home filled her with dread. The cold, dark rooms with no water, even to make a cup of tea. Yet, here were café after café, and people wandering about with cardboard travel mugs, sipping steaming lattes and hot chocolates as if water was the most plentiful commodity in the land. Perhaps she should keep shopping, she told herself. Browsing the windows like everyone else as if purchasing something was a probable prospect. It would keep her warm at least, and perhaps some of the Christmas spirit would rub off on her. She might absorb it from those for whom, a meander through the high street was a pleasurable festive pursuit rather than another nail in the shoe of her downtrodden life.

A lady with the collection bucket was smiling and thanking people for the donations, their charitable duty done, the swell of satisfaction inside that they had shared their fortune with those less so. Kayleigh felt wretched. How could she explain to the lady that she had no heat or light or water at home, that the only presents she had for her son were pre-owned and that the only money in her purse had come at a price that could cost her a whole lot more than fifty pounds?

'Merry Christmas,' the woman called with a beam. 'Can you spare anything for the homeless?'

Kayleigh patted her pockets making a show of trying to find anything spare.

'Sorry,' I haven't got any change,' she said not breaking her stride in an attempt to circumnavigate the woman's position on the pavement.

'That's okay, we take notes and credit cards,' the woman joked. 'Anything, anything at all for the homeless. So many people sleeping in doorways. They would be so grateful. Anything, enough for a cup of tea.'

Somehow, the woman had presented herself in front of Kayleigh, between a lamppost and a roadwork bollard. There was no getting around her. She didn't even have enough to get herself a cup of tea and wanted to hold onto what little she had. What price, a cuppa for a stranger?

A black eye from Tag's henchmen.

'Lots of people are in crisis,' she explained. 'Your donation could give someone a roof over their head for Christmas,' the women said, 'and a warm meal and a hot shower and change of clothes.'

A warm meal, hot shower and a change of clothes sounded like heaven to Kayleigh who had had none of which for about a week. But there was something that had resonated with her. A roof over their head. However bad things were, she and Liam at least had that. Sometimes, one had to consider how much worse something could be before finding the silver lining.

Her fingers found a pound coin in the bottom of her pocket. She had been saving it for the bus home. Perhaps she could walk instead. 'It's all I've got, sorry,' she said as she tipped it into the slanted slit in the bucket lid. She supposed the woman would take it to mean, it's all I've got on me. Not, it's literally all I've got.

'Thank you so much,' the woman effused. Her colleague, a man in a Santa hat, shook a bell and smiled a warm smile. 'Every little helps,' he said. Kayleigh supposed he meant it gratefully and not just quoting a supermarket slogan, but she couldn't help feeling a stab of injustice. It might be a little to you, mate, she wanted to say. But didn't. She smiled and put on her gloves. Her walk home would be cold. Her house would be cold, but at least she had a home.

Humbug

Darcy was cleaning the back windows when there was a knock on the door. Mr. Norton looked up with the surprise of one who never gets visitors.

'I'll get it,' she offered, putting down the cloth and removing her rubber gloves. She moved through the living room towards the front door. It was no more than a few strides. These flats were small, though she had to circumvent his recliner chair positioned in the centre of the room, his little side table on wheels on which he ate his meals, placed his newspaper and glasses, and rested the remote control for the television. A Zimmer frame was set to one side, and she slunk around it in a practiced way, like a skier on a slalom.

Observing a silhouette through the glazed top panel of the front door, she opened it carefully. Being in these flats wasn't her favourite, the stairwell smelt of urine and vomit most days, and there were often noises from the flats above and unsavory characters hanging about the entrance way and car park. She was grateful that she only ever had to see Mr. Norton in the mornings. She would hate to see what the place was like after dark.

A woman and a young boy stood beyond the doormat. Darcy guessed at her age. About early thirties she assumed, though a tiredness made her look older. The boy looked about nine or ten, but it had been a while since her children were that age, and they all seemed to look older now. They looked cold and Darcy's instinct was to let them in, but it wasn't her house. She tried a warm smile, instead, as if the radiance from her face would be enough to lift their pallor to a healthier colour.

'Hi,' the woman said, her arms around a bag which appeared to be a garden pot. 'Is, er, Mr.… I… we are from…' she pointed to above, which Darcy assumed was a flat on the next floor.

'Who is it?' shouted Mr. Norton from within, like a king on a throne demanding the name to whom he should grant an audience.

'Kayleigh and Liam from flat seven,' Kayleigh said as if she was presenting herself at a masked ball.

'It's Kayleigh and Li…' Darcy began.

'I heard, I heard,' said the old man impatiently.

Darcy raised her eyebrows in apology.

'I broke his pot,' Liam offered. 'With my football. We brought him another one.'

'Oh, I see,' Darcy replied. She stepped back into the hall and turned back to face the living room. 'Mr. Norton, Liam says he has a new pot for you. That's nice, isn't it?'

'I should hope so,' the man said without grace.

'It's freezing out there. Come in for a bit,' Darcy said stepping back to let them in.

'I don't want the likes of them in here,' Mr. Norton said. 'Druggies, who go around destroying things.'

Darcy looked at the pair. True, the young woman looked pallid and weak and as if she hadn't seen hot water or a good meal for a while and had a general air of unkemptness generally associated with substance abuse, but her eyes were kind and soft, more defeated than stoned, and the boy, well he was just a sweet child.

Liam stepped over the threshold and walked down the hallway and stood before the old man. His mother tried to stop him but was a breath behind. She followed him in, and Darcy closed the door behind them.

'Why do you think we are druggies?' Liam asked him, looking inquisitively at his face. 'I don't take drugs and either does my mum,' he said simply. 'My dad did, but he died… in our bathroom,' he added for clarification.

Darcy's hands flew to her mouth and her eyes sought confirmation in Kayleigh's. The young woman's gaze was firmly fixed on her son in a mixture of compassion and love.

Mr. Norton glanced at the television, the sound was muted but the local news reporter stood on screen, wrapped up in a white padded coat and a blue scarf, giving her something of a snowman look. She held a microphone and gesticulated behind her to indicate where whatever had happened, had happened.

'I'm sorry I broke your pot,' he said. 'But I think the one we got is nicer. Your old one had a crack in it anyway. I think that's why it broke.'

Darcy sympathized. She remembered one year, when times were hard, their car had broken down and there were no funds to repair it. The shops were at the end of the long walk, that she had made so many winter evenings, looking in at the cosy houses, and carrying the groceries was difficult. She, her sister, and her mother had trailed along, the handles cutting into their fingers wishing every step closer to home to be the last. A friend of theirs had offered an old shopping trolley. This contraption was a welcome aid, and although she had felt like an old lady pulling it along, and it was far beneath her mother's previous transport status of a course of BMWs, they had been grateful. The little wheels eating up the pavement distance, containing their weekly shop like a squat, wheeled bi-ped creature from Star Wars. It had a bit of an ungainly gait, something to do with a bent axle, her mother had explained. After a couple of weeks, the creature died. The wheels came off the wagon and not only were they back to carrying the shopping whose bags had handles made of catgut, but they had to pay the friend for 'breaking' the already broken trolley. If they had had money to pay for a trolley, they could have bought one for themselves in the first place. There was a saying, if you'd hit rock bottom, the only way was up. She didn't think that was necessarily true. There were often times when rock bottom seemed only Ground floor, there was still, lower ground and basement to go.

Mr. Norton nodded.

'We did get you another one,' Liam added. 'But it had a Christmas tree in, and we kept it.'

Kayleigh cringed. She loved her son's open honesty, but this grumpy old man seemed reluctant enough to accept their apology or efforts of restitution without learning that he'd missed out on the grand prize.

'I bought it with my own money,' he continued. 'Well, some of my own money. I haven't got that much.' He cast his gaze around the room, a small frown appeared on his brow. 'Why haven't you got any decorations?' he asked.

It was Darcy's turn to cringe. She had asked the same thing a few weeks ago, wondering if he needed assistance to get his home ready for Christmas. In truth, she rather liked its festive barrenness. It was like an oasis to her, an island of normality amongst the noise, lights, traffic, and crowds. He had explained that Christmas reminded him that he was alone. His son was estranged, some fall out years gone, the nature of which, he didn't disclose. His wife had passed away. Christmas was just something that heightened his sense of loss. He had explained how every advert on the television that showed multi-generational families all pulling crackers and laughing around the dinner table hurt him anew. He said that Covid was a blessing in disguise, because even people who had families couldn't be with them, so they were no different to him, and that though he wouldn't want to wish anyone sick, he would be quite happy if they could all go into lockdown again.

'I don't like Christmas,' the man said.

'How can you not like Christmas?' Liam asked. He rather thought that if the old man had a tree, he would feel infinitely more festive, although he loved their new little potted tree and didn't want to have to part with it. Perhaps the man could get his own for his new empty pot.

Kayleigh wondered how her son *could* like Christmas,

aware as he was that his wasn't quite the same as everyone else's.

As much as she relished being in this warm room, she thought they should leave before old Ebenezer sent them to the workhouse.

'Come on, Liam,' she said, winking at him. 'I think we should go and leave Mr. Norton in peace.' It felt strange saying his name. They had always referred to him as Flat One, and even now, they had not been formally introduced, she had just heard the cleaning lady refer to him as such. She realised that she didn't know the cleaning lady's name.

'Sorry to take up your time, er…,' she said nodding to Darcy allowing the space at the end of her sentence into which the woman could insert her name.

'Darcy,' she said escorting them to the door. 'Nice to meet you, and you too Liam,' she said smiling at the young boy. She felt sad that his friendly conversation had been met by the words of a Grinch whose heart was two sizes too small.

Placing the plant pot on the ground, they held their breath and ran up the stairwell. If not to defend their nostrils from the noxious odours, then to raise their body temperature before returning to the cold flat.

About an hour later, Darcy completed her work and making Mr. Norton a cup of tea before she left, she called goodbye from the front door, sealing him inside his emptiness. The hem of her coat brushed against something that her spatial awareness hadn't registered before, and an arm reached out and touched her leg. As she looked down, she found the arms covered in a fuzzy green sleeve. She had the Grinch on her mind. But this was different. It was a Grinch with Dalek arms, stuck out at odd angles as if it had suffered a few radial fractures and hadn't been able to get to the clinic in time. Dangling sporadically on the Dalek arms were a few baubles. There were no lights. But even so, it added a jaunty source of life to an otherwise empty pot.

The angel's candle

Straightening the Advent wreath, Jen wiggled the candles, checking that they were secure and calling to mind the significance of each.

The first, purple. The prophet's candle, lit on the first Sunday of Advent. It had already burned down low, dribbles of wax solidified down its side. Its meaning: Hope.

The second, purple. The Bethlehem candle, representing the journey of Mary and Joseph. Preparation. Its meaning: Peace.

The third, pink. The Shepherd's candle. Its meaning: Joy. The shift from repentance to celebration and anticipation.

The fourth, purple. The angel's candle. Its meaning: Love.

The final candle, placed in the centre. White. To be lit on Christmas Eve, in celebration but also in recognition of Christ's purity.

For now, Hope and Peace were all she needed. It was not yet week four, but as she did every night before he came home, Jen prayed her angel prayer for protection.

Fork 'andles
Darcy

… Of course, liturgically, or ecclesiastically, the Advent period is more than just a countdown. It is a time for preparation and reflection in and of itself. We always had an Advent wreath and observed the lighting of the candles at mealtimes and on each Sunday of Advent. The candles are set on a special stand, surrounded by a wreath of fresh greenery, a circle of evergreen to symbolize everlasting life in Christ, and each one carried its own meaning. The first to be lit is a candle for Hope, the purple representing penance and prayer. The second is the Bethlehem candle representing the journey of Mary and Joseph and the Faith they had in their mission. The third is pink, for joy, Mary's joy in her baby, but also mankind's joy in His arrival. There was another purple one, but I can't remember what that one is for now. Then the final was white, to be lit on Christmas Eve, in celebration but also in recognition of Christ's purity.

For some, these candles could be merely symbolic, and an Advent wreath could be fashioned in any rudimentary way. Not so for my mother. Our home candles had to be the same as the ones at church. It was very difficult to find purple candles in Fenwick's, or John Lewis in the eighties. I don't know if they still have Fenwick's anymore. Do they? It's like Athena and HMV, they've gone now. Anyway, long dinner party candles in those days favoured an elegant cream, or a delicate peach or pale blue if you were particularly daring; pastel pink and white were doable but never purple. Purple was for witches and voodoo practitioners, or anyone who indulged in superstitious practices (rather ironically, I think). I remember Mum panicking that unless she purchased them from the church repository, when they first appeared in October that she wouldn't have them in time for Advent. There was one time when we had taken visitors in the summer holidays, and we had taken them to see Westminster Cathedral – the Catholic mother ship, as it were. When we saw the large, church-style Advent candles in their shop, we seized upon them in delight. How ahead of the game were we? We gloated. It wasn't even August, and we were already prepared for December. We hadn't considered then that we didn't have the church-sized candle-holders at home… So, when it came to it, we couldn't use them anyway. It was unthinkable that we could make a wreath with any other colour candle, but I suggested it, nevertheless. Four red candles and one white, I mooted, (I'm resisting the opportunity to refer to the Two Ronnies sketch about fork 'andles!) Red and green were Christmassy and festive and the white one would be for Christmas Eve, I proposed. Mother wasn't convinced, thinking that to go against the church's example, with red of all things, we were teetering on the edge of damnation at most, and hedonism at least. I ventured that, surely, as long as we lit them and meditated on the meaning of each one, that was all that mattered, and wasn't it better that we focused on the significance of the candles rather than their colour? After all, that seemed a bit racist to me. She reluctantly relented, still believing, I think, that red was the colour of prostitution, and we diligently lit each new red candle throughout Advent and burned it at every mealtime throughout the week. Interestingly, as it was only the candle that burned, and not our souls in infernal hell for deviating from the colour code, she seemed happy to accept that sourcing red candles was much easier and yes, surely God would be alright with red, and we used them every Advent since.

Do you know, I don't think I've ever actually ever thrown any out, I just pop them back in the box to be kept for next year, tiny and insignificant little cylinders with burnt out wicks, dribbles of shiny, red wax, cooled into undulations like lava rocks. Well, I won't be needing them this year. When I was little, I liked to snap the dribbles off with my fingernail and use them like fragile crayons. Mum thought that irreverent in some way, even in their petrified state. They had been lit and prayed to. I suppose I could chuck them now, or in the spirit of recycling, I could use them up next time I do some yoga, or keep them in the utility room in case of a power cut.

They were just candles after all. It is only the symbolism that we layer on that confers on them a greater significance. But I do love candles. They are one thing that brings me joy, and peace. There was once when I was in my twenties. I had gone on a pilgrimage to a shrine. I had missed half of the lectures and workshops because I had found a little chapel that I didn't want to leave. I was happiest just sitting on the stone floor tiles, surrounded by candles that were set into every ledge and stand on the walls, window ledges and floor, reflecting against a mosaic of a dove on the wall. Peace. Candles are fuel and light, and peace.

I wonder now, where was the line between affirmation and indoctrination? Where did one end and the other begin? Had I confirmed and affirmed the belief and spiritual education of my childhood and youth, or had I simply been strung along long enough to get past the point of no return, where questioning became impossible, and acceptance became complete?

I don't know, and I haven't done a wreath this year, for the first time... ever. I haven't taken time to pray and focus on the significance of each Advent week. But candlelight, whether a votive for prayer, or not, is still fuel, light, and peace, and even joy. So, perhaps it is okay to just hold on to the bits that I like?

Chaos

Chaos is often described as a swirling mass of disordered matter and is used to explain something messy and out of control. In fact, in the origin of the universe, it was a void, a chasm, the abyss of infinite darkness, the separation of heaven and earth. The ultimate calm really.

So, when Darcy let herself into the back door and her mind jumped at once to the notion of chaos, it was in the commonly understood definition of disordered and out of control, rather than the origin of the universe way. Laura's house was anything but calm.

Three bun tins were upended in the sink, the mixing bowl smeared with the remains of a chocolate batter and the beaters stood in a measuring jug which looked as though it had the creaminess of whisked egg coating its sides. Powdered sugar covered the surfaces, like a layer of snow over the Cairngorms and a stack of Tupperware cake boxes stood next to the microwave, on which stood an open tub of glace cherries. Broken pretzels crunched into salted crumbs beneath Darcy's feet.

'Hello…?' she called, finding a place to set down her bag on top of a tower of cookery books and two unopened boxes from Amazon. 'Laura…?' She walked through the dining room where the table looked as though it had been clad in decorative log rolls. A large transparent bag, which in a former life, had been the packaging for a large eiderdown, now sat atop the logs with its top open, foil bows and ribbon spewing from its mouth. At the head of the table, a laptop was perched, its lid up and its screen emitting a blue light. Darcy half expected a voice to emanate from it, dispatching instructions like the disembodied mastermind in a spy movie.

Stepping over bags and boxes, she moved through to the living room, to find a beautifully decorated Christmas tree in the corner, more boxes, and bags around its base, but not of the gift-wrapped kind, these were old moving boxes with black sharpie scrawled across their faces, announcing their contents and ripped packing tape hanging in long curls, like the adhesive version of beach waves.

'Laura…?' she called again, a little louder this time. She must be upstairs.

Moving back through the dining room to the hallway, she heard the thump of feet hurrying down the stairs. Then she saw them. The feet were in pink slippers with pom poms on the top, the legs clad in jeans and the body was a large snowball, which upon closer inspection Darcy recognized was the white linen of three double beds and a king-size. There was no head to speak of, just a messy topknot on top of the snowball.

'Careful,' Darcy warned. 'You can't see, you'll fall down the stairs.'

She reached for the snowball and in doing so revealed Laura's face.

'That might not be a bad thing,' Laura smirked. 'At least if I had a broken leg, I might get away with not having to do Christmas.'

'A broken leg is the least of it,' Darcy chided. 'You could break your neck.'

Laura deposited the snowball on the floor of the utility room and began to pull it apart like clumps from a white candy floss, feeding it into the waiting mouth of the washing machine. In a few practiced moves, she added the washing tablet, scent boosters, closed the door and pressed the buttons. Within moments the clear door was filling up with water and the candy floss began turning around.

'Thank heaven for machines,' she said. 'What would we do

without them? Imagine what it was like in the olden days.'

Darcy wanted to point out that there were still many people who didn't have washing machines in their houses and had to roll their snowballs to the launderette on a regular basis. But she didn't.

Opening the dryer door, Laura pulled out another huge snowball and packed it into a waiting basket.

'I can do that,' Darcy offered. 'That's what I'm here for.'

'Actually,' Laura pleaded. 'Is there any way that you can please clean the oven today? I've done a load of baking – chocolate reindeer cupcakes for the nursing home. I thought they'd be fun, but now I'm thinking that the pretzels might prove a challenge to dentures and institute a choking hazard.'

Darcy smiled.

'I've also precooked the cranberry sauce, made a lasagne for Saturday, a casserole for Sunday, and a curry for Christmas Eve. I've prepped stuffing balls and carrot and parsnip mash and it's all in the freezer. Oh, and I made a yule log and a raspberry roulade. So, the oven is a mess, and that is the first thing that Jack's mum will comment on when she arrives next week. Ugggh?' Laura groaned audibly. 'I'm so tired and I haven't done half of my list yet. The laptop spreadsheet just keeps sitting there, as if it is a disembodied mastermind from a spy movie, giving me mission after mission.'

'That's what I thought it looked like too,' Darcy laughed. 'So, the oven, okay, but what with the rest of Tartarus,' she said gesturing to all of it.

'What's Tartarus?' Laura asked. 'Is it anything like Hell, because that's what I'm feeling at the moment.'

'Yeah, it pretty much is,' Darcy agreed. 'Looks like you've got a lot going on. Is there anything else I can help with?'

Laura looked around and saw the individual projects as one daunting whole. 'I can't put the decoration boxes away yet because there is still more to do. I've still got loads to wrap. I've got more shopping to do because Jack's sister, Linda, has said she and Owen and the three kids are going to pop in on the way to Owen's Dad in Minehead. She wasn't going to, so I didn't get presents and now it will be awkward if she brings my guys something and I haven't got anything for them. And they are all buggers to buy for because they're the type to have an opinion on everything. I keep getting light-headed when I think of how much there is still to do. The beds all need changing; the rooms cleaned; the food to be bought and prepped; the extra tables and chairs to get – Susan next door is lending me her kitchen table, because they're away in Kent, but I need to get them before she goes, but not too soon because she still needs it and I'll have nowhere to store it.'

'Can't you send the in-laws to stay at Susan's?' Darcy joked. 'Jack's mum can comment on the state of her oven and bed linen instead.'

'Believe me, I would love that,' Laura said.

'Are you sure you're okay?' Darcy said, concerned. 'You seem to have taken a lot on. What else can I help with?'

'No, honestly, I'll be fine,' Laura asserted, unwilling to belie any weakness at not being able to cope. 'It's nothing more than thousands of other people are doing at this time of year, is it? We're all doing it. It will be fine, and everyone will have a wonderful time. It will all be worth it on Christmas Day, when the food's all done, and we are all enjoying a game of Trivial Pursuit and a glass of port.'

'How goes it with the bunyip?' Darcy ventured, having learned what it was, and hoping that the packages in the kitchen might contain the elusive mythical creature.

'Oh, no. No luck. We haven't been able to find anything like it, so we are going to have to give her some modelling clay. It might blow the Santa thing out of the water, which would be rubbish for Max, but I can't say that a piece of me wouldn't be happy to have it all done with. I'm tired already thinking about Christmas Eve. Getting everything done by Midnight, only to be woken at four a.m.

'Are you going to Grace's show?' Laura asked, changing the subject, and reaching across the sink detritus to fill up the kettle.'

'I'll do that,' Darcy said, taking it from her. 'Looks like you need one.' Balancing two mugs on the only piece of countertop that wasn't under a layer of fresh snow, she popped two teabags in and added a splash of milk. 'Yes. It will be lovely. It's been ages since I've been to a school nativity. I'm sort of out of it all now. Is Briony in it?'

'Yes, she's an angel. I've made the costume. Here, look?' Laura ran to the understairs cupboard and produced a hanger, upon which hung a flowing robe of shimmering white lining fabric and a pair of wings that looked like they had been pinched from a passing snowy owl. A tinsel halo completed the ensemble.

'Oh Wow!' exclaimed Darcy, impressed. 'That is incredible. You made that? It looks like it's a proper bought costume from online.'

'Oh, angels are easy,' she said. 'It didn't take long. I had the sewing machine out anyway, because I couldn't find any Christmas cushions that I liked and so I made some. It's not like I had to make an ox or donkey, or anything.'

'Sofa, now!' Darcy said, placing the mug of tea in Laura's hand and ushering her to the living room.

Returning to the kitchen, she wiped and cleaned and scrubbed, restoring the chaos to Chaos.

A void of nothingness and calm.

More tapping than Ginger and Fred

Oxford street was teeming with bodies. Lucy had seen a programme once about pharmaceuticals. It showed all the little pills being pushed along a conveyor belt and then two steel blades funnelling them into a narrow line, then, still moving, each bouncing over the other, they were finally deposited into the bottles. She imagined that if you viewed the busy high street from above, the Christmas shoppers would look very much the same.

Aside from the jostling and jouncing, feeling like a paracetamol in more ways than one, she did admit to having a lovely time. The atmosphere was everything you would want from a Christmas shopping expedition in a major city. It was dark but not too late, five o'clock. She had left work early and had hopped on the tube, emerging from the underground into a world of light and activity, like a hedgehog on the first day of spring. Once she had determined whether she was going left or right, she waved farewell to her agency as far as directional intent went. She just had to step into the throng and be carried along.

The strong south side current led her past small stands, selling London souvenirs, their hats and t shirts spilling onto the street and their hawkers shouting and thrusting them into her face. Cafes, their golden glow and Christmas lights shone out through misty glass, the windows steaming with the warmth of sweating bodies and the cold December air. Whenever a door opened, Lucy could hear the clatter of cutlery and chatter of voices and the whoosh and whirrs of coffee machines as the baristas frothed milk and ground beans. She would treat herself to a sit down and a peppermint latte later, but for now she wanted to get started. A world of gift-buying awaited.

Lucy had a list of names rather than things. She was not the sort to peruse magazines and plan that Grandad would get a sweater, and Grandma, a gardening trowel set. She preferred to let the gift muse strike. Obviously, she had had to get something for the secret Santa at work, but Amazon had taken care of that, and they were already wrapped under the tree at home. But for her family, she wanted to wander through the stores, touch and feel the items, try them on even, and return home with branded bags full and her purse empty.

Not that she was carrying cash of course. No one did that in London, not with the pickpockets. In fact, no one did that anywhere. Cash was a thing of the past and she was grateful for it. Cash carried with it that sense of reduction which was most unsatisfactory. Like, when you see a big cake, and slice by slice, it gets less until it is gone. Sometimes, after five slices, you have to tell yourself, that's enough now, you should really save some cake for another time. But with tapping technology, you didn't even have to see the cake and could happily tap your card, your phone, your watch even, and know that the cake was always there. There was a small problem with debit cards. At some point, the cake did run out and that was severely disappointing, if not quite alarming. But with credit cards, the baker just kept baking more cakes, covering the counter with them, more cakes than you ever really needed in fact.

So, Lucy would not be returning home with an empty purse, but with a full credit balance. But that was a "future Lucy" problem. She would deal with that in the new year when the bill came in. After all, that's what the family expected. Her eldest brother had two kids, her sister had three, her youngest sister was a student and her brother, Chris had just returned from backpacking around Cambodia. She, Lucy, had a well-paid job in PR, earned a London salary and was single. It was expected that she was the one with the most disposable income and therefore able to provide the best gifts. Although it would seem, that none of them understood anything about property prices in the suburbs of the city.

So, Grandma and Grandad, Mum and Dad, four siblings, three in-laws (Simon had married twice and she still kept in touch with his first wife) and six children (the first wife had remarried, and the new husband came with an adorable six-year-old, called Natalie). That was seventeen, and she also wanted to get something for her best friend, Tamsin. Eighteen names on the list. She did also need to get a dress and shoes for two parties, one Christmas, the other New year, and unfortunately with the same circle of friends, so she couldn't wear the same thing twice. Then the was the cost of the travel to Cardiff. She had no need of a car in London, so she had intended for the train to take the strain, but the price of a return ticket over the Christmas season was two hundred pounds, and Lucy knew from past experience that that didn't even guarantee you a seat. She had spent one year sitting on suitcases in the guard's van sharing a sandwich with the porter because they hadn't put enough carriages on.

Also, she needed hotel accommodation, as there were so many visiting her parents, she thought it fairer to let her Grandparents have the spare room, and Simon, Patsy and the kids bunk down in the playroom. Rachel and Alfie weren't staying as they didn't live too far away, Shona would have her old room and Chris was sleeping her floor, which after hostels in Cambodia was a definite upgrade. Her mother had researched local places, feeling some sense of neglect that her own daughter was being turfed out onto the street, while her son's second wife, whom she didn't really like very much, had taken her place in the nest. She had found the nearest Travelodge to be the most reasonably priced, unfortunately they didn't have a trouser press in every room, but she had promised that she would happily run the iron over Lucy's slacks if she needed it.

Lucy had googled it to see if it was walking distance from her parents' house. It wasn't, which meant that she wasn't going to be able to have a drink over the whole of Christmas because she would have to be able to get back to her functional, but oh so, not luxurious room on the ring road. And not even be able to press her jeans once she got there. Instead, Lucy had booked herself into a small hotel, a pub with rooms, really, which had looked idyllic on the website. Cosy, comfortable rooms, a roaring fire and bon viveur in the pub downstairs. A bath, which she didn't have at home. London prices didn't allow for baths, too much square footage. So, when everyone was fighting over what to watch on the television and Patsy was boring everyone with her views on child rearing (and judging Rachel for hers), Lucy could bid them farewell and take an evening stroll through the snow (of course it would have to snow to complete the idyll), to the welcome and hospitality of the Fiddle and Bow. It sounded perfect.

She just needed to have the perfect presents to go with it... oh and boxes of course. Christmas gift opening was only satisfactory, to her mind, if the treasures were ensconced in elegant boxes and tied with bows of thick fabric ribbon. There was nothing more unappealing than a garment; a cashmere sweater, or a cute scarf, gloves, and hat set, wrapped in paper alone. Hanging floppy and limp from the hands of the recipient, as they pulled at the thin foil ribbon to release the goods did not bring Lucy any Christmas joy. She liked to present a firm, solid box, like they did in the American movies, or on TV adverts, bearing her gift as if it were a box of Frankincense brought from the east. Technically, she did come to Cardiff from the east, so she rather fancied placing herself amongst the most famous gift-bearers of all. There would be no tugging and tearing at paper, hunting for scissors to snip the ribbon binding, the one to whom she would bring gifts would hold the elaborate box in their hands, their eyes full of wonder and delight at what could lie within. Then in one, simple and elegant movement, would lift the box (thick, fabric ribbon bow and all) and their face would fill with joy, as beams of light shone to all corners of the room. That was how Lucy gave gifts.

Eighteen gifts and boxes, six kids, five siblings, four in laws, three nights B&B, two dresses and one return ticket. Her Christmas shopping list had the makings of a song, and it wasn't even day one yet.

Lucy sat in the café, drinking her peppermint latte, and eating a turkey and cranberry panini. Her bags sat opposite her on the empty chairs at her table, like uncommunicative dinner guests. Her feet were aching, but she was finally the right temperature. That was the problem shopping in a high street, wearing enough layers to keep warm as you are carried by the narcotics conveyor, but then being roasting when you are deposited into your crowded store bottle. However, here with her coat on the hook and her hat and gloves stowed in the pocket, she sat enjoying her well-earned rest, like Goldilocks who had discovered all of baby bear's things.

Whilst her table companions didn't share her repast, nor chatted amiably about the weather, she was aware of them muttering something amongst themselves and felt as though it was to do with how much they had cost. Lucy had never really considered the gifts having a conscience before but imagined that they would be quite happy to have been purchased, rescued from a life on a store shelf, before being sold off cheap, or worse, sent to an end of line store like TK Maxx. Like some valiant knight, rescuing an incarcerated princess from a tower, Lucy had come along and had not only freed them, but had matched them perfectly to someone who would appreciate them and treasure them for years to come, (well, not in the case of the kids, they would probably get bored or outgrow them, or be broken within the week, and possibly not Patsy, who would invariably find something wrong with it and cast it to one side ungraciously, with the intent to pass it on at the earliest opportunity), but in the main, Lucy's part in sourcing the perfect gift and uniting it with its life partner was wholly satisfying. She rather liked the credit that went with it, like the valour of chivalry. 'Behold, Lady Lucy of Londonshire, bestower of the finest gifts in the land,' or 'Lucy got me this the Christmas before last, or 'Oh, yes, that was from Aunty Lucy, George absolutely loves it, never puts it down.'

A small churn rotated her stomach like the intermittent turns in a light wool cycle in the washing machine. Not much, but enough to unsettle things within. Was it the turkey panini? Might have been the peppermint latte. Christmas was a time for all that was rich and sickly and those stomachs that tried to be mindful of healthy-eating the rest of the year found it particularly challenging to process all the requisite junk.

The sly whispers and muttered asides from the bags were getting louder. Particularly the shiny one with the tissue paper protruding from the top. The one from the boutique where she got her dresses. It seemed to be muttering something about not needing another dress, that she already had a couple in her wardrobe that she could wear to the parties, that everyone was too drunk to remember anyway, and even if they did, wouldn't they respect you for reusing what you had than going to buy more? Lucy didn't want to listen to their negative griping anymore. She looked away from the bags and out of the window at the rest of the pills, who she now saw as turtles, blissfully riding the current, getting carried along and carried away to Christmas Island. Whatever doubt or niggles of nausea that she was feeling about how much tapping she had done (because she knew that it wasn't the food that was making her feel sick), it couldn't be that wrong, she told herself, because there were thousands of people out there, doing exactly the same thing.

Most highly favoured non-binary person

Showing her ticket to the woman behind the desk, Darcy shrugged off her coat and walked into the school hall. The seats were numbered, and she found hers easily. There was something comfortably familiar about schools, she found. Of course, there were differences according to their position of league tables; sporting prowess, and teaching quality and pupil behaviour, and grounds and facilities. But, overall, most school halls felt the same; high windows with short, navy curtains, gym apparatus on the walls, parquet flooring, polished in the centre and dusty around the edges. Some sort of black box AV system, with pivoting lights suspended from overhead gantries. A variety of children's work, displayed around the walls.

Stage blocks had been erected at the front, Darcy thought of her own secondary school which had a proper built in stage, and curtain drapes, a trap door and storage beneath for props and costumes for productions. Why had she never partaken in more productions? She asked herself. No self-confidence, she replied. Too shy. Struggling enough to know who she was without having to pretend to be someone else. Always worried about making a mistake. What if you forgot your lines, or lyrics of a song? It would be shameful and embarrassing. If she had a regret, and she did (there were more than a few to mention, Mr. Sinatra), it would be that she cared too much about what people thought. If she could tell her younger self one thing, it would be, "Do what you want to and don't let anyone chip away at your pedestal. You have as much right to be up there, as anyone". Too crippled and disabled she had been over the years, too afraid to try, in case she failed. It was easier to cope with failure if people thought you hadn't even bothered. Perhaps it was her faith. Always thinking that God is watching, knows your every move, is chalking up a little list next to your name as to whether you've been righteous or sinful, good or bad, naughty or nice, like some great Santa in the sky. Yes, Darcy had to accept, that had been a part of it. That and her mother. Her words, always there. "What would people think if you did that…, wore that…, said that? Imagine the shame".

Shame has its place. We feel ashamed if we have hurt someone or caused something bad to happen by our actions. But should we feel shame it we have taken a single step outside the box of societal acceptability? If we blasphemed or missed church on a Sunday? Was that the same sort of shame?

No, Darcy realised now. It wasn't, but how could you get forty years back and have a do over?

The room was filling up. Where was Liz? She wondered. Fortunately, the seats were allocated, their being numbered meant that she didn't need to feel nervous about her coat on Liz's seats. She checked her watch. It was nearly time to start. The children filed in and took their seats, their teachers directing them to sit down and with fingers on their lips, keep quiet.

Anxiety swelled in Darcy's stomach. Perhaps something had happened. She had turned off her phone for fear that it would go off during the performance, though no one ever called her, so it was unlikely. But you could never rule out a random call from a scam artist, whose untimely call could not only serve you a few looks and tuts from your fellow audience, but also empty the life savings from your bank account.

As she typed a message, she saw a boy get up from the back row and hurriedly put on a blue robe and headdress. Strange, Darcy though. That looked like Mary's outfit.

With the ringer off, she studied the phone screen for a reply. The dot appeared on the app, and she opened it.

'Not going to make it... Mum staying with us for Xms. Wouldn't leave without her shopping bag. I said she didn't need it as shops were shut and we were going to Grace's play. Grace was getting more and more anxious as time ticked by and Mum wouldn't get in car. I said we couldn't wait any longer, wasn't fair on Grace, she would miss her part and she had been practicing for so long and that if Mum didn't come with us, she would just have to miss it. Karl away, couldn't take her. Mum started crying that I didn't care about her and how could we go and leave her. Mssged teacher to say we'd be late but would still make it by the end of the first song – decided to leave Mum- teacher said already too late, Patrick going on as Mary instead. Grace is in bits, inconsolable. I want to kill my mother. Hope you enjoy the show, sorry. Merry fucking Christmas. Xxx

In the bleak midwinter

It was the twenty-first. Midwinter. Darcy walked into the barn to find it a hive of activity. The last time she had been there, she was in borrowed overalls that Emma had lent her, and wellies and a cold north wind was blowing through a couple of broken slats at the back. They had worked hard, clearing cobwebs, sweeping, swabbing the concrete floor with disinfectant, and scrubbing down benches and chairs.

'Happy Solstice!' Emma called, running over to Darcy and her husband, hugging them both warmly. 'Welcome! Oh I'm so excited. It is the best time of the year,' she said. 'Well, Summer solstice is special too, but there are lots of long summer days and late warm evenings, so the Solstice doesn't stand out as much. But, in winter, everything is so dark and cold and wet and damp and grey and muddy, and that's just our front yard,' she joked, 'and it is the perfect time to get together and celebrate that it is the shortest day of the year, after this, every day is getting a little longer, a little brighter, and although January and February can still feel the harshness of winter, there is not much longer before the spring and we can celebrate.'

Darcy and Richard nodded and looked around at the beautiful, natural space and the friendly buzz of activity.

'Historically,' Emma continued, 'when people didn't have Tescos,' she smiled, 'it was a time to enjoy the food that had been gathered in at harvest, because you knew you didn't have to make it last for too much longer. It is a time to acknowledge the importance of the sun in our lives and the life it brings.'

Darcy smiled, feeling Emma's enthusiasm. She imagined that by now, her mother would have swept her out of the barn

386

in a cloud of disapproval for the paganistic nature of the occasion. But her mother wasn't there, and Darcy was quite enjoying the realization that perhaps there were other opinions to be had in contrast to her mother's, and that not everyone who didn't go to church were sinful heathens. Some could actually be quite lovely, warm and generous people.

Why it had taken her over forty years to realise that, she wasn't sure. Probably something to do with her faith again. God – one true faith – one true way – nothing else exists – especially winter festivals that weren't Christmas.

'I'm so glad you are both here,' Emma said greeting them warmly with a hug. 'Thank you so much for coming. We're making good progress but it's always fun to have more hands. The more the merrier,' Emma said brightly. Darcy had always thought, the more the more opportunity to spoil the broth, but perhaps that was from a lifetime of subversive control.

'Looks a bit different from a couple of weeks ago,' she said glancing at the stacks of hay placed around the perimeter at different heights like bleachers at a basketball game.

'Yeah,' Emma agreed. 'The hay is great for extra seating when the table is gone and it gives it all an 'organic' air, I think,' she said, managing to pivot on her toes as she beckoned Darcy to follow her. How was she so bouncy? Darcy wondered, feeling stooped and drab as if she was carrying stones in her pockets. 'So, here's what we're doing. The tables are going to be joined together all down the centre of the barn with the benches and chairs around. The chairs are all odd so it doesn't matter where they go, just not so crammed together so people can have a bit of elbow room, we want everyone relaxed not scrunched up uncomfortably,'

Darcy nodded and thought of Susan's kitchen furniture squashed into Laura's already small dining room.

Emma continued, waving her arms around as if she were conducting an orchestra. 'Over here, we have the bar,' she said pointing to an old Welsh Dresser that stood against the far end. A friendly-looking man was stacking piles of paper cups and lining up jugs of what Darcy presumed was cider.

Three small boys were jumping on the haystacks and Emma swatted them off as she passed, telling them to go and see if Jane needed help with the candles.

Darcy hoped the candles played some other part in the celebration as the thought of naked flames in a draughty barn filled with haystacks and cider fumes was a health and safety no go.

As the afternoon wore on, the barn transformed into a grotto of wonder. Darcy and Richard had helped, along with Laura and Liz, Sally and her girls, and a cohort of Emma and Rob's friends and farm hands. Emma had been clear that the dress code was that there was no dress code. (No dress code? What does one do when there are no rules to follow? Darcy wondered to herself) But she had chatted with her new friends and found that they were intending to wear whatever they were comfortable in as long as it was suitable for dancing.

The candles had come into the barn. But Darcy's concern was ameliorated by seeing that they were in fact little tea lights in jam jars. Each jar decorated with a bow of jute and strung on wires so that they could hang from the wooden posts and walls of the barn and suspend from a huge fallen tree branch that was secured over the centre table. The effect was magical. Thick, lush, boughs of holly and ivy, laurel and pine were wrought into swooping garlands that surrounded the room. Natural decorations of dried clementine slices, cinnamon sticks, pinecones and red apples were set amongst them. Firmly nestled in the glossy stems, rather than the south facing, like the tiny nipples of Darcy's past. She was entranced.

A ceilidh band had arrived and were settling themselves in the corner of the barn, Darcy could see a banjo and accordion resting on the haystacks, like people waiting for the dance to begin. It reminded her, not for the first time, that music was made by the music makers. The instruments couldn't do it alone. How different it was this year, to not be the music maker. To not be the one poring over sheet music, printing it out, transposing the keys, arranging rehearsal times, leading the rehearsals, panicking that they weren't ready and would sound crap. It had been part of her Christmas preparation for the majority of her life. Singing Emmanuel, in candlelit services, feeling responsible for the spiritual awakening for every soul in the congregation.

A thin man with a tin whistle and a denim jacket laughed easily and took a swig of coffee. Darcy couldn't be certain what was going through his mind, but his attitude seemed to suggest that at this candlelit service, his purpose was different. Might it be possible to play music for one's own enjoyment and that of others, without carrying the burden of a faultless performance? Interesting.

More people were arriving, walking down the lane that led from the field gate to the barn. Rob had erected braziers at intervals like an avenue of lime trees, their bright orange flames billowing slightly to the south, like windsocks on an airfield. Darcy watched as they approached, laughing, and carrying platters and casserole pots, and soup pans. Some brought cushions and wore blankets around their shoulders like cloaks.

The atmosphere was electric. Darcy felt a fizz forming on the hairs of her arms and allowed it to run up to her neck without moving. Returning to the barn, the music had begun, a quiet background acoustic sound, a fiddle and a guitar mostly and the tin whistle man. Darcy allowed the music to sweep over her and smiled. The table looked incredible. All along the centre, was a runner of the same greenery as the garlands, studded with whole clementines and candles and apples. Darcy inhaled deeply and felt a sense of wellness that she had not experienced since..., well, since she couldn't' say when. For the first time in forever, there was no dread, fear, apprehension, it seemed even as though the palpitations had stopped. The tension in her shoulders had gone and she was able to roll them back and leave them there. She felt a couple of inches taller in this attitude. She may even have the appetite for resuming her yoga or taking walks to assist her core in keeping her body in this new upright pose. It felt like Christmas, in this place, people of all ages laughing and joking around the table, or deep in conversation, the table laden with food but not a turkey in sight, no one person fraught and stressed in a hot kitchen, the labour, equally shared. No gift unwrapping ceremony, everyone simply had a pot of Emma's homemade jam to take home with them. No church service to attend, where you reinforced the beliefs of a lifetime, or sat in confusion, wondering how much of it was real. No litany of traditions to observe because to not would be an offense to your mother and all that she had taught you. No cookery books to peruse because you had made something you enjoy rather than something you had be pre-destined to learn how to produce, because you are a woman and the next in line to continue the Christmas catering legacy.

An energy swirled through her, rising like the smoke of the snuffed taper and she took a deep, contented sigh. She smiled.

The table was laden. Rustic loaves of bread and slabs of chilled butter sat next to large tureens of lentil stew and spicy parsnip soup. Roasted squashes, filled with pomegranate jewels nestled in beds of buttered green leaves. Large wooden platters of cheeses were surrounded by grapes and figs and walnuts. Slices of soft, sticky ginger cake and fruit cake lay atop each other, like layers of happiness. The cake didn't have marzipan and icing, Darcy noticed. It was light, more like a tea loaf and freshly churned butter filled small ramekins, its golden colour, looking like a tea light itself. Clementines and shiny red apples sat in wooden crates, their leaves still on, as nature had intended, their freshness filling the air. Vegetable curries and bean chilies bubbled away in slow cookers and bowls of rice and potatoes and salads were dotted here and there amongst them. Cider and ginger beer and mulled apple juice, aromatic with star anise, nutmeg and mace, were poured from earthenware jugs and people toasted each other's health, a clement end to winter, and raised their paper cups to the unconquerable sun. For without its light and warmth, there is only darkness.

*

Richard watched Darcy at the Solstice festival. Her eyes were alight, as they had been when he first fell in love with them twenty-five years ago. He wondered where that light had gone recently, how it had withdrawn into the cloud of sadness and depression. How she had withdrawn from him. How she had receded. How cruel it seemed, life, that you spent your early adulthood caring for your children. Then they left, leaving you uncertain about who you were without them. Just at the time when you might start working it out, your parents aged. They need you as your children need you. There is no time for you to work out who you are before you have to be something else.

Coincidentally, or not, it was at this time that your hormones suffered the same identity crisis. They were no longer needed for childbearing and had not yet worked out what their future looked like, so they went through the same unbalanced seesaw of thoughts and emotions, which usually included hopelessness, fear, worthlessness, dread. And just because hormones are actually really spiteful bastards, they changed your body beyond all recognition too. Possibly causing some other unassociated health issues as time marches on.

He knew that she didn't know how to approach Christmas when everything else was at sea, her faith not just in question but more like a dropped set of revision cards, disparate words and phrases scattered across the floor, and none of them with any answers on the back. What did any of it mean? What did

Christmas mean if you no longer believed in the scriptural story and saw your life's devotion as service to a thread of fabricated lies? What did it mean when you no longer found joy in following the same Christmas routines that you had done for the previous forty years, bar a few new ones that you created along the way, but still had no energy for as it loomed large towards the end of December?

He didn't know, nor did he know how to reach her, he just wished that he could stay forever in this warm and convivial barn, with its music and garlands, its hearty and nutritious food, its clementines, candles and gingerbread and to watch joy sparkle once more in the eyes of the love of his life.

Tinsel, turkey
and
statistics

Sally wiped her eyes and sipped water from her glass.

Will waited. 'You know. You don't have to go to these things,' he said. 'If there are any social engagements you don't feel up to. It is perfectly fine to decline the invitation.'

Sally nodded and felt a swell of tears form again, welling on her lower lashes.

'I thought it would be nice to be out with people I love, and it would be fun for the girls. And it was,' she sobbed. 'The Solstice celebration was amazing. It's just hard to see everyone dancing and having such a good time and laughing, and I don't feel I'll ever truly laugh again. I just have this intense sadness inside. I feel like a broken vase that has been glued together. From a distance I look like one piece, but close up, I'm just a craze of cracks.'

'It is exactly that,' Will said gently. 'Losing Peter has broken you. He was a husband who you loved, and an amazing father to the girls. It is enough to break anyone to lose someone you love. And at Christmas all of that pain that you feel everyday is intensified. Not only are you really tangibly feeling the loss of that person, but the shared joys and traditions you used to have now feel more empty and meaningless without them. Also, everyone around you is happier. Their parties and fun and laughter and sense of good cheer, whether genuine or not, is all pervasive. It is everywhere we look. There are those who are having the perfect

Christmas, or just pretending to, and whether it is real or not, it seems so to those on the outside, and just strengthens the sense that the whole world is happy and you're not. Christmas is a whole bundle of learned behaviour that we carry through from our childhoods. Some things we do because we enjoy them, but most are because it is what we think we should do based on her childhood experiences. It is the maintenance of long held family traditions. It is the pressure of meeting the expectations of other family members and what they want to get out of the season and it is doing things for the people we love, even if we don't want to (like queuing up to take your baby to Santa, even though they are too young to know any different and it is mainly to make up for the long held sadness in your husband that they never had all of the Christmas magic because they grew up in foster homes with families who were in it for the money and not for the care of the child. And you absolutely hate it, but do it, because you love that person so much) is what he wanted to say, but didn't, because he was the therapist and should be able to practice what he preached, and also because this was about Sally and her bereavement and Will couldn't imagine for a moment how awful it must be for her without Peter, because the thought of raising Olivia without Johnny made his heart sore.

'If you want to withdraw from it all – that is perfectly understandable. Your grief is your own. No one can tell you that it is time you got over it, got out there again and allowed yourself to have a little fun. It is still only less than a year. You must be gentle with yourself. You are keeping everything going as well as possible for your girls, but who is doing it for you?'

'Emma,' Sally muttered.

Will had meant it as a rhetorical question but was pleased that Sally felt that she had support from a friend.

'Did you know that 81% of people report that they find Christmas stressful rather than enjoyable, with 77% struggling with intensified mental health problems? 51% of women are more stressed at Christmas with all the cooking; buying presents; keeping kids entertained; decorating the home; cleaning up after gatherings; hosting family members they don't even like; financial pressure; guilt that they can't afford to buy the present their loved ones wish for…'

Sally looked at him through sad eyes.

Will removed his glasses and said, 'I know that sounds a bit sexist and misogynistic. I know that there are plenty of men who support Christmas, and it is not just women who do it, but statistically, it is only 35% of men who feel this. It is an incredibly stressful time. It is also winter, and many people suffer from Seasonally Affected Disorder. Our bodies need sunlight and yet, here we are stuck in these winter blues. It can be very depressing.

'Loneliness,' he added. '73% of people experience loneliness because they don't have the relationships that are promoted in the adverts. 53% of men feel lonely at Christmas due to marriage break up. They might not be able to see their children over the holidays, or they have grown up and moved away. Lots of men, don't have true friends, you know, just mates who they can't really share things with. Then there are those, like you, who are lonely through bereavement.

'There are more,' he said, 'Christmas statistics I mean.' 47% of people are getting into debt. They spend more than they can afford in pursuit of an amazing Christmas and then fear the bill coming in in January and how they are going to pay for it. Some don't pay other bills in order to enjoy the excess and some even go to loan sharks, just because Santa has to bring their child that toy of their dreams.'

Sally nodded; she had done the same to get the bikes for the girls. Fortunately, she had not had to resort to a loan shark, but she had made some other difficult sacrifices all because she wanted to keep their faith alive in Father's Christmas' abilities to make the impossible possible and to bring some Christmas joy into her daughters' broken lives.

'18.4%,' Will went on, waving his phone at Sally. 'That's

how much the rates of depression have increased between 2005 and 2015. And do you know what that's largely down to…? Social media. Everyone posting food ideas, wrapping hacks, present ideas, how to tie the perfect bow or make the perfect mince pie… then Instagramming their efforts, making the rest of the world feel worthless and inferior if they haven't managed to meet the proposed Christmas standards.

'You have all of that to contend with. It is no surprise that you feel broken.'

A punch hit Sally's heart, knocking her head forward to her knees. She just wanted the pain to stop. Coming to Will had helped, but no amount of bereavement counselling could bring Peter back. This was it; she was on her own now and couldn't imagine how she was ever going to be able to rebuild herself.

As if hearing her thoughts, Will spoke.

'It seems impossible, I know, for you to imagine what the future holds, and it won't be easy. But as with any crisis, or trauma, breaking the recovery into little steps is the only way cope. So, Christmas is the next big thing to address. My advice is to plan exactly what you want to do. Don't be coerced into celebrating if you don't want to, but also, perhaps try to make a change from your usual traditions. It can be too painful to relive them in someone's absence. Have you thought about what to do on Christmas Day?'

'Yes,' Sally muttered, sitting up. 'I'm going to Emma's. She and Rob have been there for me, and the girls like playing with their boys. Also, they don't really do Christmas, because they have just had their Solstice festival so it will feel different to being at home with all of Peter missing.'

'That's good,' Will said gently. 'I'm glad you've got good friends. Remember though. I know you don't feel like you will ever be happy again, but allow yourself to feel good if you want to do. It is very common for bereaved people to feel guilty for enjoying themselves. But these are little moments of light in the darkness, let them in.'

He wasn't expecting Sally to reply, but paused a moment to let his words sink in.

'It is good to keep exercising too. I know you have the girls, so that keeps you fit; but take some time for yourself. Go outside for a walk and get some infinite light into your eyes. It is uplifting for the soul; mood-boosting and it refreshes and refocuses the mind. We all spend too long looking at room corners,' he scoffed looking at his own room which he spent all day in. 'I know I do.

'And try to limit your social media to the absolute minimum. You can check notifications in case you have missed something important from a friend, but, on the whole, avoid all of the other adverts and clamours for your precious attention. Don't give it any of yourself. And try not to look back on the past year. If there was anything you couldn't achieve, don't see it as a failure. You have had a life-altering shock. And just try to keep everything in moderation. I know it sounds cliché and banal, but it is easy to seek solace in food and alcohol, but too many excesses only lead to mental and physical health problems in the new year, and you don't need any of those.

'Above all. Ask for help. Which you are doing by coming to these sessions with me. Allow your friends to help you. You do not have to appear strong and like you have it all together. They probably don't know what to say to make you feel better and don't know how to be around you, but let them in. If you push them away, you have lost a lifeline and they have lost a friend. If they love you, they will be there, so accept them.'

Too good to be true

There were ninety-seven presents under the tree. Darcy counted them and assumed that there were even more to come. Despite having been to Lapland and having met and received presents from the Jolly Old Elf in person, Magnus was still of the opinion that his proper presents were coming on Christmas Eve by sleigh mail.

Hildy had wanted her to come an hour earlier as she was having a cocktail party for a "chosen few" (score). Mostly work colleagues of Stephen's but some local big wigs too, entrepreneurs and local developers.

While Darcy vacuumed, Hildy Instagrammed.

Flitting through the house she arranged and titivated and placed, and replaced objects and items composing the perfect shot and ensuring that the right ambience was set. She had made sure to move the empty vodka bottles during the week. Clever. The wiles of a functioning alcoholic. You can drink, just don't let anyone know.

The fireplace flames had to be just the right height and colour. Snap. A robin had fortuitously elected to perch on a tig outside the kitchen window. Snap. She was wearing her Christmas jumper and holly wreath earrings. Selfie. The candlelight set off the plate of Maria's mince pies just perfectly. Snap. Caption – Mmm homemade! (yeah, by Maria). The parcels under the tree. Snap. Caption – not going too crazy this year. Quick change into little black dress and diamond necklace. Selfie with glass of Prosecco. Caption – It's not Christmas without a bit of Bolli! Xx. Advent calendar triangle number twenty-three and a little toy sticking out of the pocket. Snap. Caption – Day 23 and counting… not long now till the big prezzies!

As Darcy cleaned the bathroom, she thought she could detect a faint trace of vomit and urine that reminded her of Mr. Norton's flats. She squirted bleach around the toilet bowl and gave it an extra scrub, but the odour remained.

It wasn't the toilet. It was one of Hildy's dresses in the laundry basket.

Could it be that not everything you saw online could be believed?

What was real and what was fake?

Money, no object

It was after last orders and Darcy was tired. She wanted to mop the floor behind the bar and then go, but she couldn't while there were still customers. Cleaning was something you did when no one could see, like a little elf, making shoes or Christmas presents after dark, so no one could witness your labours. They just came in in the morning and all the work was done.

A man sat alone, scrolling through his phone and she busied herself straightening the menus on the tables while he supped slowly on his pint. There was still a quarter of it to go. It wasn't her job to do that, that was the preserve of the waiting staff, and she was a cleaning operative. Two worlds. But the waiting staff had already gone home and the only barman left had nipped to the toilet and asked her to keep an eye on things. It was funny how a cleaner was too lowly to carry out menial menu-straightening tasks, but could mind a wall full of optics, a fridge full of wine and a till full of Christmas party takings.

Should she wait behind the bar, so that the lone drinker knew that the bar was sufficiently secure? She asked herself. Not that she would have the courage or knowledge to know what to do if he did want to run off with the drawer full of cash. Or should she just hover in the background, wearing her yellow tabard, seemingly inconsequential in the security of the hostelry and focus on her mop as anyone within her pay grade should do?

He looked up and smiled at her.

She smiled back, then went back to her mop.

'Some people get all the good jobs, eh?' he joked, nodding to the bucket.

'Yeah,' she replied. 'Pub toilets are the best.'

He laughed and took another swig. A good sign. Perhaps if she got him talking, he would sup more quickly, and she could get home.

'Were you part of the office party?' she asked, nodding to the large area by the window, which was cleared down now but had seen a loud contingent of accountants, which seemed an oxymoron to her mind, who had shouted themselves hoarse along with Noddy Holder in a coarse rendition of his festive hit.

'Nah,' the man said. 'I was just in with my mate, but his wife called, he had to go home, and I still had my pint to finish.'

Darcy nodded. 'What are you doing for Christmas?' she asked, as everyone did. She had often found that strange. You wouldn't ask a complete stranger what they were doing on Tuesday, would you? Yet it was perfectly acceptable to pry into people's personal plans any day throughout December.

'I'm er… having my kids round,' the man replied. 'I've got two, ten and fifteen. I don't live with them. Me and their mum… split up…, a few months ago.'

'Oh, I'm sorry,' Darcy said. 'Do you see them at all? I mean are they local?'

'Oh yeah,' the man said. 'I can see them, but I didn't know what was going to happen for Christmas. It's our first one apart, and … well, it's not like there's a rule book, or anything, is there?'

Darcy agreed. Whilst she had not had to experience what this poor man had, she did often think that Christmas and where to spend it must be the root cause of most early marital conflict. She remembered her first post-nuptial Christmas discussions beginning in late August, with each family vying to be the first to claim the newly-weds into their Christmas fold. Shakespeare may believe that love be a marriage of true minds; but marriage is a minefield of Christmas booby traps, where the baubles of mothers' dreams can be shattered, if one family is chosen over the other. There is no truer test to be conquered by the infant relationship than be able to negotiate the competing demands of, 'your folks, my folks, or neither'. In a bid to try to find some compromise, days are fragmented – 'we'll 'do' your folks, in the morning and 'do' mine for lunch and evening'; weeks are segmented – 'we'll 'do' yours on the Christmas Eve and Christmas Day, and 'do' mine, Boxing Day and the Thursday…,'; tears are pre-empted – 'okay, but your Mum will be heartbroken…,'; placations attempted – 'sorry Dad, we'll come to you next year,'; appetites are tempted – 'But, I've already made the mince pies… you love my mince pies…'; relatives are exempted – 'well, she'd better not bring her mother with her, that woman would bore a statue to sleep…' For all concerned, this relationship hangs in the balance. Where a few short months ago, everyone might have stood with beaming smiles, throwing (environmentally sustainable) confetti over the happy couple, wishing them a life of blissful togetherness and the strength to face life's ups and downs in respectful union, no one thought it necessitous to mention that if you don't determine who is going to 'do' Christmas in your pre-nup, you might as well start clearing your side of the wardrobe, because you'll be in the spare room by Halloween.

Not that this had happened to her, she was pleased to note. Although, they had been some fractious discussions over the years, they had largely been able to spread themselves thinly enough to meet the wider family's expectations. She couldn't imagine how difficult it would have been had her family ever been split apart.

'So, when are you going to see them?' she asked, genuinely interested in this man's unsolicited Christmas. 'Will you see them on Christmas Day at all, or Boxing Day?' She tried to keep the inflection out of her voice, as if one had weighting over the other, which it sort of did. Christmas Day was the jackpot; first prize. Boxing Day was okay, but you'd want to try again next year if you drew that out of the hat. It was physically impossible to see everyone in one day, particularly if geographically widespread. To Darcy's mind, equal weighting should be given to each of the twelve days of Christmas, because that was the only way to appease the conflicting branches of the family tree.

'They're coming to me for about 1pm,' he said, his face lighting up with the thought. Darcy liked that. He didn't say it as a dad who felt that it was his duty to spend time with his kids on Christmas Day, but one for whom the previous Eve traditions and early morning excitement would be sorely missed, and who would attempt to make up for it in the afternoon.

'I'm cooking,' he said pride evident in his voice. 'I've never done a Christmas dinner before,' she said. 'By myself, I mean. I helped Ellie, my wife,' he explained, 'but she did most of it. I usually sat in the living room, assembling the new toys and inserting batteries,' he laughed.

'Well done,' Darcy said impressed. She didn't know why. Most chefs on the television were men, why was it impressive for a man to do Christmas dinner? She wondered whether Gordon Ramsey or Raymond Blanc had sat on the floor assembling Barbie's dreamhouse or a Playmobil Safari Park while their wives magicked a meal into fruition. Perhaps they did. When else would they get a day off? She supposed the presentation of a cookery book from her mother-in-law, passing on a mantle that all future Christmas dinners were her responsibility had something to do with her old-fashioned opinion. That and the fact that her own mother had always 'done' Christmas, the first her father knew of it being when the pub closed and he sat down to the whole feast fully formed, as if it were a banquet at Hogwarts.

Jason (that was the man's name, she learned), had gone on to explain the lengths he had gone to when he lived at home. How when their children were little, he had tied a length of fishing wire to a set of windchimes and had run it to his and Ellie's bedroom. When everything was ready on Christmas morning, with the stockings filled and the gifts by the tree, the mince pie eaten and the footsteps in soot marched across the floor, he would lie in bed and pull the little invisible string. Skye and Tim, the children, would run out of bed and down the stairs. The chime, Santa's doorbell, the proof that he had been.

He spoke with delight in his eyes. Darcy recognized it. It was the delight of all parents who had managed to create Christmas magic in their homes and who had met every one of their children's expectations, whatever the cost.

The cost, Jason had confided, was irrelevant. He had spared no expense this Christmas. There were stacks of presents, a tall tree with all new decorations (he didn't have any, being newly separated with none of the shared family decorations that accumulate over time available to him). The fridge was bursting with food, and he had bought all their favourite things. He had even bought a new television, because the video game console he had bought for Tim wouldn't work so well on his old one and he would want him to enjoy playing it when he came to visit. For Skye, he had bought clothes, her favourite Vans, or Trucks, or whatever brand it was. Jason didn't know about brands, but Darren did apparently, and he didn't want Darren giving Skye more than he could, himself. He had bought a new sofa, because, really, how could you all cuddle up together with hot chocolates and watch Christmas movies under the duvet on that saggy old thing with the smiling mouth? Apparently, Darcy discovered, Jason was a security guard at the supermarket (she felt that she didn't need to watch the bar so much now in the presence of a trusted punter who was also in the business of guardianship). Over the weeks, he had watched the customers filling their trolleys so high that they could hardly push them. Who needed that much food for one day? He had asked himself. It's not like the old days, when the shops closed for the whole festive period. Most of them would be open again on Boxing Day for the sales, so there was really no need.

But there was. Because it was Christmas, and he was going to spend time with his kids. They were leaving their family home, coming to his crappy flat and moving into a spanking new place with Darren in the new year. He was going to give them a Christmas with everything. With trimmings on the trimmings. Yes, it had cost a fortune. Yes, he had had to get a loan out (this he confided to Darcy's discomfort. She was concerned to hear that), but it would be worth it, he said. Because how else would he show them what they mean to him, how much he loves them, and how heartbroken he is that he won't be lying in bed on Christmas morning and ringing the chimes to wake them to the promise of Santa?

Santa's night off

Margaret and Holly were watching *White Christmas*, with their feet up and making good headway into the Quality Street and Turkish delight. The stockings were hung on the chimney with care, and Dave was mulling some wine in the kitchen and making a sandwich. The doorbell rang and after a few exchanges of pleasantries on the doorstep, Lucy stood in the hallway.

'I'm leaving now for my parents',' she explained. 'Want to get away before the traffic gets worse.'

'Oh, I thought you were going by train,' Margaret said remembering an earlier conversation.

'I was, but that was before I got all the presents,' Lucy said. 'I couldn't carry them all, so I hired a car instead. It costs about as much and at least I'm guaranteed a seat.' She smiled.

She was holding two presents. Margaret saw them and made a dash for the tree. 'Oh, yes, wait, we have one for you, too' she said, her slippers crossing the carpet like skis.

Lucy crumpled. She realised how her unexpected visit must appear. Her, standing there in their hallway, on the day before Christmas Eve, with two wrapped gifts. Particularly having just admitted to having bought too many presents to carry on the train. It was a reasonable assumption for Margaret to make that Lucy's booty from the pirate ship, Oxford Street might have included two small "pieces of eight" for her goodly neighbours. But she hadn't got anything for them. Hadn't even thought about it. She just had her eighteen names on her list, and London Town at her feet. All she was thinking of were her fancy boxes, memorable gifts and relaxing in the bath at her nice hotel. Why hadn't she thought of Margaret and Dave? She could at least have got a box of biscuits or something. Embarrassment crept up her neck until her cheeks were burning like the logs in the fireplace.

'Oh,' she began, fondling the packets awkwardly. 'These are actually not…, they're for…'

Margaret sensed her discomfort and put her out of her misery. 'Yours is just a bit of homemade nougat,' she said. 'Nothing special. Just wanted to give you a little something for looking after our advent donkey so well,' she said kindly.

That didn't help. Lucy felt doubly bad, not only had she forgotten to get them anything, but she was also now the recipient of a gift for doing no more than keeping the donkey out of the rain and sitting at home in the warm until the elderly lady came to retrieve it. There should be rules for moments like this, she thought. Who exactly were you supposed to buy Christmas presents for and how could you do it in a way that didn't leave someone being unreciprocated? It was a minefield.

Her mind returned to her purpose. 'Well,' she began again. 'Thank you. That's lovely and very kind of you, and there was really no need, but… Thanks,' she muttered. 'I… er… got these for my Secret Santa,' she explained, 'and I got them early; the night I found the donkey, actually,' she added. 'So, they got delivered and I wrapped them. But then the girl at work who organises these things decided that it would be better if we gave money to charity instead, which I am more than happy with, but it meant that I didn't need these anymore. They're not suitable for my nieces and nephews so… I don't know. I know it's a bit late now, and you have probably done all your Santa work, but perhaps you can keep them for next year? You can open them and see what they are. It was just a bit of fun for a guy in the design team, but it's not rude or anything…, so anyway, if you have a use for them, they're yours. Otherwise, they could just go to charity or something.'

Margaret took them gratefully. 'I'll add them to my sack

for next year,' she said. 'Thank you. I still have a couple of bits left from our trip to the children's hospital and I collect things all the time, and especially in the January sales, so I'm sure I'll find a use for them. Thank you, lovey.'

Lucy smiled and checked her watch. 'Okay, well I'd better be off now. See if I can get off the motorway sometime this side of Christmas.'

Margaret gave her a hug and Dave thrust a foil-wrapped parcel in her hand. 'A cheese and pickle sandwich,' he said smiling. 'Keep you going till the service station.'

'Thanks,' Lucy said gratefully, thinking it funny that Santa was giving her a shiny gift. 'Merry Christmas,'

'Merry Christmas,' the couple replied, waving from the doorway like Santa and Mrs Klaus on their day off, which Lucy supposed they were.

Christmas Eve

Insight

The morning dawned cold and grey. But Margaret liked it like that, the better to show off the sparkling lights and decorations. Particularly on the high street. She always thought it seemed rather a waste on a sunny day to see the large light displays suspended above the road, eclipsed by the glare of the sun.

Pulling her hat tighter over her ears and wrapping her scarf, she parked the car and opened the boot. She had washed and pressed all the cassocks for the choir and had made another batch of mince pies for after the rehearsal. She was getting a bit sick of them now, in truth, having made over forty batches since the end of November, but it was Christmas Eve. If you couldn't have a mince pie then, when could you? That was the problem with making the start date earlier and earlier, you were all Christmassed out by the time that day actually arrived.

It wasn't possible to carry it all in, she would have to make a few trips, she realised. Serendipitously, she saw Darcy coming out of the theatre. Margaret assumed that she must have been cleaning it in readiness for the matinee performance of the Panto. Perfect timing, an extra pair of hands just when she needed it. She sent up a silent prayer of thanks for God's providence.

'Morning,' Margaret said crossing the car park that the theatre shared with the church. 'How are you, Darcy? All ready for Christmas?' she asked.

'Oh yes,' Darcy replied brightly. 'All ready.'

'Oh good, I love this time now, all the hard work's done and it's time to look forward to it,' Margaret said, her face crinkling with glee.

Darcy thought of the majority of the working population who still had to get through a day of paid employment, before they knocked off and even then, were still probably going to hit the shops and begin their Christmas shopping at just gone six, with all the wrapping and Santa stuff looming ahead of them like a road with no end.

'Which service are you going to?' Margaret asked simply, assumption already embedded. Once you were known for being involved in the church, that's where you stayed regardless of any deviations in your spiritual journey.

Was Darcy going to admit to her that she wasn't planning on going to one at all? What Christian would not be going to church on Christmas Eve? Even lapsed Christians, who missed every Sunday throughout the rest of the year, still went on Christmas Eve. She guessed that meant that she wasn't a Christian anymore then.

Really? Was that true? After all of her indecision and uncertainty, had she reached a point of realization now that she had lost her faith? That seemed too final. There was a saying, when God closes a door, he opens a window. She wondered whether it worked if she were the one to close the door rather than Him. Might there remain the opportunity for her to scramble through a cat flap at some point in the future, should she change her mind?

'Erm…' she said, playing for time while her mind sought a respectable answer.

'Still not sure?' Margaret said sagely as if she were aware of Darcy's spiritual dilemma.

'No,' Darcy replied hoping that it was sufficiently vague as to whether she was referring to the time of service, or her faith as a whole.

'Well, like I said, when we met a few weeks ago,' Margaret said rubbing her hands together, 'we have the kiddies candlelight service at four o'clock and then carols and lessons at seven thirty, and then the actual proper candlelight midnight service, beginning at eleven.'

Darcy felt herself stifle a yawn, a Pavlovian response to the thought of church at midnight. For years, she had been the one organising the music, like Margaret, busy with everything for hours before the service began. Elves and cleaners again – the secret magic makers. And in the years proceeding, she had attended with her mother, it being the highlight of the Christmas preparation. She had loved it, in truth, going out at night, when the air was crisp and cold, and then stepping into the church, its dark shape silhouetted against the night sky; a little golden glow in its arched windows, the only suggestion that there was something going on inside. It was like a secret ritual meeting of a cult, that only certain people knew about, which she supposed it was really.

The carols would be rousing and exciting, the anticipation of the birth of Christ palpable and as the organ pounded out the final strains *Hark the Herald Angels*, there was nothing quite like it for the tingles. One year, as people filtered slowly out of the church, congregating outside as they wished each other Merry Christmas, a bottleneck had formed causing the aisles to block with people. The organist had stopped, their festive repertoire complete. Darcy had rallied a few of her musicians and had launched into an impromptu rendition of *Do they know it's Christmas?* The looks! Some bobbed along happily, delighted with the unexpected entertainment while they waited to leave. Others squeezed themselves through the gaps in the radiators to go and seek the Witchfinder General. The charge? Singing a secular song in church on Christmas Eve. She wondered what they would make of her now, if they learned that not only had she partaken in a Winter Solstice celebration, she had delighted in it.

'Sounds like a busy night,' she said.

'Oh, well, you know what it's like yourself, don't you? Still not singing?'

'No, not for the moment,' Darcy said, hoping that sounded like she might pick it up again at any time.

'Oh shame,' Margaret said, without any trace of judgement. 'Well. Since you are not going to your church at the moment, is there any chance you can help me to mine? I don't think I can carry everything inside.'

'Of course,' Darcy said and followed the woman to her car.

Entering the church was peculiar. Both familiar and strange. So much of it was part of her, the smell, the feel of the stone floor, the height of the vaulted ceiling overhead. The icons were like family pictures, the statues like old friends. She knew them all by name. She crossed herself at the altar. Not knowing what you believe anymore doesn't erase years' worth of habit, ritual and respect.

Following Margaret into the sacristy, she hung up the cassocks on the rack, the perfect laundering a credit to Margaret's hard work. No one would know this – cleaners and elves. So much went on in churches that was the work of the faithful. They busied away, organizing, planning, doing, arranging and no one knew. It was service to the Lord. Or was it servitude to the clergy? She wasn't sure anymore. It felt more like the latter. Like the unknown workforce in Santa's toy factory.

A woman walked down the centre aisle; her feet soft, reverential. She crossed herself and approached the door, hearing voices within.

Margaret poked her head out into the main body of the church and greeted the woman warmly.

'Jen,' she exclaimed. 'How lovely to see you.'

'Darcy, this is Jen,' she said, turning towards her, 'and these are her two wee angels, Helena and Freya.'

Darcy waved at the girls and smiled at the woman, which Jen returned but there was a meekness to it.

'I brought the donkey back,' she said. I don't think I'm going to make it for the candlelight service. I can't leave the girls, but we are hoping to be back for the children's service at four. I didn't know when you needed it, so I thought it would bring it now. The lady on the phone said you'd be here.'

Margaret took the Bag for life. The donkey was upright, looking out of it, as horses look out of their stable door. Darcy wanted to giggle, it looked a little like it was sitting in a dodgem or some sort of small vehicle.

'There was a little accident,' Jen said. 'It got knocked off the sideboard.' Her hand moved to her temple, and she pulled down a few strands of hair. Darcy noticed the merest flash of a glance with the girl who stood to her right.

Margaret made no mind. 'Oh, don't worry about that,' she said. 'As long as he can still stand up, no one will be able to see if he has a few bumps and bruises.'

Darcy smiled at the girl, who was the image of her mother, her plaits, the principal determinant of age. She had the same sad eyes and quiet posture; one that seemed to say, if I stand still and quiet enough, I can be invisible.

The girl smiled back and chewed her bottom lip.

Another little girl was peering into the large crib to the left of the altar, the figures nearly the size of her.

'Where's Jesus?' she asked Margaret directly. 'We put ours in the hay on the roof. He can't go in until Christmas morning,' she added authoritatively.

'We keep him in the back, behind the ox,' Margaret whispered, bending down to the small girl and pointing to a space in the corner.

Without really thinking about it, Darcy found herself finding Margaret's comment fairly symbolic of most people's attitude to Jesus, shove him in the back corner and just bring him to mind on Christmas Day. She could see herself becoming one of them.

Standing before the crib, a tableau so much part of her throughout her life. Darcy looked at it anew. Was there really a star? Yes, quite possibly, she told herself, but was it just an astrological phenomenon that happened to occur at that time? Planets have cycles and orbits and align with each other at appointed times. Who's to say that the Christmas star wasn't just a celestial occurrence, which whilst obviously astonishing to those who witnessed it, had little to do with leading wise and men and shepherds to the stable? Incidentally, if it were that extraordinary, it probably would have led a great many other witnesses there too. And what's with all the angels? Darcy asked herself. They were everywhere. One for the Annunciation, another appearing to Joseph, and the shepherds and the Wise Men. Always appearing in their iconographic white robes, halo bearing and huge-winged, with great news or advice to impart. It struck Darcy how few angels appeared elsewhere in the bible, or as part of everyday life. It seemed rather unfair, now that she considered it, that most people had to muddle through each day, not understanding the depth of God's great purpose for them, because visions of advice-giving angels were in short supply. Yet, in Nazareth and Bethlehem, they were on hand whenever something of great mystery befell anyone.

For most of Darcy's life, she had never questioned the Virgin birth, it would be sinful to do so. It is given and received, the knowledge, inherent in faith, bestowed and unchallenged. Much like Mary's pregnancy. But, again, now, she wondered how people could be so gullible. What was it about this generic form of mind control that was so powerful, it could stand for generations? It is because, she assumed, that we are always searching for a miracle. Miracles bring hope, and prayers are wishes. She understood it. There had been times in her life when all human involvement in a difficulty had run out, and the only recourse was to seek aid from a higher power.

Was Jesus the long-awaited Messiah? she wondered. Or just another prophet? Was He the Three in one – Father, Son and Spirit? Or was He just a charismatic leader whose depth of loving kindness reached out to those who were vulnerable? Darcy had always derived great comfort in the Holy Spirit. It was this arm of the Trinity that she felt filled and restored by each day. But how could you just take one third?

Once Darcy had begun to doubt these things and had learned that much of the bible was not in fact the true and unrefuted word of God but was based on oral tradition; centuries' old folklore and the gospels and letters of the New Testament written by people (largely men) who each put their personal spin on events and ideologies, (often decades after the fact) she began to distrust it. That was the beginning. Once you distrusted it, what did it mean anymore?

What did it mean for Easter? Did Jesus rise from the dead? How can anyone really know for sure? If He didn't, then what did that mean for everlasting life, and heaven? And if He wasn't God, then what was the point of praying to Him, because he actually can't affect your life in any real way. If you pray for something and it doesn't work out, the faithful around you say, "that was God's will, or He has a different plan for you," or offer wisdom like "He is the Alpha and the Omega. How can we, poor, simple humans, understand the mind of the Almighty?" Then the cynicism creeps in. The patriarchy of the church, the indoctrination, money and control. The subversion of other faiths, the intolerance of other sexualities. The was the main one, really, that had turned Darcy away from it all. Jesus preached the message of 'loving one another,' which was pretty broad and inclusive, regardless of whether he was the son of God or not, so how could a church still persecute and have different rules for different persuasions of their flock? A sheep was a sheep was a sheep.

'I'm getting a unicorn dressing gown,' Freya announced suddenly, her words, moving swiftly from Jesus' location of pre-Christmas repose to another subject altogether, in the way that children do.

'Lovely,' Darcy said, coming out of her existential crisis and considering whether it was appropriate to ask if this was going to be coming from Santa or not. It wasn't always easy to know people's personal Santa proclivities and it was invariably a delicate arena in which to step. One foot wrong and you could be responsible for ruining everything.

'From Santa,' Freya added helpfully. 'And unicorn slippers, and unicorn night light and unicorn cushion for my bed.'

'Exciting,' Darcy added, smiling. 'And very unicorny.' One mythical figure delivering another, she mused. Was that a good thing, that we lose ourselves in the magic of the impossible, or was it just a perpetuation of the deceit?

'How about you, Helena?' Darcy asked, turning to the quiet girl. She was reminded of her own relationship with her younger sister. Darcy, the elder, quiet, thoughtful one, Lily, the chatty, engaging one, who everyone warmed to, and thought was cute and funny, even now.

'I asked Santa for…,' she paused for a moment and looked at her mother and Margaret briefly, then back to Darcy. 'An easel and some paints. And friendship bracelets, and a basketball hoop for the back garden.'

Darcy was no psychologist, but she could imagine what Will might say to that collection of desires; two solitary pursuits and a plea for company.

'Now then. Helena, Freya,' Margaret said, in a tone that was all excitement and industry, 'shall we put donkey back up on this table together, then we could say a little prayer and then you can come with me and have a mince pie and a glass of orange. Yes?'

Darcy wondered at Margaret's endless generosity. She knew how much the woman had already done and still had to do throughout the day with all the services to prepare for and not enough time, yet she was giving up more of it to treat the children. Whilst Darcy had always tried to do things for others, she recognized that she was sadly lacking, compared to people like Margaret.

Freya jumped and ran to Margaret's side, and watched as she withdrew the donkey and put it on a small wooden table beside the lectern. On the opposite side of the altar was a tall wrought-iron stand that displayed the Advent wreath. The purple candles, all at varying stages of burnout, according to the length of time they had been preparing for Christmas.

Like most people, Darcy thought.

None of them were lit, but Margaret took the box of matches from the bag and lit the small votive. She placed it next to the donkey and held hands with the girls.

'Dear Lord,' she began. 'We thank you for returning our advent donkey safely back to us. Like the beast who bore Our Blessed Lady, Mary, on her arduous Journey, we know that we can lay our burdens upon you. You are the light of the world. You are Emmanuel, God with us. We know that you are present amongst us and see all our pains and worries. The donkey's journey has ended. Let the glory of the angels be seen, this special night. Amen.'

'Amen,' Darcy responded, feeling the familiar warmth and security that praying together induced.

'Amen,' Jen repeated quietly, her head bowed, and hands clasped.

'Amen,' Freya shouted at the top of her voice, enjoying how it echoed into the high rafters. Helena gave her a stare. The unspoken duty of the older child to parent the younger.

'Now, juice and pies,' Margaret said to the girls, clapping her hands. She lifted the votive to her face and made to blow it out.

'Actually,' Jen said, her hand raised in a staying motion. 'Would it be okay if I use it to light another candle? I'd just like to take the moment to pray, if you have the girls.'

'Of course,' Margaret said carrying it across the altar, she shielded the tiny flame with her other hand and bent it to a new tealight, kissing its wick into life.

'I'll give you some space,' Darcy said, retreating to a seat a couple of rows behind. There would have been a time when she would have lit a candle too and would have knelt or sat before it, praying the words of her heart. But she wouldn't know what to say now, or who to pray to, or what for. Being there felt both fraudulent, and invasive to Jen's privacy. She didn't even need to be there at all. Helping Margaret to carry things from the car was her purpose for being here and that had been done. She could go. But even though her prayers eluded her, and her thoughts ran wild with her re-immersion into the *living* water of her faith, she did acknowledge that there was comfort in the peacefulness found inside a place of worship. Not just church, necessarily. She had visited a Hindu temple a few years back and that had been the same. All polished wood and gleaming floors, lit candles and fragrant arrangements of flowers. The smell of burning incense was agarbathi rather than the usual frankincense, but the feeling was the same. Quiet, devotional meditation and an overwhelming sense of peace.

'No, you don't have to go,' Jen said quietly. 'Stay with me.'

The words struck Darcy squarely in the chest. The young woman may have been simply being polite; acknowledging that the space was for all, not for her alone. Yet, something deep in Darcy's heart heard their meaning as something different. Tears sprang to her eyes. Her throat closed with emotion. Of all the words that this woman could have used, she chose those.

Stay with me.

The words of Christ in Gethsemane, where he had pleaded to those whom he loved, and who he believed loved him in return. He was asking his friends to wait with him, yet they denied him.

He was denied by their lack of faith.

Darcy, the denier.

She nodded and sat next to the woman in silence. She found herself before a candle in church on Christmas Eve after all. What was it they said about mysterious ways?

She couldn't pray though. The words didn't come. Her mind couldn't get past the bruises she saw on this young woman's arms and face. In Jen's devotion, she had forgotten herself. Kneeling on the altar with her elbows on the rail, her hands were clasped, and her eyes were closed. The angle of her arm caused the sleeves of her coat to recede, revealing the dark welts and marks around her wrists and forearms. Absently, in her prayerful reverie, her lips muttered silent whispers as she swiped a lock of hair from her forehead, tucking it behind her ear. An angry-looking gash stared out from her temple and Darcy noticed a slice of dark scab where her skin should have been. She had visited a farm once, on holiday, and the farmer, a lady, who wore a nylon dress and wellies to do the milking, had been kicked by a cow on her bare legs. The wound on her shin bore a striking resemblance to this one. Just shows you what damage a hoof can do.

She looked at the donkey accusingly.

Feeling in her pocket for a business card, she found one and moving quietly, joined Jen at the altar rail. Her body assumed the humble position, her muscle memory easing comfortably back into an attitude of prayer.

Enclosing Jen's left hand in her own, Darcy used her right to insert the card into the space within her clasped palms, and enfolded them firmly, pouring as much compassion and warmth as she could through the pressure of her fingers.

Jen's eyes opened at the unexpected touch to find Darcy looking at the wound on the side of her head.

'If you ever need somewhere safe to go,' she whispered.

It was possible that she read the situation incorrectly. If she had, there was no harm done, just an impertinent assumption. If she hadn't, hopefully she could prevent it being done. Perhaps she should have spoken to the woman and found out for sure. But she doubted it. Women in that situation rarely talked about it. You just had to recognize the signs.

Darcy should know, they were the same ones she had seen in her mother.

Magic makers

Old SANTECLAUS with much delight
His reindeer drives this frosty night,
O'r chimney tops, and tracts of snow,
To bring his yearly gifts to you. (anon.1821)

Jack backed down the loft ladder stairs, while Laura held each of the children's bedroom doors. He was wearing a Santa suit, lest he was spied through a blanket; or dreamy eyelashes, heavy-lidded with sleep but stirred enough to take a peep. Yet, despite being dressed appropriately, they couldn't risk the children wandering onto the landing to find Santa making his way gingerly out of the loft. He was supposed to use the chimney. Stumbling down the last two rungs, because the fake beard had risen over his nose, to meet the fake white hair that had fallen over his eyes, Jack fell to the ground and dropped the sack on the floor, the top presents spilling out. Laura shushed him loudly. They quandaried for a moment in stage whispers about what to do with the ladder. If they took the time to return it through the hatch, its creaking and clunking might wake the children before they had a chance to deposit the gifts downstairs. However, if they did the gifts first, and then did the ladder, and the children woke, they would emerge to find the ladder down, assume it was Santa's alternative choice of access, in order to avoid getting soot on his outfit, and then rush down to the Christmas tree to open their presents. It was only one thirty in the morning. At once, both too early and too late. Too late for Laura and Jack to be up on Christmas Eve: Way too early for them to be up with the kids on Christmas morning.

The rest of the sleigh(t) went without a hitch. They crunched the carrots and spat them on the grass. They schmushed up the reindeer sparkle dust food with their boots. Jack dragged the lawnmower across the grass, not to cut the lawn of course, but to create two grooves with the wheels, that looked like sleigh marks.

Inside, they ate the mince pie, being sure to leave a few crumbs. It looked more authentic than just removing it from the plate, and Laura drank the sherry. The sweet, heavy liquor usually gave her a headache, but she didn't think she'd even notice on top of the pounding pain she had had all around the crown of her skull for the last three days; although, the pain in her temple was new. She glanced in the mirror above the mantelpiece to see if there was a little elf sitting on a tree stump, hitting it with an axe. There wasn't, but there was a sprite or goblin or some sort of creature with grey skin and dark circles beneath their dull eyes. They really should have found time to pluck their eyebrows, she thought, and to have done something with their hair. She knew that goblins weren't known for their long, glossy tresses, but this one could at least have taken a moment to see to their wispy, grey roots.

She was so tired; she could hardly think straight. The laptop had no wisdom for her now. Its work was done. Over the previous month, it had displayed lists and names, columns and figures, timelines and rankings in order of urgency, and she had obeyed. Everything had been bought and checked, wrapped, and baked. House cleaned, provisions sourced, family welcomed, hospitality given. It wasn't even Christmas Day yet and she was already done. No sooner would her head hit the pillow, but she would be up again, dragged from the soporific restful coma that her body craved. Little feet would pad down the landing, following excited voices and stockings spilling chocolates and candy canes.

It would stir a magic in her and she would look at Jack, together they would share the smile that said, we are the magic makers.

With much delight

Jason was laying the table. It was only a small fold-out one that he had got from Ikea. He didn't usually have a table. A microwave curry for one was best eaten on the sofa in front of the TV. But he had a new sofa now, he was not going to be spilling anything on that. And anyway, it was Christmas. And Christmas dinner was at the table. It always had been, over the years, where he and Ellie had built their home together.

Opening out the table in the small space somewhat impeded the hallway. Jason moved his coat and shoes from the hook by the front door and put them in his wardrobe. He wanted their special lunch tomorrow to feel like they were in the dining room of a country house hotel, not amongst the wellies in their boot room. He had bought all new crockery and glasses. It was silly really, he only ever needed one of anything. But he was taking this time to build a new home for himself, one where the kids would come and hang out and they would like his big, smart TV and comfy sofa, and they could have more dinners together. He could get into cooking, make a curry or chili or something. The hope he held for Ellie to leave Darren and invite him home was gradually slipping away. He had to accept that it was over. In January, they would all be living together in the new house, a new family home. It made him feel sick with sadness at the thought of it, Ellie and his children, living with *him*, in a whole new and shiny life. Happy New Year!

Thinking like this wasn't good for him, he knew that. He must focus on something good. The crackers. Taking them from the box, he placed them at each place setting. He had found little Santa candles and put a few of them along the centre, next to a short, fat, red church candle that sat in a little ring of plastic holly. They were reduced at the supermarket, and he thought it looked nice on the red paper tablecloth. He folded paper napkins into swans, as Ellie had taught him to do once, years ago. They were the closest thing he could get to white, more a sort of cream with red nutcrackers on. *'Three swans a swimming…'* he sang to himself as he took a swig of beer from the bottle.

He didn't have a fireplace, but the flat had come with a bookcase, and he hung the stockings on the middle shelf. The items he got were mostly novelty things; Top Trumps, a small set of magic tricks, a joke book, a felt dart board, a set of hair chalks, some sweets and chocolates. The rest had to wait until tomorrow, but Jason was so excited. If the turkey wouldn't ruin, he would put it in the oven now, he was so keen to get started. Christmas Spirit had found him and was filling him with its magic. Well, that and the money from the loan.

As he put the final bits in the stockings, he couldn't resist looking at the joke book. Flicking through the pages he found a smile forming at the corner of his lips, a motion his facial muscles were unacquainted with.

'What is a magician's favourite dog?' he read aloud.

'A labracadabrador!'

In the empty room, filled with the promise of Christmas, he laughed out loud.

Elf or Angel?

Apparently, Liam had found, Mr. Norton didn't like Christmas because it made him feel lonely. He wanted it out of the way as quickly as possible because it was too painful to be reminded that he had no family or friends. He had said that the only person he ever saw was his cleaning lady and the man who bought the meals on wheels. Liam had knocked on the door, the day after he and his mum had put the Dalek tree in the empty pot, and while he started out his usual grumpy self, by the time he had eaten some of the gingerbread men that they had given him, and they had all had a cup of tea together, which his mum had made, he seemed to have brightened right up.

Liam had asked whether the meals on wheels brought turkey and stuffing. Mr. Norton said that it did, and Liam thought that sounded wonderful, though a little unfair that only old people got nice things to eat, and it was brought to you all ready. You didn't need to have electricity to cook it, or anything.

Having said that, the strangest thing had happened, the day after they left the Dalek tree in the pot. The next morning, they had found an envelope on their doormat. It had obviously been put through the letter box, but it didn't look like the normal post. They usually had little see-through windows in and made his mum sigh and look worried. This one was plain white, but squarer than the window ones. It didn't have typed writing on either, just handwriting, like the loopy joined up writing they were taught in school. It just had their names on. Kayleigh and Liam, Flat seven.

His mum had been cautious in opening it, all sorts of odd

things went on in their flats. But she did and had just dropped to the hallway floor and cried. There was a note. All it said was, *Kindness begets Kindness*. And there were five twenty-pound notes inside. Liam was amazed. He didn't know what begets meant, but he knew that one hundred pounds made them millionaires.

He didn't know where it had come from, one of Santa's elves maybe? Or even what the kindness was that had deserved it.

It couldn't have been someone getting the wrong flat because it had their names on, and their flat number. No one knew them in the flats, or even spoke to them much, except for Tag upstairs. This was a new thing. They had never spoken to Tag before, but he often said things to his mum which made her look worried. Liam didn't know why but had noticed that since Tag was more present in their lives, they had been able to have their lights and the heater on at the same time, and he now had a warmer coat and shoes that didn't have a nail through the top holding them together. Liam had suggested that perhaps the money was from him. His mother had said that she had no idea where the gift could have come from, but it was certainly not Tag.

Liam and his mum had pinned the note to the top branch of the Christmas tree. He knew that presents usually go at the bottom. But this was too good to go on the bottom, it had to be up at the top, with the star, or the angel, if they had had one.

Perhaps they did.

Christmas, present

Grace had found it difficult to forgive her grandma for making her miss the show. Why were old people so annoying? Her mother had said that they weren't. They were actually often confused, scared and lonely, locked inside a world of their own, and afraid of the one outside. Grace thought that perhaps if they tried a bit harder not to be so self-centred and worried about their shopping bags, they might notice other people and what they needed. Elliot had said that it was good that Grace had missed it, because that had given Patrick the opportunity to play Mary, the mother of God, which was absolutely brilliant on so many levels. Liz had lauded his point of view but asked him to be more sensitive to his sister's disappointment.

Liz snipped some holly from the bush in the garden and placed it on the windowsill. It reminded her of the plum pudding she had taken into the care home. They had enjoyed it, Maureen, and Arthur and even scientist Bill, who, watching the flame, had launched into a recollection about which chemicals cause which reactions. It had been worth it. Those memories were in there, somewhere. It was just often difficult to find them. Invariably though, the magic of Christmas was often a catalyst to drag them out of the darkness into the light.

Liz had recognized the signs. Working with dementia sufferers, she knew that her mother's shopping bag obsession was the first sign of it. It was only Christmas Eve, she still had days to get through and her patience was already wearing thin. How was it that she could find endless sympathy and compassion for the residents in her home, and yet want to rip her own mother's head off?

She supposed it was something to do with the fact that it was hard to acknowledge that moment when your parent was no longer there for you. That was their role. To be someone on whom you could depend, and share things with, even if you were no longer a child. But, when they ceased to be, becoming like a child themselves, it felt like a betrayal. They may be physically there, but not mentally or emotionally, and sometimes that could be even more difficult than bereavement. Because in death, the body and soul have gone, but they are remembered with love. In dementia, the body and soul have gone but the mind lives on, albeit in a twisted, knotty, mass of gnarled, thorny brambles, and its diseased dysfunction infects all that thrives around it.

Some of the relatives had heeded her advice and had left their loved ones to enjoy Christmas in the care home. Others had not and had gone to great lengths to involve them in their family celebrations. She felt for them. It would be difficult. It was difficult for her too. It was inconceivable to have Christmas without her mother, despite Grace's huffing, puffing, sidelong glances and general lack of grace. But there would come a time, soon, as much as her professional life had taught her, when it wouldn't be possible. Either because her mother's physical needs would be too great, or because it would create too much pressure on the rest of the family. How do you make the call between those you love, to sacrifice one for the good of the others? She didn't know.

All she could do was to try to find the little moments of light in the now, like flame on a pudding.

Just another Tuesday (2)

Emma and Rob had filled the stockings with a few gifts from Santa and would hang them over the fireplace later. For now, they were enjoying warming their toes before the dancing flames and nursing a brandy in chunky mug.

Emma was working her way through a bowl of homemade chocolate Krispie cakes. And Rob was dozing on her shoulder. He had just put the last bits of bark chippings down on the ground around the second-hand jungle gym that they had found on Facebook. It was from a local woman, mum of one of the boys in Matthew and Adam's class, but he didn't know that until he got there, and they got talking. Rob had had to dismantle it all and she had brought him regular cups of tea, explaining that she would be moving house in the new year to one of the new show homes on the development by the cinema. She didn't want this shabby thing in the new garden. It was more of a champagne in the hot tub sort of place. Rob felt sorry for the kids.

Rob had loaded it all onto the flatbed and had been building it over the past week. The boys knew that their main present was from them and not Santa, but Emma and Rob had still liked to keep it a surprise, for a bit of Christmas magic. They would reveal it tomorrow morning.

Sally and the girls were coming. It would be nice for them to ride on their new bikes and play on the jungle gym. Then they could all come in and make pizza. Christmas Day would come and go, and it would feel like just another Tuesday.

Move over God,
You might be three in one,
I am five!

The bikes were wrapped exactly as she had envisioned. Sally stood back and admired them. When Rob had collected them from the shop, they were in angular cardboard boxes. You couldn't make out what they were. But the girls had asked Santa for new bikes and so concealing their identities wasn't necessary. She wanted them to look as bike-ish as possible and so taking metres of paper, she wrapped it around the handlebars and cross-frames, around each wheel and pedal, until every bit of chrome, rubber, and plastic was covered. Then, she took thick, florist ribbon and looping the lengths over and over made two huge bows.

The bikes had taken all of her Christmas toy budget, except for a few bits for the girls' stockings and she did the 'Night before Christmas boxes,' of course. They would be devastated to not have those. They liked them almost more than the stockings. Because Christmas Eve held all the magic of anticipation.

Inside the boxes were the usual things, the requisite Christmas pyjamas, matching of course, a Christmas mug with a chocolate melt stick, a packet of their favourite biscuits and a storybook.

After laying out the cookies and milk for Santa, they had their baths, and she warmed the towels and the pyjamas on the radiator. She lay in bed with Hannah, in her snowman duvet, Rosie, curled at her feet and covered with the tartan blanket. They sipped their hot chocolates and Sally read to them from the new book. It was one about a daddy who had gone to heaven and who had gone to find a special angel, who then had to find a special elf and together they made sure that his special girls got his present on Christmas morning.

Despite the sorrow they carried with them most of the time, the thought of a special present from daddy lit a spark of magic in their eyes. Sally was pleased. His present was already wrapped and on the top of her wardrobe. She would place it under the tree when they were asleep. She yawned. It was tiring being a mother, father, angel, elf and Santa. She was five in one, God was only three.

She kissed them and allowed herself to close her eyes and rest in their peace. She had found lately that she didn't really want to be anywhere else.

Mental elf

The black and white mobile spun slowly around, and Olivia slept soundly. Johnny had wanted to cover the arms of it with tinsel and hang little festive figures from each branch. Will had counselled him that not only would that put their precious child in danger of strangulation and choking, but it was also tinsel and tacky, and neither was allowed in their home.

Johnny had accepted the admonishment with regard to the hazard issues but was incorrigible when it came to tacky decorations. If something was red or green and displayed snowmen, candy canes, reindeer, nutcrackers, gingerbread, and of course, Santa, he was all over it and determined that to not allow Olivia access to this festive tut from as early an age as possible, was bordering on parental neglect.

The bags were already packed for the trip to Will's parents in the morning. They had planned to be there already but there was so much baby equipment to take, they thought it easier to have Christmas morning at home before heading off with the car not only filled with presents for the family, but also Olivia's travel cot, high chair, bottle steriliser, changing bag, clothes, bibs, toys, sleeping bag, monitor and the hideous Santa activity playmat advent calendar, which she seemed to love.

The door was open to the consulting room and the chair sat empty. He was usually in one, his patients in the other. He thought about the hours of grief and pain that the room had witnessed since December had begun. It was the same every year. Life brought its struggles in all its forms, eating away at the foundation of emotional and mental health, even physical and spiritual health. And this was ongoing and relentless. Some people took more than their fair share of burden in quiet acceptance, like a humble, careworn donkey, while others moaned a lot, over little, attributing a slight disturbance in perfection to be a panic attack or anxiety disorder.

He wasn't there to judge. Just support. To find some way to help them to navigate through their various sufferings, whether self-inflicted or not. What he had little patience with, though, was the suffering inflicted by Christmas.

O little town

They had been to the four o clock service, and it had been beautiful. As they went in, the Sunday school leaders were handing out small stars, the size of a firework sparkler, a fine wire star-shaped frame wrapped in silver tinsel, and small jingle sticks, with little silver bells. The church was mostly dark with fairy lights all around. On the altar was a painted backdrop on hinged boards of tall plywood. Jen thought that it looked like the advent calendar book, a twilit sky and the silhouettes of the low-roofed buildings of Bethlehem.

The girls turned to her, excited. She smiled at them and at the hubbub that always accompanied the moments before something began. A small worship band was playing Christmas music in the background and the church was filling up quickly. One of the Sunday school teachers, a woman in her twenties who they knew as Phoebe, moved through the assembled asking if they wanted to take part in the nativity. Helena said no and shrank back against Jen's arm. Freya said yes and followed her to the back of the church.

Before long, a hush fell, and a narrator took his place at the lectern. He began to tell the story about how there was to be a census, and all must return to their place of birth. Since Joseph was from Bethlehem, the town of David and born of David's line, he and his betrothed, Mary, were to make their way there. She was with child, and it was too far to make the journey on foot, so they were carried by a donkey.

To everyone's delight, a real donkey made its way down the centre aisle, led by a woman in purple leggings, wellies and a Christmas jumper with the face of a donkey on the front, its teeth protruding from its upper lip as if it was smiling or

433

speaking. It had reindeer antlers bedecked with flashing lightbulbs. The slogan read, 'Jingle all the neigh…'

The donkey plodded onward down the dusty road to the altar and then moved along the front of the church, returning up the side aisle so that everyone could get a look at him. The woman who led him, wasn't a member of the Sunday school, but a volunteer from the local sanctuary. She seemed to be the one in charge of navigation and speed, but Joseph walked purposefully alongside her, holding the bridle at the donkey's mouth. Unlike the animal on the jumper, this one didn't appear to be very chatty. A girl, who Jen recognized to be her daughter, sat on the back of the donkey beaming at everyone. Helena looked up in surprise and waved at her. After which, Freya, seemingly forgetting that she was supposed to be portraying a tired and humble maiden, close to the end of her long gestational period and arduous journey, smiled and waved at everyone, as if she were Queen Cleopatra in an epic movie, or a character on a float at Disneyland.

Having completed a circuit of the church, they arrived in Bethlehem and the rest of the story unfolded, about there being no room at the inn and all that. Jen dreaded to think what Freya was going to do about having the baby. She was one for playing to the gallery. But it was all done in good taste. Whenever the word star was mentioned, everyone was encouraged to wave their silver tinsel sticks, and whenever an angel was mentioned, they rang their little jingle bells. The congregation was very cooperative, and it made for a magical atmosphere that was part church service and part Panto.

A calf was the next livestock to amble down the Christian Catwalk; a little fawn Jersey whose own bell jingled as it walked. It was enchanting and Helena thought it was the most beautiful thing she had seen. In her crib at home, the ox and ass were the same size and gave a pleasing symmetry, here the donkey was bigger than the calf, which was a little disconcerting, but she supposed it might be more difficult to get an ox into church on Christmas Eve. A collection of small sheep followed, including a tiny lamb in the arms of another farm volunteer.

The service finished with everyone singing *Away in a manger* and then *Silent Night*, although, Jen thought, they probably should have collected in the jingle bells before singing that one, if they were hoping to create the mood of Heavenly Peace.

She allowed herself to bathe in the Christmas magic. This was her happy place. Her girls, her church, the sounds and smells of Christmas, (the candles and incense that is, not the animals) the reaffirmation of her faith amongst her family of believers. She almost felt sorry for those who didn't see Jesus as the reason for the season. They would miss all this. What did Christmas mean to them at all, if not this? Just a commercial shopping and feeding frenzy.

Yes, Jen was happy, here in this place. Her sanctuary.

Freya had been on the ceiling with excitement, having been cast in the leading role and Helena said that she didn't want an easel any more from Santa, she wanted a Jersey calf. They had done all the preparation, were dressed in their Christmas pyjamas and had finally settled to sleep.

*

O holy night

Jen was putting the finishing touches to the table. She had put on some Christmas music and was enjoying the titivations. She did have beautiful things. The table was laid with her bone china dinner service, a wedding present. Crystal glasses shimmered in the fairy lights from the Christmas tree. Helena had helped her get it ready, she loved all the elegant things too. She had spent time with the holly and ivy, making a centrepiece and had thought to make little serviette rings to match. Jen opened the box of crackers and placed on at each place. They were silver and offset the shining cutlery and her favourite special cranberry spoon and grape scissors that she only ever used this time of year.

Admiring her work, she moved to the kitchen, thinking that she would prepare the vegetables and leave them soaking in water overnight. She had learned from other Christmas mornings; the advancement of the lunch took second place to opening presents; marvelling at what Santa had brought; going outside to try out roller boots or new bikes or assembling toys or inserting batteries. Whatever could be done the night before, the better. She even prepared the turkey and put it on a low heat throughout the night. The aroma in the morning was divine and it hastened the meal more towards lunchtime than supper.

Laying streaky bacon on the bird and daubing it with the butter that would give it its fake tan, she wrapped it in foil and put it in the oven. Taking one last look around and wiping down the countertop, she breathed a contented sigh. Everything was ready. She thought to put Jesus in the manger but then decided that she would leave it for Freya to do in the morning as she was so fixated on it.

What should she do with the elf? She wondered. For the last night. The ideas weren't a problem. There were plenty of them on Instagram. It was her inclination that was waning. She might have to steer the girls away from this initiative next year. What would an elf do on Christmas Eve? she asked herself. Then she supposed it might be what she was, really. Doing all the work when no one else is around, so that when they awoke, all they saw was the magic.

Taking furniture from Freya's dolls house, the source of much of the elf's activity, she laid up the tiny table with place settings and set the chairs around it. Taking a tissue from the box, she folded it to make an apron and secured it around the elf's waist. Then stood him against a chair, satisfied with his last moment of Christmas preparation, that had been two months in the making.

Releasing the ties of her own apron, she took a photo of both tables with her phone and then did the same with the stockings and the tree. She was finished.

A scraping sound scratched at the door. If she slipped up the stairs now, she could get into bed before he came in. Tiptoeing down the hall, she ducked below the door window to keep her silhouette out of sight.

She had about a minute before his drunken brain coordinated his hand with his eye and found the keyhole. As she crouched, the loose tie of her apron caught around the crooked handle of an umbrella in the hallway stand and pulled her back. She tried to get the apron over her head, but it had twisted under her collar and caught on her earring and in her hair. In the seconds it took to untangle herself, the door opened, and he stumbled in falling against the banister.

'Ssh,' she said, putting her finger to her lips. 'You'll wake the girls.'

'SSh, Ssh,' he repeated loudly, staring at her through glassy eyes. He tried to close the door but hadn't worked out that his bulk stood between it and the latch.

'I'm going to bed,' she said facing the stairs.

'Whadyumean?' he said, slurring the words into one. 'It's Chistmsev. You can't have a drink with yeroldman on Chistmev?'

'I think you've had enough drink,' she said moving past him, 'and I'm tired. I've done everything to get ready for Christmas and the girls will be up early in the morning. One of us has to be compos mentis enough to deal with them,'

'I'll be up inthmrning,' he slurred. 'I'll be up. I'll just have my dinner.'

Jen sighed. 'There isn't any dinner,' she said. 'The girls and I were at the service until six-thirty and then we just had a pizza. I had to get them to bed early so I could do all the Christmas stuff.'

'Pizza?' he said. 'Pizza on Christmsve? So, I have no dinner, is that what you're saying?'

'If you wanted dinner, perhaps you could have left your precious friends at the pub and come to the service with us, like a normal dad. Do you know how many dads there were in that church tonight? I can't count them. All there with their children. And where were you? Where you always are, with those bloody loser cronies. When you could be with your girls.'

'Ah, yeah yeah…,' he said pushing past her.

'Where are you going?' she said.

'To get some fucking dinner,' he shouted.

Jen thought of her gleaming kitchen, the turkey in the oven and each hob occupied with pans full of prepared vegetables. He was going to make a mess and she'd be starting on the back foot in the morning.

'Oh, God,' she said in frustration. 'I'll do it. You can have a sandwich.'

'A bacon sandwich,' he said staggering to the kitchen bouncing off each doorframe as he went.

'No, that's too messy and the smell might wake the girls. I'll make you a ham sandwich. Go and sit down in the living room.' With any luck, she hoped, he would go in and pass out as usual and she could slip up to bed. It was getting late.

He took a crystal glass from the table and rammed it against the tap.

'Careful,' she said. 'They are our good glasses. And the table's already for tomorrow.' Opening a cupboard, she got out a tumbler and handed it to him. Deaf to her, he persisted with the crystal wine glass and chipped the delicate edge.

Jen felt tears spring to her eyes and took out the chopping board and bread.

'Here,' she said, thrusting the sandwich plate in front of him. 'I can't believe you. Look, the glass is chipped.'

He glared at her with a mouthful of bread, his bulging eyes giving him a toadlike quality.

'Ah, will you just shut up for once,' he said. 'How many of your men in the church have to put up with a moaning bitch like you? Eh? How many of them have gone home to a sandwich for dinner?'

Jen swallowed down her response. Never argue with a drunk. That was the advice that she'd been given.

'I'm going to bed,' she said turning away.

Grabbing her apron string, he pulled her back. 'Whaddymen yr goingto bed? You'regointmke me a proper dinner,'

Stealing all her courage, she looked at him. 'It's late. It's Christmas Eve and I am not going to cook now. You've had a sandwich, that's enough.'

'What's all this then?' he said lifting and clanging the lids of each pan on the hob, sloshing the water over the sides. 'I'll have this.'

'That's for tomorrow,' she said moving to get a cloth for the floor.

As she crouched, his foot connected with her chin, knocking her off her feet and back up against the bin. 'Gerrup off the fucking floor, you fucking bitch,' he shouted pulling her up by the apron. It pulled over her head and she scrambled to her knees and crawled out of the kitchen. Reaching the leg of the dining table, she pulled herself up, between the table and the wall, but he was waiting. He picked up a wine glass by the stem and smashed it on the plate, he closed in on her, holding the broken shards up to her face. Edging back, her heels found the skirting board, she was trapped. She raised her knee and kicked him in the crotch. He doubled over and staggered, falling forward onto the table. The glasses toppled and fell and as he raised himself up, his fists dragged the cloth, sending the china dishes to the floor.

The Christmas table was laid waste. China and cracker lay in smashed piles like a party at a Greek restaurant.

'I need a drink,' he said moving to the living room. 'Clean this lot up, you whore.'

Jen's whole body shook. Her hands and feet were like ice, but her head felt hot, like a fever. Her chin was cut, and her lip had split, filling her mouth with blood. Her bottom teeth felt spongy, and she explored them gently with her tongue. Fearing that the sound of shattering glass and crockery had woken the girls, she made her way to the stairs to check on them. She could not have them thinking that the noise was Santa arriving, bringing them rushing down the stairs in excitement, only to find Christmas destroyed.

Creeping past the living room door, Jen heard his breathing. The whiskey, the warm room and the comfortable armchair had been enough to knock him out.

Pulling the door to, and running up the stairs, she opened Helena's door. Miraculously she was asleep. She had heard that once, that parents worry so much about keeping quiet and tiptoeing around, but research showed that they could even sleep through smoke alarms.

She shook Helena gently. 'Darling. Helena, Darling. Wake up, honey.'

Helena stirred and frowned in the darkness. Her face

studied the gash on her mother's chin which looked similar to the one the donkey had given her on her head the other day.

'What is it?' she asked sleepily. Then suddenly she remembered it was Christmas Eve. 'Is it Santa? Is he here?' she asked, assuming that was why her mother with was waking her with such urgency in the middle of the night.

'Yes, we have to go, darling.'

'Go?' she repeated rubbing her eyes.

'Yes, quickly, put on some shoes and get a jumper and some jeans.'

Leaving Helena with confusion on her face, Jen ran into Freya's room. She pulled some clothes from the drawers and shook her awake. She spoke brightly, as if it was an adventure. Freya didn't respond well to solemn and serious.

'Come on honey, quickly get up. I think I heard Santa on the roof. If we go outside, we might be able to see the reindeer fly,'

'What?' Freya said, jumping out of bed as brightly as if she had literally just laid down her head. 'Where?' She ran to the window, straining her head to see upwards.

'Come on girls,' she said taking their hands. 'Let's go and see if we can see the reindeer?'

Bleary eyed and stumbling, Helena made it to the top of the stairs, but Jen pushed past her. She wanted to guard the living room door and give them a safe exit.

The girls followed her, and she grabbed their coats from the pegs by the door.

Pulling the door behind them, she double locked it from outside and ushered them into the car.

Freya walked down the garden path backwards, her neck bent up, straining to see the rooftop. Helena still seemed to be in a dream and shivered in the cold night air.

'I can't see them, Mummy,' Freya said, her little forehead in a frown. 'I can't see Santa and the reindeer.'

'No?' Jen said in surprise. 'Well. I'm sure I heard the jingle bells on the sleigh. Perhaps they've gone to the next street.

Shall we go, and see?'

'Yeah,' said Freya jumping up and down as Jen buckled her into the booster seat.

Helena buckled herself in and leant forward to search the night sky.

Jen started the car and reversed out of the drive. When she had gone as far as the first set of traffic lights, she finally let out a breath that she had been holding since she left the house.

She drove for twenty minutes, up and down every street. Not going far but doubling back on herself to ensure that he wasn't out searching for them. All the time she searched the rooftops in a game of chase she would never win.

The girls were getting tired, the novelty had worn off about three streets ago and they were convinced that Santa was probably elsewhere in the world. They had turned their concerns to the fact that if they weren't at home in bed sleeping like good children, he wouldn't come and leave their presents. They wanted to go home.

But she couldn't go home.

Taking out her phone, she made a call.

The reply was simple, 'Stay with me.'

Darcy had woken Richard and put him to work finding inflatable beds and sleeping bags. The cabin in the garden hadn't been opened since Tilly had used it for band practice and she had been living in Australia for six months. She gave it a quick sweep and put on the oil-fired radiator. Some fairy lights were already up around the windows and there were rugs on the floor for sound insulation. It would do.

Within thirty minutes, Jen had arrived with two worried and tearful girls. Unsure of what to tell them, she had run through a variety of excuses as far as her traumatized mind could manage. Each of them was perfectly credible at any other time of year, but not now. She had considered saying that there had been a flood warning; or worries of a gas explosion; or a bear on the loose from the local zoo. But at Christmas, when every excuse threatened the likelihood of the day being ruined, or implied that children had to be anywhere other than "tucked up in their bedrooms, fast asleep", it was impossible. She was going to say that there had been reports of burglars breaking into houses to get Christmas presents while people were out at Church. But that would have worried them more. She realised that there was nothing for it but the truth. Daddy had hurt Mummy, and they couldn't go back.

Christmas and Santa be damned.

Not that she could say that.

Freya was crying loudly, and Helena was clinging to her mother's arm in silence as they entered the cabin. As Darcy settled them, Richard brought gingerbread and hot chocolates for the girls, tea with sugar in for Jen, and brandy to settle her nerves. Poppy, their golden retriever followed him in, delighted to have new friends and access to a midnight snack of gingerbread, and, curling up on Helena's makeshift bed, nuzzled into her face.

Before long, the girls had cried themselves to sleep, and Darcy tended to Jen's wounds.

'I know that their safety is all that matters,' Jen said. 'And mine,' she added ruefully, 'But they haven't got any presents.'

'Don't worry about that,' Darcy said. 'Like you say. You had to leave, and you did the right thing. Who knows how far he would have gone? Your girls would rather have you safe and well, than a few unicorn bits and a painting set.'

Jen looked at her and smiled. 'You remembered?'

'It was only a few hours ago?' Darcy replied gently.

Jen felt like it had been a lifetime.

Santa... You're up!

The phone rang. It was one thirty in the morning. Ordinarily, a supremely anti-social time for calling someone, reserved usually only for bad news.

Yet, it was one thirty on Christmas morning, and that was different. Busy parents were still sorting out Santa presents; party revellers were still revelling. Travellers were still travelling, driving home for Christmas. And people were still getting in from Midnight services, which only finished about half an hour since.

'Hello?' Margaret answered in a cheery voice.

Whenever wasn't she cheery? Darcy wondered. 'Margaret?' she ventured, unsure for a moment whether it may have been her daughter, Holly.

'Yes?'

'It's Darcy... from... er church?' which sounded wrong because although they knew each other through church, they weren't from the same church, and Darcy wasn't from one at all anymore, yet they had been in one together today, so she hoped it covered all the bases.

'Darcy! Merry Christmas!' Margaret said warmly.

'Merry Christmas!' Darcy said, realising that it was the first time she had wished it. For over twenty years, the first person she had wished Merry Christmas to was Richard. But then, this Christmas seemed to be the first, for firsts.

'Erm... Margaret, I'm sorry it's so late, but I was wondering... do you have any Christmas presents left from your Santa visits that would suit a couple of girls aged ten and six?'

Christmas Day

Loan to value ratio

The children were going to New York. Leaving Boxing Day. Darren had bought the trip for them. So, not phone and clothes from Vans then. Jason tried to feel happy. His kids were with him. He had made a magic lunch; the new sofa was comfortable; and the TV was great. But they wouldn't be cuddling up to watch movies as he had hoped and they would be going on a trip that he had planned for them, himself. They had to get back because it was an early flight. Ellie was sorry, she didn't know. It was all part of Darren's wonderful surprise.

Skye loved the hair chalks and used them straight away, and Tim loved the joke book. Jason tried to laugh at the one-liners and riddles, but the mirth was gone. Might it have been because no matter what he did, or how much money he had, he could never compete with Darren? Might it have been because he had got hugely into debt for nothing more than a Christmas dream? Was it because Skye and Tim loved the two cheapest things Jason had bought and so he need not have got the loan anyway? Or was it because with every passing day, he felt himself disappearing?

Social Needier

Hildy was wearing two baubles from her ears and a plastic tiara on her head. She thought it gave her a 'Fun Mum' vibe, but this was balanced with the expensive white wool coat, red scarf and high-heeled black boots, which while impractical for the park, did have a very elegant Christmassy look. And how things looked were all that mattered for Instagram.

Magnus was tearing up the park paths, and some of the flower beds, with his new jeep. Seventy-five presents remained unopened at home.

Christmas pudding
on
roller skates

Liam had seen Magnus driving on the road. He had the Range Rover jeep that Liam had wanted. The one he had offered to drive his mum around in, so she didn't have to get the bus everywhere. Part of him was sad that he couldn't have a jeep like that, but as they had discussed, they had nowhere to keep it. Magnus had plenty of space, it probably had its own garage, next to the one his mum's Range Rover was in.

Liam wasn't sure that the Santa thing about putting what you want on your list and getting it if you're good, was correct. Because Magnus seemed to get everything he wanted, and he was horrible most of the time.

Although, he had to concede that Santa was still great because even though he just asked for a few surprises, he got great board games and some books and even a new pair of football boots. And Mr. Norton had bought him a pair of play goals to put up in the garages, so that he could play without breaking the Dalek pot. They had eaten Christmas lunch in flat one, with Mr. Norton, when he got his turkey dinner on wheels.

It is okay to smile

There was a massive Pete-shaped hole that, despite her best efforts, Sally couldn't fill. The girls were happy with their bikes, and the angel and elf had managed to get his present to them, which was a photo of him with each of them in an angel frame.

Being at Emma's was the right decision. They played on the climbing frame at being pirates and with a little elf alien who they called Spock. The farm was fun and festive without being Christmassy, and Sally even smiled when Rob used an elf-name generator and announced her to be henceforth known as Poinsettia Figgy Socks.

The two months and twelve days of Christmas

Briony was delighted with her mythical characters. She was surprised about the bunyip though. She really thought the elves could make everything, and they had magic. It was quite mystifying. But Santa had left some modelling clay, so she was going to make one herself.

Laura was relieved. They had got away with it for another year. Santa's mystery and infallibility remained intact. She figured that no one really knew what a bunyip looked like so Briony could just decide for herself. Perhaps her daughter's interpretation of the myth would become established in the psyche of children for generations to come, and they would add symbolism and stories and imagery to corroborate her conception. There was no reason why not, it had worked for St Nicholas.

It had been fun, but exhausting. As she looked around her, she could see the joy. She had made magic happen for all. But if her headache and the tingling in her fingers and toes were anything to go by, she had overdone it. The day was nearly over, and she could rest (once the turkey sandwiches were made). Then there were just a few more days to keep the kids entertained, a New Year's Eve get together to sort out and then grand clear down to arrange on Twelfth Night. She could do it.

Stop the clock

This brought her joy, Liz affirmed, as she watched her family around the table. The crackers had shared a variety of charades and riddles, and Karl was trying to mime something to the family which was bordering on X-rated. She imagined that the word he was trying to describe was 'sporran' but she was having too much fun watching him trying to come up with other more inventive ways as to how to secure a winning guess, for her to reveal that she had already got it. Grace and Elliot were in hysterics and Liz felt that perhaps they were doing the same thing. They had probably guessed the word ten minutes since and were just enjoying Karl's performance.

Lewis was back from university and sat with Joshua, their heads bent together in matching paper crowns, as he scrolled through pictures of his dorm room and pointed out all of his new friends. Liz loved that he was happy, but it was a reminder of the fact that he was an adult now. He had left home and lived in a world that she had not even seen, beyond the brief trip around the campus on the Open Day, let alone could influence or control. Josh and Elliot would not be far behind and then there would just be Grace. At home, by herself, the family dynamic completely altered. No more, the youngest child and only girl. But the only child. Liz was trying not to think of her in gender normative language – the Holy Patrick, Mother of God episode too fresh in her mind. But she *was* her only girl and her little girl. In a few months, she will have left primary school, embarking on her own journey into adulthood. The relentless plodding of life continuing, like the deliberate steps of a donkey.

There would be no further need for Liz to decorate the school Christmas grotto or attend PFA events. What would that mean for Liz's friendships? It is in these shared cultural events that bonds are made, and relationships strengthened. But all too soon, those commitments and responsibilities are gone. The relay baton is passed on to the next tranche of Vestal Virgins, charged with keeping the Christmas fire burning. But what happens when Hestia, the goddess of the hearth finds herself with an empty hearth to guard? Liz asked herself. Does she keep the fire burning regardless?

Yes, because that is what a Vestal guardian does. She is the one who never lets the flame of family go out.

Liz looked at her mother, anticipating the dementia decline to come. For now, her mother was happy, content to be among her loved ones, and more importantly, aware that she was. What would next Christmas be, or the one after? Would Liz speak the same words to herself that she spoke to Harry, and the other relatives? Would she accept that it would be better for everyone concerned if her mother didn't take her usual place at the Christmas table but would leave the chair empty? A reminder of the steady and irrevocable advancement of life.

This is why we do it, she realised. This is the reason for the stress and worry and cost, for moments such as this. For everyone to make the effort to be together. If Christmas were just another Tuesday, life would get in the way, as it always does. For all its stress and worry, it is this bit, when the meal is done, the presents are open, and everyone is having a lovely time. The pure bliss of contentment. Of course, it won't last. There will be a squabble soon over what film to watch, or who ate the last purple one from the Quality Street. There will be a pile of washing up and indigestion, but for now there was only joy. Comfort, Love and Joy.

Lucky Dip

Helena and Freya were mystified. They had no idea how Santa could have found them at the cabin house. He really was magical. But he had. The presents were sort of right but not exactly. Freya had a unicorn headband with a gold horn and rainbow-coloured hair attached. With it was a pair of rainbow fairy wings. The ensemble would have looked funny on the lead guy from the design team, and that's what Lucy was going for. She thought it would make everyone laugh at the Christmas lunch; and the art set would have reminded everyone of the olden days, when art was formed with paint and brushes, not pixels and mice.

It wasn't a dressing gown and slippers, but it was still unicorny. Perhaps Santa was out of stock, Freya thought. Helena was also surprised to not get her easel or basketball hoop, but she got a unicorn paint by numbers set and also a proper drawing pad with a set of acrylic paints and shading pencils, a box of calligraphy pens and a friendship bracelet set. She loved them and made one for everyone, even Poppy.

In other parcels, that were wrapped in all different papers, there were Disney colouring books and gel pens and a cuddly unicorn with a rainbow mane and a plushy dinosaur, and card games like Uno and Happy Families. Helena didn't feel right about playing that but Freya thought Mrs Baker looked like Margaret from church, which Helena had to agree with and thought appropriate because she did make a lot of mince pies.

They got chocolate selection boxes and chocolate oranges and there was a clementine and pound coin in each stocking and a packet of homemade nougat flecked with red and green, cranberry and pistachio.

Helena was worried about her dad. What would he think to wake up on Christmas morning and find his family nowhere to be seen? He would worry. Perhaps she should call him and tell him where they were. She didn't know where that was exactly, only that Darcy knew Margaret at church, so he might be able to find them that way. But then, he had hurt her mum, quite badly, lots of times. She had seen it from the top of the stairs, before pretending to be asleep. Perhaps they should just stay here, where he couldn't hurt her. That is what she had always prayed for. Perhaps the angel had heard her.

*

Darcy and Richard had laid the table with a winter feast. His parents had gone to his sister's family when they heard that there wouldn't be any turkey. Darcy's mother was with Lily and her family.

Greenery and candles, lush boughs studded with clementines and apples, ran down the centre and the room was filled with fairy lights, and the smell of ginger and nutmeg. They had not expected guests so had chosen to fill the table with all their favourite food.

Helena loved the spicy ginger cake with hot custard, it was like a warm hug. Freya had been looking forward to turkey so had been disappointed to have any but was delighted when Darcy suggested fishfingers and beans instead.

They grazed throughout the day and played with Poppy in the park. Helena thought she might love Poppy more than the calf from the service. She didn't know what would happen about going home, whether they could go back there, or not. But she hoped they could. If they did, she might ask her mum whether they could get a dog like Poppy. She was like a fluffy blanket with a heartbeat. A living blanket that could also offer protection. Perhaps they should have had a Poppy all along.

*

As the sun set on a Christmas that had none of the normal Christmas things, but still felt Christmassy, Darcy smiled. She brought cups of hot spiced apple juice into the living room. Freya was sitting crossed legged on the floor and giggling. The hurt and mystery of her father missing, somewhat mitigated by the toys and diversion provided by Poppy. It was no surprise that dogs were used for therapy, Darcy thought. The animal had nursed them today. Her silent, unassuming, intuition allowing them to pour all their sorrow into her fur. Sometimes, that was all that was needed. No words of advice or trite platitudes, simply quiet empathy. Was it coincidence that dog was God spelt backwards? Perhaps that was where He was found, in the love of a hound.

Richard had tears running down his face and was wearing some fake elf ears that had come in Santa Dave's rather odd selection of presents. His ready laugh and sense of fun had always been something that Darcy had loved in him, but even more so today, seeing him hamming up his comedic antics for the girls. Helena was still withdrawn, understandably. It was harder for the older one, Darcy knew that from her own past. The younger, more protected by earlier bedtimes and having less ability to provide support. Still, she glanced up every now and again, watching from the sidelines, like someone at the darkest edge of a carnival. Darcy had known that feeling too, not too long ago even, but she had found it easier in recent weeks to be out of the mud and in amongst the lights and music. Freya, with the "in-the-now" attitude of younger children seemed to have stored away the trauma of the previous night and the absence of her father in a box to be revisited whenever the next diversion had passed.

'What's going on in here?' Darcy asked smiling at the infectious mirth.

Freya pointed to Richard and fell backwards laughing.

'Pom Pom Toffee Bubbles,' she said holding her tummy with glee.

'What?' Darcy asked in surprise.

'That's my Christmas elf name,' Richard said. 'Look, it's online,' he said flashing his phone as evidence. 'It comes up with your elf name. It's randomly generated so you don't know what you are going to get.'

'What's mine?' asked Helena quietly, looking up from her mindful colouring book.

Richard swiped and pressed the screen.

'Cupcake Jinglecrackers,' he announced. Helena laughed and Freya was undone.

'Darcy, Darcy,' Freya said, jumping up onto the sofa and looking over Richard's shoulder. 'Do Darcy.'

Richard may have been the one wearing the pointed ears, but Freya looked impish, with a light in her eyes as if she could hop off any moment and go and make merry mischief somewhere. Darcy wanted to see that same light in her sister's and mother's eyes too. She knew it would come one day. It just took time, and courage.

'Here we are,' Richard said profoundly. 'You, my darling, are, Clementine Gingersparkles.

'Perfect,' Darcy replied.

Twelfth Night

The Epiphany

The wise men came from the east. They had followed the star. They had seen the Christchild and offered their gifts, gold frankincense and myrrh. It was an awakening. The wonder of Christ was revealed to them.

Darcy had reached her own awakening. An epiphany. She had allowed herself to explore her lifetime of Christmas traditions and memories, both good and bad, and there were many more that still lay there, too painful to be uncovered. Her sessions with Will had made her see that so much of what she thought Christmas should be had been imposed on her by external factors; her mother; family tradition; her faith; the expectations of others; the mantle of being the bringer of magic. There had been much joy throughout it all and she could still glimpse the hope and promise that Christmas had always held, but suddenly there was distance and perspective. A filter, like the anti-glare glasses that she wore for night driving. All the shine of the opposing headlights, dimmed and dulled, the bright, strobing beams drawn into plain, simple focus, like the sudden retraction of a light-sabre.

With her children grown and living away; commercialism, a rampant hungry beast whom she had no desire to feed; the duty of the daughter or in-law to provide the festive feast no longer one that she was willing to bear; and her faith not only in quandary, but in all reality probably gone forever, Darcy had to reexamine what Christmas meant to her, now. And perhaps with the wisdom, brought by the wise men (and women), she felt she had.

It had come, not in the robes and gifts of the Magi, but in the people whom she had met. It should not have surprised her, often we can only see ourselves, when reflected in others. They were the ones who had given her an insight into her own thoughts. It had begun with Jason. She had seen him at the bar one evening, the same place where she had first met him, when his face had been alight with the promise of Christmas Day with his children. The feeling of self-worth endorsed by the fact that he was on equal financial footing with his wife's new partner. That he had been a worthy contender in the who can get the best Christmas gift for the children competition that divorced and separated people engage in. But the light had been eclipsed. By a trip to New York. Darren had won. The loan, the worry, the planning, the expense, all for what? Yes, he would still have those things, like the sofa and the television for when his children came to visit but the race to get it all by Christmas had been an unnecessary waste. If it hadn't been, his body would have spoken positively of the new much needed improvements he had made to his home, sitting up straight on the bar stool, shoe comfortably on the footrest and a ready smile to all around. Instead it said, through his stooped slouch and grey, sad eyes, none of it means anything without the children. The hands turning the glass, into which he peered added, Now I'm facing the new year feeling even more alone, and further in debt. What is the point? Would they even notice if I was gone?

*

At school, when she had arrived at the end of the day to begin her cleaning, the teacher was speaking to Sally about Rosie. Darcy didn't want to intrude on their privacy, so she turned to move to another task instead. She had heard enough to note that being at Emma's for Christmas had helped the Little Women, as they had avoided all of the usual trappings which the girls would have found too difficult to endure with their father gone. However, it transpired that there had been an argument in school between Rosie and another child. The other child had mocked her for believing in angels, saying that everyone knew that Santa was real and more important at Christmas than angels. Rosie had said that angels were real, because that is how her father had got her daddy's present to her from heaven, via the elves.

The elves were undisputed, both agreed that they existed. Where did bereavement fit at Christmas? Darcy asked herself. The routines and traditions painfully reenacted but without a principal character, like a director having to call on the sound engineer to fill an absent part of a play. They might speak the words but brought nothing else to the role. No heart, no soul. The rest of the company could go through the motions, but they have nothing to work with. No chemistry. No feedback. No shared memories of running lines, or former rehearsals, or chatting with the director about where they could take the story and what emotion to add. When Darcy was younger, she had seen *Les Misérables* six times. Hugo's novel brought to stirring life by an incredible score and a cast of powerful performers. It would be hard for her to select a favourite part of the show, but perhaps the bit that resonated with her at this time, was when the friends recalled those who no longer sat with them at the inn. So much of Christmas was found in the meal. The borrowed furniture, the plastic garden table covered with a tablecloth to expand the seating facility, all to accommodate the familiar and expected persons to partake in the repast. Until they no longer could. Empty chairs and empty tables.

*

Darcy would call herself an elf rather than an angel. An

angel sounded trite and cheesy. But she was a cleaner, and like elves, they were the ones who worked behind the scenes, where no one could see or notice. That is why she had slipped the envelope into flat seven. It wasn't for her to be thought of as an angel. She didn't need credit or gratitude, or to be thought of as a holy messenger of God sent to watch over people and do His work. She just needed to know that she had made a difference to two people whose circumstances had served them a tough time, with cream on top. Except there was no cream. There was no money for the merest basics like shoes without nails in, never mind luxuries like cream. It had happened for her own family too once, in their dark days. Darcy's mother had opened the door one morning to find an envelope. Inside had been fifty pounds, and forty years ago, that was a fortune. To this day, she did not know who had put it there. She had an inkling, but the person had never sought recognition. It remained a secret. If it was who she thought it was, the woman passed away nine years since, but Darcy had never forgotten. She had thanked her at her graveside though. May Henry would never know, would never know, what that money had meant. It hadn't been given at Christmas, it was February, she recalled, when the biting wind found every gap in the mouldy windows; food was scarce, and the electricity gone. When she, her mother and her sister had eaten their meagre and irregular dinner, sitting on the kitchen floor because the sole source of warmth was from the gas jets on the cooker, which would last only as long as did the fifty pence pieces in the meter. After that, darkness and cold. With that envelope came hope, a break from the despair and worry.

Fifty pounds: Fifty lifelines.

Darcy hadn't given Kayleigh and Liam the money because it was Christmas, but because they needed it to survive. Need exists beyond Twelfth Night. People are not only in crisis at Christmas.

*

When she had let herself into Lucy's house, there was a piece of paper on the countertop. Darcy moved to read it, expecting it to be a note from the young woman with requests or additional instructions for her morning's work. Instead, she noticed that it was a credit card printout. Realising it to be private, she put it down immediately. Darcy was nothing if not discrete and respectful of others' privacy. However, it was impossible to miss the large red pen mark, encircling the total owed and the hastily scribbled word scrawled across the page.

SHIT! it said, the small four letter word conveying the despair that Lucy felt as she had written it. Each character representing approximately six-hundred pounds, the exclamation mark – about another two hundred and fifty. Darcy did not judge. She had been guilty of the same in the past. Not to the same extent but spending more on Christmas than she should have. That was credit for you. It was like a croupier at a casino, doling out card after card at a blackjack table, swift as lightning. You keep taking more and more, another tap and another tap, until you are Bust. Never play against the house. The house always wins.

*

Maria had taken down most of the decorations, but, as usual, it was Hildy that was shown posing on her posts declaring to anyone who scrolled, the efforts of her endeavours. This time it was with the cardboard boxes at various stages of disassembling, the captions detailing what a gargantuan task it had been. What better way was there to demonstrate how impressive your decorations had been than posting about them coming down as well as going up? Double-whammy. Double-Likes. Sad faces and crying emojis accompanied the captions at the departure of Christmas for another year, together with quips about tempting superstitious fate and leaving them all up until next year as they were soooo amazing, and Christmas was sooooo wonderful and Magnus was soooo happy. The ninety-seven presents were strewn about the house. And the jeep, Darcy noticed, was in pieces, apparently undergoing some sort of electrical failure after having been left out in the rain. Seemed a bit of a waste of a spare garage, she thought.

As long as there were people posting perfection, there would be people aspiring to it. Darcy often watched Hildy carefully arranging her life for maximum impression and screen appeal. Her viewers seemingly completely taken in by the falsification, if the responses and comments could be believed.

But perhaps they couldn't. Who knew what was real and fake anymore?

Wisdom is defined as the ability to act productively, using knowledge, experience, compassion and unbiased judgment. It is witnessed in the deployment of sound sense, ethical and benevolent reasoning and enlightenment. If Balthazar, Caspar and Melchoir did indeed possess the Wisdom with which they were credited, Darcy wondered whether it might have been better that they were remembered for such things, rather than simply for the gifts they brought.

*

Most of Darcy's visit to Laura had been to administer to her health needs than to help with the ironing. Somewhere between the afternoon on New Year's Day and the first day back at school, she had succumbed to nervous exhaustion. Both Jack, and the doctor, had ordered her to stay in bed. Laura was worried that she wouldn't get the decorations down and the tree undressed in time. Darcy told her it could wait another day, without the wrath of God raining down on them. It felt easy to say now, yet for years she had carried the same concern. Her grandmother had been incredibly superstitious, no new shoes on the table; no walking under ladders; a left itchy palm meant money coming to you, the right meant it going out; seven years' bad luck for a broken mirror; left for love, right for spite, with regard to burning ears and the nature of someone's gossip about you; and so on. The typical symbolism found amongst fear and ignorance of the unexplained. Even now Darcy had to take a new box of shoes off the table and despised herself for it. How had such nonsense been passed down through generations and adopted without question? Much as many family traditions, she supposed, not least Christmas ones. It did strike her as odd now, the double-standards by which the church operates. Historically, a woman could be sent to the ducking stool for belief in such talismans and supernatural intervention from the spirit world; as if you would be cursed or struck ill by not warding off such activities, yet the church quite happily built its whole doctrine on appearances by mystical figures, virgin births, magic stars, and the most powerful of all magic spells, Transubstantiation.

No one ever wanted to tempt Fate though, and if leaving up your decorations past Twelfth Night would do so, it was commonly avoided. The angel's ubiquitous address may be '*Fear not*' but life can be hard, and there can be much to fear. We exert whatever control over it that we can.

*

At the nursing home, Liz had been taking the decorations off the dining room tree and placing them carefully into a box.

As she dragged Henry in to hoover the carpet, Darcy could see the woman she knew to be Maureen in room thirty-four chatting to Liz and informing her that it was bad luck to not take down the decorations on Twelfth Night. Liz explained that as it was indeed the appointed day, they should be alright. She asked Maureen whether she knew why this was a rule that should be followed. What would happen if you dared to leave them up another day or week? Or even all year? She had asked. Maureen had said she didn't know. For once, Darcy thought, the woman's lack of understanding was less to do with her failing mind, and more to do with the fact that no one knew. Nothing would happen if you left the decorations up, except that they would get dusty and broken and you'd probably be sick of them by June.

Arthur had come by and had offered Liz a bauble from the box, believing he was helping her to dress the tree. He explained that it was good to get a head start on the Christmas decorations and that November twenty-fourth had always been the date he had begun his decoration preparations. He asked what date it was. Neither Darcy nor Liz had the heart to tell him that Christmas was over, and it was now January the sixth. But Maureen did. "September the fourteenth," she had asserted and pronounced Liz crazy to be putting the tree up so early.

Darcy thought of all of Liz's conversations with relatives. Each one desperate to involve their loved ones in their celebrations, regardless of distances to travel, and accommodations to be made for special care. They could not conceive of a Christmas where they were not present at the table. Empty chairs and empty tables.

It didn't feel right to have someone missing, a former matriarch or patriarch, the original magic makers, from whom all others had descended. But for so many, in the words of Bob Geldoff, Darcy asked herself, *Do they know it's Christmas time at all?*

*

Will sat in the chair opposite. It was the same position as always. Darcy in the client's chair, delving into the corners of her psyche and he in a relaxed pose, his long legs crossed, and a notebook placed on his lap. His questions few and direct, seeking clues to explain the behaviours found in her, in everyone he saw. The memories, recollections, childhood experiences and adulthood experiences. The thoughts and deeds of others imposed on them, and theirs on others. His quiet study of Christmas and how we are shaped by it.

It had led her to face Will in his therapist's chair from her own of the therapee, and to remind him to talk to Johnny. To not seek to perpetuate what we deem Christmas to be and the sense of loss that we feel we have if we have missed out, because that only feeds it into future generations. It is those with the babies who have the power to make the change. To turn the tide, to be the ones to reevaluate. To extract the good, healthy, uplifting parts of Christmas, and to leave the rest among the torn packaging. To allow Antarctician Christmas penguins to frolic with Arctic polar bears because it was all made up anyway. And to remind Johnny that the love we have from those around us now is what matters and we don't need to let ourselves be subsumed by what society tells us we need to purchase, to be happy.

*

There were shining lights in the darkness, Darcy had found, in the likes of Margaret and Dave. Those who give of themselves; their time, compassion, efforts, love and generosity. It was not because they are church goers and needed to do good to get on God's Nice list and secure for themselves, a place in heaven. It was just because they were thoughtful and compassionate, and wanted to make a difference, even in small gestures. Whether the Christmas story in all of its Marvel superhero technicolour was fact or fiction, Darcy knew that the Roman records of the start of the Common Era, attested to Jesus existing. So, whether or not he was Emmanuel, God with us, or simply a guy who just wanted to have a nicer, better, more caring world, did it really matter? The thing she could rely on was the same, Christmas was a catalyst for charity. Darcy pondered how, over the years, she had been a member of many church families and had noticed that being a churchgoer, did not, de facto make you a good person. Some were selfish and mean; judgmental and shallow. So, Margaret's loving touch in the lives of others came from a purity of goodness within. Such as Darcy had found in many others throughout her life, those of different faiths and beliefs, complete atheists even. Because one need not be of a specific denomination to offer kindness.

In their home, when Margaret had warmed her with tea and mice pies, Darcy had seen the bags of wrapped presents for the children at the hospital and the residents of the nursing home. She had seen Dave's Santa outfit hanging on the hall peg. These two were magic makers. Margaret and Dave: Jesus and Santa. The ultimate double-sides of the Christmas coin.

*

In the barn on the night of the far-from-bleak-midwinter, Darcy had witnessed the bounty and sharing of food, love and laughter, yet with none of the commercial stresses. She had been surprised but gladdened to find it possible to have an uplifting, fulfilling winter festival without worrying about church or gifts, or turkeys, or Santa. Indeed, the pagans had been doing it for centuries of centuries.

Her awakening had also led her to realise that it was possible to enjoy the peace of church without the angst of unanswered theological questions. It was possible to sing carols without worrying about the words, in the way you might sing something in another language that you don't understand. It was how the music moved you that mattered. She had spent many years singing about Santa coming to town or getting stuck up the chimney and his cannon universe had about as much theological foundation as did the Christmas story. So, if she could do that, she could sing about Jesus, our Emmanuel, without having to stop and pick apart the years of oral tradition, Hebrew and Greek translations of the bible and seek ultimate, all-knowing understanding of the scripture.

*

She didn't know how long Jen and the girls would be with them. It could be for as long as they needed. When she looked at the holy family, she was pulled backwards through the years.

In Jen, she saw her mother, bruised and beaten, surviving only to protect her daughters.

In Freya, she saw her sister, Lily, whom she, Darcy, had shielded from the worst, soothing her back to sleep when she awoke to raised voices.

In Helena, she saw herself. Too old to be helpless; too young to be helpful. A girl in a nightdress on the stairs, watching two people dancing, but not the dance of love. Majesty and Meekness.

Her fear for Jen was that she would fall into the same trap that many people did, which was relying on God to help, whilst ignoring the work of the people around you. She was reminded of a joke about a man who was stranded on a desert island. He kept praying for God to save him. Various forms of salvation came in the shape of a lifeboat and helicopter, in the Triduum format that such jokes usually take. Each time he sent them away saying that his faith would save him. The joke concludes with the man dying and questioning God in heaven why he could let such a faithful servant perish. God replied, what you do mean? I sent you a lifeboat and helicopter...

Emmanuel – God with us. If there was a God at all, and Darcy still wasn't entirely convinced there was, anymore, then He was to be found amongst us, in our own activities and interaction with each other. If there wasn't, then this life was all there was. A precious gift that was sometimes a struggle but was to be valued because one never knew how it could change.

Perhaps all Darcy needed to know of the Christmas story was that it stood as a metaphor. The donkey, representing the respective arduous journey that we take through life. The stable, a gesture of hospitality, the sharing of resources with others. The star, simply a waymarker, like a candle in a Scottish crofter's window, letting the sojourner know that they are not alone, that there is light in the darkness and protection to be had, found in the hearts of others.

The wooden cabin had been a centre for percussive excellence when Tilly had been out there playing the drums and jamming with the band, but now it had a different purpose. It was a shelter.

Darcy had decided. Whenever Jen and the girls were ready to move on, even if it took until next Christmas, or the one after, it would remain so. She would fill it with fresh clementines, and fairy lights and homemade gingerbread in the winter; or homemade scones and jam in the summer. It would be a place of refuge for anyone, single, or family; holy or not.

Joy to the world

Darcy knew that seeking Joy in presents, and crumpling under the burdens of Christmas; the worry and stress, debt, loneliness and anxiety and the pursuit of Instagrammable perfection, was fruitless. It is not to be found there. It is to be found in friendship and candlelight, in kindness and gingerbread. In simple pleasures like the fragrance of fresh clementines with their leaves on, cold from the December air and presented in brown paper bags. It is to be found in randomly generated elf names and spiced hot apple drinks. It is to be found in providing Sanctuary. It is to be found in love and understanding; in shared grief and empathy.

Life could be hard. There were too many real and present dangers to mental, physical and emotional health, to add the burden of Christmas on top.

That was her own awakening. Christmas joy was to be found in the things you loved and nothing more. Not the shoulds, and coulds, and have tos and need tos, just the simple, like tos and want tos, the rest could be left on the shelf, with the elf.

Who are the elves and cleaners? she asked herself.

They are the quiet ones. Industrious and secret, whose work is hidden and whose labours are overlooked, but they are the magic makers.

And magic is for life, not just for Christmas.

Afterword

According to research by mental health charities, Christmas sees peaks in mental health issues such as loneliness, depression and anxiety. Changes to appetite and weight lead to dissatisfaction in the new year. Debt on credit cards, loans or via loan sharks, rise to frightening levels, causing despair and panic, sometimes violence and injury, in the new year. Financial instability affects many, even with people electing to miss out on other opportunities earlier in the year in order to save money for Christmas. Add to that Winter Blues, reduced sunlight and low energy causing feelings of hopelessness and worthlessness.

The general atmosphere of good cheer can create a pressure to be 'up and fun' and partying and full of Christmas Spirit. But this can be intimidating, leading to the desire to withdraw. Dread, fear, palpitations, intensive music, lights, crowds and traffic can all trigger negative reactions and the desire for a calmer environment.

The statistics from research carried out by, among others, the mental health charity, MIND, YouGov.uk and Mental Health UK, high percentages of mental health sufferers find Christmas stressful, with their symptoms intensified, and the pressure to partake and enjoy in festive fun to be overwhelming (NB, the statistics I have used in the book are based on these but have been generalised. For specific results, please check original source data.) The continual postings of decoration and presents and wrapping ideas; food and drink; gifts and seasonal activities such as parties and Father Christmas and naughty elf antics bombard news feeds relentlessly. Bereavement and loss are more keenly felt at Christmas, with loved ones absent from family traditions. As is guilt for not being able to provide things that we feel our loved ones wish for or deserve. A sense of loneliness is felt by those who do not have the relationships that are continually promoted through advertising and these factors can contribute to people feeling overburdened.

In addition, a reduction in the number of people attending church and Christmas becoming a more secular cultural winter festival than a religious one, can also cause people to question what it's all about and to place the emphasis on other elements of the celebration.

During Covid, many people had to alter their traditions due to lockdown restrictions. As soon as it was over, many made up for lost time, going full out. There is much goodness to be found at Christmas, good cheer, care and generosity, greater charitable donations and a focus on family, friendship and love. However, it is interesting to note that it is a socially developed monster that requires continual feeding. Whilst charities collect food and toy donations to pass to those in need, which is commendable, it is only necessary because we have established that as a thing.

How people want to celebrate the season is, of course, entirely up to them, and can be as excessive, or meagre as they wish. The only thing to be mindful of, I think, is that it is just that. That it is what *they* wish, and not what society, or faith or tradition tells them they must do. Because therein lies the festive holy trinity of pressure, anxiety and worry.

Season's greetings! Merry Christmas! Happy Solstice!

Whatever your preferred way of celebrating the midwinter festival, I wish you nothing but Joy and Peace.

With love from
Marshmallow Hollystockings   xx

Acknowledgements

To my Marshmallows.

You continue to be my whole world.

I thank you all, for your endless support and for the individual ways that you each demonstrate your love and encouragement for me.

Nathan, for allowing me the time and space to indulge my love of writing. You continue to be at once both my rock and the wind beneath my wings. Never failing to find ways to enable me and help me to fulfil my dreams.

Hermione, for continuing to inspire me every day with your depth of compassion and inimitable joie de vivre. And, of course, for your little notes of motivation and endless cups of tea.

Tristan, as ever, for providing sage and thoughtful words of understanding. Always ready to listen and to walk with me through my various literary wanderings with humour and affection, and to be my unofficial and unpaid marketing manager and CEO!

You are all the source of my profound joy.

Everyday. Not just at Christmas!

THE EPIPHANY

ABOUT THE AUTHOR

Sarah Shanahan-Mallows lives on The Lizard, in Cornwall with her family and Poseidon the labracadabrador.
Her first novel, Lizard Legacy, is a Young Adult mystery comprising Cornish folklore, magic and an overall theme of coastal awareness and safety.
She has also written and illustrated a series of children's books about sea safety, called The Wizard on The Lizard.

Find out more on her website www.sarahbooks.co.uk

Printed in Great Britain
by Amazon